TERNION OF TARR

A Simgra Series Novel

Bethany Arliss

Paperback: 978-0-6453449-9-8

Hardback: 978-1-7635421-0-5

E-book: 978-0-6453449-8-1

First paperback edition: June 2024

Edited by Rachel Hunt Editorial and Mandi Oyster

Cover by Daniela at Stardust Book Services

Photographs by Shaliam Publishing

To every story that ignited my creativity and inspired me.

Conpieta
Region of Keplon
Ga'Razi
Region of Garr
Simgra
Carlver River
Lapana
Region of Basima
Ikra
Roselake
Padoosa
Region of Fauster
Wyndmere Sacred
Region of Erian
Unpassable Sea
Black Roil Islands

Igta
GODDESS OF BIRTH

Uros
GOD OF DEATH

First Generation Gods

DIMENSIONAL GODS

Anja • Goddess of Time Zevanna • God of Space

... and many more

Second Generation Gods

Briotl – Goddess of Magic

... and many more

ELEMENTAL GODS

Agnis • Goddess of Fire I'Kuna • Goddess of Earth

Saleal • God of Air Kikara • God of Water

IN THE GREAT DIVINE WAR, THE SECOND-GENERATION GODS CREATED DEMONS TO BE THEIR FOOT SOLDIERS

1

BRITTLE COLD STIFFENS MY bones and pebbles my skin under my thin, striped prison uniform. It comes in equal parts from the frigid stone walls of the ancient castle and from the riot brewing in the common room. Rage and fear fill the air, coating my tongue with an acrid taste.

Fuck. Another day surviving Lapana Prison.

I drop the tin tray with today's meagre ration of slop onto the table and sit, keeping my eyes fixed on the opposing gang members by the east door. Puffed chests, snarled lips, and curled fists join the rumble of voices rising and falling in angry waves that vibrate against my breastbone. They are hefty and brutal and many. I am pint-sized, benign, and ... alone.

I force my gaze away—there is nothing I can do to stop the impending brawl.

With a sighing exhale, I push my long, tangled fringe aside and stare at the meal. I swear I can see the stink of boiled meat rising from it, and is that …? Eww … a fat, dead maggot floats in the thin, pallid gravy. My stomach feels like a sack of mouldy straw, and I swallow against the geyser of puke shooting to my throat. Eyes watering, I swipe at my damp, bony cheeks with the back of my hands.

Thank the gods the prison only serves meat twice a week. Fork in hand, I push the grey animal flesh around the plate, trying to separate it from the vegetables in the sloppy stew. My hunger is brutal, and yet … gods, this is gross.

A wide shadow crosses my view, and I frown when Janga, the blacksmith—broad as a tree trunk and knotted with muscle—crashes into the seat opposite me. "You cryin' 'cos you didn't get no visitors this morning, girlie?"

Not likely. That kind of forlorn hope is for those who have someone to visit them.

I roll my watering eyes at Janga. "Oh, yes. I'm heartbroken. And you're disturbing my grief. What do you want, Janga?"

The man-mountain peels back his lips in a stained-teeth smile. The fetor of his rotten breath joins the stink of my meal, and I blink against the repulsive stench. "I'll be takin' your meal today." He rubs his belly in big, slow circles.

A sigh rises in my chest, but I hold it back. There's no point arguing, and besides, oily nausea fills my shrivelled stomach. The blacksmith's smirk makes my toes curl though, and I sniff.

"I'll keep my bread." I shove my chin forward. "I'll have your bread, too."

Janga rubs a thick, hairy finger under his nose. "Don't be pushin' me, or I might stomp on your wee little body." He pincers his forefinger and thumb in a gesture to show just how tiny I am.

Palms on the table, I lean forward, slow and deliberate. "Being short puts me closer to all nine levels of hell, and they feed me wagon loads of wicked. So, unless you want me telling the guards about the stash of tobacco you got hidden behind the loose stone in the bathroom ... I'll have your bread."

Janga pulls back, his too-small, too-close eyes popping wide. "How ...? Ah, little flea, you're a fresher fruit than most here. You can have your bread." He tosses his bread roll, and I shoot out a hand, catching it before it lands on my tray and gets meat stink on it ... then fling it in the air again when a booming shout makes me jerk.

"Fuck you, Gorn!"

I juggle the bread, catch it, and turn to the far side of the common room where the riot is brewing. The leaders of the prison gangs, Gorn and Drustan, stand off against each other, their members grouped behind them. Drustan shoves Gorn in the chest, and shouts rise to a rumbling black thunder, echoing in the cavernous common room.

Other prisoners, fresh from the visiting room, file into the common room behind them, giving the gangs as wide a berth as possible.

The bread in my fist squishes, and my throat fills with a moth-like fluttering. This is shaping up to be a big one, and although I am on the opposite side of the room, safety is a thin, tenuous thread if all hell breaks loose. Across the table Janga shifts, concern stiffening his movements.

The eyes of a few of the guards standing around the perimeter of the room dart, and some grip the cudgels at their hips, but they don't move. Their ill-fitting, drab, brown overalls and floppy, wrinkled caps are a perfect match to their lethargy. Or perhaps their lethargy matches the uniforms. Either way, they are slow as molasses in the winter. Tension among prisoners is a wick never pinched. Instead, it is allowed to spark and sizzle as if the imminent boom is bright delight in the guards' otherwise dull day.

My skin prickles as if a hundred furry stinging nettles burrow in. I smell the eruption like smoke racing ahead of fire. Around me, other prisoners have stilled. The line of men and women waiting for food from the carts breaks up as they edge away, widening the distance between them and the hostile inmates.

Then, right amid the brewing tension, the newest inmate—a young Lapanian girl—shuffles into the common room, her shoulders rounded, her eyes lowered. Arriving last evening and given the cell next to mine, she spent the night alternating between screaming her innocence and bawling like a lost lamb.

Typical Lapanian who expects to be heard. She has no idea what it is to have no voice.

She takes baby steps, her eyes stuck on the floor. Her long brown hair hangs on either side of her face like tattered, drawn curtains.

Burning hell. Wake up, girl.

To be caught in a brawl means pain, even death ... and the guards are just as likely to inflict harm as the prisoners. I chew my bottom lip. The prisoner is Lapanian and deserves everything she gets. Still ... she looks about Cassia's age, and her hair is the same shade. I shake the agonizing thought of my sister loose. Soft feelings have no place here.

"She's on her own," Janga says as if he has read my mind. "Ice your blood, Flea. You don't get nothing by being a hero." He folds his arms and tilts his head.

He's right.

The snarling gang inmates surge like milk on the boil, shoving and shouting. They swell and bubble and...

Damn it!

Flinging my fist-flattened bread onto the table, I leap from my seat and cross the floor, dodging the broiling group, ducking under arms and around twisting bodies. Heart thumping, I reach the new girl, grab her arm, and haul. The foolish thing screams and slaps my face with surprising force, laying a hot sting on my cheek.

Her scream hangs in the air, and as if it is the flick of a match, the first fist shoots out like a striking snake, cracking the jaw of the man opposite. The gang members break the invisible line between the two sides, and the fight ignites. Dull thwacks of fists on flesh melt together with shouted orders from the guards, who finally rush forward with gleeful grins to extinguish the flame of ill tempers. The sharp crack of their cudgels smacking bone joins the sour melody of the brawl.

I jam my jaw tight and cling to the terrified, wiggling girl, pulling her along. Fists and feet and torsos lash at us like the swaying branches of a forest in a storm. From somewhere within the mess, the sour smell of urine snatches at my nose hairs. Someone has pissed their pants.

Ahead, a small gap splits the writhing bodies, and I focus on it like it is freedom itself. Step by dragging step, we get closer.

Restrained magic fills the room with a voltaic scent, prowling and roaring like a caged animal. It presses against me, and I wrinkle my face against the pressure and against my magic that also surges. No inmate with power dares to use it. Not in front of the guards. No one will risk extending their sentence. So, the magic punches the air in frustration, as inhibited and persecuted as everyone else in this damned place.

The gap ahead shrinks, and I quicken, my sweaty grip around the Lapanian girl's bony wrist turning vice-like.

One more step and ... a stray fist slams into my cheek—the same one the girl slapped—with the force of a mallet. I gasp. My brain rattles in my skull, and my thumping heart surges to a gallop. I stumble but stay on my feet and keep hold of the Lapanian.

With one last pull, the girl and I spill free of the melee.

"Ow!" Stinging pain rips down my forearm.

"Retract your claws," I shout over the roar of hitting and bellowed cussing and look down at where the girl's ragged nails have peeled back my skin. Narrow lines of blood trickle towards my hand. I drag the spitting feline well clear of the fight, then release her.

Hair flying, the Lapanian spins around. Her lips are snarled, her nostrils flared. "Bitch!" Spit rides her words in an arc. "Never touch me again." She sinks to the floor like a puddle of soft pudding and sobs.

I press my hand to my throbbing, abused face, blood from my forearm dripping onto my striped prison shirt. Burning hell, my cheek is already swollen and squishy.

"Get under a table," I say. "The fight could still ..."

"Leave me alone!" The girl's eyes are wide and wild, and I take half a step back.

I want to hate her, but I understand her terror. It's the kind that drowns you. It's the kind I'd felt in my first days here.

From the corner of my eye, I spot Janga, smirking with a kind of grim amusement. Catching my gaze, he makes a big show of scooping the last of my stew with a chunk of bread. He plucks the bread I'd left on the table and shoves it into his mouth too. With a fat-cheeked grin, he leaves the table, taking his food tray with him.

Great. No food for me.

I heave a sigh and lean close to the sobbing girl on the floor, one forearm defensively raised in case she strikes out again. "Bit of advice, newbie. Stay alert. Careless gets you killed." I stretch my mouth into a smile that makes my abused cheek throb. "You're welcome, by the way."

I turn to leave, but snapping, rhythmic footsteps stop me. My throat squeezes as I spin to the west door of the common room where four Elemental guards enter at a march, their hands already raised. Unlike the regular prison guards, their black uniforms are sharp, three-piece suits atop white shirts with starched, stiff collars. Their black trilby's sit at precise, matching angles on their heads. Their expressions—sharp, precise, and black. They stretch their claw-like fingers towards the fighting prisoners.

My stomach turns to stone. I rush to the closest wall and drop, my knees barking from the force of hitting the stone. Back to the room, I press my forehead to the frigid rock and clasp my hands behind me. Beside me and around the room, all prisoners not consumed by the brawl, line the walls. All on their knees, foreheads to the wall, hands behind their back, like they are offering their heads to the executioner's block.

The prison guards retreat from the fighting prisoners who haven't heeded the danger. Who still battle with blood-spattered faces, heaving chests and curled fists. Any brawl is dangerous, but this is far from the worst I have seen. So why are the Elemental Guards here? In the past year, more dire situations have not warranted the power of the Elementals.

In seconds, dozens of prisoners—any who do not kneel—collapse. Their hands claw at their throats; their necks extend like they're trying to scoop oxygen into gaping mouths. With a flick of their fingers, the Elementals have drawn the air from their lungs. I glance towards the Lapanian girl, and she, too, writhes, her eyes bulging, her chest frozen.

Gods above.

A shout bubbles in my chest.

She didn't know. She's new. Have mercy.

I suck my cheeks into my teeth. The words will go unheard. They are a waste of energy and a risk to the air in my own lungs.

Ice your blood, Flea.

So, I stay quiet, though the foul tang coating my tongue has nothing to do with the boiled meat stink. I am no stranger to the flavour of injustice, and I let it burn as it slides down my throat.

The common room collapses into thick silence. My heart thumps, heavy and sluggish.

"Release!" The piercing voice of Duty Supervisor, Officer Segar, breaks the silence like a whip crack.

His order echoes ... then the desperate, wheezing breaths of the prisoners given their lungs back fill the cavernous room.

"The midday meal is delayed." Officer Segar lowers his chin, his eyes roaming the room like a bird of prey in search of a mouse in long grass. "All rise and take a seat."

No one moves. The rigidity of terror binds us. The new prisoner, still on the floor, mutters incoherently.

Officer Segar smashes his cudgel on a table. "Get your pile-of-trash keesters off the floor and sit at a table." He tugs at the tie beneath his stiff, white collar. "Unless you want the Elementals to ... persuade you." Segar's tone holds dark delight.

In a rush, prisoners stand. Wobbly legs and pale, sweaty faces surround me as we scramble for a seat at a table. No one speaks, but the thump of men and women taking their places rings out. Two men grab the new girl, slide her across the floor and dump her at a table where she slumps, eyes staring vacantly at the wooden tabletop.

I move too, claiming my usual table tucked into the corner, happy Janga is no longer there.

I draw my knees to my chest and gingerly finger my injured cheek.

Then Officer Segar announces they are visiting.

No wonder the Elementals were summoned to squash the riot.

2

Rill

All around the room, as if a puppet master tugs on strings, heads turn to the west door. A few gang members mop at bloody noses and split lips, but even their eyes search. Those the Elementals held are still pale, but the fear in the room fades. The Elementals remain in the common room, but it is unlikely they will use their particular brand of control while the visitors are here.

I tuck myself up tighter, wrapping one arm about my knees, and rest a cool palm on my burning cheek.

Then, Lady Keeva Dalton, daughter of the Earl of Tarr, walks through the door, skirts swishing. As always, she carries a basket of goodies over one arm, her parasol over the other, and I draw a deep, steadying breath.

Lady Keeva's benevolence scrapes at me with a friction that rubs my bitterness raw. I don't doubt she chooses charity to hold the guilt of privilege at bay. But I hate myself more because her visits are the singular thing I look forward to in this hell of a life.

Rill Narin of Ikra, looking forward to seeing Lady Keeva Dalton? My convictions have weakened. It's this damn prison. It erodes. Bit by bit, all sense of self grows soft and powdery. Rotting and peeling until everything you are turns to dust and floats away in the stale prison air.

Two years. I have to hold it together for just two more years.

Constable Sabella Rivers accompanies Lady Keeva, an arrangement that never changes. She carries a second basket, dangling from loosely hooked fingers. Sometimes the baskets hold bread or sweet cakes or fruit. Sometimes cheeses, lemonade and occasionally, in the winter, warm blankets.

Sabella trails behind Lady Keeva like a packhorse, but there the analogy ends, for Sabella's sharp eyes flash and *see*. She misses nothing. At some stage in her life, rough living sharpened Sabella. I know, because once you've endured it, you recognise it in others.

Lady Keeva wears a pretty, pale-blue, summer frock. Silk, no doubt. Her leg-of-mutton sleeves are puffed, and bows of blue ribbon run down the front of her grass-yellow, frilled bodice ending at her tiny waist. Her blonde hair is piled on top of her head and fixed with an array of blue and pink bows. It is a prison joke—among others of a cruder nature—that Keeva's smile could light the entire city of Lapana. Today, when she shines her unique wattage, her teeth seem even whiter against the glow she's built up in the summer sun. So very un-ladylike for the aristocracy.

From my dim corner, I stare. Did Lady Keeva lie in the sun? Did she recline on cool, grass, her eyes closed against the sun's warmth? Did she inhale the perfume of summer? The image makes my soul and earth magic ache, so I shove it down deep. Tucking it away, even while knowing the image will bide its time and reemerge to torment me in the darkest hours of night.

I press my lips together. The hour a day I am permitted to wander the shaded, concrete courtyard is enough.

Except ... it's not. I am bereft of sunlight.

Lady Keeva and pack horse Sabella move from table to table, handing out goodies like they are fabled fae folk granting wishes. Clean and dressed for the summer that we prisoners don't see, they stand apart from the dirt and smell of the prison, like torchlight in a dark room. They wind their way among the inmates, ignoring the sneers that follow them. Ignoring the rude gestures made by some men and not a few women. Holding themselves apart from the filth and stink of body odour, urine, and blood.

I release my knees and straighten, running my fingers through my knotted, wayward fringe. Then I lean back into the corner's shadows to hide my swollen cheek.

When the visitors reach my table, Keeva lowers herself gracefully onto the stained seat opposite me. Sabella stands tall behind her.

"Good day, Rill. Sitting alone as always, I see. Are you well?" Lady Keeva asks, her voice creamy, her vowels rounded and yet, her tone and demeanour are warm and friendly.

"Yes, thanks, Lady Keeva." I lift my eyes to Sabella. "Hello, Constable Rivers."

"Greetings, Rill," Sabella replies politely. Unlike Lady Keeva, the constable is not friendly, yet she is not unfriendly either. Her gaze snaps to my cheek, immediately seeing through the disguise of shadows.

I resist the temptation to cover my swollen cheek with a hand, though I do angle my face away from the constable's sharp eyes.

Sabella never comes in her uniform. Clearly accompanying Keeva is a favour, not an order. Although, what kind of favour, I can never decide as Keeva and Sabella don't seem like they are friends. Certainly, the idea of a citizen guard being friends with the Earl's daughter is ridiculous.

Still, Sabella has an undeniable air of dignity to her. Her simple outfit of a white shirt and light skirt is immaculately clean and pressed. A simple black bow sits at her throat. A tight bun, slicked smooth with hair creme, holds her ebony hair. Her skin and full eyes, both as dark as the loamy soil in Wolf Woods, are luminous.

Lady Keeva's blonde-haired, blue-eyed beauty is classical, while Sabella's looks are exotic, powerful. Lady Keeva moves with delicate grace while Sabella moves with sleek power. The pair are a mystery to be solved.

"I have fruit or bread today. Which would you prefer?" Keeva gives a light, tinkling laugh. "Silly question. You always request fruit."

I stretch my lips into a polite smile, careful not to wince at the pain in my cheek. "Fruit is nature's sweetmeat. I miss ..." I bite my tongue. Rule Number One in prison—never talk about anything personal. And my love of nature is at the very core of who I am.

Keeva hands me a bright red apple and a second later, a peach as well. She leans a little closer and theatrically cups her hand beside her mouth. "The fruit is less popular. Have two," she whispers.

Less popular because fruit spoils and can't be stockpiled to bribe the guards.

I cling to the furry peach, fighting the urge to hold it under my nose and breathe deeply. That would show too much.

"Thank you." I tuck the apple into my pocket and bite into the peach, savouring the sweet summer flavour.

Sabella clears her throat. "Lady Keeva. You have a party to attend this evening." Sabella gently taps the watch pinned to her breast. "We must move along, or you will be late."

"Oh, Sabella, thank you." Keeva stands. "She always keeps me so organised. I will return this week, Rill, and bring more fruit." Keeva's eyes hold steady on my face, and she purses her lips. "Perhaps, if permitted, I shall bring a small pot of herbs for you to tend." Somehow Keeva has zeroed in on my desires.

It is rare someone is able to see through my walls, and I recoil under the exposure. Vulnerability sends lumps to my belly as if I've swallowed a dozen peach pips. Not only are my convictions wearing thin, but my armour is too. Scraping a fingernail at a lump of dried food on the table, I try to swallow the bite that wants to ride my words.

"There's not enough light." I force calm into my tone. "A plant will wither and die."

Lady Keeva's mouth thins, and she drops her eyes for a second. But then, she brushes at something on her shoulder and picks a stray cobweb from her pretty dress, shaking her fingers to get rid of it.

The pips in my stomach rattle. I don't want Lady Keeva's sympathy, yet I also don't like feeling less important than a cobweb. "Why do you come here, Lady Keeva?" There is no fake calm in my tone now. "Why do you walk amongst the dirt that is Lapana Prison?" I wave a hand towards Lady Keeva's shoulder. "Aren't you frightened some webs will stick?"

I feel Keeva's brightness dim. Sadness hangs in the space between us, but I force myself to keep eye contact with Lady Keeva's sorrowful, pale blue eyes.

Around us, the hum of the mess hall seems to rise to a roar as if it rushes in to fill the silence.

Lady Keeva tilts her head and purses her lips. "The webs I am wary of, Rill Narin, are the ones constantly spun in our minds. Hatred, fear, judgement." She taps her temple lightly. "It is those that must be dusted away before they catch insects."

Somehow, her words expose me even more. I lean forward, no longer caring if she can see my fat cheek. "Spoken by someone who has never known hardship." I mirror Lady Keeva with a tap to my own temple. "I like my webs laden with bounty." Hate, bitterness, fear—they keep you safe. "A larder filled with caution, stocked and ready for when disaster comes my way." I feel my nostrils flare and struggle to reel my emotions in, to stay in control. Not only have I allowed Lady Keeva past my guards, but arguing with the Earl of Tarr's daughter can only bring trouble. Like a coward, I drop my eyes, focusing intently on the chipped table.

I sense movement—thank the gods, they are leaving—then Lady Keeva does the unthinkable. She leans in, covers my hand with hers, and gives a gentle squeeze.

The moment expands around me and freezes, holding me in a bubble. My stomach rises and falls like a bouncing ball, and my thoughts swell and churn with instant temptation.

Unbeknown to her, Lady Keeva has just touched a Tangler.

3

THAT NIGHT IN MY cell, I gingerly press my cheek to the dank stone wall, using its chill like an ice pack. From eye to jaw, my face aches relentlessly, deep within the bone. Probably broken, but it matters little. No matter the injury, I will not seek aid. The healer's wing is a bad place for female prisoners, so I find relief where I can.

Knees locked, I stand with my neck craned against the wall and forbidden temptation clashes with the ever-present despair. With a mute sigh, I breathe the fetid odour of the aged stone and wrinkle my nose. Centuries of violence, pain, blood, despair, and death have soaked into the stone, endowing the walls with a uniquely grim flavour.

With my jaw clamped, I push away from the stone wall. My heel catches on an uneven flagstone, and I windmill my arms, desperate to avoid the rough iron bars of my tiny cell. At night, they hum with magic. A single touch renders your legs useless, loosens your bladder, and sends you crumpling to the floor, where you spend the next eight hours drooling. I learned this the hard way.

Balance regained, I pace—two steps, turn, two steps, turn—my flimsy prison shoes pat quietly on the ancient floor. I curl my fingers as I step. In and out. In and out.

Some nights, I fare better. After lights out, when my cell becomes a crypt of blurry shadows—courtesy of the sparsely scattered oil lanterns in the hallway—I lie on my bed of wooden slats, pull the single, thin blanket over my head, and sink into my favourite daydream of a hero come to right the injustices of Conpieta. Just like the stories I love to read. Unlike me, the hero is always tall and strong and extraordinary. And unlike the real world, the bad guy always loses.

Some nights I even sleep.

Tonight is not one of those nights.

I gaze at the back of my hand and swallow against the opposing forces of thrill and doubt that tug at my throat.

A few cells down, Janga snores. The big man's sonorous snorts echo, slapping my ears over and over. Not that I mind. The noise covers the sound of weeping that often floats down the row of cells. Snoring does nothing on a screaming night, though. Nothing covers the wails of nightmares when they come.

Two steps, turn.

Lady Keeva touched me. Skin to skin.

Two steps, turn.

Of course, she has no idea I am a Tangler. I keep that little gem a tight secret. Not even Cassia knows.

It is a deadly power for the unsanctioned citizens of Conpieta to possess. Before King Ryker's grandfather, King Benedict, implemented the Magic Class Act, rare power of any kind was revered. But rising magical crime forced King Benedict to create a register of its citizens' powers. But in those days, anyone from anywhere could get a magical license. Until Benedict's son, King Ryker—devoid of any magic and driven by fear— restricted licenses to certain regions and wards. It was the start of the end for many. No longer able to obtain a license, all unsanctioned citizens were forbidden to use magic. King Ryker turned his citizens into criminals.

And any unlicensed person with Class Five magic, like tangling, is put to death.

Entering another person's mind and taking over their body is a rare power. And one cannot tangle with just anybody. A closed mind will resist. A powerful mind will push you out. And you must touch a person, skin to skin, before you can tangle with them.

Just as Keeva did.

Temptation tugs at me like a siren's call. It would not be the first time I used my power in prison. It saved me twice from attacks in the bathrooms when I'd slipped into my attacker's body and used the tangling control to walk them away. But even that was a risk. Once I release control, and the attacker finds themselves in a different location—seemingly in an instant—they could report me. But avoiding injury is worth the risk.

And once, in the constant battle with despair, I took over the body of a guard. He'd finished his shift a few hours earlier, and I hoped ... well, I wanted a little time away from the cruelty that was Lapana Prison. But tangling with him only resulted in finding myself in a tiny, grotty room in the body of a man who was drunk out of his mind. I only lasted five minutes before returning to my body lying on my cot. Lady Keeva though ... well, that would be a wholly different experience.

I press the heels of my hands to my forehead.

No, no. I must not do it. If I get caught ...

In two years, I will leave this place behind. I will search for Cassia. But if I am discovered tangling ...

Gods above, Sabella said Lady Keeva is going to a party. A party with light and life. A party where I can be among others and not fear for my safety. A temporary escape from pain and misery. I again rub a thumb over the back of my hand. I can feel Keeva. Feel her physicality. My magic bubbles, pressing to be used.

Slowly, deliberately, I lie back on my hard bed.

I shouldn't ... but I will.

With a deep breath, I shut out the steel-like cold of the prison. I shut out Janga's snores. Shut out the hum of my cell's bars and the ever-present stench of hopelessness. I narrow and shrink and focus on Lady Keeva. Magic fizzles under my skin, warm, insistent, and vital. I free it, and it unfurls, rejoicing. It is too easy. Immediately, I connect with Lady Keeva's body and soul. I probe her mind gently. Will she let me in?

I give a slow blink, and when I open my eyes, a young man stands before me. My heart thumps, my eyes bulge, and I breathe the balmy air of a summer's night.

I am in a narrow alleyway behind a building that bursts with music. To my left, steps lead to a door that stands open. Warm light and a joyous beat spill from the door, punctuated with shouts and squeals and the thump of dancing feet. I glance down at my body to find it is not mine at all.

It is Lady Keeva Dalton's.

4
Rill

I RUN A HAND over the soft green material of the dress I wear. It is buttery soft and silky with short sleeves and a narrow skirt. Lady Keeva's hands are smooth and free of callouses, and the sleek material shifts like water beneath them.

I draw another deep breath—sweetly relieved to have a pain-free face—and revel in the night air. It is free air. Not musty and cold like prison air. This melange of smells invigorates with an odour rich and dense with life. It's a warm summer's night with a fluttering breeze that weaves with the humidity. The aroma of food and drink and debauchery swells around me, mixing with the smell of decomposing food and dampness.

I'm close to the river. With a start, I realise I am in the Lower South district. Hell and gone from Manor Rise where Keeva lives.

What in I'Kuna's name is Lady Keeva doing here? It is no place for a society girl and definitely no place for the Earl's daughter.

"You look as beautiful as ever tonight, Keeva."

I jolt. I'd almost filtered out the man before me. His yellow-green complexion and elongated earlobes tell me he is from Fauster. He is tall with dark blond hair, deep brown eyes and, like many Faustians, is thick-set with broad shoulders. Now I appreciate how close he is and understanding hits me. My stomach squeezes and her heart leaps, a combination of panic and titillation sweeping over me. Keeva is here with a beau. Is that why she is in the Lower South district? Is she having a clandestine affair?

"Thank you, ... sir," I reply, amused by how strange it is to speak with Keeva's lyrical voice.

The blond man laughs. "So formal. You know you don't have to be like that when you come here." He places broad, capable hands on my arms and leans in.

Gods save me. This is wrong. And wonderful. I let gnawing rules and reality fall away and tilt my face to the man. His lips are soft, his kiss passionate, and he smells of soap and cedar wood. His hands run down my back, the dress is so soft it is as if he traces fingers over my skin, and the resulting shiver is delicious. I submit completely and allow Keeva's body to fold into the man's solidness. I trail my fingers over his corded arms, then over his chest, packed with muscle.

When we break apart, our breathing comes in heaves and puffs.

"You know, my place is not far," the man purrs.

Oh, no, no. I will not have sex in Keeva's body. That would cross a line. Besides, I want to follow the music and the laughter that comes from inside of what is clearly a dance tavern. I want to abandon every thought of the prison and just dance. I want to lose myself, safe behind the ultimate wall—another person's body. Just for a few hours.

"Um ..." Gods, I don't even know this man's name.

But he laughs good-naturedly. "I know the answer is no. It always is. But a man can hope." He gives me a peck on the forehead that speaks of friendship. Completely at odds with the passionate kiss from a minute ago. "Another drink?"

I nod mutely.

"Give me a second. Drinks in ... drinks out." He shrugs, gives a wide grin and moves away a few steps.

Smiling inwardly, I lean against the wooden wall of the tavern and run my tongue back and forth over Keeva's smooth, straight teeth. Somehow, this man declared he was going to take a piss without it sounding remotely boorish. I carefully keep my eyes off him as he fumbles with his trouser buttons, gazing instead in the other direction down the alley. I am sure this is Carlver Alley, only two streets from Carlver River. If it wasn't for the thumping piano and stomping feet inside the tavern, I would hear the slap of the water against the docks and the snap of the ropes that hold the boats tight.

Not the party I imagined Keeva to be at, but so, so much better.

"Did you ask your father about exploring Conpieta?" the blond Faustian asks.

I freeze, thoughts racing. Exploring Conpieta? Is Keeva leaving? How should I answer him?

"He's ... been busy," I say carefully, still turned away from the man.

Silence sits heavy. Have I made the right reply?

A blast of heat hits my back, searing and painful, like someone has opened a furnace. With it comes the most eye-watering, gut-churning smell. I spin 'round.

The Faustian is sniffing the air too, his chin lifted, his nose wrinkled in disgust. The next second, a shadow moves, and the Faustian's stomach explodes in a shower of blood and intestines.

A hot spray of moisture lands on my face, and I recoil, slapping a hand over my mouth. I press tight to the wall of the tavern, my pulse pounding in my neck, my chest heaving like a blacksmith's bellows.

The Faustian man meets my eyes, a tiny, high-pitched sound coming from him like air being slowly let out of a balloon. I watch his life fade, his stare morphing from wide-eyed shock to filmy blankness. I push my hand tighter to my mouth. Prison taught me to never scream. But my eyes stay glued to the dead man I'd just kissed ... and to the horror behind him.

It is a creature. A creature so appalling, my heart slams against my ribs. It stands on two legs, like a man, but its legs are that of a goat and its head that of a dog. A snarling, red-eyed dog with thick drool sliding from its vicious teeth. As I stare, the monster lowers its tooth-laden jaw to the Faustian's neck and, with one bite, rips his throat out. Then it lowers its mouth to his tattered neck and sucks like a vampire, its tail—a horned, black serpent—lashes back and forth in a hissing frenzy.

I can't hold back the small keening sound that rises from deep within, forcing its way past my tight throat and the hand clasped over my mouth.

The creature lifts its head, its glowing red eyes landing on me. The lips of its muzzle pull into a gut-turning smile, and a forked tongue laps at its blood-soaked maw.

"Tasty, innocent soul," it says in a voice so deep, dark, and malevolent, it drives a shudder up my spine. The words seem to come from the ground itself, rising like fire, licking at me with grotesque rapture.

The creature runs its forked tongue over its fangs and sniffs at the air, thrusting its head high. Then it grins again, its eyes darkening. "Two souls in one. Rhapsody."

It takes a step towards me, and I stumble back. My heel catches on the stairs that lead to the tavern, and I fall, slamming my butt onto a wooden step. Burning hell, I am going to die.

Deep, rhythmic words sound from further down the alley, joining the tempo of my pounding heart.

I pull my eyes from the demon—I don't doubt what it is. The smell of brimstone is overpowering. In the shadows of the alley, a black-clad man stands. He wears an ebony mask and chants strange words over and over. The summoner.

Powerful magic drenches the night air, carried on a scent of rotting flesh. I feel it as a fierce grip that holds me frozen in an awkward, half-sitting position on the steps.

The demon tips his head back and howls—a malignant sound that slices through my soul. Terror pumps in my blood, and my limbs unfreeze. I shimmy backwards up the steps on my bum, recoiling from the screaming agent of hell. Suddenly, the demon vanishes, leaving ashen smoke curling above the bloody corpse that floats in a lake of blood.

I lock eyes with the summoner. At least, I am sure he looks at me from behind his mask.

He stands, preternaturally still, staring. Then, he raises a hand and ... salutes me?

I blink, feeling like the world is off-kilter. I sway. Gods above, I am going to pass out.

Run!

Adrenalin surges. I scramble to my feet, turn, and plunge into the dance tavern.

Inside, the music is louder and yet, how nobody heard the demon scream I can't imagine. I push through the whirling crowd of dancers, wiping at blurry, tear-filled eyes and getting bumped and shoved. The wooden floor is slick with spilled drink and the dainty heels Keeva wears are like balancing on ice skates.

I crane my head back. Does the summoner pursue me? If he does, I struggle to spot him among the sea of revellers. My heart beats louder and faster than the music, and I fight against the sobs that tear at my throat.

I want to shout at the crazy dancers. Their laughing smiles, heavily lidded eyes, and twirling bodies, completely at odds with bloody murder. A blood-spattered girl in their midst doesn't rate a single glance.

One of your own is dead! Someone is summoning a demon. Help me!

But I have spent my life avoiding attention. A life of slipping around and through crowds unnoticed. A life of relying on myself. I will not ask for help.

Fear screams, ricocheting around my skull. *Leave Keeva's body!*

I could. I could return to my body, still lying on my cot in the prison. I could leave this nightmare. *Should* leave this nightmare. If Keeva dies while I tangle with her, I will die too. But Lady Keeva will have no memory of what just happened. She will have no idea a demon summoner has seen her—that she witnessed a murder. The Earl's daughter represents everything I hate in this world, but I cannot—will not—leave her so vulnerable. I must get Keeva somewhere safe.

Wiping sweat from my forehead—the heat from the crush of bodies is fierce—I make my way to the front of the tavern. To one side, a cloakroom. I do not know which coat might belong to Keeva, but it doesn't matter. I slip hands inside the pockets of the hanging garments until I find one with coin inside. I fling the thin coat around my shoulders and palm the money. Two and a half tains. More than enough to take Keeva's body to the only place I ever felt safe.

5

Rill

THE APPARITION BOOTH IS filled with dark emptiness when I step into it. My lungs scream for air. My pulse pounds so hard in my neck it is like my teeth jump to the rhythm. I ran from the tavern to the closest dirty apparition booth I knew of, looking back over my shoulder every few seconds. I'd turned an ankle twice on the cobblestones—Keeva's narrow heels are ridiculous—but I didn't dare stop. Ignoring the stabbing pain, I'd kept running.

It was worth it, for I am sure no one followed me, and I can now take a moment to assess. To decide what to do. Because I am in a wagon load of trouble.

Gulping, I suck in oxygen and wipe at the sweat on my—Keeva's—face, yet my heart still races, and my throat feels like burning paper. Nausea rises, thick and foul, making my limbs quiver. Air. I need air.

Tugging the stolen, oversized coat tighter to cover my blood-spattered dress, I take two steps and cringe. The pointy heels rap on the wooden floor like knuckles on a door, inviting someone to come and ask, 'Who's there?' I rise to my toes—a bolt of pain skewering my sprained ankle—and creep from the hut and into my home village of Ikra.

Immediately, the earthy, mossy smell of Wolf Woods buffets me. It crowds my head with swirling memories that rob me of thought and reason. Palm pressed to my chest, I try to drive back the assault. To stop the explosion that will scatter me. But the past comes, hitting me with the force of thunder and wind and rain, and I fly apart.

My sister floats before my eyes. Cassia's arms full of wildflowers as she runs over the grass in bare feet. Cassia's large brown eyes filled with wonder and hope as she chases butterflies. Cassia's wide mouth smiling at the unexpected. Cassia's sweet laugh rising from her gentle soul.

When they took my sister, the light in my world was extinguished.

It should have been me. Dullness is not missed.

I squeeze my eyes shut. Reaching deep within, I draw on my vinegar soul and fold the pain back, smaller and smaller, until it is a stone in the pit of my stomach. Nothing can reach me if I reside deep within the darkness. Piece by piece, brittle, icy bitterness brings me back together. I smooth and harden the seams until the breaks are invisible. With my armour in place, I can face what comes next.

I straighten, ignoring my trembling body, and glance down the rough dirt street. A few folks linger outside the tavern a little further along, bathed in the yellow lantern light that spills from the windows. Unlike Lapana, Ikra has no electricity. No Hismish village does. And this tavern holds no music. It is a rough-hewn, grey hut with a straw floor that serves cheap, bitter wheat wine. The people of Ikra—which had included me and Cassia from time to time—go there for quiet conversation and a few precious hours where they can put their troubles aside.

A couple holding hands walks by, and I freeze, not even daring to breathe. But they stagger, clutching at each other to stay upright, and pay me no attention. They do not stop with surprise and wonder why the Earl of Tarr's daughter stands in their poor, Hismish village. Probably too drunk to even register me. The wide band of dirt that circles the bottom of the woman's skirt tells me that even sober, she has given up lifting them free of the dust. Melting into the shadows, I retreat from the street, tucking myself between the apparition hut and the building next to it.

Safely hidden by the gloom between the buildings, I catch my lip in my teeth. If I flee Keeva's body now, she will not know where she is. She will be at the mercy of the people of Ikra, and there is no guarantee they will be helpful ... or even kind to her. But there is someone who might help. If I'm right, I can then leave Keeva knowing she is as safe as I can make her. Hopefully, she'll be returned to the Earl's manor unharmed. Hopefully, she will not figure out that I tangled with her.

Unable to think of a better plan, I release my gnawed lip and give a nod. I will go to the village elder, Esme. I will return to the woman who was like a second mother to me and Cassia after our mother had died and our father had left.

But what if Esme recognises my soul in another body? My stomach squeezes. Esme doesn't know I am a Tangler, but her empathic magic is strong and her perception sharp. The idea that I might bring trouble to Esme—accomplices to unlicensed magic are just as persecuted—well, I shudder at the thought, but it is a risk I must take.

I poke my head around the building to check that the path to Esme's home is clear, and my heart stops dead.

Emerging from the apparition hut is the summoner.

6

Rill

BURNING HELL!

He followed me here. Obviously determined to take care of the one witness to his crime. I inch back, clinging to the building, but keeping my eye on him. I wrap my arms around my body and squeeze hard to stop myself from trembling.

Ikra isn't safe either. A new plan is needed. I watch the summoner, a chilly breeze from the depth of Wolf Woods cooling the sweat on my face. At this range, I can see that his plain black clothes have the fit and look of wealth. Unless he's stolen them, he is upper class. He still wears the dark, featureless mask, and as I watch, he twists his head to look up and down the street. I hold my breath until finally he turns and walks away.

Only one chance to get Keeva's body to safety remains. Creeping as silently as the ridiculous heels will allow, I slip from the village and enter the thick, cool darkness of Wolf Woods. I try to run again, but the fine heels of Keeva's shoes sink stupidly into the soft soil. I haul on one foot to free it, overbalance and tumble headfirst over a crumbling, fallen log. I hit the ground and lie face down in the forest carpet of moist leaves, my nose buried in the sweet smell of rotting vegetation. Rolling over, I spit leaf litter from between my lips.

With a half-shrug, I squirm about in the leaves and soil like a dog in a muddy puddle. I scoop up fistfuls of leaves and rub them in my hair. To stay alive, I must mask the scent of human and meld with the forest. Then, with my jaw clenched, I slip the shoes off and rise. Dangling Keeva's party shoes over a finger, I run in bare feet, free from the encumbrance of spiky shoes.

Now I can be silent. Now I can be swift. I push, putting thigh and calf muscles to work. Thank the angels, Keeva's body is fit and strong. The woman obviously does more exercise than dancing and dinners. Which is just as well, because the woods are dangerous at night. Hags emerge from their trees and roam, gathering plants and animals for food and spells and potions. And on the lookout for any unlucky person who might take a wrong turn and become lost.

In my own body, I might have had a chance of bargaining with them. They had often traded herbs with me—although, a year away is a long time, and they may no longer be inclined to allow me passage. Still, hags are a danger I know how to avoid, but only if I stay silent. Only if I stay alert and light on my feet. They are also a danger I hope will stop the summoner from following me.

Once I get to my cottage, I—and Keeva's body—will truly be safe. Not even a demon can break my wards.

I hope.

I weave and dodge my way around trees. The forest path to my cottage is a more direct, faster route, but I know to avoid the paths at night. It is where the hags patrol, hoping to find that stupid someone who has entered the woods. But path or not, day or night, I race through the darkness with confidence. For years, the woods have been my home.

I veer now, staying clear of Web Way, the stretch of trees where Sorrow Spiders sling their webs like hammocks stretching from tree to tree in thick, sticky swathes. Being caught in one means certain—and nasty—death.

A rancid smell hits my nostrils. It is a cross between decaying wood and rotten eggs and the reek lays like damp wool in the back of my throat. My pulse jolts in my neck, and I scurry to crouch beside a gnarled tree, barely daring to breathe.

Hags.

I can't hear them, which is not surprising. They are creatures of the forest, at one with nature, and walk with the kind of step that leaves no prints and makes no sound. I press against the tree, digging my fingers into the rough bark. The odour grows stronger. They have found me.

But, no ... they are only close. The gaggle of hags pauses a few trees over. I put one eye around the tree, and there they are ... their noses raised to the currents of the night air. Their twisted bodies, dressed in rags that hang like stringy bark, are as still as tree trunks, like they've been spelled into a kind of cruel contortion.

If they catch my scent, I am in trouble.

I'Kuna save me.

But the goddess must be looking out for me because the hags move off silently to continue prowling the forest. I let myself breathe, count to ten, then run once more.

Sweet relief hits me when I reach the clearing. My clearing.

There in the moonlight, my cottage sits, patiently awaiting my return. Despite the ghastly situation that brings me here, despite my racing pulse and dripping face, joy fills my chest. It rises to my throat and trickles out in a soft smile as my eyes roam over the clearing that is my home. My sanctuary.

The herb garden has gleefully run amok without my careful tending. Basil rambles. Mint stands tall and leggy. The lavender has become woody. Thyme spreads, sending fingers that lie over the path to my front door. Many other herbs have gone to seed, some proudly displaying a mass of flowers, even in the moonlight. Around the perimeter, nettle has grown tall and threatens to dominate the garden. It is an absolute mess, and yet, the cacophonous aroma of herbs drifting in the night air is divine, and I can't help but admire nature's dynamism.

Stepping towards my hut with a cheek sucked between my teeth, I pluck a sprig of mint and hold it to my nose, letting the sweet smell unwind my muscles.

Would Keeva's body have enough magic to get through my wards? The right spell is one thing, but a spell without magic is just words. Does Lady Keeva possess any power at all? I dip into the well of Keeva's body, and to my surprise, even a little shock, I discover Keeva has a remarkably deep pool of magic. With no time to waste—the hags have likely picked up on my scent by now and are doubling back—I open the wards and slip in, closing them carefully behind me.

Now I stand before the cottage—so humble many would call it a shack—that was home to me and Cassia for the past five years. Until Cassia was taken. Until I was caught in the Gibson's home in Lapana and arrested for stealing. The little cottage has stood empty for the past year, and my heart floats, light with joy that I stand before it again. I flatten my palm on the rough wooden door, murmur the right words, and the door springs open.

Inside, it is as if being locked up has decayed my home, just as being locked up has decayed me. Cobwebs and grime cover everything, and yet ... it remains my haven, wrapping me in a warm bubble. I move to the table at the centre of the room—painted white by me and Cassia one summer—and track a finger through the dust. Like a time capsule, everything is just as I'd left it that night when I'd gone searching for clues of who might have taken my sister.

Bundles of herbs hung to dry dot the walls and even now, the ghost of their scent haunts the air. Neatly stacked plates—lovingly made by Cassia—sit on the shelf. Numerous jars—carefully labelled in my neat hand—of herbs and powders stand in rows. My and Cassia's spare dresses and aprons hang on hooks, side by side.

Several piles of faded books sit on the table, all of them taken from the trash of Lapana's rubbish heaps and barges, for I love to read, just as my mother did. To one side of the room, Cassia's bed, still as neatly made as it had been the day she disappeared. The sight of it, grey with grime beneath glistening webs, stabs at my chest with sharp, caustic pain. I draw a deep, steadying breath and deliberately turn my eyes to my bed on the other side of the room.

My thick, rough-spun blanket is dull with dust and the stain of abandonment.

I pick up the matches that lie on the table and light the lantern at the table's centre. Ignoring the spiders that scuttle away from the sudden light, I pull out a chair and sit, massaging my twisted ankle.

I've brought Lady Keeva to safety in my hut behind the wards, but I have also trapped her. And in a few hours, the guards at the prison will wake the prisoners. They will discover my soulless, unconscious body.

Being caught doing magic without a license equals trouble.

Being caught doing Level Five magic without a license equals big trouble.

Being caught tangling with the Earl of Lapana's daughter ... well, that trouble is unimaginable.

Trouble can go to hell. There is no way I am allowing strife to find me again.

Ice your blood, Flea.

Sitting at my kitchen table, a wicked plan starts to form.

7

Sabella

Rising from the small desk in my room at the guardhouse, I arm perspiration from my forehead. It's fucking hot, despite my open window, a consequence of being on the top floor. Outside, the city of Lapana sits in darkness, yet, like a stubborn infant, it doesn't sleep. The strain of music, the clop of horses' hooves, and the murmurs of revellers and workers hitch the summer breeze that floats in the open window. My lungs fill, and I relish the fan of jasmine-scented night air on my warm face. I stab my thumbs into the small of my back and stretch. Blazes, my body loathes sitting for hours on end.

"Well, too bad," I whisper, and move my thumbs in circles, working the stiff, protesting muscles.

It was worth it. Three neat piles of folders sit stacked on my desk. The no pile and backup pile matter little, but the contender pile is *everything*. Communications to arrange interviews with the contenders will go out tomorrow. I rest a palm on that important stack of folders. Somewhere in here is my fledge. My first. Someone I'll spend the next three years training to be a citizen guard. The ache in my lower back flares with a fresh twinge of pain. Swaying my hips in a slow stretch, I glance up at the wall.

The hands of my clock stand nearly straight up, the little hand tucked tight behind the big. In a literal tick, it will be a new day. A once-familiar ache hollows out my chest. A sour emptiness I haven't felt in nearly three years. An ache I thought I'd left behind.

I shake my head, flap my hands, and breathe, trying to pour confidence into the hollow. Old feelings can be sneaky bastards—visiting when you least expect and always unwelcome. A deep sigh fills my lungs. The feeling belongs in the past, and that is just where I intend to leave it.

I sit once more to unlace my boots and give myself a talking-to.

You can sleep now you've conquered your to-do list.

Easing my unlaced boots loose, I wiggle them off my feet.

You kicked your disorganisation in the ass.

Thank fuck I've *finally* sorted through the applications.

Curse the Code. Curse the requirement to take on a fledge.

OK. That last self-talk is less helpful. Boot in hand, I stare blankly at the wall while I rearrange my thoughts.

My apprenticeship with Constable Nash had been challenging, but I got through it. More than got through it. Finishing on top in every test, written and physical, earned me the moniker, Peak. The nickname sent worms curling in my stomach at first, sure the other guards were mocking me. Until Tavell told me differently. Friendly banter was a new experience—strange and unknown. After that, I worked hard to allow pride to trickle in. To push self-doubt aside.

Placing my boots at the foot of my bed, I nudge at them until they sit perfectly in sync, then cross the floor to the drawers by my bed. I tread softly, knowing even the footfall of socked feet will echo in the room below if I am not light about it. I pull a neatly folded nightgown from a drawer and lay it on the bed.

On the wall, the clock hands move. A new day has begun.

Two months ago, I'd become a fully-fledged citizen guard. My dream had come true. But now I only have one month left to choose my own fledge. As I unbutton my shirt, my fingers slow. I have put it off for so long. It is a huge decision, and my tenure with the guards relies on me getting it right. If I choose poorly—if my fledge fails or quits—I am out too.

I tug at a button caught in a thread and bite down on the urge to rip the thing from my shirt. The real reason I've dragged my feet on picking a fledge rises in my mind like a spectre, and that hollowness carves a spot in my chest again. I will have to work closely with my fledge for the next three years. Train them. Mentor them. I will have to develop a relationship with them. And fucking relationships make me want to rip my guts out.

Finally freeing the button, I peel off my shirt. A fledge fails most often when the connection is not there.

Tavell Nash took a chance on me three years ago. Eighteen years old and fresh out of the orphanage, my application had been a long shot. But Tavell had seen something in me. But he is a true teacher—confident, intelligent—and capable of getting the best out of anyone. He'd certainly gotten the best out of me. Not that I'd ever given anything less.

But connecting with others ...

I pull the nightgown over my head, sit heavily on my bed, and close my eyes.

Courage is not the absence of doubt, but action despite it.

It was something Tavell had said to me once, and it stuck with me.

"Sabella. I need help."

The words enter my mind. In a voice that is not mine. I sit bolt upright, my heart flying. I frown and cock my head, fighting to stay on an even keel.

"I am in danger."

"Who is this?" I form the words in my mind, trying to decide if I should call for help immediately. The only reason I don't is because the voice in my head sounds like Keeva. Which is impossible.

"Lady Keeva is in danger. She needs help. Your help. But ... this is Rill Narin."

I shoot to my feet, completely forgetting to be quiet. "Rill? The prisoner? What have you done with Keeva?" I speak out loud now, fear shooting to my chest, squeezing and urgent.

"Do nothing stupid, or Keeva will be lost."

"If you bloody well hurt her, I will hunt you down." Dread clutches at me.

"I won't hurt her. But if you report this, she will be lost."

"What in Agnis's name are you talking about?"

"I tangled with Lady Keeva. And while in control of her body, I hid her, locking her away."

My teeth grind and grit, my jaw flexing in time with my thudding heart. I curl my hands into fists and breathe hard through my nostrils. Then a freezing cold stiffens my skin. Keeva touched Rill today, and I hadn't stopped it. Agnis above, I should have been more alert. A sick feeling rushes over me ... I had failed Keeva.

"What do you want?" I force out, the words scraping like sandpaper in my throat.

"Get me out of prison. Get my sentence overturned. As a citizen guard, I'm sure you can manage it. Do that and I'll take you to Lady Keeva. But report me, and you'll never see her again."

I drop Diarissa's reins and sling a bag over my shoulder. Over the river and away from the city, Lapana Strip is cooler, and the light breeze coming off the surrounding farmland cools my heated cheeks.

"I'll be back soon," I say, and Diarissa tosses her head in answer, stirring the sleepy scent of cows and sheep and hay.

My fists bunch as I walk. Hard enough to make my nails bite my palms, hard enough to keep the scream in my throat from escaping. The corner Rill has backed me into squeezes. Tight. Everything feels as claustrophobic as a coffin, despite the spread of moonlit pastures around me and the immense dome of stars above. Even my skin presses and crowds, no matter how much I squirm against the pressure. Corners, both physical and metaphorical, are dangerous—a lesson imparted by my mistress, the orphanage.

The mere whisper of that history causes my chest to shrink. I draw a deep breath, expanding my lungs, forcing the memory back. Cowering hadn't freed me then, and it won't now. Action. That is the key—the master key of salvation and freedom.

In my room at the guard house and fighting panic, which action to take in the face of Rill's ultimatum had been an agonising choice. My go-to response was to immediately report the situation to Tavell. To come to the prison and demand Rill cough up where she had hidden Lady Keeva. But guilt blanketed me in dense hesitation. I had allowed Rill to touch Keeva—this is my fucking fault, and if her brother finds out ...

Passing through the outer gate of Lapana Prison, my carefully smothered fire magic flares. I have to put this right. I have to see Keeva return home safely *and* give Rill what she asks for without setting a dangerous criminal loose. I have to put my career on the line to fix this.

I stride towards the prison's main entrance, its weathered stone walls shadowed and ominous in the dark. The hefty, iron-crossed door groans when I push it open, and I clamp down on the bone-shaking shudder that ripples through me. The damn place is sombre enough during the day. At night it is just plain funereal. Even the air smells ... bereft.

The night administrator behind the desk leaps up in surprise when I enter. He is a thin man with hair so black it must be dyed—the sort of desperate dye job that tells me the man is either conceited or timid. It glows purple in the light of the lanterns, and I can't resist the comparison to a shiny balloon bobbing above the crowd at an All Hallows Eve parade. The administrator clears his throat noisily.

"C-c-c...can I help you, Constable?"

Timid then. Probably why he works night shifts.

"I need to see the Head Warden." I hold the administrator in my clutches with unwavering eye contact.

"He ...he's in bed." Balloon-head licks at his lips.

"Do not mistake me for someone who cares. Get him up!"

The administrator gives a jolt, turns, trips on his own feet, and nearly smacks his head on the door behind him. He glances at me, gives a high-pitched giggle, and scurries through the door. Hopefully to rouse the warden.

I wait. Alone, the shadows stretch, the silence thickens, and the stink of decomposing hope swells. But standing in the mouth of the monstrous prison is the least of my problems. Blast Rill and her tangling magic, forcing me to lay my career—my dream—on the line to help Lady Keeva. Gods. My teeth ache from the crushing pressure they endure. Rubbing at my jaw, I attempt to massage some of the tension away.

A short time later, the warden appears, a tartan robe tied around his sizeable stomach. He doesn't look impressed. I don't care.

"I am here to claim a prisoner," I announce.

8

Sabella

I STAND, FEET PLANTED wide, shoulders square and chin high, resisting the impulse to clear my throat.

"This is highly unusual, Constable—"

"Warden. I am not required to share details with you, but it is a matter of some urgency, and I need you to release the prisoner, Rill Narin, to me. Now."

The warden blinks several times, but he has no authority to question me. Citizen guards outrank prison guards in nearly all matters. Coming to the same conclusion, the warden nods to the night administrator, who snaps to attention.

I shove the bag I carry at the administrator. "Clothes. Instruct her to dress quickly." The black-haired man takes the bag and hurries off.

The warden reaches under the desk, and I tense, cursing the automatic reaction. Blasted childhood habits stubbornly refuse to rest. The warden draws out some forms and a pen and places them deliberately on the desk, giving the documents a little tap with his pudgy forefinger.

"Paperwork to be filed." He gives a greasy smile. "What reason shall I give for her release?"

I tell him, and his eyebrows shoot up so fast they tug his eyes wide.

By the time Rill appears, the paperwork is complete, and my feet itch with the urge to pace. Rill is dressed in the clothes I had scavenged from the lost and found hamper at the guard house. They are, predictably, too big for her. Partly because they are men's clothes and partly because she is the opposite of tall. The cuffs of the pants are rolled several times as are the sleeves. The boots are so big, she looks like a clown in comedic shoes. Putting that aside, I size her up with fresh eyes. She walks with her chin held high, despite the fact that one hand clutches at the waist of her pants to stop them from falling down. The nasty bruise on her cheek that I noticed earlier this afternoon has deepened, and the swelling pushes up under her left eye, so she rather looks like she is giving the room a half wink. Someone has clobbered her, but I bite back my questions. Now is not the time.

Rill meets my gaze, and although she hides it well, I can tell she is apprehensive and probably even a little scared. Good, she blasted well deserves to be.

I sign the document the warden pushes towards me, and it is done. My future with the guards is now filled with stormy shadows.

The warden ushers Rill forward, effectively releasing her. He sniffs loudly, his round, robe-covered stomach bobbing. His expression is sour. "You are the last person I would have imagined as a citizen guard, Narin. I'll be watching your progress with … interest."

Rill's step falters. Her mouth sags. The victory gives me a moment of satisfaction. She said I had to free her, but she didn't say how. Still … I wait. If Rill becomes flustered, this is all over … and I am ready to arrest her as an unlicensed Tangler. But she rights herself within a second and dips her head at the warden, looking for all the world like she is in charge. Impressive. I will have to be on my game with the criminal if she is to be my fledge.

Without a word, I turn and exit the prison, trusting Rill will follow. The slap of the too-big boots behind indicates she is.

She waits until we are out of hearing range of the prison.

"What'd he mean, guard?" Rill's voice does not emerge with fear or apprehension. And the polite tone she normally uses when Keeva and I visit the prison is gone. In its place, the snap of sharp insistence.

Ah. So, here is the real you.

I keep walking. "You said I had to get you out of prison. There was only one way I knew of doing that. And that was to make you my fledge. So, congratulations, Fledgling Constable Rill Narin."

Rill's boot slap stops. "I don't want to be a guard. I won't—"

I spin 'round and step close to Rill. "We made a deal. I get you out of prison and you take me to Lady Keeva. Are you telling me that in addition to being a thief, your word is also worthless? If you prefer, I can take you back to the prison. I'm sure the warden would be happy to make not-yet-lodged paperwork disappear. Particularly when he hears you are a Tangler."

I'm taller than Rill by a head, and her sharp chin tilts until she locks eyes with me. Even though one is swelling shut, the other pierces the moonlit night with hostility. Tension weaves threads between and around us. Neither of us moves, both waiting for the other to crack.

Will Rill be stupid enough to run? She will not get far in too-big boots and pants that threaten to sink to her ankles at any second. Then, without dropping her gaze, Rill lets out a breath.

"I am not a thief." Her voice is clear and trimmed with dignity and pride.

Surprise tickles at me, but I keep my expression neutral.

"And my word is good," she adds. "I just hadn't expected yours to be dishonourably devious."

"Pot, kettle," I snap back.

Rill narrows her eyes, flinching from the obviously painful injury to her face. She purses her lips. "I'll take you to Lady Keeva," she continues, still meeting my gaze. "We must get to an apparition booth and go to Ikra."

I give a curt nod and turn to walk once more. "We are not going via booth. I have a mount."

"A mount? We can't take a horse to Ikra. It is way too far." Rill's tone is contemptuous, like she can't believe I could be that stupid.

I just smile to myself as we clear the outer wall of the prison. To where I left Diarissa, who stands with her white, dappled coat glowing in the moonlight. She stamps a feathered foot and flares her wings when she sees me, a sight that never fails to delight.

A sight that never fails to fill my heart with gratitude that this magnificent creature chose me. I stop to take in Rill's reaction.

She stills, her one good eye is wide but not from shock. It is filled with wonder.

"Oh! You have a Pegasus?" she whispers and takes half a step forward, then stops. "Will she let me ride her?"

I reach into a saddlebag and withdraw two pairs of goggles. I hand a pair to Rill. "She will if I request it of her." I give the goggles a light shake. "Do you think you can wear these over … that?" I point to her swollen, bruised cheek.

"I'm used to pain," she mutters and takes another half a step towards Diarissa like she desires to be close but knows enough to stay clear. She accepts the goggles. "She's … magnificent. What's her name?"

"Diarissa. I'll make introductions but stay alert. Pegasi don't take kindly to people with … dark souls."

A flash of hurt crosses Rill's face, but she swipes it away smartly. I tuck that tiny flash away—perhaps the criminal has a heart, after all. Though tangling with Lady Keeva and using her to blackmail her way out of prison is heartless. And I don't regret what I said because it is true. A Pegasus sees a person's heart and soul and will judge them six ways to Sunday. Rill is a thief. She might declare her innocence, but every prisoner does.

"Diarissa. This is Rill." I nod to Rill to come closer.

She steps forward. All her attitude, her pride, her defiance has vanished. In its place, a softness. "Hello Diarissa," she says, her voice gentle and humble.

Diarissa lowers her head and snorts, regarding Rill with large, dark eyes. Then … she pushes her velvety nose into Rill's chest, snuffing acceptance. I suck in a breath, and my chest stills. What is Diarissa seeing?

Rill runs a hand over my Pegasus's face—her other hand still clinging to the waistband of her pants. Diarissa goes down on one knee and lifts her wings out of the way—an invitation for Rill to mount her.

Amazing. Maybe, just maybe, my career is not as over as I fear. Maybe Rill Narin has a good soul.

Still, I hesitate. "We will ride together. It will be too easy for you to touch my skin. How can I be sure you will not tangle with me?" Concern presses at me, torrid and burdensome. If Rill takes over my body, anything she does while in it will be my responsibility. The fear that kind of lack of control sparks is fucking breath robbing.

Rill has the decency to look chagrined. She runs her free hand through her unkempt short hair. "Can't Tangle with someone if their mind's not receptive." She cocks her head. "Doubt very much if yours would allow it."

"You managed it just fine earlier," I say, concentrating hard to hide the fear that holds my stomach tight.

"I didn't tangle with you. I just ... communicated. And even that was only possible 'cos I came to you from Lady Keeva's mind. You know her. Trust her."

It only just now occurs to me properly. "You have left Keeva now—um, untangled from her. Will she remember anything of the ... entanglement?"

Rill shakes her head and winces, no doubt from that damned injured cheek. "Won't remember anything. That's the problem."

Rill ducks her eyes for a second. When she lifts her gaze back to me, her throat bobs. "I saw a murder while I was in her body."

The scream of a barn owl fills the night and a shiver of shock ripples over me, but I draw on my training to speak with calm authority. "You witnessed a murder?"

Rill's peaked face turns pasty white. "Yes," she whispers.

"You can identify the murderer?"

Rill shakes her head more gently this time and gives a noticeable swallow. "A man was killed by a ... demon."

Anger flares, rising from chest to throat, and my carefully applied professional exterior crumbles. "A demon? It's bad enough you used Lady Keeva—who has only ever been good to you—to wheedle your way out of prison, but to fucking make up stories—"

"No," Rill all but shouts. "I didn't. I swear." Moonlight catches the silvery tears glossing her eyes. "The demon ripped a man to pieces right in front of me. The summoner was behind him, down the alleyway. He saw Lady Keeva ... I mean, me in her body. And he knew she saw him. Even though he wore a mask, a black mask, he still came after her. I had to help her. Had to get her to safety." Rill's breath catches in her throat, and she clings to her trousers with a white-knuckled grip.

For a moment, I think she is going to let her tears spill, but then her chin comes up, and her features settle into a bland expression.

"She is safe for now." Her voice holds only the slightest quiver. "In my hut in the woods. I drank a sleeping drought before I left her. But if she wakes, I'd imagine she'll be frightened."

I nod, anger dampening. I don't doubt Rill is telling the truth. In my three years as a fledgling guard, I'd talked to enough witnesses of violent crimes to recognise the trauma.

"If you didn't tangle with Lady Keeva to hold her to ransom, what, in the name of Agnis, were you thinking, tangling with the Earl's daughter?"

"Tying a knot in my rope," Rill says quietly, as if to herself.

"What?"

Mouth pursed, she lifts her hazel eyes. "Nothing."

Cicadas sing. Diarissa rustles her wings. In the distance, a cow low echoes softly.

I sigh. "Show me where your hut is, and we'll retrieve Lady Keeva."

9
Keeva

I STIR, MY FINGERS drifting lightly over my covers, seeking the silky texture I find so comforting upon waking. Instead, my fingertips meet with rough and scratchy, and with eyes still closed, I frown, annoyance rising. What has the laundry staff done to my bedclothes?

I draw a deep breath ... what in Saleal's name is that smell? A sense of wrongness penetrates my drowsy mind, and I jerk awake, my eyes flying open. My heart leaps, thundering into panicked action. These are not my chambers. Not my room. Not my home. It ... it is a hovel.

A musty odour of mildew rises from the rough blanket I lie under, and dust fills the air, swirling lazily in the muted light of the dim lantern on the table. Flinging back the blanket, I swing my legs from the narrow cot. Terror sends my head into a pirouette, and I pant. Where, in the name of all things holy, am I? How did I get here? And am I alone?

Sitting on the tiny bed, my fingers curled fiercely around the wooden frame, I look around, rational thought spinning out of control. The last thing I remember is the tavern with Thorn. This was a nightmare ... nothing more. I stomp my feet on the floor. Wake up! Yet, the nightmare persists.

Chest heaving, I peer into the dimly lit room. Every shadow appears to be an assailant crouching in wait, but it is merely my galloping mind playing tricks. I am alone.

The hovel is a tiny hut, clearly abandoned. Cobwebs hang from the rough-hewed rafters and lace the bundles of herbs that dangle from every surface. The desiccated plants thread the mildew stench with a sallow herb scent. In one corner of the single-roomed hut, a ring of rocks nestles into the dirt floor forming a fireplace with a rusted iron pot at its centre. A shelf runs the length of one wall. Upon it, rows of chipped jars, a stack of thick, misshapen clay plates and chunky clay mugs with crudely fashioned handles.

I have been taken prisoner. That much is clear. Anti-royalists? Slavers? I inhale deeply in an attempt to stitch my wits back together and drop my head ... oh, gods! A crash of fear and churning horror hits me. My dress ... it is blood-spattered. I tug at it, looking down at what was once my favourite dress. Tiny dots mix with great blobs of red. Over my gown, I wear a ... man's coat. What the heck is going on?

Sobs force their way past my throat, and hand over mouth, I race to the door of the dim, gods-forsaken hut. But the door will not budge, no matter how hard I throw myself against it. The wheezing strips of my breath are loud, and the sound intensifies my panic. I stumble to the single window, grope at the latch, and haul on the sill. It does not shift, not even a little. Holding back a scream, I hoist a chair and hurl it at the glass. The chair, however, merely ricochets back at me, and I duck, narrowly avoiding getting smacked in the face.

Chest heaving, I spread my palms on the table and lean, trying to catch my breath. Trying to fight the rising hysteria. Whoever locked me in this shack will be back, and I do not wish to be here when they return.

Collect yourself, Keeva.

My father's words play in my head.

"There are bad people in this world. People who would love to get their hands on the Earl's daughter. You must know I only wish to keep you safe."

It was the same speech every time I slipped my personal guard, Alex, and sneaked out of the manor.

Gods. He will relish the opportunity to say *I told you so.*

Strangely, thoughts of my father tut-tutting calm me. My thoughts cease tearing around my brain, and I manage to *think*. Someone has obviously spelled the place, locking me in. But unlocking spells are my strength. I straighten my spine and cross the dirt floor, grimacing at the grit beneath my stockinged feet.

The wooden door is rough beneath my palms, but I narrow my focus, murmuring an incantation.

Under moonlit sky, where shadows play
I call upon Briotl, guide my way

Goddess of magic, in realms so vast,
Set me free, from bindings cast.

It doesn't work. I attempt several more, varying the words, locution, and meter, but with no success.

I tap a finger to my lips. Anyone brazen enough to kidnap the earl's daughter would not make breaking free easy. Still ... I repeat the unlock spells on the window, but it remains firm ... no matter how hard I rattle it. Fear and frustration drive my heart to my throat.

Escape is imperative, and I study the floor. It is hard hard-packed dirt, but maybe, just maybe, I can dig my way out.

Glancing around the room for an implement I can utilise as a shovel, my eyes land on the small pile of books on the table. Specifically, the book that sits atop the pile. It is my favourite childhood book. A volume of stories of high adventure, set in the time when the fae folk still roamed Conpieta. A tangle of dread sits in my stomach. Did they hold children in this hut?

I pick up the book. It is well worn;, the letters of its title, *Legends Unleashed – A Collection of Extraordinary Adventures* are faded. The pages are yellowed, and when I open the book, a few leaves fall out. It is an old copy, often read and probably loved once upon a time. The thought it might have been the last bit of joy a child had makes me ill.

The next book on the pile is an academic book for school children, *The History of Magic in Conpieta.* Gods, did a child leave it here? Did they have it with them when they were kidnapped? With increasing horror, I spread the rest of the books over the table.

They are a strange mix. From basic herbology to university-level politics. From royal biographies by tabloid authors to the breeding of Pegasi. There is even one book on carpentry. What is this place—?

Voices sound outside the locked door, and my heart jams in my throat. Terror-stricken, I whip my head around, this time for anything that might serve as a weapon. The door rattles slightly, and I leap for a pan that sits on the dusty shelf. Putting the table between me and the door, I stand with my *weapon* raised in sweaty palms.

Two figures burst through the door, and I grip the pan fiercely. But the yellow light of the dim lantern on the table reveals ...

"Sabella?" I squeak, disbelief mixing with fear.

Sabella takes a step, her hands raised with palms forward. "It's me—here to return you to the manor."

I lower the saucepan, my hands trembling. Then I notice someone else standing behind Sabella. "Who is that?" I lift the saucepan again—it gives me a ludicrous feeling of power. But the whole situation is ludicrous, so it is fitting.

"It's Rill. You remember, from—"

"Rill Narin? From the prison? How?" I feel like my brain is buried under a pile of rocks, and I struggle to find a way out from under the weight.

"I know this is confusing," Sabella says. "And we ... no, *Rill* will tell you everything." Sabella turns to Rill. "You can speak the words of your betrayal. I won't do it for you."

Sabella looks twitchy. Her shoulders are tight, her arms rigid by her sides. Rill, too, shifts from foot to foot, and neither will make eye contact.

I stare at Rill, my fists tight around the saucepan handle and wait … for three seconds, then my patience expires. "Tell me what?" I snap, my eyes darting between Rill and Sabella. It is all I can do to hold back the scream that boils in my throat.

Sabella spins on Rill. "Rill!"

Rill lifts her chin and finally meets my stare. Oh, my goodness, her face is dirty … no, not dirty, it is bruised and swollen. Dread rises in me. My dress is bloody, and Rill's face is battered. What in the heavens has happened?

Rill steps forward and closes the door behind her. Slowly, as if I am a timid wild animal, she reaches over the table and turns up the lantern, filling the little room with warm light. I cannot resist a tiny backward step, and the action sends a flame of shame over me.

Timid wild animal, indeed.

I fill my chest with air and resolve to stand steady.

"I am a Tangler, Lady Keeva," Rill says. "I tangled with you this evening. I got no excuse except … your life seems so … exciting. Exotic even. And prison life is gruelling. They take your soul and squish it …" Rill takes a ragged breath. "You touched me earlier today when you visited, and the temptation was great. Sabella said you were going to a party, and … I thought if I could have a little time. A tiny break from the emptiness." For a second, Rill's chin drops, then she catches herself and thrusts it high. "I abused your kindness. I'm ashamed … and very sorry."

10

Keeva

COLD, STEELY BETRAYAL CHILLS my skin. Typical that a criminal would control me. Goodness knows everyone else did. I feel my lips twitch in anger and battle to still them.

"It seems you have only told me part of the story," I say, relieved when my voice emerges tight but steady. "You tangled with me, Rill Narin. You entered my body without permission, like the common thief that you are. You are quite correct in your summation that you abused my kindness."

Rill flinches but keeps her head high as if held by tensioned wire.

The situation still makes little sense, however. I place the saucepan back on the shelf in a slow, careful movement, taking the time to gather my thoughts. Indignation overtakes my fear, and I step out from around the table, my cheeks aflame. "There is more to this story, and I rather wish you would get on with it. How …" I sweep my hand about the hut. "… is it that I am here? Was I also a pony to be taken on a joy ride?" I step closer to Rill, determined to maintain my decorum, despite my bare feet and ruined dress. "Why was I locked in? And why, in the name of Saleal, is my dress covered in blood?" I cannot stop the squeak that rides my voice with the last word. I tug hard on the strange coat I wear, ripping it from my body and flinging it to the floor. "Why am I wearing a man's coat?" A sob catches in my throat, and I swallow, desperate to retain a modicum of dignity.

Sabella pulls out one of the chairs. "Perhaps we should sit while we tell you the rest."

"No, thank you, Sabella. I will stand."

Rill flicks her eyes to Sabella, and my stomach tightens. I am not going to like what they tell me.

"When I tangled with you," Rill says, with a lick of her lips. "I found myself … well, you were in an alleyway, behind a dance tavern."

The blow of my jaunts to the Lower West district being discovered hits me, and I grip the back of a kitchen chair. If my father finds out … my poise falters, but I manage a weak nod.

"There was a man." Rill continues. "I … talked to him. He went to take a … to relieve himself. I waited. He said we'd get a drink." Rill is dressed in clothes that are ludicrously large on her. She swaps the hand that holds up her trousers and wipes the other on her thigh.

"Then I felt heat. And the reek of brimstone. I turned and …. there was a demon behind the man. The demon …" Rill's throat bobs. "… killed the man."

My decorum splinters. I clap one hand over my mouth, and my other arm crosses my chest. "Thorn is dead?"

"I don't know his name, he—"

"A blond Fauster man?"

Rill nods, eyes downcast.

Sabella gently takes my arm, and I allow her to direct my trembling body to a chair.

"Oh, gods. Oh, gods." I rock on the painted wooden chair, then snap my head up. "Why am I here?"

"Keeva," Sabella's intense stare demands my full attention. "Rill will tell you everything, but you must listen carefully. And I'm sorry because Rill will have to give you details. All the details. Because unless you plan to turn Rill in for tangling with you illegally, you will need to say you witnessed the murder. You will have to make a statement to the guards."

Understanding slowly, slowly seeps into my brain. I drop my hand from my mouth and release the other shielding my chest, then fold my hands deliberately in my lap. "I will listen to everything without interrupting. And once I understand, I shall decide if I should bring Rill to justice."

Sabella rights the other chair from the floor, the one that clashed with the spelled window, and indicates that Rill sit. Rill's face, already pale with prison pallor, has turned positively pasty—a stark contrast to the nasty bruise that covers her left cheek—but she sits. And starts telling me the entire story.

I listen to the gory details of blood spray and spilled guts, horror sitting in my stomach and spreading to my chest and throat. I want to cover my face with my hands, to shut out this revulsion, but I force myself to listen. Rill whispers the words the demon spoke, and I sense she is just as terrified, just as reeling as I am.

Rill tells of the summoner, dressed in black and masked. Of how she ran in my body and used a dirty apparition booth to come to Ikra, trying to bring me to safety.

"A dirty apparition booth?" I thought they had all been discovered and decommissioned.

"An apparition booth created by illegal magic. By someone not licensed. Authorised booths are expensive, and they record ..."

I wave a frustrated hand at Rill. I know what a dirty booth is. She swallows her words and continues with her story.

An ominous crush of danger presses when Rill says the man pursued her ... well, me. Finally, Rill finishes her tale, telling of how she came to her hut with its wards. How she had managed a kind of fleeting tangled communication with Sabella.

"I needed to bring someone here," Rill says, her voice steady despite the impactful words she speaks. "No one else can get through my wards. But ..." her head drops again for a second before she lifts her chin once more. "I didn't want to be caught as a Tangler. Didn't want to be put to death, so I made a deal. I asked Sabella to get me out of prison. Which she did, but the clever witch put me right back into a different kind of prison."

"What do you mean?" I ask with a glance at Sabella who stands with crossed arms.

"There was only one way I knew of getting her out of prison," Sabella replies. "And that was to make her my fledge." Her face is tight, her lips pressed into a line.

"Oh, Sabella," I say softly. I know how much Sabella agonised over whom to choose as her fledge. What a critical decision it was.

Now, she has risked it all to help me. I stand and slowly pace the room, softly touching items as I go, trying to straighten my thoughts.

"Keeva. We need to get you back to Lapana," Sabella says, uncrossing her arms. "I'm sure the body ... sorry, Thorn, will have been discovered by now. Tavell will almost certainly be looking for me. And your family might have missed you. We must know how you wish to proceed." Sabella shifts her weight.

I stop pacing and point to the bed. "I awoke in a dusty bed that smelled of mould and neglect. I did not know where I was and how I had come to be here. I tried to leave, only to find the door and window locked with magic." I turn on Rill, a flush of anger heating my face. "I was terrified. I thought radicals had drugged or spelled me, and my life was going to end. Or worse." I inhale deeply.

"Instead, I find that my friend Thorn has been killed. By a demon, no less. A gods-damn demon. And some lowlife, black magic, demon-summoning man pursued me, presumably to end me, too. I find I am here, not because of radicals with nefarious plans, but because I was being kept safe." I stare at Rill, who sits rock-still. "You could have abandoned my body as soon as the demon appeared. You could have left me vulnerable and ignorant. You could have saved yourself. Saved your life and protected your secret. But you did not."

No emotion shows in Rill's expression.

"Staying in my body, you brought me to Ikra, where you hoped your friend would help me return to the manor. But when the summoner appeared, you brought me here." I look around the room which is much less scary now the lantern is turned up and I am no longer alone.

"Tell me, Rill. You grow and sell herbs, don't you?" I gesture to the jars lining the shelves.

"Yes," Rill replies in a small voice.

"Then why did you try to steal from a good family? I read the reports. That is what landed you in prison, was it not? Were you hungry? Was the person you shared this hut with ..." I sweep a hand towards the other bed in the corner. "... sick? In need of help? Or did you steal merely because you are greedy?"

Rill stands in a rush, her chair scraping against the hard dirt floor, her back ramrod straight. "I did *not* steal from that family. My sister, whom I shared this home with, went missing. Like so many others from Hismish, she simply vanished. She went to work one day and never came home. The citizen guards did nothing. They didn't care. They *laughed* at me." Rill flashes a look at Sabella. "I went to my sister's employer's home in search of clues to where she was. Instead, I was discovered and arrested for stealing. No one believed me. And now, it has been a year, and my sister is still missing. Yes, I bargained with Sabella because I wanted to avoid the death penalty—" she curls her hands into fists, her eyes flash and her jaw flexes "—but more than that, I wanted to get out of prison and search for my sister." She abruptly sits again like her body has folded under pressure. "I said I was sorry, Lady Keeva, and I am. But I won't beg."

I look again at the two beds. At the personal items still sitting on the small bedside tables.

"What is your sister's name?" I ask softly.

"Cassia. She was nineteen when she was taken. Because I'm sure she was. By traffickers."

I notice Sabella nodding as if she thinks Rill is correct, and I feel my decision click into place.

"I understand what it's like to want to escape your life for a while," I say. "It is the reason I go to the dance tavern. I am treated like a normal person there. I have friends who do not perceive me as good for nothing except for wearing elegant clothes." I turn to Sabella. "What is your plan, Sabella? I cannot simply return to the manor and quietly say I witnessed a murder."

The tension holding Sabella falls away, her shoulders rounding.

Rill noticeably relaxes, too, as if the invisible wires holding her taut have slackened. She reaches out slender, pale hands and carefully re-stacks the books I had spread across the table. Once again, she places *Legends Unleashed - A Collection of Extraordinary Adventures* on top of the pile, carefully reinserting the loose pages. She runs a wistful finger over the cover, then drops her hand in a gesture of resignation.

Saleal save me, I feel for this lost and lonely girl, despite what she has done. My father always says I am too soft.

"We came on Diarissa," Sabella says, moving towards the door. "I figure we go back to the stables and say we found you there, hiding in fright." She points at the man's coat crumbled on the floor where I had discarded it. "You'll need that. The skies are cold."

I give myself a mental shake. "Best we get going then." I direct a grim smile at Sabella. "I certainly hope I am around when you tell Constable Nash you have found your fledge."

Poor Sabella flinches.

11

Rill

I PRESS AGAINST THE wall at the back of the room, recoiling from the pink light the rising sun sends through the window of the guardhouse. I wrap my arms tight around my middle, squeezing against the churn in my belly, the burn in my chest, and the bloody deep ache in my cheek. In the last few hours, I moved from one hellish prison to another unimaginable situation. The gift of tangling with Lady Keeva turned to stone when the demon killed the man I had just kissed. Then, being chased by the summoner sent me to my cottage where memories, both sweet and bitter, filled me with determination. I could turn this ordeal around and use it to get out of prison. I could finally be free to search for Cassia. But Sabella took my hope and brutalised it, leaving me bruised and dazed. Gods ... A citizen guard.

I'd been here before, in this very room. At the start of the nightmare when desperation had stripped my reluctance bare. When anguish had driven me to the Lapana guards to report Cassia missing.

It had been summer then too and the room just as airless. The front desk just as ludicrously large and shiny. It dominated the room. A monolith that served as the first barrier, a test of your worthiness. It set the standard, declaring I was not shiny enough, important enough ... that I didn't belong here. The duty officer had stood erect behind the desk, his dark blue uniform prim—all straight lines and crispness. His hair trimmed, his face shaved smooth, the perfect symbol of shiny and worthy. Any personality or compassion he might have had, groomed away with scissors, razor, and an iron.

I had hovered in the space between the door and the desk, scared to speak in case my words were as dusty as my threadbare dress, as limp as my matted hair, and as hopeless as I felt.

I wondered what the hell I was doing here.

"Yes?" the duty officer asked, his shiny eyes sweeping over me in a wave that was judge, jury, and executioner.

I swallowed. "My sister is missing." Gods. Speaking the words made it real, and a raw, aching lump lodged in my throat.

The guard pressed his lips together, picked up a pen, and plucked a form from one of the precise piles of creamy paper that sat on his desk.

"How old is your sister, and how long has she been missing?" He stared at me, his well-groomed eyebrows arched over dark, soulless eyes.

"Nineteen. Two days." I curled my fingers, partly to fight back the tears that threatened and partly to hide the dirt that lay beneath my fingernails.

The guard put his pen down and returned the form to the pile, tapping at it until it lay perfectly square.

"You're Hismish, aren't you?"

I nodded.

"Come back when she's been gone a week." He waved a hand to dismiss me as if I was nothing more than a stray dog begging for a scrap of meat.

I blink and return to the here and now, my chest heaving from the memory.

I'm still a stray dog.

A mongrel who is now apprenticed to Sabella Rivers as a guard. A guard, for I'Kuna's sake! I had gotten out of prison, and Lady Keeva was not going to expose me for being a Tangler, but the cost was high.

My hatred for the citizen guards lives in my marrow like an infection. A disease spread by their subjugation and oppression. They claim they are 'doing their job' when they arrest decent people for using magic, ignorant and uncaring to the fact they are only trying to feed or clothe their families. They claim they are only 'enforcing King Ryker's laws' when they imprison people for crimes they didn't commit ...

I glance about. It is the same desk, spread with paper and ink wells, as that horrid day a year ago. The same uniform on the young man behind the desk, though it is a different man. I suppose the red velvet sofa under the window where Keeva sits, wrapped in a guard-blue blanket, is there to provide comfort for the gentry. The rest of the room is all function. Shelves take up the wall behind the desk and upon them sit numerous communication boxes. I reach twenty before I lose count. Burning hell. The whole of Ikra has one communication box, held in reverence like it is a god to worship. This kind of excess feels lewd ... and wondrous.

A surge of desperation rises in me and wraps around my chest making it hard to breathe. Three years of being a fledge is unthinkable. I need to look for my sister. My stomach twists like it always does whenever I think of what Cassia might, right now, be enduring. I have to find a way out of this nightmare.

"Is Senior Constable Nash here?" Sabella asks the young desk constable.

"I don't believe so, Constable Rivers," the guard replies. "He was called out..."

The door to the guard house opens in a rush and a striking-looking man strides in. He is Faustian. His yellow-green skin, elongated earlobes, and broad shoulders are a dead giveaway. Carrot-red hair sits above a strong, square jaw, and his deep-set, knife-like eyes take in the room with one sweep. His gaze flows from Sabella who stands at attention, to me, clinging to the wall and still hugging myself, and finally lands on Keeva who sits on the sofa with her feet curled under her and the blanket wrapped tight around her.

"Lady Keeva," he says with a sharp incline of his head. His voice holds a kind of gentle dominance. The kind that makes you think you'd do anything for him.

The kind that makes him dangerous.

"May I inquire why you are here?" the Faustian guard asks Keeva.

I squeeze my fingers tighter around my arms. This is it. If Keeva cannot give a convincing performance, or if she changes her mind, I will be back in prison … on death row.

Keeva lifts her head to the man. "Senior Constable Nash, I …" She bursts into tears, rocking slightly and bringing a trembling hand to her forehead. "I saw … I saw." She sobs harder and flings the blanket open, exposing her blood-stained dress. "I saw a murder. I saw Thorn Newton killed."

I blink with surprise. Either Lady Keeva is an excellent actor, or she is drawing on the emotion of this truly fucked-up situation.

The Faustian guard—clearly the Tavell Nash who Sabella mentioned had been her prime—turns to Sabella.

"She did, sir. I found her in the stables earlier. She was frightened and hiding."

I note Sabella does a fair job of lying, too.

Tavell motions to the guard with whom Sabella had made inquiries. He immediately sits at the desk, slides a clean sheet of paper towards him, and dips a pen into an ink well.

Satisfied the scribe is ready, Tavell eases himself onto the sofa with Lady Keeva. "The body of Thorn Newton was discovered a few hours ago. Near Jackal Tavern. Are you sure … I mean …" Tavell's voice fades like he can't think of a nice way of asking what Lady Keeva was doing in such a place. But he cannot ignore the blood that not only stains her dress but also lies in splotches on her face.

I swallow at the memory of Thorn Newton's exploding stomach. The feeling of warm wetness hitting my face.

Lady Keeva, however, displays no insecurity. "I often frequent Jackal Tavern, Senior Constable Nash. I sneak out of the manor and dance and drink and laugh with people who do not tiptoe around me as if I am as delicate as gold filigree and just as inclined to bend or break. Last night, I witnessed my friend, Thorn, killed by a demon in Carlver Alley. The Demon King's minion opened his belly and tore his throat out. He spoke. He said ..." Keeva takes a breath "... 'Tasty, innocent soul.'

We had agreed not to share the demon's other comment, 'Two souls in one. Rhapsody.' Those words might give too much away.

"The creature then decided my soul might be a tasty morsel too." Lady Keeva's tears mix with Thorn's dried blood on her cheeks. "The summoner stood behind, further down the alley. He was dressed all in black and wore a black mask. He chanted something, probably encouraging the demon to rip me apart, and so I ran. I fled through the tavern and out the front door. I ran and hid under buildings. I was terrified and couldn't make my thoughts cooperate. Finally, I came to Sabella. She always makes me feel safe. But the door to the guardhouse was locked, and I did not want to be seen ..." she heaves a shuddering breath and gathers the blanket once more "... in such a state by just anyone. So, I hid in the stables, hoping Sabella would attend to her Pegasus when morning broke."

Keeva meets Tavell's eyes, raising a finger to gently sweep at her tears. I get the sense Keeva is far from *delicate gold filigree*, and she is whip-smart too.

"Why do you believe it was a demon, Lady Keeva?" Tavell's voice is rounded, but his gaze is sharp.

Keeva sits straighter and firmly pats her damp face with her fingers. "Do you think I am stupid, Constable? I might not have street smarts. I might not have travelled extensively, but I am educated, and if the demon dog head with red eyes did not convince me, then the eye-watering, burning sulphur smell did. Along with the heat, like a blast from an oven. I am here to tell you—Thorn was not just murdered. A demon ripped his soul from his body. A demon that was summoned by a man in black."

I am impressed. Keeva remembered every detail. She shared it a bit like a shopping list, but the emotion she displayed made up for that. But this Tavell fellow is going to be a problem. I narrow my eyes at him and hope I am wrong.

Senior Constable Tavell Nash holds Lady Keeva in his intense gaze, and I can't shake the feeling that he can tell she is lying. I resist the urge to gnaw on a fingernail. Showing nerves now will not do. I settle for wiping at the sweat beading on my forehead and nose. Gods, it is hot in this room. The kind of heat I hadn't felt for the last year.

But Tavell nods slowly. "I saw the body, Lady Keeva. The ground beneath it was scorched, and the victim's clothes still emitted the smell of brimstone. As crazy as it seems, because there hasn't been a demon summoning in Conpieta for hundreds of years, I also concluded it was a demon attack."

Lady Keeva slumps on the sofa as if relieved and overwrought.

Tavell pats her hand gently. "Do you remember anything else? Any tiny detail could help."

Keeva makes a show of thinking, then shakes her head. "It was all a bit of a blur."

Tavell questions her further, asking what time it was when Thorn was killed and clarifying a few other details. "Alright. If you think of anything else, you can send for me. You'll need to sign the witness statement now, Lady Keeva. Then I will escort you back to the manor."

Tears well in Keeva's eyes once more, but she gives a regal dip of her head to Tavell from under demurely lowered lashes.

I pray that the words written on the paper by the young guard don't expose our deception. I pray no one looks too closely at Keeva's dress, which bears not only blood but also the brown and green stains of Wolf Woods.

Tavell invites Keeva to sit at the desk and read the statement, then he spins 'round and lays his impressive gaze on me.

"Who are you?"

12
Rill

I JOLT AND WANT nothing more than for the wall behind me to swallow me whole.

"This is Rill Narin," Sabella says, saving me, although Tavell's grey-eyed stare doesn't falter. In fact, I am sure he looks right through me. "She is my fledge."

That rips Tavell's gaze from me, and he places it squarely on Sabella. "Your fledge?" His eyes narrow, and his full lips pucker. "I don't recall the name from the list of applicants."

Sabella clears her throat. "She wasn't one of the applicants. Rill ... you know Lady Keeva and I regularly visit the prisoners." She pauses as if waiting for Tavell to acknowledge this, but he doesn't so much as move a muscle, so Sabella ploughs on. "And you know I was having a difficult time deciding upon a fledge."

I watch with fascination as Sabella collects herself, drawing in confidence like it is air. In a smooth, elegant gesture, she runs a finger over a lock of curly hair that sprang loose from her bun.

"I have gotten to know Rill over the last year. She expressed interest in being a citizen guard. Initially, I thought the idea crazy, but I couldn't shake the feeling she would make an excellent guard. Whenever I read the applications, I could not stop thinking of Rill instead. Finally, I decided she was the one. So, last night I fetched her from prison."

Tavell's eyes flick to me, then back to Sabella. "She's a criminal."

"No, sir," Sabella says. "She is innocent of the crime she was imprisoned for. I am sure of it."

A spark of gratitude snaps in me, then winks out just as fast. Sabella is putting on an act for Tavell. It is nice to imagine she believes me innocent, but dreams are for rich people.

Suddenly, Tavell stands right in front of me. He is broad and tall—although everyone is tall when you are pocket-sized—and I have to lift my head to look at him.

"Released from prison as a guard fledge, hey? Tell me, Rill Narin. Why do you wish to be a citizen guard?"

Standing so close to Tavell Nash, I can feel his magic. It seeps from him with a faint scent of ginger and pepper that rides on a current of power. And I swear his eyes change from grey to green, and for a second, it almost looks like swaying yellow grass patterns his irises. But he's missed our deception. He thinks I have scammed Sabella into releasing me. He doesn't have a clue I am a Tangler or that I was the one to witness the demonic murder. And why would he? No one would imagine such a situation.

My mind races. I have no intention of being a guard, but convincing Tavell I want this is crucial. I will find a way out later, but if he doubts me, I might end up right back in prison. And I am convinced he will know if I lie.

"I wish to bring justice to the people, Constable Nash. To all people, regardless of their place in life. Justice shouldn't depend on who birthed you, or on how much money you have or where you are from. My sister went missing a year ago. I fear traffickers took her. My mother and father ... well, let's just say I know what it's like to lose members of your family and have no one listen. I hope to be the sort of guard who listens." I meet his keen, intimidating eyes without flinching.

Tavell slowly looks me up and down.

"And this?" He jabs a finger towards my cheek. "A fist to the face if I am not mistaken. How did that happen?"

My heart does a little leap at the question I am not prepared for. "Caught in a riot. Stray punch found me."

The scent of ginger and pepper swells for a moment and unease settles over me. Is he using magic on me?

"Not very clever, being caught in a riot. I hope you display more sense as a guard."

Indignation rises, chasing my unease away, but I swallow the acid words bubbling in my throat. I think of the girl I'd pulled from the riot and the slap she gave me. This Tavell fellow is right—I was not very clever. So, I say nothing despite his continued scrutiny.

He sniffs, then blows through his nostrils like something unpleasant has lodged there. He pivots back to Sabella.

"For Kikara's sake, get her a uniform ... and a bath." He pauses. "And a cataplasm for that face." He turns and taps a finger on the large desk. “Fledge Ryan, please have the contract drawn up for Rill Narin to sign.”

Contract?

Tavell gently plies his fingers to Lady Keeva’s elbow. “I shall escort you home now, milady.”

Lady Keeva stands, and Tavell pivots, once more drilling his sharp eyes into me. “It is a magical contract. Signed with your blood. Quite unbreakable.”

My stomach plummets to the floor.

“Come. I’ll take you to the bathroom upstairs,” Sabella says. Her words and expression are tired.

We reach the door behind the monstrous desk when a man and lady crash through the front door of the guardhouse. A female guard tears after them, distress contorting her expression.

“Is it true?” the lady shouts in the high-pitched voice of hysteria. Her eyes are red-rimmed, her mouth contorted, and she clutches at a handkerchief held tight to her breast. The man beside her—his tie crooked and loose like he’d dressed in a hurry—clings to her arm, his grip fierce. I can’t decide if he is holding her up or using her to hold himself up.

“Is it true?” the lady shouts again, her eyes snapping from person to person and finally settling on Constable Nash. Perhaps because the couple are Faustian and drawn to their own, or perhaps because Tavell has an air of authority about him despite only looking to be in his late twenties.

“Are you Nash?” the man asks. “My wife and I are here to ask about our boy. The young constable that came to tell us ...” He glances behind him to the guard who stands with her hands tightly clasped. The man’s voice cracks, and he takes a second to collect himself. “She said a demon murdered him. We want to know if it is true. Has our son’s soul been taken to the nine hells?”

Oh, gods. They are Thorn’s parents. Pain stabs at my chest, scraping along my sternum and piercing my heart. I flick a look at Keeva, whose expression reflects my horror. Beside me, Sabella turns stiff as a stone pillar.

Calmly and smoothly, Tavell tugs the blanket tighter around Keeva, ensuring nothing of the bloodstained dress shows. Gently, he guides Keeva so she stands behind him.

“You are Mr and Mrs Newton?” Tavell asks.

"Yes. Yes, we are.”

“I am sorry to inform you, what you have heard is true. Your son was murdered by a demon.”

Mrs Newton collapses to the floor, her cotton gown puddling around her, her mouth hanging open in a soundless wail.

Mr Newton’s now empty fingers, open and close like he is trying to grasp something that is no longer there.

13
Keeva

I do not have to fake the trembling in my body on the carriage ride from the guard house to the apparition booth. The happenings of the last few hours have taken their toll. Constable Nash stays silent and does not press me for more details. Thank the gods. Though his presence is ... large. Insistent. Impossible to ignore, no matter how much I curl up within myself and tussle with my thoughts.

By the time we step out of the apparition hut near the manor's main gate, the sun has risen fully over the horizon, bleaching dawn's pink light. The shadows in the city below sprawl from the foot of Manor Rise, but the harsh glare of day paints the city in an honest light. A city of merchants and craftspeople. A place of innovation and invention.

Two hundred years ago, when the Benedict System drove magic from an art form to a business tool, it was the licensed witches of Lapana who mastered electricity. Lapana became the first city in the kingdom of Conpieta to bring working electric power to its citizens. The capital, Simgra, quickly demanded the same. But Lapana's love affair with being first had begun, and innovation and invention quickly became a part of its identity. The city had bulged to the west like a swelling tumour when factory after factory pushed the city's boundaries.

As Constable Tavell and I walk up the rise to the main gate, I cast out, my gaze wandering over the stately homes on Manor Rise. I sweep my eyes to the crowded residential district to the east, then slowly follow the transition to the central market district. Carlver River, lined with restaurants and taverns in the east and central districts, already crawls with barges and boats.

Only a few hours ago, I had been at one of those taverns, gleefully shucking the bonds of being the Earl's daughter. I had considered myself oh, so clever. Courageous. Breaking free and flying. Fool.

To the west, hulking depots stuffed with goods ready for transport crowd the riverbanks. I mentally cross the river, wandering over Lapana Strip with its farms and market gardens and scarred by the hulking medieval Lapana Prison. Then beyond into Hismish. I am unsure where Wolf Woods lies, but I had been somewhere out there, held in Rill Narin's hut.

My stomach shrinks in on itself, shame sitting like a leaden weight. Asinine. That's what I am. I had been convinced I was experiencing real life when I frequented taverns. I imagined I was bravely expanding my views and knowledge, pushing the boundaries like a gallant pioneer. Last night brought my childish fancies crashing down. Real has many layers. Many more than life as a royal and a sliver of pretending to be a Lapanian citizen. The life of Rill, for instance, living in that tiny hut in the woods with her sister, might be foreign—unthinkable—to me, but it is real to Rill. My sheltered existence closes in on me, and I press a knuckle to my chest. *Where has all the air gone?*

Last night's breeze has vanished, and flies buzz. It is going to be a hot day, yet even the uphill walk has not warmed me. I wave a hand over my face, chasing sticky flies from my eyes, while Tavell snaps orders at the guard on duty.

"I need to see the Earl of Tarr." The compelling urgency in Tavell's voice sends the guard scurrying. He does not so much as spare a look in my direction. No doubt, he does not recognise me wrapped in a blanket with my hair standing on end. Without the trappings of ladyship, I am little more than an empty vessel. A few brief moments later, the guard escorts us to the morning room.

There, I cross to the window, careful not to touch any of the silk-covered sofas with my filthy hands. I stand, clinging to the guard blanket pulled tight around me. The room smells of pine and lavender from its daily cleaning by our Hismish staff. Fresh tulips, arranged in the epitome of elegance, sit on the marble mantle in a turquoise and gold vase. I lower my eyes to the enormous yellow and olive rug at the centre of the morning room. The mahogany legs of the chairs and sofa placed just-so inside its edge. Aunt Pippa had specially commissioned the rug from weavers in Keplon, and it had cost a small fortune. On the wall, ornately framed paintings by the great artist, Len Bright of Simgra, hang in flawless, straight lines.

The comparison to Rill's little home with its dust and cobwebs and musty herbs is stark. She has a dirt floor, for Saleal's sake.

My life is as dirt-free as one can get. Living in the manor, being schooled as a respectable lady should be to develop a broad understanding in all areas of study. Not for self-improvement, or to make a difference, but so I can converse with people from all walks of life. But only people worthy of the social scene. The types of people who might be invited to royal gatherings, balls, and to drink tea from fine china.

The most important part of my day is what dress to wear, while Rill and her sister eke out a life growing herbs and living in a dirt-floor hut. Day after day until one is kidnapped by human traffickers and the other is imprisoned in her desperation to find her sister.

The inequity of the society King Ryker created had always struck me like off notes. But seeing Rill's home and learning more about her situation has turned the off notes into a thunderous fortissimo.

I shake my head, unable to decide if now is the wrong time for such thoughts or exactly the right time. I pull the blanket tighter and bathe in the gentle morning sun, filtered by the leadlight window, wishing it held more warmth because I can't stop shivering. Shock perhaps, but also a good deal of apprehension. My father is about to find out I sneak from the manor at night to visit the Lower West District. Saleal save me.

Yet all of that—Rill's pointless life, my father's disapproval—is nothing next to the image of Thorn's parent's grieving the loss of their son in such an evil way. *That* is burned into my mind, and the burn smoulders and aches. It infects me like an illness, and I shiver and sicken from their sorrow and my own.

My skin prickles, and my pulse leaps when my father enters the morning room, his soft boots barely making a sound on the polished floorboards.

He wears his favourite, gold-buttoned, navy waistcoat, over a crisp white shirt which is flawlessly paired with cream breeches. His thick, salt 'n pepper hair sits in waves about his face; his fastidiously groomed white beard and moustache frame his mouth. A mouth that is set with tension. His forehead is furrowed with its usual frown, and his ice-blue eyes snap to me in an instant.

Behind him, Alex Albo, the man employed as head personal guard for me and my brother, Finn. His boots, heavy and stiff, clop noisily, but he comes to a halt a short distance into the room, keeping his place in the background.

Alex is not a good-looking man. His face is long and horse-like, his nose bulbous. His hair is short and brown and his eyes narrow. But when he gives it, he has the most brilliant, wide smile, and he has always treated me and Finn with respect, kindness, and on the odd occasion, tenderness. He has served as our guard since we were born.

Gods. I hope he will not be in too much trouble because of me.

"Good morning, Lord Luca," Tavell doesn't waste time. "Were you aware your daughter was hobnobbing in the Lower West District last night?"

I hardly need to look at Father's face to know how his expression will shift, yet I cannot stop my gaze from landing on him. As I suspected, his ever-present frown deepens, his eyes cloud with concern, and he rubs a knuckle on his bearded chin.

"No, Senior Constable Nash, I was not aware." He looks at Alex with all the warmth of a snake charmer, but Alex's tight expression makes it clear he is just as ignorant of this revelation. Father returns his gaze to Tavell. "Is she in trouble?" My father's resonate voice rises and falls melodically, echoing slightly in the large room.

Tavell's stiff stance softens slightly. "No, and yes. I'm sorry to report that your daughter witnessed a murder last night."

The news draws a snap of heads and sharp inhales from both my father and Alex.

I swallow hard, my throat as dry as the desiccated herbs in Rill's hut.

"She became frightened and hid much of the night, then found her way to the guardhouse. She has made a statement."

My fingers grip the blue guard blanket around me, and I have a ridiculous desire to pull it over my head. They don't know the half of it. The vile summoner had pursed me. Or, at least, had pursued my Rill-controlled body.

"Are you referring to the murder purportedly committed by a demon, Constable?" Father looks more shocked than I had imagined.

Tavell nods. "Yes, milord. She saw the summoner, but he was masked. If you are concerned she is in danger, I would estimate she is not, as she cannot identify the man."

I am used to being spoken about like I am not in the room, but today it rankles at me more than usual. The lack of sleep, the fear, and grief rise in me, and I want to shout, 'I'm right here.' I hide my clenched fists in the blanket. Displaying anger will not help right now.

But finally, *finally*, Father turns to me. "Are you hurt?" He takes a step towards me, studying, intense. "Is that blood on your face?" His eyes roam over my body like he might spy an injury.

Blood on my face? Gods. No wonder Constable Nash shielded me from Thorn's parents. They did not need to see their son's blood.

I shake my head and drop my eyes. My ankle aches for some reason, and one buttock is bruised, but it is not bad. It is nothing compared to having your stomach ripped open. To having your soul taken. Thorn had been a good friend. Goodness, we had even kissed occasionally. My heart, my lungs, my chest ache. I will never see him again. Suddenly tears well. Real ones this time—not the fake ones I let flow when Tavell questioned me.

"No, father." I drop my gaze, willing my treacherous leaking eyes to dry. Praying the tears will hold off until I get to the privacy of my room.

Warm fingers gently pry the blanket from me, and I lift my chin to look into Father's pale eyes. "Good gods, you are freezing." He rubs my bare arms up and down. Then he takes in the state of my dress, and his expression hardens. He turns to Tavell.

"I assume you have all you need from her, Constable?"

"Yes, milord," Tavell says.

"Good. I have more questions, but they can also wait." He kisses my forehead with surprising tenderness, then turns to Alex.

"Alex, would you see my daughter to her room, please? And have an attendant assist her."

Alex gives a slick bow in response.

Father places a finger under my chin. "Go. Bathe, eat, and get some sleep. We will talk later."

It was more than I could have hoped for—although the talk later will not be comfortable. I cross the floor to join Alex.

"Alex," Father adds. "When you have seen to Lady Keeva, I'd like a word with you."

"Yes, milord."

My heart sinks. Alex *is* going to be in trouble for allowing me to sneak from the manor. But then, I had always known that ... and it had never stopped me.

14

Rill

UPSTAIRS IN THE GUARD accommodations, I bathe as Tavell ordered. The cataplasm Sabella brought me sits on the side of the bath. The wad of cloth arrived with tendrils of steam and smoke emanating from the pungent, thick green goop plastered over it that smelled of a mix of charcoal, mint, aniseed, and honey. I had wrinkled my nose but held it to my cheek for ten minutes as instructed, and the poultice now appears lifeless. However, the magic within worked wonders on the pain and swelling. Healthcare in Lapana—with access to magical healers—is so different to healthcare in Hismish which must focus on herbs and water and bandages. Even the secret, illegal magical Hismish healers don't measure up to the fully trained doctors of the sanctioned areas of Tarr.

The bath is deep and the water hot. I finger the soap that smells of pine and which actually lathers. So unlike the hard prison soap that is as useless as scraping your skin with stone. I wash my hair, my fingers pushing hard into my scalp. My mind races and pivots, spinning faster and faster. One minute, I am replaying Thorn's mother falling to the floor, the next, the impossibility of being a citizen guard consumes me.

A magical contract. Dammit.

I have to get away before I sign the cursed thing. But that poses a problem because, apparently, it awaits me downstairs. The chances I'll find a way out between bathing, dressing, and returning downstairs are slim to none. Particularly when Sabella stands on the other side of the bathroom door.

One thing at a time.

Right now, I can wash my hair and bathe with good soap and hot water and without fearing another prisoner, intent on brutality, will appear at any moment.

I scrub harder at my scalp, trying to push Thorn's grieving parents from my memories. Mrs Newton's gaping mouth and Mr Newton's fingers clasping at the air replay over and over. I'd seen their son die. I'd felt his blood hit my face. My throat burns, and tears fill my eyes. Safe in the privacy of the bathroom, I cover my face with a washcloth and sob my heart out.

By the time Sabella and I make our way back down the stairs, full morning blooms, and the sounds of the city surrounding the guard house ring out. Sunlight streams in the numerous, large windows, and I make a conscious effort not to squint. I have not seen full sun in over a year. Instead, I lower my eyes and tug at the pants and shirt of my brand-new guard uniform. It is dark blue, of course, and decorating my shoulders is a single dashed stripe in white that denotes my rank as Fledgling Constable. The cut of the uniform is masculine—we would not want female guards to stand out—and firm fitting, and I squirm and sweat. The prison was perpetually cold, and my prison clothes had been loose. In Ikra, Wolf Woods is delightfully cool even in summer, and my favoured flowing cotton dresses allow me to … breathe.

Everything here feels claustrophobic. Everything feels … wrong.

We reach the ground floor, now filled with milling guards who come and go via a door to my left.

"The duty office is in there. We share a desk," Sabella says, pointing to the door that is the source of so much traffic. "I'll do a full tour for you later," Sabella offers a half smile. "Right now, we need to do our assigned rounds—we're already late. After we sign our contract."

"We?"

"Yes. We both sign in blood. It binds us together for the next three years. The only thing that can break it is if you fail any of your tests."

I come to a stop. "If I fail a test, I'm free?" Is the solution that simple?

Sabella sighs. "We both are."

What? I frown.

Sabella correctly interprets my frown. "If you fail any of your tests, it is deemed I also failed by choosing a poor fledge. My time with the guards will end."

I hold the trickle of compassion at bay. My sister needs me. She might, at this very second, be being beaten or tortured … or worse. I don't have the luxury of feeling bad for Sabella. So what if Sabella is in this situation because I illegally tangled with Keeva? I give my shirt another tug, my guilt making it feel even more snug.

We walk into the reception room—Mr and Mrs Newton are gone, thank the Gods—and I eye the contract that lies on the monolithic desk. Beside it, two shallow dishes, a small knife and two pens. I reel. This is it. Once I sign that contract, I am bound to Sabella. My heart stammers with rising panic.

"How long 'til the first test?" I mumble. It seems it is my only way out.

"Three months." Sabella leans close. "My fate is in your hands, Rill Narin." Her tone is acidic, but beneath that ... a plea.

I slam my walls shut ...

Then, just as he had earlier this morning, Tavell marches into the guard house reception, his face tight with tension.

"There has been another murder." He holds up a strip of paper with communication box print on it. "From the description, it looks like it was demonic." He looks at me with eyes that are not unkind. "It occurred in Ikra."

My chest caves in, and a rush of nausea hits. I'Kuna save me. I led the summoner to Ikra. I thought only that he was after Keeva and didn't consider my hometown to be in danger. Stupid! Did he summon the demon in a fit of pique when he couldn't find me? He'd taken an Ikraite, and it was all my fault. I gulp short, shallow breaths.

"Have you signed the contract yet?" Tavell is asking, his words are like a feeble breeze wafting over me.

I barely hear him over the roar of blood pumping in my ears.

"No, sir, we were just about to," Sabella answers.

"Well, get on with it. I want the two of you on this. Perhaps our new fledge here can be useful on this one."

I slowly draw my guilt-soaked eyes to Tavell. He returns my gaze ... probing, assessing.

"What do you think, Fledge Narin? Want to take a shot at some of that justice you so crave for your people in Ikra?"

Time slows, the world quietens, and it is as if the room splits into puzzle pieces. Tavell, his face as heated as his red hair, his grey eyes cool within the glow. Sabella, rigid, waiting, yet stitched together by poised control. The guard behind the desk, like a piece of blue sky in a jigsaw—impossible to identify yet vital to the picture. Everyone is still, silent, and expectant. The desk itself looms unapologetic, sure of its place. And upon the desk, the contract that will see me become a citizen guard of Tarr.

Ignoring the grip of agonising pain, I straighten my spine, and time snaps back to normal. The volume of voices and movement within the guardhouse and the city beyond return to a steady hum.

I march across the floor to the desk, pick up the knife, and slit my fingertip. Beads of blood drip into one of the shallow dishes. Such a tiny amount, and yet, the copper twang fills my nose and coats my throat as if it is poison. My fingers tremble when I dip the pen into my blood. I press the red-soaked nib to the paper, and a blob spreads on the creamy surface. It soaks into the page and webs out in tiny random threads.

A demon killed an Ikraite.

My hand steadies, and in a rush, I scratch my name on the contract.

Steady and resolute, I hold out the knife to Sabella but look at Tavell.

"I'd like to bring justice to my people."

Beside me, Sabella signs the contract, and I feel it fall into place. The magic tingles and slides under my skin.

"And for that young Faustian victim, too—" I hesitate for a beat "—sir."

15
Keeva

A HOT BATH DRIVES away the shivery feeling—and washes Thorn's blood from me. In fact, I scrub my skin raw, wanting to be rid of every fleck that might be burrowed in my pores.

My attendant, Amelia, insists on a nightgown and breakfast in bed. I eat, astonished—and mildly appalled—to find I am famished. After I finish the porridge and eggs, Amelia takes my tray, and I snuggle under the covers. She closes the drapes, shutting out the blooming summer's day, turns out the lights, and leaves. I lie, fingering my silky sheets but feeling instead Rill's rough blanket beneath my fingertips.

Rill's home had disgusted me. Repulsed me even. How quickly I had judged when driven by fear. Only once the fear had gone did I see clearly. See Rill's dwelling for what it was. A home. A home shared with her sister. My reflex prejudices sit like a rusty ball of wire in my stomach.

My thoughts coil and knot and burr. No matter how much I try, I cannot smooth them out. I cannot stop them from prickling.

Thorn, killed by a demon. Killed by heinous, demon-summoning magic. The blackest of black magic. Thorn will never rest, his soul eternally caught in hell, the plaything of demons. We need to discover why. *I* need to discover why. Why had someone summoned a demon? Bringing some form of justice to Thorn is the least I can do. I will not allow anyone to push me aside. Not this time.

Flinging the covers off again, I swing my legs out of bed. I need to talk to Finn. He might have ideas about why someone would summon a demon. Maybe even who.

Quickly, I pull on a simple cream skirt and a white, short sleeve blouse. Choosing house slippers instead of my boots with their time-consuming hook and eye fastenings, I go in search of my brother. At this time of day, he is usually ensconced in his study, piles of books surrounding him. Research is his passion. His escape. His dance tavern.

I traverse the hallways of the manor, hoping I do not encounter Alex or my father. Staff in black uniforms and white aprons pause their dusting, polishing, and sweeping to curtsy as I pass. I dart around a hovering broom that swings back and forth—the servant using level-one magic to animate it. Ducking under a feather duster dancing about the light fitting above, I slip around another servant, cleaning a window. The thin woman polishes the glass by hand. Applying magic to glass is tricky. If the pressure is a little off, the glass will shatter. I observe the maid's spindly frame and the sweat beading on her face and think again of Rill.

All our staff are from Ikra, or one of the other unsanctioned villages scattered around Hismish. The only positions open to them under the Ryker laws are jobs like cook, cleaner, gardener, groomsman. The ball of wire in my stomach tightens, but this time, I thrust my ponderings of social injustice away. A demon-summoning killer takes precedence.

I reach the door of Finn's study, voices from within floating into the hallway. I halt and listen. Inconveniently, it sounds like Finn is talking with our father.

"Do you think anyone suspects?" Finn says.

"No. I do not," Father's smooth voice replies.

My chest tightens, and I dare to step closer to the study.

"What if we are discovered? With a heightened level of excitement in the city, it's possible. I mean, the Ryker Festival will bring enough attention, but when combined with demon killings ... perhaps we should stop for a time, delay the next?" Finn says, his voice thick with concern.

An icy fist of dread encircles me. I cover my chest with a hand, sure they will hear my thumping heart.

"It is too important to stop," Father answers, his voice low, but I can hear him clearly. "We go ahead as planned tonight."

What in Saleal's name are they talking about?

"Excuse me, milady." A maid passes me, carrying a bucket in each hand.

Drat.

All conversation within the study cuts off abruptly.

With a thick gulp, I burst into the room, determined to get answers. Finn and my father appear relaxed when I enter. Too relaxed. Their conversation, no matter what it was about, had been tense. Finn sits at his desk, leaning back in his chair. Father perches nonchalantly on the arm of another chair beside the desk. Both look like players on a stage—carefully arranged.

"What were you talking about?" There is no point pretending I did not overhear them.

After a darting glance at Finn, Father sweeps his fingers down his beard. I know the gesture means he is thinking. "Why are you not in bed? Are you feeling well?"

"What were you talking about? Do not thrust me aside. I may only be *Lady* Keeva, but I am not deaf, nor stupid."

"Of course not," Father says quickly. "I was just concerned for you. To answer your question, your brother and I were discussing the proposed amendments to the Magic Class bill. You know it is being drafted in secret. If our detractors get wind of it, they will be appalled at the notion of easing magic restrictions within Tarr. We must get it right before we present it to the council."

I stare at Father. It is true they have been working on the Magic Class bill for some months, and my father and Finn are often deep in discussion about it.

Each year, King Ryker holds a festival to celebrate his rule, and a part of the festivities is that the realms can introduce a new law or amend an existing one. A single change not dictated by the king and applied only to the realm that makes it. He calls it the Liberty Law Grant. But the law still needs to be ratified by the realm's counsel, and the counsel always includes a royal representative.

The festival is next week. And Father and Finn have been working hard to make the bill ready.

I draw my lips in, catching them with my teeth. Perhaps my overwrought mind is jumping to foolish conclusions. Then again, Father and Finn seem skittish, but perhaps merely because they fear being overheard. I shake my doubts away. This is my father and brother, for goodness' sake. I draw a deep breath and give Father a slight nod.

"I came to talk to Finn. It seems to me he may be able to help discover why someone would summon a demon. It is dangerous magic, after all. No one has summoned a demon for years. Why would they risk it? Finn is so good at research, perhaps he could help the guards with information."

Father opens his mouth to speak, so I rush on. "It might also help *me* come to terms with seeing my friend killed right before my eyes."

That seems to work. Father's brow smooths, and Finn taps a forefinger to his lips, interest lighting his face. He will relish something new to study.

"Keeva is right, Father," Finn says. "A demon summoning is highly troubling. As leaders of Tarr, we would do well to assist in the investigation."

Father strokes his beard, then dips his chin in acquiescence. "Very well. Tell Finn what you can of the killing, Keeva. I have a few things to attend to, but then you and I will have that talk."

Without waiting for an answer, he sweeps out the door.

Finn lounges even further back in his chair, brushing his blond hair from his face, and props a foot on the desk. Something he would not dare do while Father is in the room.

"A murder, hey, Kee. That must have been horrible." His brown eyes—a copy of our mother's—hold concern.

I settle into an armchair and smooth my skirt. "It was. I was ... terrified." I shudder at the memories of last night.

Finn swings his legs off the desk and comes out from around it to sit beside me in the armchair's pair. "Sorry you had to see that. Go through that." He offers a brief smile, his dimples making a fleeting appearance.

I shrug. "It is worse for Thorn. He's the one who's now dead." I do not desire anyone's sympathy. Partly because I did not witness the cursed murder, but mostly because I am alive and well and Thorn is not. It is him and his family who need sympathy. Thorn's mother looms in my mind. "His parents came to the guardhouse while I was there. A young guard had notified them, but they were in shock. Constable Nash had to tell them all over again that Thorn's soul had been taken to hell." Tears prick at my eyes, and I retrieve my kerchief from a pocket and dab at them. "His mother collapsed." I look at Finn. "It was horrible." A tear escapes and rolls down my cheek. "I greatly desire helping to find who was responsible. It is the least I can do."

Finn reaches out and gives my hand a squeeze.

"Let us get on with it, then." He twists towards his desk and slides a notepad and pencil across it. He sits back and props the notepad on his crossed knee. "Tell me everything about the demon. What did it look like? Did it speak? Any detail at all could be useful. I think we should start by finding out what *kind* of demon it was."

I lean forward and rest my elbows on my knees in a rather masculine pose. "It reeked, like sulphur. It produced heat, too. It stood like a man but had the head of a rabid dog with red eyes and a slavering mouth. Its legs were that of a goat ... and it possessed the tail of a serpent. It did talk. It said, 'Tasty, innocent soul.'" I shiver. I may not have heard the words firsthand, but they give me the cold creeps like someone has walked over my grave. I draw a breath and make a mental note to talk to Rill again. Any minor detail she might not have told me could be useful. Suddenly, I sit up.

"You will require access to the Heinous Section of the library."

Finn taps his pencil on the top of the notepad. "Yeeesss." He draws the word out. "*Official* access to the Heinous Section will make it easier."

I start and stare at my brother. He tucks a stray hair behind his ear, his eyes shamelessly shining with mischief.

"Finn! Have you been sneaking into the Heinous Section?"

16
Keeva

Finn smiles like he is pleased with himself. "Old Hanna is getting, well, old. She dozes. And when she does, I pinch her key ... don't look at me like that, I only borrow it and take the opportunity to sneak in."

"Poor Hanna," I murmur.

Hanna has been the Manor librarian for the Earl of Tarr nearly all her adult life. She served my grandfather, then my father after that. But there is no doubt she is now failing. Her once strong stride is as wobbly as a newborn foal, and while she always remembers who I am, she does sometimes forget what day it is, or even what month.

I am surprised Father has not replaced her. Perhaps because she continues to look after the library adequately. The filing skills and knowledge earned when she was younger hold firm in her fading memory. And unlike a public library, she does not need to work swiftly. However, most public libraries do not have restricted Heinous Sections. Over the years, generations of Earls have gathered books and artefacts related to black magic, satanic worship, and demon summoning. The collection should be better protected.

"Why would you go poking around in the Heinous Section? You know it's dangerous." I am a little shocked my brother would be so brazen. But then, his thirst for knowledge is unquenchable.

Finn taps the end of his pencil on the notepad. "Because I'm not supposed to. Don't look so appalled, Kee. I don't stay in there long, and I'm careful. I won't succumb to any voodoo."

"Mother says too much time studying the black arts can turn your soul black."

Finn snorts. "Only if you're an idiot." He taps the notepad again. "Anything else about the demon?"

I sigh. "The summoner chanted. I did not understand the words, but ... I think the demon vanished when I ran."

"Would you recognise the words if you heard them again?"

Rill might.

"Maybe."

"Alright. Let's go and talk to Uncle Sean. He already has access to the Heinous Section and may know something. Additionally, he can guide me to the best books."

Uncle Sean is a keen academic. The family often comments it is from him that Finn gets his scholarly curiosity.

Finn and I find Uncle Sean sipping tea with his wife, Pippa, in their wing of the Manor. Thick velvet curtains shut out the morning sun. When we enter the room, Pippa rises from her chair and comes directly to me.

"Keeva, darling. I hear you had quite the night. How ghastly that you had to endure such a nasty experience."

I relish the warmth of Aunt Pippa's arms coming around me in a hug. Pippa is a genuinely kind, gentle woman who cares for Finn and I like a second mother. I return her hug with a light squeeze.

"I am well, Aunt Pippa. Truly."

"Sit. Have some tea with us." Pippa gives me a pat on my arm and smiles. Her hair, groomed into a high bun, would look severe on many, but the style does nothing to harden Aunt Pippa. Instead, together with her ever-present, double-strand pearls, she looks regal. She is a handsome woman, and her years have not dimmed her in the slightest.

I return her smile and lower myself into a chair, while Finn sits next to Uncle Sean.

Uncle Sean immediately offers me a plate loaded with fruit pastries. "Here, love. Food helps everything, I find." He gives me a wink. "You're a tough one. You'll be fine I fancy."

Uncle Sean is the only person in the manor, besides Finn, who does not treat me like I might break if handled too firmly. He talks to me the same way he does everyone else. No subject is considered inappropriate. From politics to society gossip. From business strategies to party planning. From love to sex. He is a warm-hearted man with a big laugh and a generous spirit. I love him dearly. Everyone in Lapana loves Sean.

I take a pastry. "Thank you, Uncle Sean."

"Keeva thought we might undertake some research into demons and demon summoning," Finn says. "We hoped you might be able to help. Tell me where to look in the Heinous Section."

Uncle Sean sucks his lips in and runs a hand across his shiny, bald head. Then he gives his trademark, sparkling smile. "You don't have access to the Heinous Section, my lad."

Finn licks at a piece of flaky pastry stuck on his finger. "I am going to make a request to Father. He agrees anything we can find out could be useful. We can't have a demon summoner on the loose in Lapana."

Uncle Sean's eyebrows shoot up. "No, no, indeed. Well, of course, I'll help you. Provided you gain permission to access the Heinous Section, I'll show you the ropes. Show you the things you need to be careful around."

I dart a look at Finn. I *knew* sneaking in there unsupervised was dangerous. But Finn deliberately avoids my gaze.

"Thanks, Uncle Sean, that would be great. I'll go and find Father now."

"There is no need." Our father walks into the room, and I know immediately something is wrong. His expression is tight, his eyes filled with concern. "I grant you access to the Heinous Section, Finn. I'll let Hanna know. But I want your uncle to be with you at all times."

I stir in my seat. I would like access too. The thought of exploring demonic artefacts and spell books of black magic terrifies me. Yet it also thrills me.

"Father," I begin, but it is Lord Dalton, Earl of Tarr who turns to me, and the look on his face reminds me something is amiss.

"Keeva. I want you to remain in the manor. Do you understand? You are not to leave for any reason."

"Why?" A sick feeling sits in my stomach. I am tempted to think this is punishment for sneaking out, but something else is going on.

"There was another murder. Another demonic murder. In the Hismish village of Ikra. I just received word from Constable Nash."

My hand flies to my mouth, and ice scrapes at my skin. Gods above. The summoner took someone in Ikra? I pant, trying desperately to maintain my composure.

Finn stands, concern clearly written on his face.

"I've ordered our App Booth guarded," Father says. "No one is to use it without the say-so of the guard. That goes for everyone. But Keeva, they've been given orders that you are not to use it at all."

I feel my body deflate. As usual, I am being treated like I am something precious. I wish Mother was here. She might, just might, talk sense into my father.

"When is Mother due back?" I ask. She is currently on a trip south to Edgewind to see her cousins.

"I have sent a communication to your mother. Until this demon summoner is caught, she is not to return to Lapana."

I sink back in my chair. There is nothing for it. I will just have to use my fall-back method of leaving the manor and sneak out using the old root cellar in the servant's floor.

17
Sabella

THE SHOCK OF ANOTHER murder scorches the weariness from me. Earlier, when Rill had been bathing, sleep scratched at my eyes and tugged at my lids. No surprise when I'd been up all night.

What did surprise me was Rill's sudden resolve. Dread had soaked into my bones with Rill's focus on how to break the contract, but when Tavell informed us of the second demonic murder, she became like a newly oiled sword, glinting and sharp. Sure, the victim was one of her own, but I sensed—or perhaps merely hoped—it was more than that. At the very least, it proved she was inclined to take action. Exactly the kind of trait that is needed in a guard.

I glance at Rill now as we step from the apparition booth in Ikra. She looks good in her uniform. Despite being short and slight, she gives the impression of being a powerhouse, as if tenacity wires her joints and heats her blood. Her short brown hair is no longer matted but still hangs about her face in shaggy layers though it is brushed back from her broad forehead. Her large brown eyes sit under bushy brows, and her pointed nose is bracketed by angular cheeks, the left one sporting an impressive black bruise. The cataplasm has removed the swelling and progressed the bruise from fresh red to healing black. Now that her cheek is no longer puffy though, it is obvious she isn't well nourished, and a wad of guilt sits in my gut. I should have insisted we eat before we headed out. But Rill's narrow, sloping chin juts at a defiant angle. She clearly isn't focused on such mundane issues as food.

Tavell stands by the hut's door, all but tapping his toe in impatience, and I hustle to follow him from the booth hut. A silver-haired woman awaits him and behind her, a small crowd of villagers. No matter what, murder is an exciting occurrence. Rich or poor, it always draws macabre interest.

My eyes travel up and down Ikra's main road. I'd only been here once before, and it had been winter then. The covering of white snow had softened the village, cleaned it. With the mountains in the distance on one side of the village and Wolf Woods on the other, it had almost looked pretty. Not today.

In the harsh light of the summer sun, the village is laid bare. The road is dusty, the buildings are bleached and crumbling. Most are built of thin, splitting planks, and in places, rot allows the flow of air.

The villagers themselves stand staring and hostile. In Lapana, we are seen as heroes. Here, we are the worst kind of enemy—sneaky, brutal subjugators. The blistering hatred stings my face like it's a searing flame.

The villagers' clothes are plain and as worn and weathered as the buildings. The children are painfully thin, and the scent of poverty—decay, boiled cabbage, and human waste—hangs in the air.

Shoving a ramrod down my spine, I take up a rigid guard posture and set my face to an expression of authority, but inside, I ache. This is a town held hostage and battered by King Ryker's laws. This is Rill's hometown. And I have made her a fledgling guard. My mistake sends a surge of apprehension through me—what, in the nine hells, was I thinking? I know what it is to be unsanctioned. The orphanage I was raised in may have been in a sanctioned town, but all orphans, regardless of location, are considered unsanctioned. Their final designation is decided only upon adoption when they are matched to their new parent's status. And yet, for all the uncertainty, I was fed enough to survive and grow, and I was schooled. I could not relate to the thin, starving faces before me. I swallow my musings, and although they lodge in my stomach, hard and unyielding, I force myself to focus on the job at hand.

The woman who stands before us leans slightly on a crooked stick. I recognise authority when I see it and know this is probably Ikra's elder. Unless I am much mistaken, I am also sure she is a witch of considerable skill. Interestingly, she doesn't try to hide her magic. There is no dampening, no wilting, no trying to appear smaller. Even in the presence of Tarr guards who can rightfully arrest her if we suspect she has used even a drop of magic, she stands tall.

The woman is defiant and proud. Both can get you in a lot of trouble.

"I am Senior Constable Nash," Tavell greets the woman with a dip of his head. "We are here to investigate ..."

Tavell's words trail off because the woman isn't listening. She looks straight past Tavell—an occurrence as rare as never. Immune to his commanding presence, her gaze lands on Rill.

"Daughter. It is good to see you." Her eyes hold a mix of joy and wary confusion.

Rill goes to the woman and kisses her cheek. "Hello, Esme." Emotion wafts from the two, but they hold themselves apart from it, like now isn't the time. "Constable Rivers here ..." Rill indicates towards me. "... took me as her fledge, and so I am released from prison. But it's not the day for social chats. As Senior Constable Nash said, we're here to find out about the murder." Then she sucks in a breath. "Who was it?" Her voice is small and filled with trepidation.

Esme's face clouds. "Yalda. I'm sorry, Rill."

Rill goes still, though her chest rises and falls rapidly. Then she takes a big, expanding breath and turns back to me and Tavell.

"What do we do first?" Her eyes are bright with pain.

"Esme. Could you please take us to the body?" Tavell asks it as a question, but his delivery makes it sound like a command.

Esme nods and grips her cane with both hands.

"Fledge Narin," Tavell continues. "If you knew the victim, this might be difficult. You may stay here if you wish."

"I do not wish," Rill replies.

There is no doubt this was another demon killing. The dirt around the eviscerated body is blackened, and the pungent smell of brimstone hangs in the air. The victim's bright red hair fans out on the dirt, almost like it pays homage to the blood-soaked ground she lies on. Her green eyes stare vacantly at the sky, and I imagine I can see the terror of her sudden death in them.

"We record our findings into a com box," I tell Rill, pointing to the small communication box in Tavell's hand. He crouches beside the body, his sharp gaze wandering slowly over the victim. "When we return to the guard house, we activate the recording into writing. Alternatively, guards at the GH can obtain a transcribed copy via the linked box at their end. That way, if needed, the analysts can commence their work promptly. We are all issued with our own com-box." I tap the large pocket on the vest I wear. "You'll get yours this afternoon."

"Victim is a woman of approximately thirty years of age," Tavell speaks into his com-box.

"She was thirty-two," Rill interjects. "Her name was ... is Yalda Lott."

Tavell gives Rill a small nod. "The victim's abdominal area and chest has been torn apart and her intestines spilled." Tavell pauses and dips closer to the body. Then he plucks something from the woman's tattered chest, carefully avoiding the white ribs that gleam grotesquely in the sun.

"What is it?" I ask.

Tavell rolls the item slowly between his finger and thumb, seemingly caring little about the dried blood that covers it. He glances at me but speaks into his com-box. "Found what appears to be a broken claw in one of the chest wounds. This is consistent with the demon theory, but the item will be taken to Lapana Academy for Professor Meade's analysis." Tavell once again studies the body. "Victim's throat has not been injured, unlike the first body in Lapana."

Tavell gently rolls the girl over, the sun setting his red hair aflame like a macabre reflection of the victim. I keep a close eye on Rill. Many fledges lose their stomachs or even faint when faced with their first body. And this is a particularly gruesome one. But Rill simply looks on intently, her eyes moving slowly from the woman's head and down her body. She doesn't tremble. She doesn't swallow against rising nausea. Still, shock can be delayed.

"The shirt on her back has been shredded by what appears to be claws," Tavell continues recording. "The skin is similarly ripped. First thought is that the initial attack came from behind."

Tavell stands. Over his shoulders, the foothills of the Haunted Peaks roll into the distance. At my back, Wolf Woods stands, dark and menacing, even in the bright sun. The looming presence of the woods fires my imagination, and I fancy the summoner is a hag who has taken her black magic too far. Rill is sure the summoner is male, but hags can change their appearance.

Surrounding us—although at a distance after Tavell snarled at everyone to stand back—are the villagers. Men stand with crossed arms and wide stances. Women cover their mouths or pluck at items of clothing. A few weep, some moan, and others simply stare, anger and grief making their faces rigid and raw.

"Sabella, could you and Rill please take statements? I'm going to talk to Esme about taking the body back to Lapana," Tavell says.

"She won't like it," Rill says in a matter-of-fact tone.

Tavell pauses. "Perhaps you could accompany me, Fledge Narin. If the mortician can examine the body, he might be able to assist us to identify the kind of demon. There are many, from numerous low-level demons, right up to King Ravana himself. Combining his findings with Lady Keeva's statement will give us valuable information. If we can narrow down the type of demon, we can assess what kind of power is needed to summon it. It may bring us closer to finding the man responsible." Tavell's eyes soften. "We will return Yalda to Ikra when we are done. You knew her, didn't you?"

Rill's throat bobs. "She sometimes looked after me and my sister when we were little. Then, when she had her own children, we helped Yalda care for them." She spins on her heel. "We'll talk to Esme."

I watch Rill and Tavell go, then turn to the crowd. "I need to speak to anyone who had contact with Yalda. To anyone who might have heard or seen anything. Please."

A murmur goes through the crowd, and the hostility returns. Hoping I am guessing correctly, I let my guard persona fall. I round my shoulders and soften my face. "I only want to find out who did this. I want to bring justice to Yalda and to Ikra," I say. "But I need your help."

A white-haired lady in a stained, greyish dress and tattered apron steps forward, her demeanour as sharp as the juice of a lemon. Her face and body are angular like she is made up of dozens of crooked elbows. "You can conduct interviews in me house." She jerks her thumb, looking like she is trying to bruise the air rather than give directions.

"Thank you." I nod and cover the body with the tattered blanket that had been over her when we arrived. "Will someone stand watch over Yalda?"

A man with red-rimmed eyes and a deeply grooved face shoulders his way through the small crowd. He takes up a soldier-like stance beside the body.

"I will watch over my wife, Constable."

My heart cracks wide open.

18

Sabella

The home of the sharp, all-elbows woman is tiny—only one room which is lounge, bedroom, and kitchen combined—but it is surprisingly cheerful, given its owner. It is like the woman has given the home all her softness leaving her bereft. Every item, every piece of furniture is thin and worn, but it is clean, and brightly coloured rugs adorn many surfaces. Candles of all shapes and sizes are scattered about, snatching any available surface. At the moment, none are lit, and the room is dim after being in the morning sun.

The home-owner orders me to sit at the table, which when I lean on it, rocks on the uneven floor, so I sit back in my chair and drop my com-box onto my lap.

"My name is Sabella. Thank you for offering your home."

The Ikraite woman stares at me with a kind of resigned repugnance as if I am none other than the murdering demon in disguise.

I lick my lips. "What is your name?"

She folds her arms, her chin shooting out to one side. Awkwardness billows off me …

"Aubrey Burke," she spits with the kind of venom that normally accents swear words, and with rapid, jerky movements, she gathers three mugs and after filling them from a jug, slams them down on the table, the water sloshing over the edges.

I try to gather my wits. Normally I am wrapped in guard armour—straight back, lifted chin, snapped orders—but having discarded it for these people, I am whisked straight back to the orphanage. I am a child again. A child without friends. A child who is constantly teased and bullied. I try a smile and gulp at my water which leaves a sour aftertaste.

Aubrey returns my smile, looking like a wolf baring its teeth, and the drink's sourness spreads from my stomach to my chest.

"Hello …?" Tavell's voice sounds at the threshold of Aubrey Burke's home.

Thank the gods.

He and Rill enter, and Tavell immediately sits at the table uninvited. He leans his forearms on the table, seemingly oblivious when it bucks like a boat in rough water and grabs a mug of water with enthusiasm. He has it halfway to his lips, when Rill sweeps in and snatches it from his hand.

"What in the name of …" Tavell's expression cracks with thunder.

"Aubrey," Rill says in the tone of a governess scalding a child. She sniffs the water and shakes her head, lips pressed tight.

"Rill," Aubrey replies like she's working up a spit ball and crosses her arms.

Rill turns worried eyes to Tavell who, keeping his dark gaze on Rill, reaches out to my mug and sniffs at the water within. He dips a finger in it and dabs it on his tongue.

Rill has gone so still; I don't think she breathes.

Tavell turns, treating Aubrey to one of his flinty stares. Her only response is a swallow, though I notice her fingers press into the soft flesh of her arms.

"How much water did you have, Constable Rivers?" he asks without taking his eyes off Aubrey.

"Oh, um ... a mouthful." A horrid sinking feeling washes over me. "Was it poison?"

Tavell finally breaks his stare with our dubious host. "Not poison, no. Fledge Narin, remove these mugs of water. And ma'am—" he turns back to Aubrey, anger holding him tight "—thank for you the use of your home, but we need privacy, so, unless you know something about Yalda's murder, you can leave ... now."

At his words, Rill breathes again and quickly gathers the mugs. But Aubrey doesn't move. Rill tosses the water into a tub that serves as a sink then grabs Aubrey's arm.

"Nine levels of hell," Rill squeezes out between clenched teeth. "Leave."

Aubrey gives Rill a look that would spoil food, then quick as a mouse, stabs a finger into Rill's bruised cheek. She turns and stomps from her home.

"Hope that hurt," she flings over her shoulder before slamming the door behind her.

Agnis save me, what a woman.

"Get our first witness, Fledge Narin," Tavell orders.

I want to ask Tavell what was in the water, but the rigid set of his jaw and shoulders stops me. If it was anything to worry about, he would take action, so I shove the whole situation to the back of my mind—though I fully intend to grill Rill over it the first chance I get—and turn to greet the first witness Rill brings in.

A middle-aged man takes the last seat at the table when Rill indicates he sit.

"When did you last see the victim?" Tavell doesn't waste time.

The male witness looks directly at Rill.

She sits with shoulders rounded; her hands clasped between her knees. "Yalda baked the best bread in Ikra, didn't she, George," she says in a soft reminiscing tone.

George folds his arms, his fingers squeezing his biceps.

"Was yesterday baking day? Did you see her delivering?" Rill asks.

George drops his head like he is praying. "Helped her run the loaves out," he says into his chest. "I like the smell and after delivering bread, it gets in me clothes. Stays with me a while." He unfolds his arms, looks up, and gives an embarrassed half-smile.

I fancy I can smell freshly baked bread on him even now.

"Finished 'bout ten in the mornin'," George says, absentmindedly scratching at his elbow. "I tended me garden after that. Didn't see Yalda again ..." His breath hitches, and though he opens his mouth again, no more words come out.

I blink ... then gasp. The room has turned monochrome. The colourful blankets now varying shades of grey. Tavell's hair, like charcoal.

"Easy, Constable. It will pass soon enough," Tavell says without so much as a glance my way. "Thank you, George. You can go now."

Fuck. The water was spelled. Or was, perhaps, a potion. Unlicensed magic, audaciously performed right in front of citizen guards. No wonder Rill looked frozen with nerves. Tavell could have arrested Aubrey. I can't help but scrub at my eyes while Rill fetches the next witness.

Hold it together, Sabella. Do your damn job. I suck in a deep breath and unclench my fists.

The next villager is a woman around thirty years of age. She wears a faded beige apron over a thin cotton dress, but both are clean. Her hair is short with the appearance of being hacked by shears, but it too, is clean. The woman holds herself with pride.

I clear my throat. "Did you hear anything last night? Any shouting? Or chanting?" I ask, determined to not let Aubrey's blasted spell get the better of me. Once again, the potential witness looks to Rill.

"Yalda was a wonderful mother," Rill says. "Her girls so well-behaved. Her memory will live on in those girls."

The woman's cheek twitches. "She ran a tight ship, right enough. Never no crying or shouting from *her* household." The woman tugs at the neck strap of her apron. "It were no different last night. Not a peep could be heard."

Witness after witness, Rill shares the villagers' grief and fear and then gently directs them with memories and words honouring Yalda. She takes their heartache and turns it deftly into tenacity. Or perhaps she knows the tenacity is there and simply accesses it; for once they start talking, they openly share.

Unfortunately, nobody saw or heard anything of use.

Until a young couple steps into the hut, bringing with them the stench of sour alcohol mixed with acrid body odour. Out of the corner of my eye, I am sure I notice a monochrome Rill stiffen slightly.

"I'm Lars, and this is me wife, Jane. We think we saw the summoner," the man says immediately.

Tavell straightens. "Go on," he says.

"Me and Jane had been at the tavern. We was walking home and we saw … a stranger. A woman. Standing out front of the apparition hut." Lars glances at Jane. "She didn't look evil exactly, but she sure looked like she was trying to hide. Shifty like. She wore a coat pulled tight around her. It was a warm night. No one needs to pull a coat that tight unless they are hidin' something."

My stomach twists, and at the same time, flashes of colour pattern my vision. I don't dare so much as a glance at Rill.

"Did you see what she looked like?" Tavell asks.

"Not well," Jane replies. "T'was dark, but she had blonde hair. She had stuff on her face too, like … paint. You know …" She leans forward. "… camouflage."

"How tall was she? Did you see what colour her eyes were?"

Jane and Lars exchange looks. "Tall," Lars says, and Jane nods in agreement. "Like she'd been stretched long and skinny. She was right tall for a woman. Didn't see her eyes. Too dark."

"Did you see where this blonde woman went?" Tavell holds his com-box out a bit further as if in hopes it might catch something useful.

"Skulking, she was," the man takes over. "She crept off into the shadows. Right creepy, she were."

My heart races. Shit, shit, shit. There is no doubt they'd seen Rill in Keeva's body. I had to do something.

"I don't suppose you saw a man dressed all in black?" I ask and suddenly, everything turns back into full, steady colour.

The couple start and look at me like I'm crazy. But the woman looks thoughtful, and I hold my breath.

"There was a man. But he weren't creepy. He walked like he was busy. Like he had chores needed seein' to."

Tavell clears his throat. "Did this man wear black? Did he wear a mask?"

"I only saw him from the back, out me window. He was heading towards ..." Jane stops and claps a hand over her mouth.

"Towards Yalda's house?" Rill asks, her quiet voice somehow loud.

Jane's face reddens and beads of sweat form on her nose and upper lip. Her eyes dart back and forth between Tavell, Rill, and me. "Angels save us. I didn't know .... I didn't ..." She covers her face with her hands.

"Did you see the blonde woman again? From your window, perhaps?" Tavell asks.

Jane lets her hands fall and lifts her face. Her mouth twitches. "Nah. She was gone."

"And what time was this?"

Jane licks at her lips, then shrugs.

Lars gives a chest-vibrating hum. "Hmmm. Reckon it were just after midnight."

Tavell nods. "One last thing. How much drink would you say you had at the tavern? A lot or a little?"

Lars beams. “Oh, a lot, sir. We were celebrating our wedding anniversary. We had a right ripper of a night.”

Obviously deciding he got all he could from the couple, Tavell tells them they can go.

I allow myself to breathe and risk a glance at Rill. She sits, still as a mouse caught in a trap and just as startled.

“Fetch the next person please, Narin.” Tavell stands and stretches his back.

The next interview is with Yalda’s husband. He sits with his spine straight, like if he locks himself in place, he won’t fall apart. He wears stained, rough-spun work clothes but holds himself with a kind of dignity.

“Tell us what happened,” Tavell says, gentleness in his voice.

“Yalda went to check on Emma. She’s sick, you see. She took bread ... everyone likes Yalda’s bread.” He takes a shuddering breath. “When she was late comin’ home, I figured she was needed a while longer at Emma’s. I got the girls to bed and turned in myself.” He pauses and swallows. “I didn’t wake ‘til mornin’. Of course, when she weren’t home, I went looking for her. Went to Emma’s who said Yalda had stayed a bit but left around midnight. I got right frantic then. Started lookin’ everywhere. But Jameson found her. He ... he came and got me. Told me not to look. But it was the least I could do, wasn’t it? She was murdered. Torn apart. What sort of coward would I be if I couldn’t even look at her?”

He leans forward and grips Rill’s hands. “You’ll make sure she’s cared for proper, won’t you? In Lapana. Make sure my Yalda is returned to me.”

For the first time in all the interviews, Rill looks uncomfortable. But when Tavell shifts in his seat like he is going to intervene, Rill shakes her head at him.

"I'll do everything in my power to make sure she is looked after and returned safely to you, August."

August squeezes Rill's hands, then stands, giving Tavell and me a small bow.

"I gotta get back to the girls. They're grievin'."

Then, forgetting to straighten his back, he leaves the hut with shoulders that look like the weight of the world sits upon them.

Which it probably does.

Interviews finished, I carefully secure my com-box, murmuring a small prayer that my sight is back to normal. No harm done, but that didn't stop me wanting to tear strips off Ms Aubrey fucking Burke.

The morticians arrive to collect Yalda, and Tavell steps from the kitchen to give them instructions on where she is to be taken.

Tension sits between me and Rill, and I am at a loss as to how to break it. Perhaps it is unbreakable. The chasm between us yawns. The level of loathing by Hismish people towards guard authority is apparent in Aubrey's little prank. Though Rill had prevented us from drinking more and enduring days of colourless vision, I suspect she was saving Aubrey rather than us.

"Come on," I say with a sigh, and we leave, stepping back into the bright sun.

Tavell has finished talking to the mortician, and when we emerge, he sets off towards the apparition hut.

"We'll take time for lunch when we return," Tavell says as we walk. It is likely he'd heard my stomach growling during the interviews. "Then we'll visit all the booths within ten minutes of Jackal Tavern and retrieve the transport information. If that couple, Lars and Jane, are accurate with their estimate of the time when they saw the summoner, it would mean he came to Ikra right after the demon killed Thorn. Lady Keeva saw the demon just before midnight, and Yalda was killed a short time later, so the summoner had to use a booth close to the Tavern. Unless he had a Pegasus, although I think that unlikely. No Pegasus would choose someone who clearly has darkness in their heart."

19
Sabella

BACK IN THE ENORMOUS kitchen of the guard house, we partake in a brief, but welcome lunch at the kitchen table, sitting among the flour and rolling pins that take up a good part of its surface. It is too late in the day for the mess hall to be stocked or manned.

The mess sits beside the main guard house, connected directly to the kitchen by an enclosed walkway. A second enclosed walkway takes the guards from the GH to the mess hall for all main meals and any functions. But the kitchen is always stocked. Strange hours often mean guards whip into the GH for a bite, and they can always find something ready and waiting for just that purpose in the kitchen.

I notice Rill cleans her plate of sandwiches in a minute flat—after sliding the chunks of meat from their centres and placing them to one side. I give a subtle nod to Cook Calista who immediately makes another sandwich—this one meat-free—and slaps it on Rill's plate. Rill hesitates for a second, jerks one shoulder, then eats it too. Calista presses apples in our hands as we leave, and Rill immediately bites into hers.

I am glad to be on the move again. Tiredness descended once more while we ate, and I need to shake it off. We are nearly at the front door when a guard rushes down the hallway to intercept us.

"I have Fledge Narin's kit here, Constable Rivers."

"Thank you, Fledge Peters." I take the vest and belt and hand them to Rill. "We'll go over the gear in the cab."

Rill barely meets my eye, and dread stales the sandwich in my stomach, particularly when I feel Tavell's intense stare on us. The man is too damn clever to buy my story of Rill *wanting* to be a guard.

Outside the guard house, the heat of the city, amplified by the stone buildings and cobblestone streets, smashes into us, adding sweat to the stench of brimstone, poverty, and death that clings to me. It only takes a second before I am batting my first sticky fly from my face. I yearn for a bath, but there is a demon summoner on the loose, and we have work to do, so I set my jaw against the dry, oppressive heat.

Tavell hails two cabs. He is going to visit the apparition booths along Carlver River, and Rill and I are to check those on the north side of Carlver Alley.

The black, horse-drawn carriages pull up, and Tavell wastes no time in entering his. I encourage Rill forward.

"Never been in a cab before," she murmurs. "Never been in no carriage."

Funny, Rill's Hismish accent is normally light and tinged with what I could have sworn is a Lapanian accent. It is as if our visit to Ikra has drawn the Hismish out.

I understand Rill's unease. My childhood home, New Hope Orphanage—dubbed No Hope by the children—is situated north-east of Lapana close to the Keplon border. It sits on the outskirts of the small town of Balter which consists of just four streets before it breaks apart into scattered homes that quickly melts into farms. It certainly has no cabs.

When I'd first arrived in Lapana, the noise, the people, the carriages, and the smells had been overwhelming. Tavell had been patient though and soothed my nerves with information. He showed me around the different districts of Lapana, explaining the market section, the warehouse section, the industrial section, and even took me to Manor Hill where I'd stared at the fancy homes, the wide streets, and the well-dressed people. I make a mental note to do the same for Rill.

I give her what I hope is an encouraging smile and, knowing her eyes are on me, place my foot slowly and deliberately on the tiny, round peg. With a light spring, I enter the cab. A second later, Rill is beside me having mimicked my entry.

Inside the cab is stuffy and smells faintly of body odour and pipe tobacco. With a wrinkled nose, I drop the window and indicate Rill do the same with hers. Now the city passes through the square spaces beside us. A cacophony of city sound rings out, swelling and receding as we set off. Horses' hooves striking the cobblestones, drivers yelling at pedestrians who cross the road with little care for swift-moving horses and carriages, vendors pedalling their wares in loud voices that have drooped against the heat. They've lost their singsong lilt and veer towards plain old yelling. Deep summer turns the city into a pressure cooker. Tempers are short, energy is low, and the air is thick. I try to draw oxygen into my lungs and allow Rill to lean and look for a while.

I want to talk to her about Aubrey, but for some reason, the words stick in my throat. Instead, I call her attention to the vest and belt.

"Why doesn't Tavell have a fledge?" Rill asks, ignoring the items on her lap.

I consider redirecting Rill's attention, but curiosity is something to be rewarded. At least, that's what Tavell always tells me.

"As you know, I was Tavell's fledge. After graduating, the Code dictates I take on my own fledge, but I have three months to make a selection." I give Rill a brief, pained smile. "I only had a month left to make my decision. It was a difficult choice to make." I pause to reel my emotions back in. It still stings to have had my options squashed. "I was Tavell's second fledge, so he has six months before he must gain another. Though he may do so earlier if he wishes."

Rill pivots in her seat so she faces me directly. One of her cheeks glows red with the heat, the other black from her bruise. "What's this Code? Why do you lose your job if I fail? Seems an unfair system."

I lick my lips. "The Code was introduced shortly after King Ryker amended the Benedict Magical Class laws. As you know, his amendments caused segregation and poverty, and suddenly, positions with the guards were highly sought after. Apart from the army, it is now the only career remaining where anyone can apply no matter if they hail from a sanctioned or non-sanctioned area. Anyone can become a guard regardless of birth, wealth, and magical skill. Faustians like Tavell, Keplons like me. Hismish like you." I pause. "Even prisoners." I fidget with the cudgel that sits on my belt. It often digs in when I sit, and I shift it to be more comfortable. "So, for many, being a guard was a way out of poverty. While allowing anyone to become a guard made for a robust and fair guard force, it caused some issues. Numerous people applied, even if it was not a life they were cut out for. Even if they had no interest in justice. Some guards took in family members and friends as their fledges, merely to give them a job. The quality of the force suffered. So, it was decided the prime must be responsible for their choice. It ensures they strive to train their fledge well, but also ensures they make a wise choice." I take a breath.

A prime is not supposed to choose someone to aid a friend in need. Like I had for Keeva.

"When my sister went missing," Rill says, "I came to the guards. They wouldn't help. They made me feel like I was nothing. Like my sister was nothing. I don't think the force is *robust and fair*."

I resist the urge to squirm. "Not all guards are good at their jobs, or even good people, I'll grant you that." I catch my top lip in my teeth. I detest talking about my childhood, but perhaps sharing a little would go a ways to building our relationship. It might let her know that I am not ignorant to her hesitancy to join the guards.

"I also had a bad experience with the guards. I was only young and ... well, I was raised in an orphanage you see, and a girl I was friendly with was adopted." I cannot bring myself to tell Rill the girl I referred to was the *only* friend I'd ever had in the orphanage. "Anyway, she was adopted by bad people. I saw her once after, in the street. She was covered in bruises, and her eyes ... they'd lost all their light. I begged the headmistress to report it, but she ignored me, so I sneaked out of the orphanage one day and went to the guards myself." I go quiet for a minute, waiting for the wave of distress the memory brings to ease. "They didn't listen. They returned me to the orphanage where I was ... punished."

My punishment had been five wacks with the strap on my bare back. My skin had split, and then I'd gotten two additional straps for getting blood on my sheets. I slept on the floor after that until my wounds healed. "Two months later, my friend was dead." I breathed, slow and steady, grasping for control.

Rill's large eyes show no reaction. So much for sharing.

"So, I understand. Not all guards are good. But most are. Most care very much. I'm sorry you had a bad experience, but you have a unique chance now, Rill. Just as you said to Tavell, you can be the voice of those who don't feel they have one. You can bring about change from the inside. And once we have caught this son-of-a-bitch summoner, we can work together to find information about your sister." I purse my lips, hesitating. "Or you can sit around and moan about how unfair life is until you fail your first test and are free to go."

Tension sits between me and Rill. It charges the hot cabin. Rill's brown eyes drill into me, unblinking and intense.

Fuck. I went too far.

20
Sabella

SECONDS TICK ... SLOW and strained. Beads of sweat roll down my nose.

"Tavell didn't arrest Aubrey," Rill says in a small voice and meets my eye. "Neither did you."

Rill looks small and unsure, and an irritating kindheartedness comes over me. "Yes, well, no harm done." The anger at being fed a potion is gone, burned off by Lapana's heat. "Now, your kit." I tap the vest and belt resting on her lap.

Rill gathers the items. "She only wanted to show you the world is not meant to be black and white," she whispers.

A million responses come to me, but they all stick to my tongue, and I say nothing.

Rill holds out her kit. "Show me what's in here."

I hold in a sigh of relief and pat the small space of seat between us. She places her kit there, and I reach into one of the vest pockets and withdraw a small black box.

"Here is your com-box," I say, happy my voice is steady, despite my racing pulse. I thought I'd lost Rill with my hard words, but she *saw* more clearly than I imagined. "Its matched pair now sits on the shelf in reception. Whenever you are out, investigating a crime or on patrol, you use it to record your observations." I flick a switch on the box. "If you are onto something important and want it looked at straight away by staff at the GH, you toggle this switch, and it will automatically transcribe your recording to its pair at GH. Just make sure you record *who* you want to look at it. Which analyst or superior I mean."

Rill's eyes widen.

"Don't worry, we'll go over that in more detail another day. For the first year, you don't go out alone, anyway. I'm always with you."

Would Rill see out a year?

I slide the com-box back into Rill's vest and withdraw a pair of handcuffs.

"Self-explanatory, but I'll show you how to use them on our first training day." I tuck them away again and draw the belt onto my lap. From it, I pull the short wooden cudgel from its loop. It is smooth and thin for a cudgel. A gold crown is foiled into the wood, and a smooth polished black gem sits at the top. I lay it across my fingers and hold it out to Rill. "Your cudgel."

Rill's eyes travel the weapon, coming to rest on the black gem. "Is that ... a tourmaline crystal?" She looks at me with wide eyes.

"Is this a wand? You're giving me a wand?" Her fringe falls over her eyes, and she sweeps it back impatiently.

"Not a wand, no. Though there is some magic stored in the crystal. It's a cudgel, but we guards just call it Jack."

Rill takes the cudgel from my outstretched hands like it might turn her into a gnat, then squeals when the cab takes a corner a little fast and she drops Jack. She retrieves it from the floor quickly. Her face glows even redder, and her lips curve into a wry smile. Yet her eyes gleam, and she runs a fingertip over the black crystal.

"Jack? They are ... all called Jack?"

"It's a nickname. Officially, it's a guard's cudgel. Unofficially, it's Jack. My Jack, your Jack. Um, like, 'Have you got Jack?' 'Did you hit him with Jack' type thing."

"Not a wand, then?"

"No. It does contain two spells though. A light so it can act as a torch and a freezing spell. If you need the light just point Jack and give the command, *Lux*. It will last about an hour before it runs out."

Rill's gaze flicks to me, filled with the unasked question.

I smile. "Go ahead. Try it."

Rill holds Jack before her. "Lux," she says, and there is no mistaking the spell experience in her voice with the commanding lilt she puts on the word. Jack bursts into light, filling the cab with white brightness. Rill briefly opens her mouth like she is about to say something, then gathers herself.

"The word to turn it off?" she asks, suddenly becoming stiff Rill again.

"Umbra."

Rill gives the command, and the cab falls back into dimness.

"And if you find yourself in danger, you can use the freeze spell to incapacitate your attackers. Just point the stick at them and use the command, *Immotus*. However, you can only use it three times before the freeze magic is depleted and the Jack requires reloading." A sharp crack rings out when I slap the solid wood into the palm of my hand. "You can also use it to smack someone. It'll do a fair bit of damage." I slide it back into the loop and set the belt aside.

"I ... I'm permitted to use magic?" Rill asks. Her resolute boldness has vanished.

"Of course. All guards are automatically granted a level three license. If you have a particular talent in higher magics, like you do, you can even be granted a level four or five. I ... I hope to get my level four one day."

Rill's eyes widen. "You're a red witch?"

I nod, fighting the unease that is a constant companion to my fire magic.

"Show me."

Because Rill is looking at me in awe, I figure a tiny boast can't hurt. And I can control something small, so I conjure a tiny ball of flame in the palm of my hand. I let it flicker for a moment before closing my hand around it to snuff it out.

Rill's face holds absolute delight and admiration. "Awesome," she whispers.

Well, that worked better than sad orphanage stories.

The cab stops with a lurch, and I hand the vest and belt to Rill.

"There's more to show you, but it can wait. Wear both at all times when you're on duty."

I pay the driver through the trap-door above us, and we exit the cab. Outside the air is marginally cooler, a little fresher, but the day is still and heavy, and I long for a breeze to cool my damp face. I wait while Rill threads the belt through the loops on her trousers, buckling it with nimble fingers. Then she shrugs on the vest and buckles it.

"I'Kuna save me. I thought the uniform was uncomfortable before." Rill tugs at the vest and wiggles, pulling a face. I just smile and lean towards Rill, giving the vest a rap with my knuckles.

"Armoured. You might be glad of it one day."

Still grumbling under her breath, Rill follows me into the first apparition hut.

This particular hut operates six booths. A few citizens come and go. Those that go, tap in their ID on the control panel and are gone in the blink of an eye. Those that arrive materialise before our eyes, step from the booth they'd used, and leave the hut without a backward glance.

The hut attendant is reading the *Lapana Townsman*, a low-brow newspaper. The starched collar of his shirt appears to have melted as it sags in a mess of wrinkles. He has removed his jacket and sits in his waistcoat, sweat patches blooming under each arm.

"Half a cup within the realm, full cup for inter-realm travel," he says in a bored voice, not even looking up from the newspaper.

"We'll be retrieving information today, not travelling."

That draws the attendant's attention, and he finally lifts his eyes to take us in.

I show him my guard ID, and he shrugs and nods at the same time then buries his head in his paper once more. It is too hot to pull him up on his disrespect.

Instead, I give Rill a run down on how to retrieve booth information.

"Each booth retains a memory of who was sent and where."

Rill folds her arms and gives me a withering look.

"Sorry. You would know that." I push a few buttons on the control panel and enter my guard code. "But we only want information about anyone who travelled to Ikra last night." I tap out another combination, glancing at Rill to make sure she is watching.

"We send the information to our com-box and take a printed list also." I withdraw my com-box from my bag and hold it in front of the booth.

A soft whining sound accompanies the roll of paper that emerges from beneath the booth controls, and my com-box shakes in my hand. I smooth out the curled paper and read. There is only one name, and it is a woman. I notice Rill leaning close.

"This is a waste of time," she whispers into my ear. I brace against the prickly annoyance needling at me.

"A lot of guard work is mundane, but it is required just the same. Did you watch closely? Do you think you can do the next booth?"

Rill gives a soft snort. "Of course. But that's not what I mean." She glances at the booth hut attendant.

"If the summoner followed me," she whispers so softly, I have to lean closer, so our foreheads nearly touch, "he probably used the same dirty booth I did."

Rill pulls back as if awaiting my answer, but I catch her by the elbow and direct her out of the hut and onto the busy, noisy street. I don't want to have this conversation where we might be overheard by the booth attendant, despite his apparent lack of interest in anything beyond the *Lapana Townsman*. We hug the apparition hut wall to avoid the harried pedestrians flowing along the path.

"Rill." I take a breath to steady my frustration. "You are not entirely wrong. It does seem like a waste of time that we are checking regulated booths, however, unless you feel up to telling Constable Nash it was you who witnessed the murder and you whom the summoner followed, then we must do as ordered. In other words, it is part of the ruse. A part of the investigation that you, by your actions, has made more difficult."

Discomfort floats across Rill's face.

"Furthermore, something has been troubling me. You were quite sure you were not followed to the booth, yes?" I had been putting off sharing this with Rill.

"Yes. I ... was frightened, running scared, but ..." Her chin comes up in a gesture I am sure I am going to see a lot of. "... I know how to ensure that I am not being followed."

"Exactly. If you took a dirty booth, the summoner would have to watch you enter your destination to follow you. He'd have had to have been in the hut with you."

Rill's face ripples in a series of twitches as if controlled by the turning cogs in her brain.

"Are you sure the booth you took was dirty?" I ask.

Indignation holds Rill. "Yes. I didn't have the money for a—"

"The guards are constantly uncovering dirty booths. Mostly, we close them down." I grip Jack on my hip. "But we let some operate and ... secretly install monitoring."

Rill looks like she's been slapped, betrayal showing in her wide eyes, her fists, her clenched jaw. I rush on.

"We can't identify *who* has travelled, only *where* people are travelling. It has helped us in many investigations. You must know, dirty booths are often used to transport slaves."

For once, Rill's face is an open book, emotions flooding her expression in a twist of confusion and hatred and deception.

"Point is ... there is only one kind of person who can access booth data, registered or otherwise."

Shocked understanding lights Rill's eyes. "A guard," she whispers.

I nod. "So, the summoner is either a guard who followed you to the dirty booth which happened to be a monitored booth and accessed the data to find out where you went ... or it was a complete coincidence that he went to Ikra right after you. He may not have been chasing you ... or Keeva ... you know what I mean. And if it was a coincidence, it's highly possible he took another booth."

Rill sweeps her fingers through her fringe, combing it back over her head and then her bland expression snaps back into place. "OK. We *do* need to check all the booths. In addition to the one I took. Will you know if it is ... one that the guards monitor?"

I shake my head. "Not as such. The information is above my pay grade, but it doesn't stop us from trying to access the booth data. If it's monitored, I'll be able to. If not ... well, it's not a guard-monitored booth. Will you take me to the booth you used? I promise I won't report it if it is not already monitored."

Rill is still for a moment, and I sense she is contemplating her next move. I hold her gaze and wait, mentally crossing my fingers.

"I will. And if it is not monitored, I guess, we could ask around, in case anyone saw anything?" Rill shifts her weight, runs her fingers through her hair again, and turns back to the apparition hut. "And, we should get the information from these booths, and the others in the area." She walks smartly back in the door of the booth hut.

I gnaw at my cheek. Rill has every right to be angry that the guards she hates so much monitor booths used by her and other Hismish to get around cheaply and without detection. She has every right to be angry at the very suggestion the summoner might be a guard. Goodness knows the thought makes me sick. Yet Rill quelled her emotion and opted for action.

Still, I can't help but wonder, when this is all over and we have caught the summoner, what Rill's next move might be.

21
Keeva

"KEE, I FOUND SOMETHING."

Jolting awake, I am immediately vexed. I sit in an armchair by the window in Finn's study where the afternoon sun streaming in the window coaxed my eyes shut. I was supposed to be reading the book Finn brought me. It was not from the Heinous Section but was instead a scholarly tome on the history of black magic and included several chapters on summoning a demon. It was a dry read, however, and my lack of sleep had beat me into submission. I stare at Finn, struggling to push torpidity aside.

"What?" I ask, losing the struggle.

"I found something. Something important." Finn is not remotely sleepy. He is animated, and his eyes shine. He has pulled his hair into a bun, and a few escaped strands hang around his face.

Galvanised, I sit up. "What did you find?" The dusty tome on my lap—the one I was supposed to be reading—slips to the floor with a dull thud.

Finn holds his open notebook, and I notice it is covered, top to bottom, with his sloped handwriting. He sits in the chair opposite me and taps at the scribbled page in his book.

"Mid-level demon. I am certain what you saw was a mid-level demon. While they can take many forms, what you described fits perfectly with one of the depictions I found. Which, in turn, directed my research and drew my focus to mid-level demons only." Finn stands and paces. "Then I found ... well, this." He looks down at the page and stops pacing.

"Mid-level demons are known to grant favours," he reads, tracing a finger over the writing. "Which makes them the most commonly summoned demon. The summoner must be a witch of considerable power as the summoning requires great control. A failed summoning attempt will result in the demon being called from the underworld only to kill the summoner and roam free. If this happens, the demon goes on a killing spree, gorging itself on souls until it is sated and returns to hell." Finn takes a breath. "The price demanded for favours from a mid-level demon, is always the same." Finn lifts his eyes and stares at me. "Six souls over three nights."

I leap from my chair. "But ... that means ..."

Finn nods. "It means, the two people killed last night were the first instalment. And if I am right, another two souls will be taken tonight."

"Oh, Finn, we have to warn the guards." My heart gallops.

Finn nods again, reaches out, and picks up my half-drunk cup of tea from the table between us. He throws it back then pulls a face. "It's cold."

"Of course, it is, silly. It was made nearly an hour ago." I look at the giant grandfather clock that stands in a corner. Four o'clock. "I'll go and see ..." I trail off and despondency weights my heart. I am forbidden to leave the manor, and much to my disgust, Alex has hovered nearby all day. Even now he stands outside Finn's study. Which means sneaking out is going to be tricky.

Finn places his fingers gently on my arm, and I look up into his deep brown eyes. "I know it's difficult, but Father is right. It's not safe right now, and you did see the summoner. He might be after you."

More than might.

The earlier news that someone in Ikra was killed still makes me queasy. They were killed because the summoner had chased me. Or, at least, chased Rill in my body. Gods. The situation sends my head spinning.

Finn gives my arm a light slap. "Send your friend, Sabella, a com. Tell her what we've found. I'll go and see Uncle Sean and show him too. He set me up with a few books from the Heinous Section, but now I'll see if there is anything specific to mid-level demons who grant favours. I'll keep researching, Kee."

I smooth my hair and draw my shoulders back. This is no time to feel sorry for oneself. "Let me know if you find anything else."

Finn closes his notebook, snaps the band around it, and slides his pencil into his breast pocket.

"I will." He spins and leaves the room.

22
Sabella

Rill and I arrive back at GH after a long and fruitless afternoon of gathering names from apparition booths and interviewing would-be witnesses—both of which amounted to zilch. The dirty booth Rill used to go to Ikra wasn't one the guards monitored, and we could get no information. Which also, thankfully, puts an end to the idea the summoner might be a guard.

As we walk in the front door, I glance down at my uniform. Damp with perspiration and grubby from the stains of Ikra and the city, it has lost its crisp, ironed lines. Rill too, seems to have wilted, her face red and beaded with moisture. We both need to bathe and change, but I insist we first tour the guard house. I try to put enthusiasm into it, but lack of sleep tugs at me. Still, I have come to develop a fondness for the GH—my first home—and pride lends some vigour to the tour.

The guard house is a large, three-storey place, built of wood. Everything is wood—the walls, the floors, the furniture. Not fancy wood that glows with rich tones and holds whorls of grain that are nature's artwork, but plain, hard-wearing wood that makes every room feel similar. Like the warehouses and factories, it is a newer build, different to most of the centuries-old buildings of Lapana. And it has been built for function, not form. All straight lines and square rooms. Although the mess hall was added as an afterthought, resulting in the side-by-side, joined by covered passageways, arrangement.

Rill, however, is less than impressed ... bored even when I show her the duty room with its rows of desks. Her expression is as wooden as the numerous offices for the higher-ranking guards that are tucked in behind the duty room. She yawns at the long, wide briefing room at the back of the building. She has already seen the kitchen and reception at the front of the building, so I skip them and take her upstairs to the living quarters to show her her room.

“I have a room to myself?” she asks. “I don’t share with you?” She stands at the threshold with one hand encircling her opposite wrist. The hand she clings to is bunched. I can’t decide if it is a gesture of nerves or excitement.

“Fledges don’t share with their guard, no. Usually, when a guard becomes fully fledged—once their three years of training are complete—they move out of the GH, but I ... I still have a room here.”

Rill flashes me a look with the first spark of interest since I started the tour. “Why?”

"Well, rent is expensive. Normally, the money you earn when you graduate is enough to gain you humble lodgings. But I spent my money on ... something else. So, I'll remain here for a while. It's cheap—the board includes meals and ... it's convenient."

The truth is, I yearn for a place of my own. My whole life has been one of communal living, first at the orphanage and then at the GH. The idea of living alone, of having my own place, my own kitchen, a private bathroom ... well the thought makes me giddy. It will be a sign I've finally made it. Finally left my past behind.

"What?" Rill asks, her tone more demand than question.

I frown.

"What did you spend your money on?" This time Rill softens her voice.

"Diarissa," I reply quietly.

"Your Pegasus. Of course." Rill's eyes seem to find the floor fascinating, and she still stands in the doorway.

I take charge and step smartly into Rill's room. "The bathroom is down the hall. Your uniforms should be hanging in your wardrobe already." I fling open the door to the wardrobe and indeed, a line of neatly pressed uniforms greets us. I grip the round wooden handle of the wardrobe door. "If you like, we can go shopping together on our day off." I speak to the row of hung clothes in the wardrobe. It feels like the safer option. "For casual clothes. For when you are off duty." I close the door. "Only if you want," I add quickly.

Rill doesn't reply, and I turn back to face her.

"How did you come to get a Pegasus?" Rill asks. She runs a hand through her hair and finally steps into the room. Like the first step is the hardest, she now crosses quickly to the bed and flops down on it, leaning back on propped elbows. "I'm surprised you could afford one, even after saving for three years. How much money does a fledge make anyway?"

I hesitate, but this isn't a sad story. It is astonishing and joyful. I pull the straight-backed wooden chair from Rill's desk/dresser and straddle it, facing Rill who now sits with her legs crossed, her hands clinging to her ankles. My lips twitch with the desire to tell her to get her dirty boots off her bed, and I try to ignore the dust they have already smeared over her blanket.

"Tavell helped me. I mean, it was because of him, that it even happened. I'd never, in my wildest dreams, ever *thought* of owning a Pegasus. But Tavell helped me with a loan too."

Rill sits motionless. Listening.

"Tavell is from a village in Fauster called Padoosa. It's a farming community of Pegasus breeders. An old friend of his from Padoosa came to Lapana to sell his Pegasi at market. He let Tavell know he would be in town and invited him to come to the choosing. Tavell thought I might like to come along and watch the Pegasus selection too. The process fascinated me, so I agreed."

Rill's face remains blank, but I fancy she leans a little closer.

"It was just over a year ago, in spring. I remember because it was a perfect day. You know the sort, when winter finally lets go, and the sun holds warmth. It brought people from all over Lapana out to come and watch. A Pegasus selection is entertainment for many.

"And it *was* amazing to watch those magical creatures. The registered potentials—the buyers—lined up at one end of the ring, and one by one, the Pegasus were led in to judge the buyers. They tossed their heads and flared their wings, prancing like they knew everyone was there to see them. I swear I held my breath each time one was led out. Would they pick someone? And some Pegasus didn't. They sniffed and looked and turned away. Some, though, pulled their handler—Tavell's friend—across the ring, going straight to a particular potential. They would lower their heads and snuff at their chosen's neck. They had chosen. It was a breathtaking sight—a wondrous treat to just be there." I smile at the memory.

"Finally, there were six potentials left and only two Pegasus. The second to last chose a man, and the joy on his face was a thing to behold." I rest my chin on my folded arms across the back of the chair. The memory of the day taking such a firm hold I almost forget Rill is here. "Then the last Pegasus was brought out. She lifted her head and surveyed the arena like she was royalty. She gave the potentials the barest of looks, then ... she tore across the ring ... straight to me watching on the sidelines."

Rill takes an audible breath, and the sound brings me back to the tiny guard room. Rill is definitely leaning closer now, and her eyes shine with ... passion. Her wide mouth is slanted in a slight smile.

"I was shocked and unsure of what to do. Diarissa neighed and tossed her head and refused to go with her handler to the waiting potentials. She was causing a ruckus. I didn't know it at the time, but it is a rare thing for a Pegasus to choose someone who has not declared their interest. She mesmerised me, of course. Her big eyes, her soft nose, her magnificent silver-white coat and wings. She was like an angel. And ... she'd chosen me."

To my horror, tears prick the back of my eyes. I'd endured a different kind of choosing many, many times. Couples who'd come to the orphanage looking for a child they could call their own.

Word would spread like fire among the children, drawing them to the staircase and balconies, where we could peer down at the couple. If they looked horrid, we scattered, hiding, even while knowing it would earn us a punishment later. But if the couple looked nice, we lined up, waiting to be called. Each child hoping they were the right age, the right sex, the right colouring. Hoping they might be chosen.

Potentials were called to meet the couple, and it was always the same. A stilted hello followed by inane questions.

How old are you?

What's your favourite colour?

The prettiest and youngest girls were always chosen and the biggest, strongest boys. I learned early on not to hope, but sometimes, when a black couple arrived, I could not stop the slither of longing that crept over me. Maybe they would want me. But they never did. I was never chosen. When Tavell accepted my application as his fledge, I didn't think I'd ever again experience such happiness. Until Diarissa, the Pegasus, looked into my heart and soul and wanted to be with me.

I slap the back of the chair and stand. "Long story short—Tavell suggested I buy her. He said he'd help me, not only financially, but he'd teach me how to care for her. Even how to ride. I'd never ridden a horse at the time." I force a laugh to make light of my admission. "And so it was, that Diarissa became mine. And I became hers." I push the wooden chair back under Rill's desk. "And that's the reason I still live here. I've got another year before I can pay Tavell back, and then I'll be able to save for my own home."

I walk to Rill's door. "I'm going to take a shower. Our shift is finished now, so you are free to do as you like. Dinner is at six o'clock in the mess hall. Cook Calista makes a truly delicious summer soup." I go to shut the door, then pause. "There will be vegetarian options too." I close the door and leave Rill to contemplate her new life as a citizen guard of Tarr.

After my shower, I am about to don my casual clothes for the evening, when my com-box gives a shake and emits a chime. Quickly buttoning my skirt, I play the recording, reaching for my blouse and pulling it on as I listen.

The message is from Lady Keeva. Halfway through doing up my blouse buttons, I freeze.

Shit.

If what Lady Keeva says is true, we will not get the night off at all. Without bothering with shoes, I snatch up my com-box and fly out my door to see if Tavell is still in the GH.

Fifteen minutes later, I am back in uniform, and the GH has become an explosion of activity with slamming doors, booted footsteps and excited chatter.

I'd found Tavell at his desk, talking with Senior Sergeant, Victor Parker. The printouts from all the booths in Lapana were spread across Tavell's desk. With a quick salute to Sergeant Parker, I slammed my com-box on the desk and pressed play. Which was what caused the explosion of activity.

Sergeant Parker and Tavell both snapped out orders, recalling all guards on-site to duty. Com-boxes buzzed with recall messages to the guards off-site. They were to gather in the briefing room in forty-five minutes. I fled to my room, heart clanging, to change once more into my uniform. Now I have to fetch Rill.

I bang on her door but get no answer. Frustration and dread swell, and I open Rill's door with force. The room is empty. Where in the name of Agnis is the girl? Somewhere in the building, surely. I would have felt the tug of our magical contract if she had left. Swearing softly under my breath, I march back downstairs in search of her.

After five minutes of nothing, I catch the arm of a constable as they rush by.

"Have you seen Fledge Narin?"

The constable is the same one who'd taken Lady Keeva's statement this morning, so he knows who I mean.

"I think I saw her head into the kitchen," he replies with a mild scowl of annoyance.

Relief trickles over me. The kitchen makes sense. Rill will be hungry. I march in, trying to rein in my tired grumpiness. After all, I had told her she was free to do whatever she wanted, and it wasn't her fault we'd been recalled to duty.

But the kitchen is empty. Not even Cook Calista is there. Alarm rises under my skin, like a fiery itch. Surely, *surely*, Rill has not found a way to break the contract's magic. Surely, she has not fled. I am about to leave when I hear ... a muffled rattling. Concerned someone is trying to break in, I tiptoe down a short, narrow hallway, not the one that leads to the mess hall, but one that connects the kitchen to the storeroom. I crack open the door and put my eye to the gap.

The light is on in the storeroom, and I am grateful I stand in the dimness of the hallway, for across the storeroom, is Rill. And she is not alone. She and another young fledge, Eli Palmer, are having frenzied sex up against one of the tall, storeroom shelves. The fledge constable's bare backside—his trousers around his ankles—flexes with each thrust. Rill's head is tossed back, her eyes closed in ecstasy. Her hands are wrapped around her lover's hips, encouraging each frenetic plunge. The young man's panting breath grows faster, and Rill lets out a low moan.

I pull the door closed silently and creep away.

23

Rill

When Sabella leaves me in my room, it is as if the walls close in on me. Despite the decent-sized window, despite the fact my room is not dark and cold like my prison cell, I feel caged. I cross to the window and fling it open, desperately seeking fresh air. But the city, with its stone and brick and concrete, bakes like a stew pot, and only heat greets me. Sucking on the harsh, dry air, I tug at the wretched, firm-fitting uniform and vest.

I'm off duty. The ludicrous idea of being *off duty* almost makes my mouth curve.

But I quickly undo the vest and remove the belt with its surprisingly heavy cudgel, Jack. I massage my ribs, tender from wearing such a fitted garment. Then, with my thoughts in a jumbled mess, I slip into the hallway and back down the stairs to the cooler ground floor.

I will put the magical contract to the test and try to leave the guard house. If it works like I think it does, Sabella will know exactly where I am. She will know if I leave and will be able to locate me anywhere. The very thought that I can be tracked tightens the bars of my cage. But a walk outside on my own, even in the suffocating city, appeals. I need to celebrate the absence of the cold, Lapana prison walls around me. I need it to feel real.

Not wanting to navigate the front room with its mammoth desk, I go in search of a back door, but passing the kitchen, I pause. My stomach tugs at me, hunger making it growl. For the first time in my life, I have unlimited access to food. As much as I want. It is a heady thought, but one that also drowns me in guilt. I can eat, while so many others cannot.

My stomach gives an extra loud grrrr, and I slip into the kitchen ... and come to an abrupt halt. There is a guard in the kitchen already, scouring through the cupboards.

A head of close-cut blond hair pokes around a cupboard door. "Hello," he says with an easy smile and brown eyes that peer at me through wire-framed spectacles. "I'm Eli Palmer, analyst fledge."

"I'm Rill ... Narin." I'd sooner pull my fingernails off than add Fledge to my name. Even introducing myself by name sounds so ... real. Like maybe I really am here. Like maybe I really am a guard. I shake my head. A ridiculous idea and one I'm not ready to accept yet.

Eli, however, ignores my discomfort—if he even notices it at all. He opens more cupboards.

"If you ever need a snack, there's always stuff in here." He withdraws a large tin marked Biscuits. Holding it with two hands, he gives it a rattling shake. "These are like a lucky dip … a delicious lucky dip. You never know what Cook Calista has made. Vanilla, cinnamon, oatmeal, shortbread, … well, you get the idea." He wags his eyebrows. "Always good though." He shoves the tin back in the cupboard and points to the bench opposite. "That bowl of fruit is for the guards to snaffle any time we want." He swings open the door of the giant fridge. "Cook always leaves good stuff in here, too. Like sandwiches and … oh!" His voice takes on a hollow sound with his head stuffed in the fridge. "Apple pie?" he says suddenly, spinning around, his eyes gleaming behind the lens of his specs that catch the electric light above us.

"Sorry?" I dart a look at the door to one side of the kitchen. Does it lead outside?

"Want some apple pie?" He holds up a dish with half a pie in it. "It's scrumptious." He grins again.

With a shrug, I flop down on a chair at the kitchen table.

Eli takes that as a yes and cuts two large slices, slapping them into the bowls he'd fetched from a shelf. Then, after sticking his head deep into the fridge once more, emerges with a jug of cream. Without asking, he gives a generous pour to both slices. With a wink, he collects spoons and collapses in the chair opposite me. He scoops a pile of pie onto his spoon, shoves it into his mouth, and chews while grinning madly.

"New fledge?" he asks, his full mouth spraying crumbs across the table.

I elect not to answer and instead, take a spoonful of pie. I'Kuna save me, it is delicious. My tongue sings with the sweetness and the woody, slightly citrus flavour of cinnamon and from pastry that is buttery rich. But Eli stares at me, clearly waiting for an answer. Not completely sure what he is asking, I opt for the relative safety of a nod.

"Thought so. New fledges have that look." He stabs his spoon in my direction, splattering a blob of cream onto the table.

"What look?" I feel indignant. I don't have a look. Or, if I do, it's drab. That's my look. Most people tell me I have a drab face, with a drab expression and drab personality. That's alright with me. Drab means they can't see anything. It's safer that way.

"Shock, mainly. Nerves, sometimes even a bit of fear." Eli smiles again, and I wonder if he has heatstroke. I've never known anyone to smile so much. Not even Cassia. "I've been here just over a year, and I tell you, it will go away."

I lift my eyebrows. What is he talking about?

"The shock, nerves, and fear," he says, by way of explanation. "They go away." He scoops at the cream in his bowl, ensuring his next spoonful of pie is drenched. "The loneliness takes a little longer."

I pause mid-chew. *That* is what's bothering me. Loneliness. The sticky greyness of it settles on me as soon as he says it. I've been lonely ever since I'd been locked up in that damn prison. It's a dull ache that has never left, and now is such a part of me, I no longer notice it. Much like the smell of the prison's stone walls, it has seeped in and fused with me. But the loneliness unfurls now, like a seed pushing sprouts through the dirt, it rises, triumphant. Maybe it was being in Ikra, talking to the only people I'd ever known. Many of whom I considered family. Maybe it was being back in my cottage last night, seeing my sister's empty bed.

No longer hungry, I put my spoon down, a thick mist of misery sinking over me.

"The shock at being accepted will go first. So many apply for so few spots that everyone wears a kind of shocked disbelief in the first few days." Eli beams, pie crumbs lining his lips. "The nerves take a little longer. But after your first few assessments, you'll feel better. More confident. I mean, let's face it, no guard takes on a fledge they don't think will make it."

Burning guilt mixes with my loneliness making my insides feel like a swamp.

"Finally, the fear eases. Though, I must admit, mine never really did go away." Eli licks at the cream on his spoon, his bowl all but empty and runs the back of his hand across his mouth.

"You ... don't look frightened," I say. I don't miss the irony that I'm too scared to ask him what he is afraid of. I am sure any *normal* fledge would know.

Eli leans back, looking at me over the top of his glasses.

He has nice eyes. Brown with flecks of gold. They hold amusement, intelligence and not a hint of heat stroke. My stomach even does a crazy little flip-flop, and I press down hard on the feeling, disappointed I'd even noticed his damn eyes. Stupid heart, beating faster in my chest. But to be fair, I'd been in prison for a year, and there was no sex in there. Just violence.

"Well, I'm not frightened anymore," he continues. "I recently finished my first year, so I've done my time on the streets. Now I get to stay in GH with Captain Wallace, safe and sound."

I still struggle to understand.

"A year on the streets ..." I fade off, out of my depth and drowning in confusion.

"Ah. Yes, see, I'm a fledge analyst. I need to do my time on the street, patrols and all that, but now I get to stay at my desk and study the data. It's my thing, seeing patterns. I'm good at it, too."

I let out a breath as understanding creeps in. Sabella had mentioned the analysts. "Is it really that dangerous on the streets?" I had spent enough time scouring the rubbish dumps near Carlver River to know it certainly could be. But not all areas of Lapana are as rough.

Eli fixes me with a look. "You tell me? You get that on the street?" He points at my face with his licked-clean spoon.

What? Oh, shit, my cheek. I'd seen it in the mirror this morning after my bath. No longer puce, the magical healing poultice had hastened the stages, whisking me straight to a black bruise. I finger it gently. Still tender but no longer throbbing.

"This was ... a misunderstanding. Not one that happened on the streets."

"Oh, well. The streets can be dangerous. I helped investigate three murders, two rapes, several burglaries, and many, many magical use infractions in my year on the beat." Eli shudders. "The murders and rapes were horrid. Seeing it. The blood. The distressed victims and the grieving relatives. The shattered lives." He scrubs at his forehead. "Behind a desk, you read reports. Read data. You are separate from it. It all becomes cold, emotionless information. I know that might not be *right*, but holding myself separate from it means I can see the patterns clearly." He smiles again.

He has a warm, friendly smile. The kind that sinks into your skin and makes your bones liquid. Burning hell. I can't stop the bubble of attraction that rises. I realise I am biting my lip and stop immediately.

"You probably think I'm a coward." Eli flings an arm across the back of the chair next to him. "*You* look like a tough one. Like a scrapper. And I don't just mean because of the bruise." His eyes roam over me, appraising. "That's a compliment, by the way."

I *am* a scrapper. Years of sneaking into Lapana and searching the rubbish barges have made me light and swift of step. It taught me to take in my surroundings with a keen eye, avoiding the gangs and guards alike. But none of it had prepared me for prison. I was soft when I went in. I came out hard. Still, I don't judge anyone for feeling fear. If I'd been presented with an opportunity to get away from the horrors in prison, I would have taken it. Hell, I *did* take it.

"I don't think you're a coward." And because Eli's gaze is making my chest tight, I take another spoonful of pie to give myself something to do.

Eli seems to be the sort of person who takes people at their word because he grins broadly, pushes his glasses back up his nose, and gives a tiny nod.

For a moment, the only sound is of me chewing. Swallowing, I work up some courage. "Do you, I don't know, ever feel trapped?" I hesitate. "Like, you can't get out of the guards without ... being responsible for your prime losing their job."

Eli looks thoughtful and drums his fingers on his chin. "I don't. I love my job. But I know some who do. Some who feel like they made a mistake in becoming a guard. But they stick with it because, as you say, leaving is a brutal act for your prime. Of course, there is *one* way out where your prime doesn't lose their job."

My breath hitches. “Oh. Yeah.” I act like I know what he is talking about, hoping he will elaborate.

“But nobody wants that on their record. Being found unstable. Or overly violent. No. No one wants that.”

Interesting. I tuck that bit of information away. I’ll have to find out more, but just maybe there is a way out of this for me and for Sabella.

“Missing your family, are you?” Eli asks and gives me a kindly look.

I sigh and nod.

More than you can imagine.

“I know of a good way of keeping the loneliness at bay,” Eli says and there is no doubting the brazen innuendo he loads into his wink.

I take him in. I’Kuna knows it has been a long time, and he is an attractive man. I’d erected such strong walls while in prison, keeping myself apart from the corruption and violence and cruelty of the inmates. Human contact was ... pure luxury. And my loneliness makes me crave human touch.

“Where?” I ask, and with my eyes fixed on Eli, I slowly slide my half-eaten bowl of pie to one side.

His eyes widen. “I was joking, really. But never let it be said that I’m not one to help a maiden in distress.”

My mouth twitches. He is just the right sort of ridiculous I need right now.

Eli licks his lips and stands. He jerks his head towards the door I had been studying moments ago. “Storeroom. If you are sure?”

Instead of answering, I rise, go to the door, and turn the handle. I look back at Eli.

"You coming?"

"Gods, yes."

24

Rill

I AM SHOCKED BY the frenetic activity when Eli and I emerge from the kitchen.

Eli snaps to attention. "Something's up." He gives my arm a quick but gentle squeeze—perhaps a thank you, or a good-bye—then scurries away at pace.

The number of guards has swelled, and the atmosphere is tense and urgent. Men and women in crisp uniforms stride about, looking self-important and oh, so busy. What is happening? Perhaps a Hismish has ... gasp ... used magic. Thankfully, Sabella appears within a few seconds, almost like she's been waiting, and leads me to the briefing room, quickly explaining what is going on.

Shock prickles my skin, and I rub at my arms. Another demon attack? Tonight? Perhaps the officiousness of the guards is warranted after all. The repose I'd taken with Eli in the storeroom flees, giving way to sharp tension.

The briefing room, located at the back of the guardhouse, is huge and yet, with so many guards attending, it is packed beyond belief. Thankfully, Sabella and I are among the last to arrive, so we stand at the back near the door. Which means I can breathe. So many people crammed together seem to sponge up all the oxygen. I concentrate on making my chest rise and fall evenly. I don't want Sabella to notice I am ... nervous. Anxious.

Sex with Eli had been exactly what I needed. For a few brief moments, I wasn't Prisoner Narin. I was not an illegal Tangler and not a reluctant fledge. I was not even Hismish as he didn't seem to care where I was from. Instead, I just was, and the act held no strings. After, I'd been ready to go back to my room and attempt to sleep. Bloody, shit-stuffed demon summoner.

An older guard stands at the front of the room and lifts his hands. Everyone goes quiet, the room filling with tense expectation.

"Captain Declan Wallace," Sabella whispers to me.

Eli's prime. I spot Eli sitting at a small desk to one side of the captain. He holds a pencil and is poised, ready to write.

"We have reason to believe the demon summoner will be active again tonight," Captain Wallace begins with no preamble. His voice is even-toned, piercing, and carries the room easily. "If the intelligence is correct, he will attempt to harvest two more souls. We must ensure that doesn't happen."

Murmurs ripple around the room.

"All apparition booths are closed, so the summoner cannot leave Lapana. All taverns and brothels are closed. Night shifts in the warehouses are cancelled and all non-essential manufacturing shifts cancelled too. A curfew is being put in place. Citizens are being ordered to stay in their homes. I want guards on the streets, patrolling. We need a strong presence as the summoner may attempt to break into a home to gather the souls. Constable Rivers and her Pegasus—" His eyes briefly land on Sabella, and I resist the urge to tuck in behind her "—will take to the sky and watch the city from above. Two guards will man the GH to receive and pass on communication of any sightings from citizens and any reports from patrols. It will be a busy night. Citizens will be jumpy, and reports will flow. Constable Rivers and her new fledge will be the first to investigate as they can cover the ground more quickly. I know some of you have just come off shifts and will be tired. But we must protect our citizens from this evil. We cannot allow black magic in our city."

I nearly leap out of my skin when the room erupts into a cheer. My jaw clenches, and I have to force myself not to step back. Beside me, Sabella doesn't cheer. She stands with arms crossed and feet wide—firm and silent.

Captain Wallace continues, and Eli writes furiously. I notice a lick of his hair is sticking up where I'd curled my fingers into it. I catch my top lip in my teeth and wonder if relations between guards are frowned upon.

"If anyone encounters the summoner, take him down by any means necessary, but keep your heads. I don't want to hear of random men dressed in black being spelled, arrested, or worse. Bear in mind, there is no guarantee the summoner will even wear black tonight."

Captain Wallace takes a deep breath.

"We have vials of holy water being delivered as we speak. If anyone encounters the demon, throwing holy water on it should make it flee back to hell. Assuming it is a mid-level demon as we suspect. I don't want heroics. No one is to attempt an incantation to trap the demon or return it to hell. Demon-controlling incantations are Level Five magic. And, as you are all aware, only one guard has a Level Five license and the skills and years of practice that go with it. Do we all understand?"

Murmurs once more.

"Right. In an orderly fashion, I want everyone to file through the mess, where you will be provided with your assignment, location, and holy water. Cook Calista has food bags for anyone who would like to take refreshments with them as it will be a long night. Any questions?"

I feel the press of tension from the guards. Fear mingles with anger and determination. When there are no questions, Captain Wallace dismisses everyone.

And that is when I spot him. The same guard who was on duty when I'd come to report Cassia missing. He hasn't changed one bit. He still looks as put together as a pencilled drawing. His lines, some artfully curved and others die straight, are clean and filled in exactly. Then, gods save me, he spots Sabella and makes a beeline for her. I shrink back, the memories of that day like acid in my belly.

"Peak," the guard says when he reaches us. His voice is smooth and monotone. He stands straight, arms by his side, his feet shoulder-width apart. His hands hang loose, but not too loose.

"Nolan," Sabella replies. I notice she doesn't smile or seem particularly pleased to be talking to this man.

"I heard you'd taken on your fledge." His eyes find me, and I wonder if he will remember me. Will he still see right through me and label me as Hismish scum?

"Hello. I'm Constable Nolan Fawns."

I stare at Nolan, every part of me screaming that he is bad news. I can't put my finger on why, but something about him is ... wrong. Sabella presses against me, and though I know she is urging me to speak, my mouth refuses to form any words.

"This is Fledge, Rill Narin," Sabella finally says, and I flinch at the impatience in her voice. No doubt she is wondering what in I'Kuna's name is wrong with me. But then Nolan smiles, and I know there is nothing wrong with me. It is all *him* for the smile is perfect ... and greasy and creepy.

"Does she not talk?" he says, the smile flicking with amused condescension, his gaze spending far too long on my bruised cheek.

"I do. When warranted," I shoot back at him, anger freeing my tongue. His smile freezes on his face. I'd hit my mark.

Nolan clears his throat and gathers himself, his lips pressed into a straight line. "Welcome to the guards, Rill." He gives me one last sharp look, then marches away.

I wonder if he ever walks, or if he marches everywhere to a beat that only he can hear. I dare a glance at Sabella who is looking at me with questions written all over her face.

"I don't like him." I study the floor. "He was the guard who sent me away when I came about Cassia ..." Suddenly worried I sound whiny, I meet Sabella's eyes and shrug. "He's ..."

"Arrogant," Sabella finishes for me. "If it makes you feel any better, I don't like him either, but he's an excellent guard. Amazing at solving crimes. He has ... a gift. Unfortunately, he knows it, too." She gives a wry smile when I snort softly, relieved that Sabella hasn't made me feel foolish. "Ready for another ride on Diarissa?"

I nod. I might be a phoney—a guard pretending to be a guard—but I can't deny the thrill that comes with the thought of soaring high above the city.

25

Rill

"WHAT DID HE MEAN by calling you Peak?"

We are in the stable preparing for our night of flying over the city.

"It's just a nickname." Sabella is bent over, head in a cupboard gathering items.

"Why Peak?" I cross my arms.

Sabella stands, balancing an arm full of goodness knows what. I annoy her with my questions, I can tell. She takes a breath. "Because I ... did well in all my tests as a fledge. Finished top of the class and everyone started calling me Peak." With a little shake of her head, she rearranges the items in her arms and holds out a set of goggles, gloves, a hat with woollen ear flaps, and a leather jacket. "Here."

I eye the jacket and curl a hand against my chest, fingering the clasps of my guard vest.

"It's leather." Many would call me mulish, but damn it, I have my principles.

Sabella hesitates, her expression softening to what I am coming to understand is her thinking face.

"Yes," Sabella finally says. "But it will be cold on Diarissa tonight. Next week, we can arrange for a water-proofed, lined cotton jacket, but for now ... well, I can assure you, you will be glad of it when we get high." Sabella cocks her head. "Were you cold last night when we flew on Diarissa?"

It had been bloody freezing. The night air of the sky had cut through me like shears.

Sabella nods, even though I haven't answered. "That was a short ride. We'll be on Diarissa's back all night tonight. Plus, we are tired. We'll become cold faster because of that." She gives the jacket a light shake. "The animal that gave its life for this jacket is dead. Not wearing it won't change that."

In the stall beside us, Diarissa tosses her head, then leans over the stall door, and nudges at me.

Heaving a sigh, I take the jacket. Diarissa is either manipulating me or giving me permission to wear the skin of a dead animal. Either way, it is effective. A spark of wry delight flickers in my chest. I am fast falling in love with the Pegasus.

The jacket is surprisingly heavy. I run a finger over the soft, supple leather and murmur a prayer to the goddess, I'Kuna under my breath, thanking the creature for its sacrifice. I slide the jacket on, wiggling my shoulders to settle it. It is wool-lined and immediately, its warmth seeps into my bones. Sabella is right. My exhaustion and lack of sleep have made me shivery, despite the heat that clings to the evening and despite having sweated buckets most of the day.

Sabella leads Diarissa from her stall, then slides a knee-high box to the Pegasus's flank. She heaves a saddle from a peg on the wall and climbs onto the box. When she taps Diarissa's back, the Pegasus unfurls her wings, up and out of the way so Sabella can fling the saddle onto her back. Diarissa is huge. Her stall is larger than those of the other horses in the stable. It is wider to accommodate her wings, and the roof is raised in this section of the stable for her height.

Night creeps into the stable, the electric lighting becoming brighter against the deepening velvet. Worms wiggle in my stomach. The demon summoner will be preparing to go out into the night and find another two victims.

"How do we know the summoner didn't flee Lapana earlier? How do we know he won't take a dirty booth out of Lapana? Closing the booths won't stop him taking a dirty booth. What if he goes back to Ikra?" I brace against the needle-sharp pain that pricks at my sternum.

Sabella pulls on the saddle's girth, tightening it, shadows dancing across her rich black face. "We can't be everywhere. That's the cold, hard truth. We could send guards to Ikra, but what of the other villages in Hismish? It would take more than eighty guards to man all of them across Hismish." She leans her forehead on the saddle for a second. "I know it doesn't seem fair ... hell, it isn't fair, but we can only do what we can with the numbers we've got." She becomes businesslike, allowing the saddle flap to fall into place, and pulls the metal stirrups down along their leather straps. "As far as the dirty booths go, the curfew will help. It makes it hard for anyone to sneak around when the streets are empty."

With Diarissa saddled, Sabella dons her own jacket, gloves, and hat. "It's the best we can do." She sounds more like she is trying to convince herself than convince me. She slips her goggles over her head, leaving them hanging around her neck like a necklace and leads Diarissa from the stable.

Shuffling my feet, I tuck in behind Diarissa's rear, patting at my vest, reminding myself of what is in which pocket. The focus on looking after Lapana stings, but I also understand the hopelessness of trying to protect everyone. They could guard Ikra only to find the summoner goes to a different village. This is my best chance to help find the summoner and get justice for Yalda. I tap a forefinger to each vest pocket.

Com-box, handcuffs, knife I recite under my breath.

I pull my goggles over my head, letting them sit 'round my neck like Sabella. Then I slap on the hat and slip on the gloves. The thrill from moments earlier electrifies me again. Flying atop the magnificent Pegasus is wondrous.

Outside the guard stables, Sabella turns to me. "Initially, we fly over the city, looking for any citizens who are not obeying the curfew. We land and instruct them to move inside. Then we will respond to any com-box reports." She reaches into her vest and fishes out her com-box. "Here. The messages will come to my box." She holds it out to me. "How's your night vision?"

I purse my lips and frown.

"The box will vibrate when a report comes through," Sabella explains, leading Diarissa out of the narrow alleyway that lies behind the stable. "We'll receive the reports the guards on the ground can't get to. You can play them on the com-box, but it's too easy to mishear, so we always print reports in the field. You'll need to print them, read them, and shout in my ear to tell me where we need to go."

Sabella comes to an abrupt halt. "Gods, Rill, I never thought to ask ... can you ... how is your reading?"

My pride stings, but it's a fair question as many Hismish never learn to read. There are no Hismish schools, and while it isn't forbidden for them to attend a Lapana school, it is frowned upon ... and the cost of uniforms and books makes it impossible anyway.

"My mother taught me and Cassia to read. She was a farmer's daughter and went to school."

"Your mother was from Lapana?"

"Ah-huh. She was from Lapana Strip, right on the Hismish border."

I cross my arms. I don't want to talk about my mother. Sabella takes the hint and urges Diarissa forward once more.

"What kind of reports will we get?" I ask, falling in beside Sabella, feeling like a fish out of water.

"Sightings of the summoner. Reports of break-ins. But be prepared. People will be scared, and any little noise will drive some to panic. The neighbour's cat on their roof will suddenly become a demon about to crash through their ceiling and take their soul. But we must check any and all reports, because the very one we don't take seriously, will be the very one that is serious."

"And the guards on the ground are doing the same thing?"

"Yup." Sabella gives Diarissa a light tap behind her front left knee.

"And we investigate ... the overflow?" I ask.

"Exactly. Or simply when the guards can't get there quickly enough."

Diarissa goes down on one knee, unfurling her wings. The city lights catch her feathers, making them glow snowy white. Sabella mounts, then holds out an arm for me. Every cell in my body rebels against accepting Sabella's outstretched arm, yet I am barely able to hold back a smile. I am about to ride a Pegasus … for the second time in two days. It is … miraculous. So, I grip Sabella's forearm and leap up behind her, hugging the com-box to my chest.

The tight uniform pinches at my belly when I lean closer to Sabella. "My night vision is excellent, by the way."

I feel Sabella's shoulders shake with the laugh she gives. Many people have told me I am too dry. Dreary. Insipid. Blah. Just a few of many words used to describe me. But Sabella doesn't seem to think so.

"Up," Sabella commands, and Diarissa flaps her wings in giant swoops that immediately lift her a few feet off the ground. She seems to unfurl her wings even further, and with two great flaps, we soar.

The saddle is made for tandem riding and has pegs for me to rest my feet. The back of the saddle curves sharply behind my backside and curls slightly around my thighs. All in all, I feel secure and certainly much better than last night when we left my hut for Lapana. I had to sit awkwardly on Lady Keeva's lap, praying she would not shift about too much.

Diarissa wastes no time in climbing high into the sky. From reading one of my rubbish-scrounged books, I know the Pegasi mix their size and sheer strength with magic to fly. No one understands it completely. Scholars have studied the creatures for years and are no further forward in understanding. I always thought, 'You can't know the unknowable.' Regardless, the magic of Pegasi is cherished and revered by all in Conpieta.

Achieving a height that allows for a good view, Diarissa levels off and glides on invisible currents, giving the occasional flap of her mighty wings. I look down on the city of Lapana. Everyone has been instructed to keep external lights on to make it difficult for the summoner to hide. So, the city blazes brightly. It sprawls before us, and from here, I can clearly see the different districts. To the west, factories spew smoke and steam into the air. Even tonight, many will continue to operate, providing electricity and warmth and clean water to the homes of Lapana.

The factories morph slowly into the warehouse area. Huge square buildings without adornment. It is the largest section of Lapana and stretches east and south until it meets with Carlver River. Beside the warehouse section is a depot area. It is the mid-point for goods and parts coming and going via the river or by rail.

In the centre, the shopping district is bordered on the north and east by residences. Lapana City is bounded by Carlver River in the south and Manor Rise in the north. Cutting around and through the city is the train track that arrives from Ga'Razi in Keplon and leaves heading for the capital of Simgra in Basima. Along with Carlver River, the trains take goods to the other regions. They rarely take passengers any more since the introduction of the Apparition Booths.

Sabella directs Diarissa north, soaring higher as the land rises. The base of Manor Rise marks the start of the wealthy section. The homes grow in size and the tree-lined streets widen. The higher up the hill, the bigger and more opulent the homes become. Then finally, seated on the huge plateau, is the Earl's manor. It is several hundred years old and more like a castle than a manor, except it lacks the turreted towers of a castle. It is several storeys high in some places and only one or two storeys in others so that it rises and falls like a small city of its own. A huge wall runs 'round its circumference, complete with guard towers.

Sabella turns Diarissa before we fly over the manor, however.

"We're not permitted to fly over the manor," Sabella shouts. "Which is OK. We need to inspect the city. Did you see any people in the streets while we flew over?"

"Yes," I shout back. "In the warehouse section."

Diarissa banks under Sabella's direction, and my stomach rises, pressing to my throat. But I can't stop the huge grin that stretches my face.

26
Rill

We sweep along at quite a rate, and the wind batters at us with a coldness that makes the heat of the city seem like a distant memory. I am glad for the warmth of the hat, gloves, and jacket.

"There." I point at a group of three men standing outside a warehouse.

Sabella signals Diarissa, and we descend. The trio look up as we come in to land, their mouths dropping open. They are burly-looking men, their chests puffed behind filthy, open-neck shirts and loose overalls, but they shuffle back, pressing themselves to the wall of a warehouse. They snatch their caps off their heads, so their greasy hair lifts when Diarissa gives a final flap of her wings and lands before them.

Sabella places a hand on Diarissa's withers, and she goes down on one knee.

"Dismount," Sabella says softly.

I appreciate that Sabella has a way about her. She requests rather than orders me, and just as well, or my normally prickly back would turn porcupine.

I quickly slide off Diarissa, breathing in the warm, metallic air, and eye the men. They smirk. Probably at my short size. But when Sabella dismounts, the smirks falter. Sabella may only be of average height, but somehow manages to look ... more. For the first time, I appreciate how the trim, clean lines of the uniform lend an air of authority. Sabella walks towards the men without hesitation.

"Is there a reason you're out after curfew?" she asks in a firm but not unfriendly tone.

"We gonna take care of the demon-summoning fucker," the man on the right says. The other two, twisting their caps in their hands, nod vigorously. The one who spoke is clearly the leader of this little group. Now I can see them better, I realise they are younger than I first thought. Early twenties—around my age—I guess.

"Ah," Sabella says. "Gotcha." She turns to me. "Record this, please."

I fumble with the com-box and press record.

"Tell me. How were you planning on taking care of the *demon-summoning fucker*? I imagine you must have strong magic."

The two smaller men look to their leader who shakes his head. "Nah, love. We're good with our fists. We'll knock him unconscious." He folds his arms across his broad chest like he's just provided the most obvious solution. "And bring him to the guards ... of course," he adds, beads of sweat forming on his top lip.

Sabella heaves an exasperated sigh. "Gentlemen. The demon summoner is likely a Class Five witch. You would not get within spitting distance before he rendered you inert ... or worse. I'm afraid I'll have to take you to the lockup for the night. For your own safety and the safety of everyone else."

Alarm spreads over the faces of the men. Even the leader looks uncomfortable.

"We ain't gonna hurt no one else—"

Sabella steps forward, and the man bites off his words. "We hope to stop the demon summoner tonight," she says, one hand resting casually on her guard cudgel—her Jack. "Hope to stop him taking any more souls. Stop him mutilating any more bodies. All the guards are patrolling the streets in the vain hope we might prevent him from bringing a demon from hell to Lapana." She advances again so she is only a foot from the men. "The last thing we need is to have to rescue idiots who think they can take on a Class Five witch with their fists. You could cost lives this evening, gentlemen, and I'll not stand for it."

The men have the decency to look chagrined.

"I'll message GH and arrange for some guards to pick you up." Sabella's expression hardens. "It's bad enough that we will waste time dealing with you. I hope taking our attention from the summoner doesn't provide a window of opportunity for him."

I've dealt with these kinds of men before—Ikra had its fair share of them, both born and raised and passing through—and an idea forms. I hope I'm not about to overstep. "Where do you all live?" I ask.

The men seem to have forgotten I am here as they look at me in startled surprise. The leader jerks his head.

"Workers quarters. Few blocks over."

"By yourselves?"

"Hey?"

"Do you have wives? Or do you live with your folks?"

The leader puffs his chest out. "I got a wife. These two live with their mothers."

I nod. Thank goodness this is going my way. It's hot on the ground in a leather jacket and hat, and I hope my sweating face doesn't make me look apprehensive.

"And you choose to leave your mothers and wife home alone with a demon summoner threatening the city? You should be ashamed." The men don't like having this pointed out, and I can see they are about to argue. "Constable Rivers, I think we should return these men to their homes. Tell their wife and mothers where they were. I'm sure each gentleman would like the opportunity to make this right and be the man of the house they should be."

The men flat-out panic. They drop all attitude, and their stances turn pleading.

"Don't tell me wife."

"I don't want me Mum knowing."

"She'll take to me with the rollin' pin."

They all speak at once, babbling like children.

Sabella presses a knuckled forefinger to her lips. From where I stand, I can see the side of her mouth twitching.

"Thank you, Fledge Narin. An excellent idea." Sabella recomposes herself quickly. "You all get home. We'll follow on my Pegasus and speak to your families." She leans in a little. "And don't even think about running because my Pegasus will enjoy the chase. And I can assure you, she won't be gentle when she catches you." She straightens and moves aside so the men have a good view of Diarissa.

The Pegasus seems to grow. I blink, wondering if her magic has actually made her bigger or if the raising of her head and tail has simply made her look bigger. She stares at the men, paws at the ground with a feathered foot, and gives a snort. It isn't the gentle snort of a horse either. It is more like the snort of a dragon, and I swear she puffs smoke from her nostrils, though it is probably just hot breath in the cooling night. Whatever it is, it works because the men look terrified.

"Go," Sabella orders, and the three flee instantly, their boots loud on the cobblestones in the still evening.

Sabella turns back to me, a huge grin on her face. "Come on. We'll make sure these three are, in fact, dealt with by their women folk." She reaches Diarissa, mounts, and I jump on behind.

"Good call. Well done," Sabella says as she gathers the reins.

Stupidly, I find I like the praise.

27
Sabella

We fly low, following the three men to their respective homes. One mother takes her son by the ear and drags him inside, a stream of filthy language echoing in the night even after she slams the door. I can't help the giggle that escapes me.

Rill was bang-on with her assessment—an assessment I could never have made. I'd never had a mother to disappoint. But Rill had read the men perfectly and come up with a solution. Now we are saving time not having to take them to the GH lock up, and we are not wasting guard resources. I have a feeling the men are going to be punished by their mothers and wife far more than a night in lock-up ever would have done.

When the door closes on the last of the three would-be heroes, we take to the skies again. It is becoming cooler, and I tie the flaps of my flight hat under my chin.

We sweep the city twice over and do not spy any more citizens breaking curfew. Then the com-box vibrates. I can feel it faintly through the saddle. Behind me, Rill wiggles, obviously working to print the com-box message.

Her mother was Lapanian, I muse. It explains the slight Lapanian accent and her ability to read. I am getting to know my fledge better, and the rising hope and even satisfaction take me by surprise. Now to see just how good her night vision is. I wait.

"Man in black spotted," Rill yells in my flap-covered ear a moment later.

My heart thumps.

"Twenty-two Parrside Street, West District."

OK. Her night vision really is excellent.

I ask Diarissa to bank and urge her forward towards the West District. As usual, my signals form only a small part of my communication with Diarissa. I am sure the Pegasus can read my mind. Or, at least, my emotions. She seems to pick up on the urgency and flies at an impressive rate towards the West district.

We land on Parrside Street which borders the west and residential districts. Rill dismounts without being asked as soon as Diarissa sinks to one knee, and I quickly follow. We both pull our hats off and tuck them into the saddle bags. I pull Jack from my belt, and instantly, Rill copies the action with her own cudgel.

I look at Diarissa. It is not the first time she's been used in guard business, but it is the first time she's been involved in something so dangerous. Would a demon want her soul? Some say Pegasi are representatives of the Gods. Would that make her soul more attractive, or would it give the demon pause? I place a hand on Diarissa's forehead.

"If the demon shows up, you run, OK? Fly away and be safe."

Diarissa gives a gentle snort, and I swear it's a snort of derision. Pegasi can take care of themselves, this I know. Anyone who tries to take a Pegasus by force usually ends up dead. Diarissa rises from her bow and stands tall, her head turning like she is scanning the area. Her long, thick mane and tail ripple. She looks impressive and not a little intimidating. I have to trust she will be alright.

I study the house numbers and walk smartly with Rill on my heels. I find Number 22 and knock on the door.

"Who is it?" A man's voice calls out.

"Citizen guards, sir," I reply. "You made a report."

A curtain in one of the windows moves, and a moment later, the door is answered by a man-and-woman couple. Their eyes are wide, their features tense. They look up and down the street like a werewolf is about to appear. They are genuinely frightened. I brace against the chill that snakes up my spine.

"Tell me what you saw," I say, keeping my tone steady and authoritative. Rill, bless her, steps up beside me, providing a stronger front.

"A man dressed in black. Black mask too." It is the husband who speaks.

"We watched," the wife adds. "He went down Bexmark Lane." She points down the street.

I can see the street sign to the side laneway and nod. "Go back inside and keep your doors locked."

"Don't have to tell us twice," the husband says and slams the door in my face.

"Com-box," I say, holding my hand out. Rill gives it to me, and I press record. "Link Duty Constable box. Report at 22 Parrside Street says a man in black clothes and mask was seen turning down Bexmark Lane, off Parrside Street. Fledge Narin and I are going to investigate but request backup as soon as it can arrive." I click send on the com-box and place it in my vest.

I grip Jack. "No heroics," I tell Rill. "Freeze if you must, but otherwise we locate and watch until backup gets here."

Rill's throat bobs, her deep-set eyes intense. She gives a small nod.

I walk to Bexmark Lane and peer down the narrow street. I can't see any movement. Luckily, house lights illuminate the lane, so it isn't too dark. But there are still plenty of shadows that could hide someone dressed in black.

"Stick to the middle of the street, and stay close to me. You look left, and I'll look right," I whisper to Rill.

Rill raises her shiny new guard cudgel, and together, we set off down Bexmark Lane. Breath-robbing unease wraps around us, drawing us close, and making us one. I concentrate on breathing steadily through my nose, keeping panic at bay. I can't afford to make a mistake. A part of me wishes Tavell was here and taking charge, but I'd trained for this, and it's my turn to lead.

A clatter rings out ahead of us, the sound of a rolling tin on cobblestones, and Rill and I crouch slightly and point our Jacks. Then a tabby cat mews, darts across the street, leaps a fence, and scurries away into someone's garden.

"Shit." My heart pounds.

Beside me, Rill's breathing races in an audible pant. There is no breeze in the laneway to shift the scent of garbage combined with the lingering odour of evening meals. The stone beneath our feet holds the sun's warmth which somehow seems to signal that we are stepping on hell's door.

We continue. Slowly. Carefully. I try not to imagine a demon suddenly appearing before us.

Where is our backup?

Then we hear a scuffling sound. This time, it definitely isn't a cat. It is too loud and too ... ungraceful. It is coming from the side access of a house to our right. I stare, and my stomach tightens when grey mist curls, spilling outward, reaching towards us with cold, wispy fingers. Dread drives a chill over my skin which leaches into my bones, and I swallow noisily.

Step by step, Rill and I advance on the house, our Jacks extended in a kind of desperate defence. Suddenly Rill presses tight, leaning a shoulder into me.

I glance at her and catch the incline of her head. I look where she indicates, and I can just make out a shape, crouching in the bushes. Fear squeezes at my chest, and my breath grows raspy. My words to the men breaking curfew ring in my head. This is a man who is probably a Class Five witch. But I have a job to do. I take a step ... and the figure starts to chant.

I freeze, my heart lodging in my throat. The mist reaches us, and it smells of ... rotten eggs. Gods. I picture the demon materialising before us. He will take my soul and Rill's, and in a single summoning, the man in black will have met his quota for the night. I grab Rill's arm.

"Run," I say and pull on her, swelling panic rippling over me.

But Rill resists. "No," she breathes. "It's not ... it's gibberish."

It takes a second to sink in, but then I realise. Rill has heard the summoner's incantation. She will know if this is different.

"You sure?" I ask. I still cling to Rill's arm. Coiled. Ready to run. Mist swells around us in a leaden soup.

"Yes." Rill keeps her eyes on the shape in the bushes. "The words are rubbish, and the magic ... the scent and the ... thrum ... it's all wrong."

Doubt holds me. If I make the wrong decision, I might get us both killed.

Courage is not the absence of doubt, but action despite it.

I straighten. "Come out of there," I order the crouching figure. "Now."

The shape explodes from the bushes and runs at us.

"Stop," I shout and point Jack at the assailant, only to have the cudgel fly from my hand as if by an invisible force. Having disarmed me with magic, the shadowy figure comes at me, and I brace against imminent impact. A second later, I meet the unyielding, cobblestone laneway, and air whooshes from my body. My attacker is on top of me, pressing my shoulders to the ground. Teeth gritted, I forcefully raise a knee, and I'm rewarded with a yelp of pain. I'm not sure where I connected with the man, but I hope it slows him. Trying to draw breath into my winded lungs, I struggle to my feet, but now I can't see. The grey mist has spread and grown, rising to form a wall around me. I crouch, fists raised, my head jerking with every tiny sound in the slate nothingness.

The tap, tap of footsteps ... and I lash out but hit nothing but the mist. I gulp for air, and tendrils of mist seem to solidify and slide into my lungs, choking and … drowning me. Agnis save us, the attacker is using water magic.

"Sabella … fire." Rill pants and gurgles and coughs. "Burn … burn it away."

Every cell in my body locks. Fire. A gift from the gods. A gift that comes with a price if you can't control it. I'd learned that lesson all too well. A ghost that haunts me still. But if I don't chance it, we might both die. But this is no tiny ball in my palm. I will need to let it flow and spread. With a shaky gulp and cough, I raise my shaking hands. The mist turns more and more watery, seeking us out like wet octopus tentacles, and dampness clings to my face, my lips, my nostrils.

I try to recall a spell, one that will control the fire. There is a reason fire elemental magic is Level Four … it is notoriously difficult to control. But instead of the words to chant, all I see is the charred paint on the desk and the raw, bubbled skin of the young boy. The one I'd burned when anger sent my fire magic roaring across the orphanage classroom. The screams of the other children echo in my head.

"Sa … bella …" Rill sounds like she's underwater, and the horror we face snaps me back into focus.

Before memories can grip me again and I lose my nerve, I draw on my training and send a narrow stream of fire into the thick, dripping mist, setting it aglow with redness. Now I see Rill, her hands before her mouth making a scooping gesture like she is trying to swim from the mist. Just past her is our attacker, standing with arms extended. His hands twist like he is conducting a curling, soggy orchestra.

In that second, Rill points her Jack at the man in black. "Immotus," she splutters, water flying from her mouth.

The man in black solidifies, caught by the Jack's magic in a pose of hands outstretched. Without the controlling flow of enchantment, the mist loses its tendrils and drops to the ground, sinking and dissipating. I close my fists, cutting off the fire and cough violently, expelling water from my lungs and throat.

Rill is bent, hands on knees, caught in paroxysm hacking. Her Jack hangs loosely from her fingers, and I look around in the thinning mist to see where mine ended up. I find it by the front fence of the house on the opposite side of the laneway. Picking it up, I go to Rill and give her a slap on the back.

"You, OK?"

She stands and wipes her mouth. "What the fuck was that?"

"Water magic." I nod towards our still-frozen attacker. "Kikara gifted him."

Rill steps towards him, but I hold her back. "Before we approach, would you say he's the summoner?"

Rill shakes her head. "No. Too short and the mask the summoner wore wasn't woollen like this man's. It was ... I don't know ... hard. Moulded."

I nod and walk straight up to the frozen man and pull the woollen mask from his head.

"Oh, for fucks sake," I say.

Rill is beside me. "Who is it?"

"Tommy Eckles. A petty burglar. And a pain in our collective butts."

Just then, our backup arrives.

"Oh, ho! You caught Eckles," Constable Aires says. He takes in our damp hair. "Got you with the water magic, did he?" Aires grins like our predicament is a great joke.

Dickhead.

Ignoring the question, I give a report, and a couple of guards slap magic inhibiting bands on Eckles' wrists before they unfreeze him.

Tommy smirks at me as I watch the regular handcuffs go on a moment later.

"I nearly fooled you, Constable. Did you like my brimstone-flavoured mist? I've never smelt brimstone before, but I read once that it smells like rotten eggs. I give credit where credit is due though, you got me a good one in my meat-basket." Eckles laughs. He is the son of a judge, and his father always manages to ensure Tommy does no prison time for his crimes. He is the proverbial thorn in our side.

My foot itches to give his *meat-basket* another kick until my com-box vibrates. My stomach turns over when I read the message.

"Come on," I say to Rill. "There's a body. Reports say it's a demon killing."

28
Sabella

Diarissa's hooves ring out when she lands on the cobblestoned street near the reported location of the body. She dances a little as if enjoying an unheard rhythm, but when I ask her to kneel so we can dismount, she refuses. As if the music is abruptly cut off, she stops dancing and stands rigid, her neck arched.

"What's up, girl?"

Beside us, Carlver River rushes by, coal black in the night although the city lights twinkle on its inky surface. Moored boats, largely in silhouette, creak and moan as they rock to the water's current. Musky dampness—damp wood, damp rope, damp rocks—scents the air. I follow Diarissa's line of sight and gasp.

"Ahuizotl," I say.

Rill shifts behind me, and I can tell she is looking over my shoulder at the small dog-like creature. It sits, clinging to a gently swaying rope that ties a boat to the dock. It stares at me and Rill, its sharp pointed ears directed towards us. Its marbled, spiked, black and silver fur blends with the night.

"It ... won't come onto land, will it?" Rill asks.

I shake my head. "Shouldn't. At least, they don't normally, and everyone knows to keep clear of the water at night. Though I've heard of drunken fools being taken when they stumbled too close to the river." I shudder. Ahuizotls like to eat the eyes, nails, and teeth of their victims, and the hair on the back of my neck rises at the thought. It is said they are drawn to death—past, present, and future—and a sighting is a black omen. I push against the dread that fills me and take a steadying breath.

"It's OK Diarissa. You can let us off. We won't go near the ahuizotl."

But Diarissa still refuses to kneel. She stamps a foot at the creature, and when it doesn't move, she screams at it, the sound rising in her chest and sending vibrations rippling through her body.

At the ear-splitting sound, the ahuizotl dives off the rope and disappears under the dark, fast-flowing water. Diarissa gives a snort as if to declare her satisfaction the creature has gone, and then bows to one knee.

As soon as she does, Rill dismounts quickly and smoothly but gives the river edge a wide berth. I don't blame her.

Swinging a leg, I drop to the ground a second later and, ignoring the churning unease the ahuizotl has caused, head towards the alleyway with firm, deliberate steps.

The giant depots of this part of the Lower West district loom into the night sky. I always think buildings only used during the day have a sadness to them at night. A desolation as they wait in the darkness to once again be relevant.

"We are not far from the dance tavern," Rill says pointing, her voice low and taut and somehow, ominous. "A block that way and one street back." The shadows on her face make her nose appear to shift, and a shiver vibrates between my shoulder blades.

Damn the bloody ahuizotl. It has made me jumpy.

I fight against sparking dread, my skin feeling electrified. The summoner has returned to a familiar haunt. Images of the bloodied body in Ikra float before my eyes, and I steel myself for what I am about to see.

"You have nothing to prove here, Rill. If anything is too much, just step away." I make sure my tone holds efficient reasoning. One drop of pity will have Rill stubbornly resist. But she has witnessed more than her fair share. Watching Thorn die. Standing in the presence of the demon. Having it speak to her. Then having to deal with the gruesome body of one of her own. Yes, more than her fair share, and it would be ignorant, even cruel, not to acknowledge that.

Rill turns her large eyes to me, her face, as it so often is, blank, though I am starting to recognise the tiny shifts caused by the flinty determination beneath.

Just as we reach the entrance to the laneway, a figure exits in a rush, nearly knocking us over. My hand flies to my Jack ... until the figure doubles over and empties his stomach into a sad, bedraggled bush. It is a guard.

Rill stares, and I know I don't have to say anything further.

"Fledge Monaghan," I greet the guard who is now wiping his mouth. He gives a weak smile in reply as Rill and I walk to the mouth of the alley.

I lean close to her. "That is Constable Fawn's fledge," I whisper.

Rill stops mid-step. "That creepy guard. He'll be ..."

"Down the alleyway, yes."

Rill takes an audible breath, lifts her chin, and walks on mumbling an obscenity under her breath.

Unlike the last laneway, this alley is dark. It isn't a thoroughfare, but rather a narrow space between the rear of two rows of depots. Ahead, two guards stand holding their Jacks in illuminate mode over a prone figure on the cobblestoned ground. Despite the hour, the darkness, and the unlikely location, a couple of onlookers stand a little further back.

"I told you to get back inside," one of the guards snaps. "Or I'll arrest you for breaking curfew."

It is Nolan Fawn.

The onlookers scramble into the rear door of what I can only assume is a narrow home squeezed between two hulking depots. The house looks like it inhaled to fit in such a tiny gap and has held its breath ever since.

A breeze shoots down the alley and lifts a few strands of my hair that have been pulled loose by my flight hat. It also brings the metallic odour of blood with it. My pulse pounds urgently in my temple.

When we reach the body, I deliberately ignore Nolan.

"What have we got?" I direct my question to the senior constable, Justin Buckman. He'll be in charge anyway.

"Male victim. Throat torn away, stomach ripped open. At first assessment, I'd say the demon has struck again." Buckman rubs a hand over the back of his neck.

Staring at the scene, I feel a tickle—that weird sense you get when you know something is not right. I peer down at the body to confirm my suspicions. Black scorch marks surround the body, however, and I purse my lips. Perhaps I am wrong, but one vital detail is missing ... there is no smell of sulphur. Someone has sure done a number on the body though. The victim's throat yawns, his windpipe curling from his skin like it forlornly reaches for oxygen. The man's intestines are peeping from wounds on his stomach in a gristly echo of the demon's brutality.

"Do we know who he is?" I ask, taking in the victim's shaved and tattooed skull. "Looks gang to me."

"Agree," Senior Constable Buckman replies. He rubs at his belly as if the sight of the body makes him hungry, though I know Justin well enough to know he is assessing. He is a methodical guard, and I wonder if his instincts are nibbling at him too.

"If the demon took a gang soul, he's welcome to it," Constable Fawn says in a clipped voice. "The bastard will fit right in in hell."

"Any witnesses?" I ask the senior constable, once again ignoring Nolan.

"No one saw anything of worth ... that we know of, but that couple ..." he tips his head towards the narrow house "... heard shouting and then screaming. They peered out the window just in time to see someone running from the scene. Someone dressed in dark clothes." The rubbing of his belly slows.

"It wasn't a demon," Rill says quietly.

Senior Constable Buckman directs his lit Jack to Rill, his expression one of intrigue, but Nolan flashes an irritated look, his eyes narrow, and his lip curls.

"I hardly think a neophyte like you would know—"

"She's right," I cut in, fury making my chest burn. "Senior Constable Buckman, Fledge Narin and I attended the murder in Ikra. We saw the body. The smell of sulphur was strong, even hours later. There is no sulphur here."

Rill folds her arms, cocks her head, and stares at Nolan with a truly contemptuous look. The girl knows how to poke at bears.

"My guess," I continue. "This was a gang killing."

"Damn it, Sabella, you're right," Senior Constable Buckman says. "I couldn't figure out what was bothering me." He turns to Nolan. "Fetch your fledge, and go interview that couple again. What we got here is a garden variety gang hit. Unless I'm much mistaken, I'm guessing that couple know a bit about the gangs. They live right in their midst for Saleal's sake."

Nolan's cheek twitches, then he comes to attention, and moves off smartly, yelling for Fledge Monaghan. He pounds on the door of the narrow house.

"We have a problem though, Constable Rivers," Justin lowers his voice, his face in shadows now that it is just his Jack illuminating the scene. "Whoever murdered this poor bastard, tried to make it look like a demon killing. The details—slit throat and sliced-up gut—are not generally known. We kept the gory particulars out of the papers, mostly to stop all-out panic."

"But the person who did this knew," I murmur, an old worry resurfacing.

"Yup. We've either got someone who flapped their mouth, giving the killer the details they need, or someone in the know is responsible."

"You think it was a guard?" I breathe the words quietly like they are sacrilege.

"Oh, hell, I don't know." Senior Constable Buckman looks grim. "But we'll do everything we can to find out."

29
Keeva

I TIPTOE TO MY bedroom door and crack it open.

"Good morning, Lady Keeva," a deep, male voice greets me. "Although it's not *quite* morning yet." The voice holds amusement.

It isn't Alex who guards my door—I imagine he needs to sleep at some stage—but is one of his team, Dawie Klerk. I sigh.

"Good morning, Dawie. I ... can't sleep and thought I might take a stroll."

"Certainly, Lady Keeva. I will accompany you."

Of *course*, he will.

Despite the early hour, I am already dressed, so I slip out the door. "I only wish to walk about the manor. I will not venture outside."

"Very good, milady." He still follows me down the hallway.

I had slept in snatches only. The summoner and the demon are firmly lodged in my thoughts. Did the summoner reappear? Have the guards caught him? At least, with the city under curfew, there is nowhere for me to go. No dance taverns open. No chance to visit Sabella and Rill for they are on duty in the city, so being a prisoner in my own home rankles less. But it does nothing to quell my restlessness.

I wander aimlessly about the manor at first, then think I might go to Finn's study. When in the grips of a research project, Finn rarely sleeps. But when I get there, the room is in darkness.

"Do you know where Lord Finn is, Dawie?"

"I believe he is in the library, milady." Dawie is from Keplon. He is a large black man who seems to be made of muscle. Even his jaw, his chin, his cheeks look muscular. Beside him, I feel like the epitome of a delicate flower—just as everyone treats me.

"Thank you," I murmur and begin the long trek to the lower levels of the manor.

The library is situated in the second to lowest floor. The only thing under it is the basement which, in truth, is mixed with the manor foundations like a series of caves. Really, the library is the bottom of the heap. Lower than the servants' quarters, or the laundry and kitchens. Lower than the storerooms and the boiler room. Its location in the manor might tempt one to think it is a lowly room. Nothing is further from the truth.

I finally descend the last of the stairs, the heavy footsteps of Dawie behind me, and take in the huge double doors that lead to the Earl of Tarr Library. The doors have always given me mixed feelings, even as a child. They are intimidating doors. Made of heavy iron that has been worked into swirls and veined leaves and depictions of the sun and moon. The two door handles, shaped like human hands, seem to reach for each other. Fingertips stretching in an eternal yearning to touch. A yearning that will never be realised. Something about the doors ignites dread, like they hold in bad things. Which, at least in part, they do.

And yet, the doors also whisper an invitation. They beckon, calling to me to enter and be transported to different and wonderful places. It isn't a ridiculous idea. The library not only contains academic books but also hundreds of copies of picture books, fairy tales, love stories, adventure stories, stories of wild imaginings, and even horror stories. They are portals to other worlds and lives, and I do adore to travel by book. The memory of Rill's faded books on her dusty table leaps to mind. Perhaps she too, likes to travel by book.

But tonight, I am here to see what Finn has learned of demons. Smothering a shudder, I join hands with the cold iron doorknobs and enter the library.

To my left, the librarian's desk sits empty, a lonely, single light hanging from above casting more shadow than light. But in front of me, sitting at a massive table, is Finn. Mountains of books surround him. Some in piles and some lay open. The oversized light above the table blazes, making the rest of the cavernous library seem even blacker.

"You may wait outside," I tell Dawie.

With a bow, he retreats to wait on the other side of the doors.

I cross the parquetry floor to Finn. "Have you uncovered anything of interest?"

Finn looks up, a surprised look on his face. "Kee. How long have you been standing there?"

"Oh, about half an hour."

Finn's eyes widen, then he grins.

"Good one, sis."

I flop on the chair next to Finn, tiredness making me gauche. From where I sit, I look directly at the gated section, walled off from the rest of the library by a tight mass of welded iron circles. The boundary to the Heinous Section. And the gate stands open. Gods. I feel a pull. A keen desire to enter and browse. Probably because it is forbidden to me, but it is also possible that some dark magic within calls to me.

"Found anything?" I ask again.

Finn nods. "I think the demon was Garmr." He slides an open book towards me. "Look familiar?"

I stare down at the picture. It is *the* demon. Or, at least, the one Rill described. In the artistic painting, it holds a human heart in one hand, blood dripping from its taloned fist. Its red eyes glow, and even though it is only a painting in a book, I get the distinct impression it stares straight at me. Right into my soul. The expression on its face is hunger. Desperate, all-consuming hunger. I place a finger on the book, careful not to touch the picture, and slide it away.

"Yes," I whisper.

"Level Five magic is required to summon one. No big surprise, really, but the incantation needs practice. Lots of practice. If one gets the pronunciation a little wrong—if the summoner allows their magic to drift, even a little ... well, suffice to say it requires discipline. Only powerful witches can summon and maintain control. Know any Level Five witches?" Finn gives a sardonic grin.

"Yes."

Finn snaps his head to me. "Who?"

I squirm, unease prickling at me. "Constable Nash is a Level Five witch."

Finn sits back in his chair giving a long, low whistle. His arm comes around the back of the chair I sit on. "I never knew."

"Well, why would you know? You're not close to Tavell. I only know because of the time I spend with Sabella. She told me."

Finn stares at me for a second then ducks his head and tidies some of the books, although he appears to simply shift them from one spot to another.

"What?" I ask. Finn is acting odd.

"Oh, nothing. Nothing, seriously. I suppose I was just thinking how unlikely it is that Constable Nash would be the summoner." He takes a breath and turns to me. "Which puts us no closer to discovering who the summoner might be."

Silence fills the cavernous library. It presses on me like a living thing.

"Finn, were you and Father really talking about the magic class bill yesterday in the study?" The words I overheard had stayed with me, replaying over and over.

Do you think anyone suspects?

What if we are discovered? Perhaps we should stop for a time, delay the next?

We go ahead as planned tonight.

It was the *tonight* that really got to me, sliding under my skin like probing icicles. I am certain they were not talking about the magic class bill. I stare at Finn waiting for an answer, desperate that he explain. Desperate that he clears the whole thing up and stops the churning worry.

Finn runs a hand over his face and takes a deep breath. "I can't tell you." Pain and confusion show on his face.

"Finn. Tell me what's going on."

A lump of sadness grows inside me. Finn and I had always been close. We leaned on each other when Father was stern. We told each other everything. We'd never had secrets. Until now ...

Finn shakes his head. "Kee, you're going to have to trust me when I say I can't tell you. The risk is too great."

"Risk? What risk—"

"Do you trust me?" Finn's blue eyes hold me, begging for my faith.

I slump, unease mixing with the fact I *did* trust Finn. "Yes. Of course, I trust you."

Finn's relief is obvious. "I hope I can tell you one day. And if that day comes, I *promise* I will." A smile twitches the corner of his mouth. A smile of hope.

I swallow down the unease and give Finn an equally tiny smile in reply. "Alright."

Silence descends again.

Finn rubs a finger back and forth on the corner of one of the books. He'd had a security blanket when he was a small boy, and he did the same movement with its satin edge. My heart melts at the sight of my brother seeking comfort. I force my thoughts back to the demon summoner.

"Could say, a Level Four witch learn the summoning spell? The control needed?" I ask.

Finn starts at my sudden comment, then gives himself a physical shake.

"I guess. It would be risky, but with enough time, yes. Yes, anyone could learn the incantation." Finn strokes his chin, a gesture he'd inherited from our father.

"And how many libraries in Lapana have a Heinous Section?" I ask.

His eyes light up, and I am certain he understands the direction of my thoughts. "Two. This one and a small one at the University." He kisses my cheek. "I'll start here and take a peek at everyone who has access." His eyes wander over to the Heinous Section Gate.

I follow his line of sight. "What is in there? Just books?"

"There are artefacts too." He grins, acting much more like his normal self. "Want to take a look?"

30
Keeva

AN IMMEDIATE NO BUBBLES in my throat. A symptom of the good-girl, well-trained part of me. The part I fight against. I stand.

"Yes. I want to look."

Finn's eyes widen a fraction. "Kee. You rebel." His dimples sink deeply with the slightly crazed grin he gives. Clearly, he expected me to decline. "Come along then."

I follow Finn, trying not to make it too obvious that I am sticking tight to my brother. As soon as we step past the iron-worked walls, I feel hot. The darkness beckons like sticky fingers on my skin.

"Don't touch anything," Finn says.

I press closer to him, no longer caring if I am being obvious.

Before us, six rows of shelves run directly from the gates. Finn goes left, taking me to the first aisle between the floor-to-ceiling shelves.

"These shelves contain all the books on enchantments, including glamours, love spells, luck spells—good and bad—hexes, and memory spells." He sniffs. "Lower-level stuff really." He moves to the second row. "This one contains information about voodoo, conjuring, and a bit of alchemy." He winks. "A bit more interesting."

We go to the third row. "This holds everything you could want to know about necromancy and summoning the dead. Fascinating stuff."

The fourth row holds books on how to summon mythical creatures and the Gods. "Ludicrous. Truly. Like a God would come when we mere mortals called." The tone of Finn's voice is mocking.

"Finn!" His comment and tone are close to sacrilege. I whisper an apology to Saleal.

"OK, on to the fifth row. The most dangerous and the most interesting. It holds all the books on demons, hell, and how to summon the creatures of the pit. And it's where I have been concentrating my research."

"What does the last row contain?" I ask. I want to move away from the demon row. I can *feel* the darkness coming from it, and I swear I smell ... burning? Sulphur? Off meat? The odour wafts and wanes, faint enough that I doubt myself. My imagination is playing games.

"Ah. The most interesting of all. That row holds the artefacts. Books that are possessed, items that are possessed. Gemstones and wands and daggers that hold spirits or special powers. We can look, but we need to be cautious. If we trigger any of the protective wards, the alarms will scream and reveal us meddling where we shouldn't be."

An icy thrill goes through me. "Scream?"

"Yes. Once triggered, the alarms actually scream. A scream that can be heard right throughout the manor."

My stomach twists at the thought.

Finn leads me down the row. On the left side is a stone wall embedded with glyphs that are wrought in iron. He clings to it and holds my arm tight. On the other side of the row, glass cabinets. A shimmer ripples across the panes of each. Protection wards. The shimmer swells and recedes in rippling waves, and I can understand why Finn clings to the opposite wall.

I stare at the first glass case. Within, a transparent, gleaming orange gem that appears to hold a rainbow at its centre. It sits on a thick pad of green moss. Above and around the gem, filigree moons crafted in silver hover in continuous orbit.

"The orbiting moons keep the gem in place. I'm not sure what this gem is or what it does," Finn says.

My stomach somersaults. To think the heinous gem is held in place by magical moons feels tenuous. What will happen if the magic fades and the moons fall? I swallow and sidle along the wall to the next case, ignoring the rancid wafts of black magic that are definitely not my imagination.

In this one, a black velvet pouch holds ... something, the shape of which I can't identify.

"That's the Mirror of Shalott," Finn all but whispers. "It's kept covered as it holds the spirit of an ancient black witch, Tenni

Shalott. She tried to open the gates of Hell and release the Demon King Ravana. Apparently, she wanted to make him her husband. She brought hundreds of demons to Conpeita before she was finally stopped by the dimensional gods. It was the last time the dimensional gods appeared in our world. It is said, that if anyone looks into the mirror, they will become possessed by Shalott, and she will once more wreak havoc on the world."

I give Finn a nudge to indicate we move on. I swear I can hear Tenni Shalott calling to me.

The next case holds the muscular arm of a monstrous creature. The arm is thrust skyward, emerging from a gnarled piece of volcanic rock. The arm ends in a hand that has not fingers, but claws. Long, vicious-looking talons. Held tightly in the clawed hand, a yellowing scroll.

"It's the Claw of Whiron. Myth says it holds a document providing instructions on how to call to a Simgra."

"You mean ... do you mean Simgra the capital city, or ..." I snorted in a very unladylike manner "... a unicorn?"

Finn waggles his eyebrows. "Unicorn." Even he seems to regard it as a joke. "But it is myth only. Whatever the document may be—incantation, potion instructions, map—it is held by the claw of the demon Whiron. Touching it will cause demonic possession. And so, it is contained."

The next case holds a book bound with human skin made by a bedlam witch, Azami.

"Many say the cover of the book is made with the skin of Azami's mother," Finn says in the exaggerated voice of a moaning ghost.

I shudder and rub at the goosebumps that rise on my arms. Suddenly, the evilness of this place is too much. It riots in my veins, stirring feelings of fear and aggression and hate.

"I've had enough. Let's go."

Finn's mouth quirks, and he nudges me gently towards the door. "You did well. Most people don't make it past the first two cases before they want to turn back."

Keeping my back to the opposite wall, I sidestep my way towards the end of the row, keen to get back to the relative safety of the library common room. "Have you made it to the end of the row?" I ask Finn.

Finn sighs. "No. I can't get past the Vampiric Heart."

I nearly stumble. "A vampire heart? Saleal save us."

"Yes. It's extremely seductive ... and incredibly spine-chilling. Just being near it, you hunger for sex and blood and at the same time, feel dead inside."

We reach the end of the row, and I rush from the gated section. Back in the library proper I draw a deep breath, then grab Finn's arm, squeezing him tight.

"Promise me you will never go down that row again!"

Finn's eyes and curved mouth send me a calm-down message, but I shake his arm. "Promise me, Finn. The evil, it's contagious. No one was meant to spend time in there. Look at the books in the other rows but stay away from those horrid cases."

Something about my desperate plea must reach him. He clasps my hand which still rests on his arm. "OK, Kee. I promise." He glances at the books and papers spread over the desk. "It will be time for breakfast in an hour. Go, and I will investigate who might have signed into the Heinous Section here. After that, I'll go to the Lapana University library and ask to see their sign-in records. If I don't make it to breakfast, tell Father and Uncle Sean where I am. The curfew will end at daybreak, so I might head straight there then."

"Do you think they stopped the summoner? Perhaps even caught him?

Finn rubs at this chin. "I think, whoever is summoning the demon is desperate. And clever. Unfortunately, I doubt if patrols will stop him."

I leave the library with nausea thick in my stomach.

Keen to be rid of the evil that clings to me, I change before I go to breakfast. I can't help the tiny sigh that escapes me when I walk into the sunlit morning room, leaving Alex, who has taken over from Dawie, at the door.

Uncle Sean, Aunt Pippa, and Father are already here, and it is bright and normal and ... safe feeling. Uncle Sean wears a cheerful, brocade vest that matches the burgundy of Aunt Pippa's gown. The gold chain of his old-fashioned monocle swings with movement when he turns to me as I enter.

Father, dressed in sensible grey, is reading a com-box printout. He offers me a small smile. "First reports say there was no demon attack last night. It is early yet, but it appears the summoner didn't show."

Every cell in my body loosens. "Thank Saleal for that," I say and kiss Aunt Pippa's powdered cheek before taking the seat next to her. Uncle Sean wears a broad beam, his eyes sparkling.

"It's good, isn't it? Our guards have done their duty and prevented further deaths. Thank the gods." Uncle Sean lathers his toast with jam and takes a big bite, still grinning like a madman.

Beside my plate is an envelope addressed to me. "What is this?"

Father puts the com-box printout down and pours himself a cup of tea. "It came for you this morning. Perhaps you have an admirer." A teasing smile twitches on his lips.

The news the summoner hadn't appeared has obviously put him in a good mood. This morning, one may have believed he was Uncle Sean's brother. Father's serious nature normally clashes with Sean's happy-go-lucky way. But Sean isn't the Earl. Maybe responsibility smothers lightheartedness.

"Perhaps it is someone from your nighttime jaunts in the city." This time Father did not smile.

There it is. The chance to reprimand me. His good mood has vanished in the blink of an eye.

I ignore his comment. The letter is likely from Sabella. Although she usually messages me via com-box. I pick up the letter opener that sits on a silver dish to one side, slit the envelope, pull the letter out, and read. It isn't from Sabella.

It is from the demon summoner.

I give a cry as I read, my hand flying to my mouth.

"What is it, dear?" Aunt Pippa puts her spoon down with a clatter against her bowl of fruit.

Uncle Sean and Father stand and hover behind my chair.

"It's from the summoner." My voice is tiny. My heart leaps like a frog in my chest, lodging in my throat one moment, then falling to my stomach the next.

Father takes the letter from my fingers and reads. "Alex!" he bellows.

Alex enters the room at pace, the fear and anger in Father's voice demanding urgency. Aunt Pippa's arm comes around my shoulders.

"Find out who delivered this letter," Father orders Alex. "Use as many men as you need to find the swine."

Alex spins and heads for the door, already punching out orders to staff and guards.

Uncle Sean's normally jovial face is tense and lined. "Luca. What does it say?"

Father doesn't answer, and Uncle Sean steps towards him, flapping his monocle back and forth as if desperate to read the letter.

"Answer me, Brother. What does it say?" Sean all but shouts.

"The summoner. He said he'd kill her. If she said anything. He ..." Father breaks off, and I understand why.

I cover my face with my hands. I will never forget the letter. Never forget the words on the page. In a matter of seconds, it has become imprinted on my brain.

> *Listen well, you fucking privileged bitch. Keep your fucking mouth shut and your snooty nose out of it. If you don't, I'll have my demon rip your head off, suck your soul from your headless neck, and take it to hell where it will burn for all eternity.*

Is this because the guards stopped him last night? Did frustration drive him to send the letter? I realise I am shaking, and I take my hands from my face and fold them in my lap. It is like the evil of the Heinous Section has touched me—magnetised me—and I now draw darkness to me. I wish Finn was here, but he has obviously gone to Lapana University. Which means, he didn't find anything in the borrowing records of our library. Not that I anticipated he would. Visitors are permitted in the Earl's Library by prearrangement only. Other than that, only members of the manor's household can access the library.

Uncle Sean and Father are now locked in a whispered conversation, and I become aware that Aunt Pippa still has her arm draped around my shoulders. I turn to my aunt, whose face is pinched with concern.

"I'm alright, Aunt." I gently slide out from under Pippa's arm and stand, ignoring my rubbery legs.

"We need to report this to the guards," I say, looking at Father and Uncle Sean. Deep in their conversation, they ignore me.

Suddenly, I snap. "I am talking!" I shout. "Stop ignoring me. Stop treating me like a possession to be set aside whenever it is not being used."

Silence descends over the room. Then Uncle Sean puts on his tender voice. "Keeva, dear—"

"No! No, *Keeva dear.* No, *poor Keeva.*" I push my chair under the breakfast table, slamming it against the polished wood. "I'm going to send a com to Sabella. This vile letter is nothing more than a clue to be used to find this low life."

A ball of tears rolls into the back of my throat, and I flee the room.

31
Sabella

Dawn's soft glow lights our way as we fly back to the GH stables. Pink hues light the terracotta-tiled roofs of Lapana making them blush like a summer peach. Below, citizens emerge from their homes, and businesses bustle, preparing to throw open their doors. To the west, the docks of Carlver River are coming to life, and the train depot wiggles with movement. The long, tense night is over.

Exhaustion tugs at every part of me. Rill droops too, her face pallid in the thin light of daybreak. But there were no souls harvested. No sign of the summoner or the demon. Beneath the tiredness, pride sits quietly in my chest. Unless a report arrives from a Hismish village, it seems we'd stopped him. We'd prevented further souls being sent to hell.

That, or Finn was wrong about the six souls over three nights. But I don't think he is wrong. His intelligence is one of the things I love about him. Once I've managed a few hours of sleep—bed called to me with intense urgency—I'll send him a message. A rendezvous at our secret place is overdue.

Diarissa lands by the stable, and Rill slips off. Upon hitting the ground, she staggers slightly as if her legs struggle to hold her upright. I dismount and offer an empathetic nod.

"You've certainly had a busy first twenty-four hours as a guard. It's not always like this. And we get to sleep now. In fact, you go in, and I'll tend to Diarissa."

The night had been crazy. The busiest shift I'd ever encountered, even busier than the annual Ryker Festival. Reports of sightings had continued through the night. Once we'd inspected the scene of the dead gang member and made our reports, we were relieved by the arrival of several additional guards and ordered back into the sky. Diarissa had flown us back and forth over Lapana, landing and assessing every reported threat. All of them had been from people spooked by shadows.

Rill leans on Diarissa's flank. "I'll help with Diarissa. She carried us all night. Caring for her now is right." She walks on wobbly legs into the stable.

I catch myself smiling, and a startling realisation hits me. Not only does it seem Rill has it in her to become a good guard, but—and I wonder if my tired mind is making me emotional—I am actually starting to like her.

I lead Diarissa into the stables where Rill and I work side by side, giving the Pegasus a rub down and gently combing out the feathers on her enormous angel-like wings, ensuring they are grit-

and soot-free. We fix her a good breakfast and leave her happily munching on wheat and oats, drizzled with molasses.

The relief that there were no demon attacks seems to pile on top of the lack of sleep, and I feel boneless. Walking from the stable, I turn to Rill.

"Breakfast? Or straight to bed?"

As if in answer, Rill's stomach gives a loud rumble. I nearly stagger when Rill gives me a small, embarrassed smile. A smile!

"Food. Then sleep," she says.

I hold back a sigh. Bed can wait a *little* longer.

There are two guards behind the reception desk. A prime and her fledge. Both look tired and, with slow movements, are placing com-boxes back on the shelf. They'd acted as the communication hub, relaying reports from citizens to the guards. Our share of the coms last night had been numerous. I can't begin to imagine how many these guards must have dealt with overall.

"Morning, Sabella," the prime says. "You are the first to return. Calista arrived about two hours ago. Said she'd be rustling up a hot breakfast for everyone. She'll be in the mess hall by now, I imagine."

"Thanks, Jasmine."

We file past the desk and into the inner GH house. The most magnificent aroma of fresh bread, eggs, and sausages drifts down the mess hall walkway, and my mouth waters. Rill is right. Food is a good choice. I lead Rill down the covered walkway into the mess hall where Cook Calista and a couple of kitchen hands are frantically laying tables and placing jugs along their length.

Calista looks up when we enter. "Good morning, Constable. We will be ready momentarily." She snaps her fingers at one of the kitchen hands and points at the serviettes. "I spoke to Captain

Wallace when I arrived a couple of hours ago. He is in the briefing room. Could you let him know breakfast is nearly ready?"

My feet bark, and my eyelids droop, but I nod and turn back down the walkway and into the corridor that leads to the briefing room with Rill still trailing behind.

"The captain doesn't go into the field?" she asks.

"Not usually, although I have known him to suddenly arrive at the scene of a crime to assess the guard's performance. Everyone dreads it. The captain is fair, but strict, and being watched by him is nerve-wracking. Last night, however, he would have acted as central control. Ready to move guards around as required." I push open the door to the briefing room.

And freeze at the blood bath that greets me.

Upon the floor, lies Captain Wallace, his arms and legs spread out like he is making a snow angel. Beside him, his analyst fledge, Eli Palmer. The young man Rill had shagged in the storeroom. Both lie in lakes of blood, and Eli appears to be reaching for the captain, his fingers stretched in his direction. Their throats are torn open, and the clothes and skin of their bodies lie in tatters. The reek of sulphur hangs in the air, burning my nostrils and making my eyes water.

Nausea rises to my throat, horror and devastation chasing it. I try to block Rill from entering the room, but I am too late. Stepping up beside me, I feel her go rigid, hear her breath catch. Tension wires me to her, a connection that grows tighter and tighter until I am sure something is going to snap.

Then she breathes one word. "Eli."

I only just catch her as she collapses to the floor in a dead faint. Sinking to the ground with Rill in my arms, I sit cradling my unconscious fledge, staring at the body of my Captain and his young analyst. We hadn't stopped the summoner at all. Instead, we'd forced him here. Ironically, the GH was the least guarded location in Lapana. Tears of frustration and devastating loss prick at my eyes. The last twenty-four hours have been hellish. Forced to take Rill as my fledge. Rescuing Keeva from the hut in Wolf Woods. Chasing down a gods-damn demon summoner.

Everything that has happened to me and Rill and Keeva is because of the demon. All because evil is called to evil. Anger burns in my belly, deep and glowing. It rises, burning through the horror, replacing it with white-hot rage. Snapping out of frozen disbelief, I tip my head back and shout. I shout for help and shout against the abomination of a soul-sucking demon taking the lives of good people.

I hear the sound of running feet. I hear someone shouting ... or is it still me? I feel hands, pushing me and Rill—who still lies across my lap—out of the way. I hear moaning and swearing and then ... weeping. In my lap, Rill stirs, and I plead with her to stay unconscious. To not have to deal with this, because it is too much for such a new fledge. It is too much for me.

Then, I feel fingers ply at my shoulder. The weight of Rill disappears when someone scoops her up in their arms. A voice sounds in my ear.

"Sabella. Get up."

It is Tavell. I tilt my head and take in the man who had been my prime. His face is etched in pain and fury. But his fingers on my shoulder are gentle. His voice is soft. I demand my legs work and somehow manage to stand. Ahead, a guard carries Rill, but she's regained consciousness and is struggling and batting at the guard's arms with her fists.

"Put me down," she cries.

I hurry to her. "I'll take her," I say to the guard and with a nod, he lowers Rill to her feet. I wrap an arm around her.

"I got you," I say, and Rill allows me to direct her towards the staircase.

"Where are we going?" she asks.

"Your room. You need to lie down."

"No. Can't sleep. We ... we need to find the summoner. We ..." Rill's head flops, her mouth seeming to work hard to form words, and her eyes roll.

Tavell gives me a firm nudge and jerks his head towards the next floor up. Keeping a solid grip on Rill, I mount the stairs with Tavell close behind in case Rill's legs give out.

"To her room," Tavell says when we reach the third-floor landing, and I blindly obey. The redness of the blood in the briefing room seems to colour everything I look at. The walls, the doors, the air. But I push on and reach Rill's room. There I lower her onto the bed where she sits, fists tight, her face set in a mask of shock.

"Rill. You need to sleep. If we don't get some rest, we won't be able to find the summoner. Just a few hours, then we do whatever we need to stop him from taking the last two souls tonight. Sometimes, knowing when to step back is just as important as knowing when to act."

Rill lifts her face to me. "You don't understand. Eli ..." Her eyes brim with tears.

I lean close. “I do understand. I saw you. I understand. And I promise you. We will do everything we can to bring the man responsible to justice.”

Rill’s eyes widen, and her tears overflow, rolling down her cheeks. She gives a tiny nod and curls up on the bed like a small child.

Tavell steps forward and lays his hand on Rill’s head. He murmurs a spell, and Rill’s breathing deepens, and her body goes floppy.

“She’ll sleep for a few hours. You too, Sabella.” Tavell’s tone offers no argument.

I draw a blanket over Rill and follow Tavell to my own room.

32
Keeva

I HALF WALK, HALF run when I leave the morning room, trying to hold back the sobs that rip at my throat. Alex trails behind me.

"Lady Keeva," he calls.

I ignore him and keep going until my feet, with a mind of their own, bring me to my room. I go inside and slam the door behind me. Inside, I pace, my chest heaving against the pressure that squeezes at my ribs.

There is a gentle knock at my door.

"Lady Keeva."

I lower myself onto the edge of my wingback chair and rock back and forth, my arms wrapped around my body.

Knock. Knock.

"Keeva." Alex doesn't use my title this time, and it makes me sit up.

"Come in, Alex." I dab at my tear-moistened cheeks.

Alex slowly opens the door and steps into my room, staying by the doorway as protocol dictates.

"Talk to me," Alex says with one of his rare smiles, though it is restrained, soft.

"I have nothing to say." I suck in a breath. "We need to find the summoner. It is all that matters."

Alex takes one step towards me. "Milady. If anyone can find who this evil man is, it will be you and your brother."

I huff. "Finn perhaps. But not me. I am good for nothing other than parties and prettily accepting guests while my brother learns what it is to be the Earl." I shrug. "I am all but useless. I'm surprised the summoner even thought it necessary to threaten me. It is rather like a cat fearing a mouse."

"I don't think you give yourself enough credit. You witnessed—"

"I didn't ..." I feel like such a fraud. "... cope well with that. I ran away. I hid in the guard stables while a killer was on the loose." I wonder what I would have done if it had been me who witnessed Thorn's demonic murder.

Alex doesn't say anything. I know he is only trying to help, but I am in no mood to pander to him. No more than I wish to be pandered to.

"Look at you," I say. "You must follow me, day and night. Never more than a few paces from me. Finn doesn't have a guard. It's clear what my father thinks of me. His precious little Keeva who might bruise if she gives so much as a hard sneeze."

"Your father loves you." Alex holds up a hand when I go to speak. "And you would do well to acknowledge how lucky you are to have a loving family. Many don't. You are supported. You just need to figure out *how* you want to be supported. If you continue to act like a spoiled child, you will be treated as one."

My mouth falls open. Alex has never spoken to me like this before.

"And you should note. Your father has ordered Finn to be guarded too. As soon as he returns to the manor, he will have a guard on him ... day and night. And I can assure you ... he will not moan about it. He may express his distaste, but he will then get on with it. In other words, Keeva, act like you wish to be treated, and sneaking out of the manor to go to dance taverns won't help your cause."

It is like a blow. A slap to my face. Gods. How long has Alex had these thoughts? He's been like a second father to me. Guarding me since I was a baby. I think of Rill, living in that hut in the woods with no family, her sister taken. She doesn't moan and complain when she has every right to. Sabella too. She has no family other than the guards. And yet, she holds herself aloft like she was born into royalty. I suddenly feel the burn of shame.

"You know. I trained as a citizen guard," Alex continues, ignoring my discomfort. "I was good, too. Before I was honoured by the invitation to come to the manor and be a personal guard for you and Finn. I may be able to help. If you want to talk it out."

I rise from my chair. How much can I tell Alex? Certainly not about Rill. Despite what she'd done, despite that she'd tangled with me, I have no desire to see her back in jail. Plus, it will end Sabella's career.

But there are things I can share. "Finn has researched demons," I say. "He's narrowed the likely demons down to a mid-level demon called Garmr." The name is burned into my mind just like the image of it in the book Finn showed me. "Summoning it requires Level Five magic, although it is remotely possible a Level Four could learn the required incantation. Like many mid-level demons, it grants favours, but the price is souls. More specifically, six souls in three nights." I slowly pace the room, gathering my thoughts. "It seems the guards prevented any souls from being harvested last night, but does this mean the favour won't be granted, or does the summoner merely need to start again? If he goes out tonight and takes two souls and does that again for the two nights after that ... If he is a patient man, he could wait a week, then harvest all over again." I press the heel of my hand to my forehead. "Saleal save us, this is not over. We need to find out who summoned the demon."

"Or why," Alex says. "The answer to that question might give you a good idea of who is responsible."

I cease pacing. "Indeed. But the why could be like saying 'How long is a piece of string?' It ... it would be impossible to find out."

"Now, I don't think that is necessarily true. I don't know much about demons except what I've read in history books, but I do believe there are a limited number of favours. You can't just ask a demon for anything. What they offer is ... limited. And different demons, offer different favours. Of course, the history books are ancient. The information may well have become skewed over the millennia."

My mouth drops open. "I don't think Finn got that far in his research. I'll tell him when he returns."

"Where has he gone?" Alex asks.

"Last I spoke to him, he was checking the records in our library to see who might have accessed the Heinous Section. Then he was going to the university's library to do the same. I assume, because he wasn't at breakfast, that is where he's gone."

Alex nods thoughtfully. "Do you think he would have taken his com-box? You could message him with this information. You could also message your guard friend, Sabella. It is good for the guards to have all the information. Even information not confirmed as correct as yet."

A surge goes through me. The summoner threatened me, but I will not let that stop me. And Alex, gods bless him, isn't treating me like I should retreat.

I cross the floor to my bedside table where my com-box sits. "Thank you, Alex. Thanks for everything."

Alex bows. "You are quite welcome, Lady Keeva. Let me know if I can be of any further assistance. I shall be outside your door."

33
Keeva

ALEX LEAVES AND I send a message to Finn, asking when he might return to the manor. Then I sit my com-box down and wait for a reply.

I take the time to wash my face and brush my hair, piling it into a bun. With a dab of my pinkie finger, I apply lip balm, then swipe on mascara and finally smooth the blouse I wear. A deep sense settles over me—it is important that I *appear* to be holding it together. I am going to show the world who I really am. And continue to do so until they see me.

Then, because Finn still hasn't replied, I gather my com-box and go to join Father, Uncle Sean, and Aunt Pippa once more. But when I enter the room, Senior Sergeant Parker is there, and the atmosphere in the room is thick. Charged. The look on Parker's face tells me all I need to know.

"More souls were harvested," I say quietly to no one in particular. I cling to the unravelling determination Alex instilled in me. Sergeant Parker, however, seems to think the comment is directed at him.

"Yes. Guards. The bastard went to the guard house."

My heart freezes. "Sabella?"

Parker shakes his head; his no-nonsense face is haggard. "The captain and his fledge. A young man named Eli Palmer."

Oh, gods, the captain. I scan the room. Aunt Pippa sits with one hand on her breast, and her eyes glisten with unshed tears. Uncle Sean squats beside her chair, his polished head as shiny as Aunt Pippa's tears. His large hand pats her forearm in a consoling gesture. My gaze lands on my father who stands beside Sergeant Parker.

"What can we do?" I ask. "There must be a next step. If Finn is correct, he will seek another two souls tonight. We can't let that happen." My voice is clear and steady, and I hold Father's gaze. "Or, more specifically, what can *I* do?"

"Where is your brother?" For a change, Father's voice is thin and tremors slightly.

"I believe he's at the university library. I sent him a com but have not heard back as yet. Which is quite typical when Finn is deep into one of his research projects."

"That's your job, then. Get him back here. And ... perhaps, if Alex thinks it would be safe, you could visit the captain's family and the family of his fledge. Offer our condolences as my representative." Sorrow paints his tone.

Normally the assignment of such a task would sting, but context is a great leveller. “Certainly Father. I will ensure Finn returns to the manor; then I will visit with the bereaved families.”

Mild surprise crosses Father’s face. No doubt he assumed I would argue.

Aunt Pippa gently shakes herself loose from her husband. “I will come with you to visit the families. It is good to do something.”

I go straight to the manor’s library with Alex trailing behind me like a lovesick puppy. It occurred to me that perhaps Finn is still engrossed in his books and hasn’t left at all. But when I reach the library, only Hanna, the librarian, is there.

“Oh, no milady. I haven’t seen the young lord for the longest time.” Hanna’s voice creaks and hisses even more than I remember. Her eyes are cloudy, and she shuffles rather than walks. She also has a sour smell about her, like she hasn’t showered in some time. I resolve to speak to Father about Hanna as soon as this is over. She should retire now and be cared for. She should rest. Goodness knows she’s earned it.

I flash a look at Alex, who stands nearby frowning.

“You mean you have not seen him since yesterday, Hanna?” I prompt gently.

The comment makes Hanna look up from the stack of books she is sorting with gnarled hands. “Yesterday …” Her expression is vacant, and she floats away, her eyes going to the ceiling like she can see something I cannot. I place a hand on Hanna’s arm.

"Hanna. Lord Finn. He was here yesterday."

"Yesterday. Oh yes. Lord Finn. Yesterday."

Poor Hanna. How in the name of Saleal have we left her here to work when she's become so bad? Suddenly she snaps to attention, and I wince, worried the movement might crack her brittle bones.

"Lady Keeva. How nice to see you! Your brother was here ... yesterday, I believe."

"Hello, Hanna. It is nice to see you too. And thank you. I was looking for Lord Finn. You have been most helpful."

Hanna gives me a pleased smile and goes back to sorting her books, humming a tune.

I climb back up the stairs, along several corridors, then knock on the door of Finn's bedroom.

I need to check, to ensure Finn *has* gone to the university library. I hope instead, I might find him collapsed on his bed, sound asleep. I really want to talk to him. Apart from completing the task given by Father, I want to tell Finn about the threatening letter—the warning that says I should stay out of all things related to the demon summoner.

Now that I'd thought about it with a clearer head, the threat must mean that either I—meaning Rill in my body—had seen something that could identify the summoner, or I must *know* something. Some little thing that gives him away. Rill said the summoner was masked, so surely, he can't be concerned I can identify him. I just need to figure out what Rill saw. Unless it is me who knows something. I sigh. I am no guard and do not know how to untangle my thoughts.

Finn doesn't answer my knock, so I push open his door.

"Finn?"

No answer. The room is in darkness. Definitely at the university library then.

I am about to leave when an unease settles on me. Something is … wrong … wrong with his room. I flick on the light switch by the door and look about carefully. His bed is made, neat as a pin. That is normal, for Father demands nothing less than perfection from the staff. They would have been in earlier to make sure everything was as it should be. The curtains at the tall west-facing window are flung back, and the morning light glows.

Everything is clean and dusted and orderly. My breath catches in my throat. His desk. It is tidy too.

"He's not here," I say to Alex. "I might just leave him a note for when he returns."

Alex gives his usual polite bow, and I enter the room, closing the door quietly behind me. Finn's desk in his study is where he does most of his work, but like he cannot bear to be too far from his research at any given point, he has a desk in his room too. And like his study, this desk is usually piled high with books and strewn with scrolls and notepads. The staff are under strict instructions to never, ever touch his desk. Today, it is tidy. Only a few books sit in a pile. Beside the books, two notebooks. There are no scrolls. No mess.

I cross the floor and stare. I can't shake the feeling there is something amiss. Finn would never have tidied up like this. He certainly would not take the time to do so in the middle of his demon research.

I look around again. The fireplace sits cold, but ash-free, as it usually is during the summer months. Then I fling a hand over my mouth to stop myself from exclaiming out loud. One of the fire pokers is not hanging with the others. It sits, leaning against the hearth, pointing up. It is the code Finn and I used as children when we used to leave messages for each other.

I fly to the fireplace and reach up to the mantle. Gods. The box is the same. I haven't thought about it for years. But Finn has kept it. And kept it in the same place as it has always been. Tenderness warms me. He'd not thrown it away. Despite the fact he is only two years from becoming the Earl of Tarr, he has held onto this precious childhood memory.

With shaking fingers, I twist the base of the box. It is where we have always placed our secret messages to each other. I have a box just like it in my room—though mine is buried somewhere in a storage crate at the back of my dressing room. Peering into the hidden compartment, my heart leaps. There is a note.

I pry it free and open it.

34
Keeva

Kee,

The entries in the library ledger are false. They show Alex Albo accessing the Heinous Section. Except, on the dates and times recorded, I was in the library and can attest Alex was not. In fact, on at least two of those occasions, I was alone in the library. And while there is no denying the entries are in Hanna's handwriting, I still believe there is something illicit going on.

I'm going to ask Uncle Sean to see if he thinks Hanna's memories may have been tampered with. I now worry that someone in the Manor is the summoner. Or,

at least, helping the summoner. I'm going to visit the Guard House and report this, but I leave this note for you, Kee and say ... be careful. Keep this to yourself for now. We don't know who we can trust.
Finn

ALEX?

The fact that he stands outside the door right now sends a chilling vibrato through me. As a manor guard, he has access to the Heinous Section, but he'd have no reason to visit it. But he *had* been keen to find out what I knew. I shake my head. I cannot believe Alex is capable of such a thing. It would also mean he sent the threatening letter to me. *No, no.* He would not write such a thing.

And yet, he is my guard. If anyone has the opportunity to do me harm, it is Alex.

Folding the note, I tuck it into my skirt pocket. I take a moment to rearrange my face into a smooth expression, take a deep breath, and leave to find Uncle Sean, trying not to care that Alex trails behind me.

Uncle Sean isn't with Aunt Pippa who sits in her personal morning room, sewing. She puts it aside as soon as I enter.

"Are you ready to visit the families?"

"Not yet Aunt. I just have something else to do first. I need Uncle Sean."

"I think he's with your father, dear."

"Thanks, Aunt Pippa."

With my skirt gathered in one hand, I all but run to Father's study, knowing he will no longer be in the main morning room and hoping he is still in the manor. Hoping he hasn't left to do business somewhere in Lapana. Particularly if Uncle Sean is with him.

I burst into his austere study to find, not only him and Uncle Sean, but also ... a king's guard. My abrupt halt is joined by a cry I can't hold back. "Oh!"

"Keeva. Not now," Father says in a tense voice.

Uncle Sean gives me a quick, strained smile.

The king's guard turns to me. "Lady Keeva, I presume?"

The man is all harshness. He is like dark alleyways at night and shadows under the bed. He is repellent and frankly, terrifying. I force myself to examine the pips on his shoulder so I can address him properly.

"Yes, Commander. I am she."

"Commander Cadel Lewis of the king's guard." The Commander gives a sharp bow that drips with arrogance. "You witnessed the first demon murder, correct?"

My stomach somersaults. "Yes, Commander."

"And you gave a statement to the local guards?"

"Of course."

"I will examine your statement when I visit their House, but I may have further questions for you, so stay available, Keeva."

I can't stop the swallow that snags halfway up my throat. "Yes, Commander."

"Lady Keeva," Father says, a deadly calm in his voice. "You will refer to her as Lady Keeva."

Commander Cadel drills Father with an expression that would send the most stoic of attack dogs yelping for their kennel, but Father stands his ground. When Commander Cadel finally brings his eyes back to me, the sneer on his face makes me wonder if *he* is the demon who has been rampaging through Lapana. His eyes seem to look right into my soul, catch hold, and pluck it from my body. I strain to keep my posture upright and my face neutral.

"My apologies, *Lady* Keeva."

In all my life, I have never known anyone to make my name sound as much like a vile insult as this Commander just did.

"And you, Lord Luca, would do well to show me a little more respect. Understand that the King is not pleased. He is trying to decide if he should strip you of your title and replace you with someone more worthy. My report, poor or otherwise, will go a long way in assisting his decision."

Father wiggles his shoulders, which I know means he is seething. "If King Ryker sees fit to make my son, Lord Finn, Earl of Tarr before he is of age, then I will, of course, adhere to his wishes." His voice and expression show nothing of his anger, his words are even and calm. He speaks, in short, like a sage politician.

Commander Cadel snarls. "If you think the King would deem to put an underage pup in your place, you are mistaken. It is more likely he would succeed you with your brother, Baron Sean."

Uncle Sean wears a mask of shock. His eyes flit about the room like flies at a picnic, and his fingers pluck at his silky vest. Father, however, maintains his composure. "A fine choice."

Commander Lewis holds my father in his gaze for a moment, like he is trying to decide if Father is sincere, or merely being patronising. "Either way," he finally continues, "King Ryker has decided to remove your Liberty Law Grant for the Ryker festival. Consider it punishment for not apprehending the demon summoner."

Oh, no. The Magic Class Bill. Father and Finn have worked on it for months. The unfairness of it stings. Father, however, merely bows.

"As he wishes."

The Commander's smug smile is filled with cruelty. I wonder if the man is ever truly amused.

"Now. I will take my leave and attend the guard house to review all the reports related to the demon killings," he says, and his tone is a perfect match for his smile.

He looks around the room pointedly.

"And where, pray tell, is your son, Lord Luca?"

35

Rill

I WAKE IN A sweat. Sunlight pours in the window, sending a burn across the bed that heats the covering over me. With a kick, I send the blanket to the floor, but confusion covers me, just as dense and just as suffocating. How did I get to bed? Then it all comes back to me with breathtaking vividness.

The bodies of Captain Declan and Eli. Their throats ripped out so thoroughly, only their spines held their heads on their bodies. Sweet Eli who had given me just what I needed. Smiling Eli who had faced his fears on the street and who thought he was finally safe in the guard house. I remember the room turning black. Vague memories surface of Sabella cradling me, and someone carrying me ... then Sabella again. Tavell was there too. He said ...

I shoot to my feet. Tavell spelled me to sleep. Shame hits. I should be helping find who is summoning the demon. Finding who killed Eli and the captain. I should not be lying in bed like a small child. Gods! It must be close to midday judging by the sun at the window.

Thankfully, I am still dressed in my uniform and not caring how crumpled it is, I fly from my room and run smack into a guard in the hallway who has a towel slung over his shoulder.

"Where is Constable Rivers?" I snap.

"I … believe she is in her room," the guard replies, surprise widening his eyes.

"Her room?" I am puzzled. Why would Sabella be in her room?

"Yes. Sleeping. Constable Nash's orders."

Oh. Maybe I am not the only lazy one. I look up and down the corridor. "Where is her room?"

The guard thumbs over his shoulder. "Room five."

I don't even bother to say thanks.

When I find room five, I thump on the door. "Sabella. You in there?"

A second later, the door is flung open by my prime. She is halfway through doing up the buttons of her shirt, and her curly hair is free, creating a glorious frame around her face. "Come in."

I step into Sabella's room and look around. It is the same as mine. A single bed with a wardrobe, desk, small bookcase, and a bedside table. My room is soulless … bare, just as you would expect when I have just moved in. But Sabella's room is also austere. It is as neat as a pin—her bed wrinkle-free, the items on her desk neatly lined up—but there are no pictures, no plants, no colour.

"Plants," I say.

"Sorry?" Sabella replies and pulls out the desk chair to sit and pull on her boots.

"You need plants in here."

Sabella glances around. "Don't have time to care for plants." She tugs on her laces.

"I'll look after 'em for you." I take a deep breath. "Perhaps when we go shopping for clothes, we can get you a couple of plants."

I cringe inwardly, waiting for Sabella to laugh at me. Or reject me outright. After all, she hadn't exactly *wanted* me as her fledge. In reality, she has every reason to hate me.

Sabella pauses mid-tying, then with deft fingers, finishes her bow and tucks the ends under the crisscross of laces. She stands and thumps her feet as if settling into the boots.

"Sounds good." She points a finger. "I always thought that corner looked bare. A plant would be pleasing there."

Unfamiliar gratitude floods through me. Sabella had held me when I fainted. Though I had drifted in and out of consciousness, I remember lying in her lap. For a guard, Sabella is alright.

Her room has a clock, and I note it is eleven o'clock. "What now?" I ask. "We need to find the fucker that killed ..." I swallow. "Killed the captain and Eli."

Sabella deftly sweeps her hair to the top of her head, creating a high bun, and secures it with a tie. A few coils instantly escape, but she leaves them be. She slings her guard vest on over her uniform. "Couldn't agree more."

"I'll just get my vest," I say and fling open the door. But before I leave, I turn back to Sabella. "Thank you. For ... you know. ... helping me."

"You're my fledge." She gives the softest of smiles.

For the first time, the words don't send ringing alarm through me. Instead, there is a minuscule feeling of ... belonging.

"And Rill. Change your uniform when you get your vest. You can't be on duty looking like you've slept in your clothes."

A more familiar feeling of angst rises, but I take in Sabella's pristine shirt, pants, and hair.

"OK," I say and rush back to my room to start my second day as a fledgling constable with the citizen guards.

Tavell is getting an hour or two of sleep in what Sabella calls 'the cots,' so she takes me into the duty room and shows me our desk. I cannot believe I have a desk. Me! And yet, I plonk down on the seat and pick up the leather folio that is tagged 'Demon Murders.'

I glance at Sabella, and when she doesn't make any movement to stop me, I open the folio and read. It is a briefing on everything to date. It includes the killing I witnessed—though the report says it was witnessed by Lady Keeva. It details Yalda's murder and the killing of the captain and Eli. It is written in cold, factual language and I want to hate it. I want to stand and scream at the room of guards, typing on typewriters and writing reports and reading com-box printouts. I want to yell—where is your compassion?

But the atmosphere of the room is already like that of a funeral. Drawn faces, slumped shoulders, red eyes, straight mouths. I cast about the room and know the death of their own has hit hard. Hell, it has hit me hard enough, and I barely knew Eli and had only set eyes on the captain yesterday for the first time. Weirdly, the matter-of-fact language used in the report makes sense. Reading it that way allows me to *think* instead of *feel* about the killings. Maybe, just maybe, there is a reason for the tidy uniforms and the prim expressions. Maybe there is a reason for their cool exteriors. Perhaps it keeps them from falling apart. I sigh inwardly and lower my head to read again.

Guards have begun investigating the murder of the captain and Eli. There is no doubt it was another demon attack, and it seems the summoner gained access via the kitchen's delivery door.

"Look," I say to Sabella, pointing to the page. "The summoner came in the back, through the kitchen storeroom. Wouldn't that suggest he knew the layout of the guardhouse?"

Sabella pulls up another chair and squishes in close so we can read together. She purses her lips. "Maybe. Maybe not. Most businesses have a delivery entry 'round the back. It wouldn't take much for someone to find the GH rear door. But it should have been locked."

We read a bit more.

"Ah. I see. The door was forced." Sabella jerks her head. "Let's go take a look."

I stand ... and he looms before me. Nolan Fawns, spruced like he has buffed away any imperfections that make him human.

"Fledge Rill." Nolan's glassy monotone voice is like snot running down the back of my throat. With equal apprehension, I fight the urge to swallow and the urge to vomit.

"I hear you and Peak found our Captain and his fledge this morning." He swings soulless eyes Sabella's way. "I also heard Lady Keeva came running to you after she witnessed the demon killing that Faustian man. And you and your new fledge attended the body of the Ikra woman with Tavell." He turns his greasy stare back to me. "Fledges on their first day do not usually attend a murder case." He lifts a hip and perches on the edge of the desk. "I made some enquiries and found out that you, Fledge Rill Narin, are from Ikra." He folds his arms like a genie, fists tucked under his biceps, elbows raised. "Not only that, but up until two days ago, you were in prison."

36
Rill

I FEEL MY PROTECTIVE wall crack. It splinters, and with each pounding beat of my heart, the crack grows. One of my eyes twitches, and I gulp against the sick feeling in my gut.

Fuck this guy.

Nolan has spoken quietly, but some of the guards in the duty room stop working and stare at me.

"Typical chauvinistic Lapanian guard," I mutter.

"Typical biased Hismish criminal," he fires back without bothering to keep his voice low.

I clench my jaw so tight, my teeth nearly splinter. How dare this piece of ...

"But your prejudice doesn't concern me. I am much more interested in the fact that your name is attached to nearly every demon killing. Tell me, where were you when the demon first attacked? Still in prison, or had Peak already taken you as her fledge?" Nolan sucks air through his teeth. "I wonder, just how you got that spectacular bruise on your face. Demon get away from you, did he?"

Sabella is on her feet in an instant and, in the blink of an eye, stands over Nolan, thrusting her face in his and shoving her knee between his legs, trapping him on the desk. He uncrosses his arms and leans back, mild alarm crossing his face which he tries to hide behind a smarmy sneer.

All the guards in the duty room now stop what they are doing, and dozens of eyes bore in our direction.

"You need to shut the fuck up, Nolan," Sabella spits at him. "If I ever hear you denigrating my fledge again, I'll kick you in the balls so hard, you'll look like a chipmunk with nut-stuffed cheeks." Sabella presses her knee into his crotch to make her point. "Do you understand me?"

Nolan nods, but his carefully applied exterior has vanished. For the first time, I think I am seeing his true face. And it isn't pretty. Redness flushes his cheeks, and rage shines in his eyes.

I take great delight in coming to my feet and standing beside Sabella. I fold my arms in a parody of Nolan. "Gee, Constable Rivers. You mentioned you were talented at cracking nuts, but I misinterpreted your meaning. I thought you meant you were good at dealing with the deranged ..." I unfold my arms and let my mouth drop as if I am surprised. "Oh! Maybe I *didn't* misunderstand."

The watching guards snigger.

"What's going on here?" The voice behind us holds barely restrained anger.

I turn to the man who'd spoken. I don't know who he is, but I do note he has three stripes under an embroidered gold crown on his shoulders. Doubtless, he outranks Sabella, so I stand back with my hands behind my back. Clearly, it is the right thing to do, because Sabella releases Nolan and comes to attention.

"Nothing, Sergeant," she says. "A misunderstanding."

"Nolan?" The sergeant is a short, older man with a growing middle, but he sure doesn't look like he cares two figs about such trivial things like how he looks.

Nolan rises from the desk, running his hands down his shirt. He flicks a glance at me, rage simmering deep in his eyes. "Yes, Serg. A misunderstanding."

"I expect better of you, Nolan." The sergeant glares with a look I think would wither even the most seasoned of guards. "Get back to work."

Nolan gives a nod and marches from the duty room, his rigidness firmly back in place.

"We were just going to have lunch, Serg," Sabella says.

The sergeant just jerks his head in the direction of the kitchen, and not needing to be told twice, Sabella immediately makes for the duty room exit. I follow, noting Sabella's stiff shoulders.

As soon as we are in the hallway, Sabella stops. "You were right, Rill. Nolan is ..." Her face is tight, anger still holding her features rigid.

"A dickhead? A ball sack? An ass?" I help her out when it seems Sabella can't find the right words. "Dangerous?"

Sabella's shoulders slump as she lets out a breath. "Yeah. All that. Except I don't think he's dangerous. He's just an arrogant fool. I'm sorry he was such a dick to you, Rill."

Genuine distress plays on Sabella's face, and a curl of surprise tickles me. It is as if she really cares.

"Not your fault. I've dealt with plenty of dickheads in my life. I think I can handle Nolan Fawn."

I don't add that I think Sabella is wrong. Not that Nolan isn't an arrogant fool because he is, but my instincts also scream that he is dangerous. I resolve to be alert around him.

The cook is in the kitchen rolling pastry, flour misting the air and working its way up her arms to her elbows. She pauses when we walk in, and I notice her eyes are swollen and red-rimmed. The churning angst that Nolan fired in me fizzles. Captain Wallace and Eli are much more important than a dickhead who doesn't like me.

"You two will be needing a feed. Sit down," Cook urges like it is any other day. But I recognise the need to keep busy. To get on with it. The villagers of Ikra respond to tragedy the same way. They get on with it.

"I know someone has already looked, but we wanted to take a look at the storeroom's rear door," Sabella says. "But when we come back, some food would be wonderful. Thank you, Calista."

Calista wipes her hands on her flour-covered apron. "Workman is back there, fixing the door. Constable Nash said he'll be warding the GH tonight." She takes a deep breath and stills, hands frozen in mid-wipe. "It would have happened while I was right here, cooking. How he got past me, I'll never know. Perhaps I was in the mess hall." She shudders, then scurries off to gather items from the fridge.

Keeping busy.

I follow Sabella into the narrow hallway that leads to the storeroom, trying to shut out the memory of walking the same path yesterday. I carefully keep my eyes away from the spot where I'd dallied with Eli and follow Sabella towards the back door.

"Why wasn't the Guard House warded last night?" I ask Sabella.

"Keeping out a Level Five summoner would require Level Five wards. Which would also keep everyone out of GH. No one could come and go. It just wasn't ... practical." She holds up a hand as if she knows what I am going to say. "Hindsight is always keen. Tavell is kicking himself he didn't insist to the captain."

"Tavell? Why would Tavell insist?"

"He's a Level Five. He—"

"Fuck. He's a Level Five witch?" Burning hell. No wonder the man emanates power. And it's the sort of power that makes me nervous. "What is a Level Five witch doing being a guard?" Level Five witches can earn very good money using their magical power in so many ways.

Sabella gives me a familiar look of mild frustration. "He was trained from childhood to become the head witch in his hometown of Padoosa. But decided he wanted to be a guard instead." She pauses like she is waiting for me to ask more questions. "For reasons that are his business."

Fair enough.

"Anyway, he could have warded the GH. He wishes he had. He told me so right before he spelled me asleep."

We reach the back door to find a man in overalls, sweating in the summer heat, working with a hammer and nails … and a wand. I start. I know magic is allowed in Lapana, but the openness with which it is displayed still takes me by surprise.

The carpenter directs the wand to the damaged timber, and it peels away from the door frame. With a flick, it flies outside, landing in the dusty laneway with a dull clatter. A mild lemon and thyme scent accompanies the magic.

"Constables." He greets us with a dip of his head.

I have to stop myself from looking behind me for the source of the plural constables.

"I apologise if you've already been asked," Sabella says. "But in your opinion, was the door forced by brute force or—"

"Ah, no Constable. It was magicked open, right enough. No doubt about it." He beckons Sabella over, and I trail behind. "See here." He points to the metal lock which looks like melted ice cream. Re-hardened drips run down the frame of the door. "Melted. See?" He points to the timber upright he'd just sent into the alleyway. "The timber's blackened too. Whoever it was, sent magic at this door and not just any magic. Level Four at least."

Sabella nods. "Thank you." She turns and walks back, muttering under her breath. "He was a good man, the captain. Thirty years with the guards."

I know Sabella is talking to herself, but I quicken my pace and catch up with her. We reach the door to the kitchen corridor, and I dare a look at *the* spot.

"Do I remember right?" I ask quietly. "You said you knew? You … saw us?"

Sabella comes to a halt. “I was looking for you.” She drops her head. “When I found you … I … let you be. Goodness knows I’m not one to judge.”

“I was lonely,” I say softly.

“I know.”

Sabella opens the door, and I take one look back … and something shiny on the floor snags my eye. It is under a tall rack loaded with sacks of flour. I cross the floor and get down on my hands and knees. The light catches the item, whatever it is, and I reach in and draw it out. It is a heavy gold button. A button with the Earl’s crest on it.

37

Rill

"Oh."

Sabella is beside me in a second. "What is it?"

I hand it over silently, watching Sabella's face. As I suspected, her eyes pop wide. She grabs my arm and hauls me from the storeroom and into the short corridor that leads back to the kitchen.

"It's the Earl's crest," Sabella whispers.

I nod mutely.

"Shit. I'll have to show Tavell, but until then, keep it to yourself, OK?"

Rill nods again. "It doesn't mean it's the Earl's button, does it?"

Sabella gnaws at her lip. "Afraid it does. He is the only one permitted to wear his crest. Not even his son, who will become Earl on his twenty-fifth birthday, can wear it until then."

A sudden memory comes to me—something I'd not thought to share before now—and I gasp. "The summoner. I got a better look at him in Ikra when he came out of the apparition hut. His clothes, there weren't fancy, but they were ... rich. Shit. I forgot. Forgot to mention it."

In the yellow light of the hallway, concern creases Sabella's face. "Fuck." She slips the button into her pocket.

"Let's eat, then wake Tavell." Sabella looks like she is carrying the weight of all the mountains of the Haunted Peaks.

Cook Calista has whipped up a full, cooked lunch, and Sabella and I make short work of the pie and vegetables. Calista even has the presence of mind to serve me a meat-free pie.

"Thank you. Calista, isn't it?" I ask.

"Aye, that's me."

"Well, thanks. For remembering and not giving me meat." I study the round-faced woman. "Where are you from?"

"Me? Oh, born and raised, right here in the city."

My chewing slows. Calista's kindness convinced me she was from a Hismish village. That plus the fact she is a cook—a typical Hismish occupation. To find she is from Lapana sends confusion coursing through me. I'd never imagined native Lapanians to be decent folk or to become cooks voluntarily.

"And you're quite welcome, Constable."

"Rill. My name is Rill."

"You're quite welcome, Fledge Rill."

A flicker of pride licks at my stomach at the title, but I swallow it down. Sabella said she'd help me find Cassia, so maybe, just maybe, staying with the guards for a short time is the best idea. But I don't have to *like* it.

We finish our meal, and I place a hand on my full belly. It's a sensation I haven't felt in ... forever. Funnily enough, I almost find the feeling to be unpleasant, and I clap a hand over my mouth when a gurgling burp rises in my chest.

Suddenly, commanding voices and booted footfalls ring out from the front reception room. I follow Sabella to the kitchen door and peer out.

The raised voices of an argument float down the hall to the kitchen. In seconds, the shouts are joined by the excited murmurings of other guards in the house. One guard shoots down the hall at pace, and Sabella sticks her hand out to halt him.

"What's going on?"

The guard comes to a skidding stop, his face wide-eyed and tense. "The king's guard are here. They're taking over the GH."

"What?" Sabella immediately strides down the hallway, and I scurry to keep up with her.

Just as we approach the door that leads to the front desk area, it opens, and a man steps through. He wears the King's colours of black and gold, and I involuntarily shrink back against the wall. I have never, in my life, encountered such an intimidating man. Steel dark-grey eyes sit beneath sharply arched brows. His beard and moustache are groomed into a square shape, the sharp lines matching his angular cheeks. Dark brown hair hangs straight to his chin and does nothing to soften the cruel twist of his lips.

Even Sabella presses against the wall when the man sweeps passed us. Behind him, four more royal guards step together in an angry beat. Following them, the sergeant that intervened in the duty room earlier, his face red with rage. And finally, bringing up the rear, Tavell.

I thought Tavell was a man of perpetual stern expressions, but what I've seen so far is nothing compared to now. His brow is creased, his mouth pressed so tight his lips are blanched, and his eyes flash. The strong magic within him creates an unhappy vibration that ripples out in waves.

Sabella takes half a step. "Tavell—"

"Not now," he snaps and leaves me and Sabella wearing the same expression of confusion as all the other guards who line the corridor and fill the doorways.

Sabella, however, grabs my arm. "Come on," she says and heads down the hall after Tavell. We round a corner just in time to see the door to the captain's office being closed in Tavell's face. He stands, hands fisted and chest heaving. Then he leans against the wall beside the door and listens.

Sabella creeps closer, and I tiptoe after her. From inside the office, a voice that scrapes down my spine. I am sure its source is the intimidating, dark-haired man.

"The King is displeased you have not found and stopped the summoner. Demon killings are an embarrassment to his reign. As your captain was killed—interestingly by his own incompetence—I will take charge of the Tarr Guards until a replacement can be found."

I flick a gaze between Sabella and Tavell. Both wear bitter rage and indignation on their faces.

"Get me the rosters for the guards, and I shall decide how best to deploy them. I want all guards in the briefing room within fifteen minutes. That includes recalling any who are on duty."

"That will take time ..." the Sergeant replies, repressed anger lacing his words.

"Fifteen minutes." The tone of the King's guard is beyond an order. His words are denigrating and filled with disgust as if he has just been served dog shit on a plate.

Silence for a minute.

"We will catch him tonight, sir. I guarantee—"

"*We* will catch him, Sergeant. We already have one suspect in custody and plan to have two more before the sun goes down."

I start, as do Sabella and Tavell. They have arrested someone? Perhaps caught the summoner? All three of us lean a little closer towards the door.

"You ... you have made an arrest?"

"Yes, of course. It did not take much to discover the likely fiend. It is Alex Albo, personal guard to the Earl's children. He is being held in the prison now, but we will be taking him to Simgra to stand trial and receive his sentence. King Ryker has lost faith that you will achieve the desired results here in Lapana."

At the news of Alex Albo's arrest, Tavell spins on his heel and marches away.

At the same time, Sabella's guard vest dings.

"Shit," Sabella murmurs under her breath and puts her hand on her vest pocket, as if to quieten it and hurries away down the hall, ducking into the nearest unoccupied room—which happens to be a broom closet. I squeeze in after her, my heart thumping. I don't understand what is happening, but I am sure it isn't good.

"Who is this Alex person they have arrested?" I ask quietly as Sabella pulls her com-box from her vest.

"Personal guard to Keeva and her brother Finn. I seriously doubt he is the summoner, but ... he would have access to the Earl's clothing ... I don't know what to think." She presses the button on the side of the com-box. "Unless I'm mistaken, that king's guard who says he now commands the Tarr guards, is Commander Cadel Lewis. He's got quite the reputation for being a nasty piece of work." She presses another button on her com-box and goes quiet to listen.

"Sabella. It's bad." It is Lady Keeva's voice, and she is whispering. "They've arrested Alex, and I need to find Finn. I need your help. Meet me in the stables. I'm here now, waiting. Don't tell anyone."

I meet Sabella's eyes, her worry reflecting back at me.

"Right," she says. "We'll go out by the storeroom door."

38

Sabella

Rill and I head back through the kitchen to the rear storeroom door. The carpenter is still there, though he is nearly finished. I pause as we leave, thinking of Commander Lewis's order that all guards assemble in the briefing room in fifteen minutes. I have a strong feeling we won't be there, and a roll call will expose our absence.

"The king's guard have arrived in Lapana and taken control of the Tarr guards," I say to the carpenter. "While I can't insist, we would appreciate it if you didn't tell anyone you saw us."

The carpenter's eyes narrow. "King's guard, you say." His nose wrinkles like there is a foul smell about. "You don't have to worry about me. I know how to keep my lip buttoned."

"Thank you."

I hurry with Rill into the glaring afternoon sun, and around the corner to the stable that stands beside the guardhouse.

"Keeva," I hiss when we enter the building. Thankfully, there are no grooms about, although that will change in a few hours when they come to feed the horses and Diarissa.

"Here," Keeva whispers back. She stands beside Diarissa's extra-large stall.

When we get closer, I become alarmed, for her face is wild with worry. She chews on a lip, and her eyes dart about restlessly. Despite the relative coolness of the stables, beads of perspiration dot her forehead and nose.

"Finn is missing," she says, wringing her hands in agitation.

My heart turns inside out and be damned if my knees don't turn to jelly. I lock them tight and take a breath through my nose, forcing my teeth to unclench. "What do you mean, missing?"

"No one has seen him since the early hours of this morning. I ... I believe I was the last person to see him. It was around three in the morning. I reported him missing to the king's guard—did you know they are here? In Lapana? Anyway, rather than sharing my concern, they say that being missing makes him a suspect. That he might be the summoner and has fled. But it makes no sense because they also suggested my father is a suspect." Keeva starts pacing. "Apparently, a report details a witness who saw my father entering the guard house last evening. Yet they have arrested Alex." Keeva stops pacing and snaps her eyes to me. "Did you see Finn this morning?"

Diarissa's head comes over the stall and nudges me as if she senses the twist of anxiety in my stomach. From sheer habit, I place an absent-minded hand on her face.

"Did I see … why would I have seen Finn this morning?" I hold my breath, alarm making my heart pound. Does Keeva know about me and Finn?

She paces again, her usual calm poise has vanished, replaced with clenched fists, fixed shoulders, and rolling chest.

"He said he was coming to see you. To report what he'd learned. But he also said he was going to see Uncle Sean, and Uncle Sean said he never did. See him. No one has. I really hoped you might have. Oh, Sabella. What are we going to do?"

I pull my com-box from my vest. "We send Finn a com. He will let us know where he is."

"Don't you think I tried that," Keeva nearly shouts.

Rill and I both hush her at the same time.

Tears shine in Keeva's eyes, but she gulps a few breaths. "I tried that," she says again, quietly. "Of course, I did. He hasn't replied. I'm so worried, particularly after the death threat I got this morning."

"Death threat?" I grip Keeva by her shoulders. "What death threat? Keeva. You need to tell me everything from start to finish."

But Keeva is hyperventilating. I contemplate slapping her in desperation when Rill steps forward.

"Look at me." Her voice is calm and somehow, hypnotic. Keeva raises her eyes to Rill. "Do I have your permission to lay my hand on you, Lady Keeva?"

Keeva gives a mute nod, and Rill presses her palm to Keeva's forehead.

"Imagine trees swaying in a summer's breeze. Swishing. Back and forth. Back and forth. Think of grass on the meadow rippling with the wind. Folding and flattening and rising."

The twitching in Keeva's body calms, and her breathing slows.

"Picture a spring brook, running over rocks, making music as it goes. Winding this way and that. Around stones and reeds and logs."

The rise and fall of Keeva's chest are steady and even.

"Finally, think of Diarissa here. Of when she spreads her wings and flies. See the majestic downward sweep of her wings, pushing against the air so that she rises. So that she soars."

In her stall, Diarissa unfurls her wings and, with one mighty downward flap, sends a rush of air over me, Rill, and Keeva. The straw on the floor of the stables rises and swirls in tiny eddies. It is like it breaks the trance Rill has woven, because Keeva blinks, pulls her shoulders back, and straightens her spine.

"That ... was amazing. Thank you, Rill."

Rill inclines her head in a tiny nod, and I stare, vaguely aware my pulse still thumps in my neck.

Rill jerks a shoulder. "Don't know if it's because of my tangling ability or my earth magic, but I can often calm people."

Pretty handy ability for a guard.

I pull my attention back to the now calmer Keeva. "Please tell me ... tell us, everything. From start to finish." I drag Diarissa's mounting block over and invite Keeva to sit.

"Finn identified the demon." Keeva lowers herself onto the block beside me, folding her hands like the lady she is. Rill perches on a bale of hay opposite, elbows on knees, hands under her chin.

And, as if she wants to hear it all, Diarissa hangs her head over the stall door, looking for all the world like she is part of the meeting.

"It's a mid-level demon called, Garmr. It requires Level Five magic to summon. Finn was going to look at the records in the

Earl's Library to see who had accessed the Heinous Section recently, see if any Level Five witches were on the list. Then he was going to check the only other library in Lapana with a Heinous Section. A … a university library he said. He said he might not be at breakfast because he'd go straight to the university when it opened, so I didn't worry when he wasn't. Oh, Sabella, I should have known; I should have realised."

"How could you know?" Fear smoulders in my belly, but none of this is Keeva's fault.

"Anyway, I sent him a comm, and I went to his room to make sure he wasn't there. That was when I found his note." Keeva pulls a piece of paper from her pocket and gives it to me.

I read it, and my fear bursts into flames, searing and painful.

39

Sabella

"SOMEONE IN THE MANOR? Gods, Keeva. Any idea who?" I think of the Earl's gold button burning a hole in my pocket.

Keeva shakes her head, looking sad. "Then there was the threat."

I listen as Keeva tells me and Rill about the threatening letter that accompanied her breakfast. Now anger mixes with fear, and I want to pace. I want to leap up and take action, but I have no clue what to do next. Running aimlessly around the city looking for Finn and the summoner will be useless. And stupid. Plus, Commander Lewis wants us assembled in the briefing room.

Keeva continues her story, telling of the arrival of the king's guard. Then, when her worry for Finn grew, how she finally reported him missing to Commander Lewis and informed him of Finn's suspicions. The commander, living up to his reputation, looked down his nose at Keeva and ordered his men to investigate the library records. Unlike Finn, he took them at face value and had Alex arrested. But most important of all—no one has seen Finn since Keeva was with him in the library in the small hours of the night.

Rather than being concerned about Finn's disappearance, the king's guard seem to think his absence is a sign of guilt, and he has become a suspect. He had tried to steer attention from Alex, after all, which Commander Lewis views as a strong indication that Finn is working with Alex. But with Alex arrested, and in the ensuing confusion, Keeva was no longer closely guarded, and she sneaked out of the manor and came to the GH.

"I was concerned enough when Uncle Sean said Finn never came to see him, but now I know he didn't see you either. He's in trouble, Sabella. I just know it." She heaves a heavy sigh. "Nothing is right. This horrid Cadel Lewis has arrested Alex, and I'm certain he would not do something like this. But Cadel also suspects Finn or Father. He says he will continue to investigate until he is sure he has the right person—"

Marching footsteps sound outside the stable. I leap to my feet, grabbing Keeva's arm at the same time. I open Diarissa's stall door and, none too gently, push Keeva inside. I put a finger to my lips as I pull the stall door shut on Keeva's surprised face.

As sharp and swift as ever, Rill jumps from her bale of hay and picks up a shovel and bucket. The door to the stable opens just as I grab a brush and apply it to Diarissa's face. Commander Cadel Lewis walks in with two king's guard ... and Nolan Fawn.

Blasted man.

Concentrating on Cadel, I come to attention as I've been trained to do. The king's guard outrank me. They outrank everyone.

Commander Lewis peers at me, his grey eyes narrowing. "Constable. What are you doing in here?"

"Sir?" I say, arranging my face in one of confused innocence. "I … I am attending to my Pegasus." I incline my head to Rill. "Teaching my new fledge how to care for her."

The commander eyes Diarissa who stands at full height and snorts like a bull about to charge. She stamps her feet with vigour, and I hope Keeva is alright crouched in the stall with her. I am sure Diarissa won't hurt her intentionally, but a stray hoof could do some damage.

Commander Lewis's gaze leaves Diarissa and falls squarely on me, heavy and loaded with malice. "This Pegasus is yours, Constable? That is … unusual."

The condescension in his voice riles me, but I hide it behind my guard exterior.

"Yes, sir." I am not remotely inclined to explain how I came to own Diarissa. Then, because I can't resist. "Would you like to pat her, sir?"

As if understanding, Diarissa flares her nostrils and snorts again. She stares at the commander, her eyes wide and wild.

Commander Lewis curls a lip, his eyes glowing with outrage. He knows very well I am challenging him … laughing at him.

"I think not, Constable. I am here to look for the Earl's son, Lord Finn, and his daughter, Lady Keeva. Both are missing and are wanted for questioning over the demon murders." He cocks a head at me like a bird of prey sizing up its next meal. "Have you seen either of them?"

I allow my eyes to widen. "No, sir. The last I saw Lady Keeva was yesterday morning when she reported witnessing the murder of Thorn Newton. Constable Nash accompanied her back to the Manor, I believe."

Commander Lewis takes a step towards me then stops when Diarissa lets out a bone-splintering scream. Clearly, she thinks this Commander is as dangerous as an eye- and teeth-eating ahuizotl. The commander brings his hands to his ears.

"Control your Pegasus, Constable. If you cannot, I will commission the breeders of Fauster to have her removed from you. An uncontrolled Pegasus is dangerous."

For a split second, my stomach tightens at the threat, but I know Tavell will never let that happen. The commander can petition all he likes, but no one from Fauster will agree to have Diarissa removed from me. Still, antagonising the commander probably isn't the smartest move. I need to be cleverer.

I reach out a hand. "Diarissa," I murmur, and immediately she moves back in her stall and lowers her head.

Commander Lewis drills his intense eyes into me. "Constable Fawn tells me that after Keeva witnessed the murder, she ran and came to hide in here. So, I thought it was worth a look to see if she was hiding here once more."

Blast Nolan and his shit.

"I am aware, Commander. It was my fledge and I who found Lady Keeva here when we returned from a ride on Diarissa." I nod towards my Pegasus. "But she wasn't exactly hiding. She was sitting right here ..." I give the mounting block a tap with my foot. "If she is hiding in the stables now, Commander, I have not seen her." I snap my head around to Rill. "Fledge. Have you seen Lady Keeva?"

Rill leans on the shovel, looking like she doesn't have a care in the world. "No," she says, her voice measured and clear. Then she swings her gaze to Cadel. "I have not." This time there is a bite in her voice, and I cringe. I need to set a better example.

Cadel presses his lips tight, and his eyes flash with something dangerous.

"She was sitting in front of the Pegasus stall?" He gives a twisted smile.

"Well, yes. Like I said, we were on a ride, so my Pegasus was not in her stall. I highly doubt, Commander, if she'd have sat there if Diarissa had been in residence."

As if to underline the point, Diarissa gives another angry snort.

The commander snaps his fingers at his men. "Search the stables."

40
Sabella

The two guards with him immediately peer into the stalls of the horses and look behind barrels of grain and bales of hay. Nolan moves as if to assist.

"Not you," Cadel orders with a curled lip, and I am sure I've never heard a more contemptuous tone, not even from the headmistress of No Hope orphanage.

Nolan stands at attention, barely restrained anger wrinkling his normally smooth exterior. Suddenly I know Rill is right ... there is something disturbingly wrong with the man. How had I never seen it before?

The king's guard open the doors of every single cupboard as they search, even those too tiny to fit Keeva. They drive a pitchfork into the pile of dung-filled straw that has been mucked out of the stables.

From the corner of my eye, I catch movement in Diarissa's stall. A flash of Keeva moving to the back corner. Diarissa immediately stands with her rump to that corner, and I once again hope she will not trample Keeva. Careful to appear disinterested, I move to stand beside Rill, watching the guards search like it is a mere inconvenience.

They search all the stalls, caring little that they startle the horses. Diarissa once more lifts her head at their worried whinnies and looks ready to attack the guards. I don't bother to soothe her. Once the guards finish searching all the horses' stalls, they reach Diarissa's who stands with her neck arched and her ears laid back. Fear flickers across their faces.

"Ensure your Pegasus stands back, Constable," Cadel orders. There is a look of amusement on his face. He is enjoying the discomfort of his men. What a slimy worm.

"Stand back," I say, taking the opportunity to look into the stall. If the guards inspect it properly, they will spy Keeva behind Diarissa's rear legs. I can only hope they will not linger.

Indeed, they approach the stall with trepidation, keeping a close eye on Diarissa, knowing her mouthful of teeth can rip muscle from bone. They lean over her stall door and their eyes range into the corners, but not the corner Diarissa stands in. They assume no one in their right mind would hide behind a Pegasus. Suddenly Diarissa flares her wings, and the guards reel back.

Her stall is the last, and the guards turn to their Commander, coming to attention.

"No one is here, sir."

Commander Lewis stares at me, and I have an uneasy feeling he can see right through my deception.

"If you see Lady Keeva or Lord Finn, report to me or one of my guards immediately. And Constable, you are due in the briefing room now. I expect to see you there." His eyes burrow into my skull, and I forcibly stop myself from writhing.

"Yes, sir."

With a spiteful twist of his lip, Commander Cadel and his men march from the stable. At the rear and the last to leave, Nolan looks back at me, and the expression on his face is truly troubling. He gives a vile, knowing smile and exits, leaving the door wide open behind him.

Quick as a flea, Rill darts across the stable to the door. She peers out to make sure they are gone, then pulls the door closed, turning and nodding at me.

"Keeva," I whisper, still frightened we'll be overheard. I lean on the door to Diarissa's stall. "You, OK?"

Diarissa takes a step forward, releasing Keeva from the corner. Her blonde-haired head peeps around Diarissa's butt. "Are they gone?" In the dull light of the stable, her face hovers, white and drawn.

"Yes. You can come out."

Keeva slides past Diarissa. "Thanks, girl." Keeva looks at me with an expression of disbelief. "She hid me."

I run a hand down Diarissa's face. "Yes. She sure didn't like Commander Lewis much." Diarissa tosses her head like she is agreeing, and I close the stall door after Keeva.

"They are looking for Finn *and* me," Keeva says, her bottom lip trembling. "You know, Sabella, don't you? None of us are capable of such a thing. Not Alex or Finn or Father … or me."

Rill turns from her watch by the door, exchanging a look with me, and discomfort falls upon us.

Keeva's hands find her hips. "What?"

I slip a hand into my pocket where the Earl's button lies, finger it, and wonder if I should tell Keeva.

"What is it?" Keeva asks again. "Gods, please tell me. If Finn is in trouble, any bit of information might help." She gives me a long look. "Even information that may be difficult to hear."

With reluctance, I pull the button from my pocket. Keeva is right. Finn needs our help and that trumps Keeva's feelings.

"I assume you heard the summoner attacked the GH last night. We lost two souls." I close my eyes for a second. It still doesn't seem real.

"Yes. I'm sorry," Keeva says softly.

"The summoner broke into the GH via the storeroom door at the back. And when we investigated … well, Rill found this on the floor." I hold the button out to Keeva, watching her face carefully.

Keeva takes the button and rolls it around on her palm. "It's my father's." She lifts her gaze. "Oh gods. You don't think … it can't mean." Her whole body slumps.

"I can't believe it. Why? Why would father summon a demon? What favour could he possibly need?"

"Favour?" Rill asks, leaving the door and joining me and Keeva.

Keeva turns pain-filled eyes to Rill. "It was something … Alex told me. He said demons grant favours but only a select few. Not just anything is within their power. They are not like a …" She flings a hand in the air "... genie. He said if we could find out what favour the demon Garmr grants, it would help us to figure out who the summoner might be."

Keeva shakes her head, like she is trying to dislodge a distasteful thought. "If Father has something to do with this ... and I'm not saying he does, he might have become concerned that Finn was getting close to figuring it out." Then she shakes her head again, this time with strong determination. "No. Father would have more to lose than he had to gain. Unless a demon can help a bill get passed." Pain spreads from her eyes, painting her face and tugging at her mouth.

"A bill passed?" I ask. "What bill?"

Keeva slumps. "It doesn't matter." Her eyes drop to the straw on the floor, and I get the sense there is something she isn't telling us. When she lifts her gaze, it is set with steely determination. "If Finn knows enough that the summoner thought he should get rid of him, we need to find Finn. And fast. Because if it is not Alex, then the summoner is still out there and will take another two souls tonight. We cannot let that happen. Not only because lives will be lost, but because this favour, whatever it is, can't be good."

"I agree," Rill chimes in. "Sounds to me like Lord Finn is the answer. The real question is, where would we even start to look for him."

"Commander Lewis has taken over the guards, inserting himself as captain. With him calling the shots, we might not be permitted to search for Finn. You heard him. We are expected, right this minute, in the briefing room. I'm sure someone will come to fetch us at any moment." I chew the inside of my cheek.

Rill folds her arms across her chest. "If a guard is not free to try to help someone in trouble ... if following the rules is more important, then I ..." She trails off. I know what she is going to say ... she doesn't want to be a guard. The bitter unfairness of her attitude hits me in the chest. I draw myself upright.

"Rill. I didn't follow the rules when I got you out of prison to help Lady Keeva." I speak through my teeth in a quiet hiss. "And I sure as shit, will break the rules again to help Lord Finn. So, if you don't mind, you can pull your head out of your ass."

Rill cocks her head, then grins. A full, actual smile. Not a half smile, not a smirk. A full, beaming smile. It suits her.

"Keeva," I continue. "We must start somewhere. And seeing as Commander Lewis will send someone to collect us at any minute and seeing as we only have a few hours left of daylight, we don't have time to debate the pros and cons of our choices. So, if we assume your father is somehow involved, do you have any idea where he might take Finn to get him out of the way?"

Keeva strokes her chin, then grows animated. "Yes! I followed my father and Finn once. I was sneaking out one evening and saw them. Curiosity got the better of me, and I followed them. They went to a warehouse in the East Section. We could start there?"

I give Diarissa a pat. "We can't take you, girl. We need to be sneaky, and you attract too much attention."

Diarissa tosses her head like she understands.

I grab a long coat that hangs on a peg.

"Put this on," I hold the coat out to Keeva. "You have dressed sensibly, thank the gods, but you still look like money." I open a cupboard and pull out a floppy canvas hat. "This too. It would be best to fit in once we get to the East section, but we also don't want anyone recognising you. If the Commander has ordered the guards to be on the lookout for you …" The situation makes my throat go dry.

Keeva swings the coat around her shoulders and shoves her arms in without complaint. Despite the heat, she buttons it, so her clothes are mostly hidden.

I tug on my guard vest. "I'll go out first and check no one is watching the stable. I'll give a whistle if the way is clear, then you and Rill follow."

We go to the stable door.

"East district is not far." I crack the door and look outside, grimacing against the breath-robbing heat. "Here we go."

41

Rill

SABELLA'S LOW WHISTLE SOUNDS, so I catch hold of Keeva's arm to guide her as we creep from the stables. I am an expert creeper, well used to slipping in and out of places unseen. I never stole, but many thought that taking items from the rubbish was just as bad. Which I find ridiculous. Lapanians discard belongings without a care, but gods forbid they be used by a Hismish.

I step lightly, keeping to the shadows, begrudgingly admitting that the firm-fitting uniform is better than the long skirt I used to wear. Except for the damned guard cudgel. It pokes out enough that I must be constantly aware of it, so it doesn't catch on edges, or scrape the wooden planks of the stable. Beside me, Keeva's footfall thuds a little, but she seems to take her cues from me and follows my every move, content to be led.

The bizarreness of the situation hits me. Two days ago, I was in prison, and now I am leading the daughter of the Earl of Tarr in a clandestine sneak to avoid the king's guard. A giggle almost escapes me, and I realise I am nervous.

We make it to the back of the stable where Sabella waits.

She jerks her head and sets off. I follow, still firmly directing Lady Keeva. A block from the guard house, I release her, and she gives me a smile of thanks. My attempt at a bow turns into an awkward nod. I am not used to being appreciated, least of all by someone like *Lady* Keeva. Having a demon on the loose breaks down barriers, I suppose. And that horrid commander has the same amount of contempt for Keeva as he does for Sabella. I guess there is always someone who thinks they are better than you.

The three of us make good time as Sabella sets a punishing, sweat-fest pace, taking alleyways and side streets to stay as hidden as possible. Every time we pass someone, I tense, but no one seems to pay us much attention. It is like they are all consumed by the very act of coping with the intense, dry heat. It's even hotter than yesterday, if that's possible, and the burn combines with the scents of the city, tinging everything—rubbish, horse dung, food—with a blazing smoky flavour. It is like hell is preparing the landscape for the demon's last harvest. Licking my dry lips does nothing, as my tongue is leathery, like my spit is stolen to be used as fiery sweat.

I finger the guard cudgel—my Jack—on my belt. As annoying as the thing is, I am glad to have it with me. I have the feeling I am going to need it.

"Do you know why your father and brother went to this warehouse," I ask as we walk.

"I don't," Keeva replies. "Even though I watched them in an attempt to find out. It all seemed so clandestine. They went inside for about an hour, and when they came out, they had a young woman with them. Her face was hidden by scarves. Intrigued, I continued to follow them. They took her to a Lapana home, and I remember it well, because a man answered the door, thanked them profusely, and drew the woman inside."

I fall quiet, a sickening apprehension settling in the pit of my stomach.

Lady Keeva's father and brother are involved in slavery.

Burning hell. Thoughts fill my head in a tumbling mess. Sabella has fallen in love with the wrong man. Because I saw her response to the news of Finn's disappearance. The way her eyes widened and her mouth twitched. The way her normally cool exterior crumpled momentarily. She is in love with him, I have no doubt.

But more importantly—did Lord Dalton and Finn take Cassia? The thought burns at me even more than the summer heat. Maybe, just maybe, if we find Lord Finn, I can make him tell me where she is. Keeva's and Sabella's feelings be damned. I will do whatever it takes to force it out of him. I try again to lick my lips—the attempt still dry and useless.

It doesn't take us long to leave the shops and homes of the central district behind. Soon, gigantic warehouses rise around us. Some are new with straight walls and roof tiles of fresh, bright orange, while others are faded with broken windowpanes and dull, mossy roofs. A few workmen mill about, but they too, take no notice of us.

"This way." Keeva points down a side road.

Eventually, we reach a particularly decrepit-looking, red-brick building. I guess it to be abandoned, and I understand why Lady Keeva had waited for her father and brother to reemerge. Definitely clandestine.

The three of us look around. We are alone, so we creep to the massive front entrance, built to allow wagons to enter and be loaded. Cut into the big doors, is a regular, man-sized door, locked with a heavy chain and padlock. Sabella tugs upon it, but it is as useless as my parched licking.

"Let me," Keeva says and steps up to the lock. She places a hand on the rusty metal padlock.

Unchain the bound, release the hold,
Unlock the secrets, in from the cold.
With mystic force and strength untold,
Let this padlock's grasp unfold.

The waft of cinnamon ripples in the hot air, and with a loud clang, the padlock falls open.

Sabella and I stare at Keeva.

She gives a restrained smile. "I excel at unlocking spells. Perhaps from a lifetime of seeking to escape." She slides the chain from the clasp and pushes on the door. It opens with an eye-twitching screech.

Inside, shafts of dust-filled light cast fingers across the vast room. The concrete floor is cracked and lifted in places. High above, pigeons coo and flap and decorate the floor with a splatter of white and grey droppings. To one side of the room, under windows that have been haphazardly boarded up, are three narrow beds. Next to them, a paint-splattered desk and a chair with cracked leather upholstery. In the corner, an ancient printing press that is a mass of dials and wheels and levers. Bottles of ink sit on the floor against the wall behind it.

My stomach shrinks to a pebble as I stare. Sabella and Keeva look about too, taking in the scene with confused expressions. I am not confused. I know exactly what this place is.

Sabella walks to the desk, her footsteps echoing in the cavernous room. She tries to open a desk drawer, but it's locked.

"Keeva."

Lady Keeva lays a hand on the drawer, murmurs a spell and it pops open. We all peer inside.

"Goodness," Keeva says.

Inside the first drawer is a seal. The Earl's seal. It is clean and sits upon a velvet cloth. Beside it, several pens and small ink pots. In the next drawer, a stack of muted yellow paper. Official document paper.

Anger slides under my skin and rises to my cheeks. I take a step back, like the horror here might infect me.

"It's a slavery weigh point." I glare at Keeva. "Your father and brother are involved in slavery. They have been taking my people and selling them." My anger surges, and to my dismay, tears prick my eyes. The thought that Cassia might have been here, having ownership papers prepared, then being delivered to her new master ... Gods.

Sour disgust floods me. Disgust for myself. I had actually started to think I might make a go of being a guard, that I might stay and learn from Sabella. Now I shudder, feeling dirty and ashamed.

Ashamed that I'd even contemplated joining a system so corrupt and so evil. I point at Lady Keeva, and it is like rage flows from my finger, streaming toward Keeva.

"You go out and dance at taverns and visit the prisoners, thinking you are hard done by and making yourself feel better by giving charity. And all the time, right under your nose, your family are taking people—good people and selling them!" My chest heaves. "I was stupid enough to think you might be different, but I see now that you are just as blind to injustice as the rest of the Lapana people. You stay blind; because if you opened your eyes, the truth might be too hard to bear." Spit flies from my mouth, lit by the shafts of sunlight.

Keeva clasps her hands, her bottom lip wobbling, and her eyes brim with tears, but hot rage fills me, and I don't care.

I direct a searing look at Sabella. "And you. You are a red witch, filled with fire and passion that should make you fly as high as Diarissa, yet you smother it every day. You curb and douse and subdue who you are. You're so desperate to belong to something, to anything, that you have sold your soul to the system. The guards and the rules are your crutches, and you lean so desperately, dreading the thought it all might shift out from under you. You think that keeping everything precise will give you control. You think having clean boots and a pristine room will make your life better. You go with Keeva to the prison, not because you think it a good thing to do, but because you are in love with her brother, and you think it will endear you to him."

That hits the mark. Keeva's head snaps to Sabella who won't meet her eyes. Instead, she glares at me, her features set in reddening rage.

"How dare you. You know nothing—"

I spread my arms wide, ignoring Sabella and putting my focus back on Keeva. "It's clear your brother is not here. I'm starting to think that whatever has happened to him, he deserves it. And Sabella ..." I swing my gaze back to her burning red face "... I tell you now. I want no part of the guards."

I undo the clasps of my vest with trembling fingers, tugging and pulling, desperate to get the thing off me. "Eli told me there is another way out, *Constable* Rivers. A way you saw fit not to tell me. *You* can fail me by saying I am unstable." I manage to undo the vest, and tearing it from my body, I fling it to the floor. "So, you'd better do just that because if you don't, I will make your life a living hell." I undo my belt buckle. "I no longer care if you expose me as a Tangler. A death sentence is preferable to working with people I hate and for a system I detest."

A death sentence will mean abandoning Cassia to her fate, but I am so angry right at this second, that I don't care. The stupid fucking belt with the stupid fucking cudgel joins my vest on the ground. I stand with fists clenched, jaw tight, and my pulse roaring in my ears.

Sabella and Keeva say nothing. After all, what *can* they say? I am right, and Sabella and Keeva both damn well know it.

Keeva drops her head, then lowers herself unsteadily onto the edge of the desk.

"My father ... is not who I thought he was. I ... I can't believe ... and Finn too. Oh, gods, it makes sense." Her face turns as white as the pigeon poop that covers the ground. "My family ... are slave traders."

"They most certainly are not."

The male voice comes from the door, and we all jolt and spin to face the man.

42

Rill

Shit. Tavell. How long has he been listening?

Heart-pounding panic fills me. I am about to be arrested and returned to prison. This time to await my execution.

"Tavell. What are you doing here?" Sabella asks. She tries to put on her professional guard demeanour but fails, her body drooping under the truths I had laid bare.

Tavell's yellow-green skin holds a red glow from the heat. "I followed you, of course. I heard the king's guard saying they were looking for Lord Finn and saw you sneak off after Cadel confronted you in the stable. I figured you either knew something or were about to do something stupid. Either way, I followed."

And I thought we'd not been seen. Wiping sweat from my eyes, I glance around the warehouse again, this time looking for another way out as Tavell blocks the door we'd entered by.

Keeva slips off the desk, clasping her hands, and her whole body trembles. "Constable Nash. You said my father and brother are not slave traders." Her voice is thick with pleading.

The pang of sympathy I feel for Keeva irks me. She has just had her life torn down around her ears and is reaching for any hope she can. But I don't trust Tavell. I cannot trust anything he says. He is a guard, through and through. Besides, what would he know about the slave trade?

Tavell strides across the uneven floor of the warehouse on long, slightly bowed legs. His carrot-red hair is set aflame by the sunbeams when he passes under them. "Lord Dalton and Lord Finn are part of a secret, underground network that *helps* the Hismish, not enslave them. They help anyone who wishes to become a Lapanian citizen."

I snort. "Why would anyone from Hismish want to become a Lapanian citizen?" My anger flares, and I grit my teeth because I immediately think of numerous reasons why they might.

Tavell turns his steely-grey eyes to me, and I am once again struck by the man's persona, by his broad shoulders and cutting eyes. By the powerful magic that thrums around him.

"A few reasons," he replies. "But two are most common. One—talented Hismish witches who wish to practice magic ... and two—a Hismish who is in love with a Lapanian." Tavell turns back to Keeva. "Your father and Finn provide new identities and forge Lapanian citizen documents. The Earl uses his seal and signs them. The refugees are provided with the appropriate magic permits, then smuggled out of Lapana to start a new life in a new sanctioned city. It is too risky for them to remain in Lapana."

Tavell steps towards Sabella. "I have been helping the Earl and Lord Finn for the past year." His tone is earnest and regretful. "I'm sorry I have hidden my activities from you—even lied on occasion, but I could not put you at risk by telling you such information."

Tavell levels a stare at me. "Tangler, hey? Fascinating. And it explains much." He rubs his chin and nods thoughtfully.

Shit. He had clearly been listening long enough.

"I am sure there is quite a story to go with it, too, but we don't have time right now. But I will tell you one thing, Rill Narin. Your sister Cassia is now Jasmine Gibson, and she lives in Martou with her husband, Seth Gibson. She came under the second reason ... she fell in love."

I feel the blood drain from my face. It rushes through my body and pools at my feet, and it is like my heart sinks too, bobbing about in a lake of blood by my ankles. The warehouse spins around me in a whirl of horror and ... hope. Relief battles with disbelief and a good dose of rage. I'd worried myself sick for my sister. I'd gotten arrested trying to find her. I'd spent a year in jail. And the whole time Cassia has been living happily with a beau? She'd fallen in love with her employer's son? Burning hell. Jasmine Gibson. She is living happily with her *husband*? My chest tightens, and I am vaguely aware I am gasping for air.

Yet ... Cassia is safe. The release of the weight I'd carried for a year makes me feel unanchored like I might float and join the pigeons above my head. Like I am a delicate, swelling balloon that will burst at any minute. I lean, hands on knees, drawing in oxygen so I don't faint.

"Why didn't she tell me?" My voice is strained ... small. Gods. I had no idea she was even in love.

"She said she tried ... before she and Seth found their way to the network. But ... she said you didn't understand." Tavell puts on his kindly tone. The one I'd heard him use with Keeva and with Thorn's parents.

I squeeze my eyes tight against the spinning warehouse. Cassia never told me ... then I gasp. A conversation looms in my memories—a memory that cuts at me, slicing painfully at my heart—of Cassia, her face bright with hope and shadowed with doubt, asking me if I thought I could ever love a Lapanian. I remember responding with scorn and hostility. I think I'd even demanded to know why she would ask me such a stupid question. Then I'd ranted about how horrid Lapanians are. Cassia had quietly pointed out that our Hismish father had loved our Lapanian mother.

"Mother was an exception. The *only* exception, I am sure." Then I'd stormed off, knocked off kilter by her question.

Fuck. Cassia was right. I did not understand. My legs give out, and I fall to my knees on the gritty warehouse floor.

I'd lost my sister because of my hatred. It had destroyed her trust in me. Gods. A hatred so strong, I'd even contemplated giving up on my sister rather than staying with the guards.

I lift my gaze to Tavell. "I searched for her. I went to the Gibson's home in search of clues of where she might be." Bile rises to my throat, nasty and burning. "That's when I was arrested."

Constable Tavell blinks. "You really weren't thieving?" Something like regret flashes across his expression.

I shake my head and swallow hard. “Did she not care? Not care I was in prison?" Pain expands in my chest, pressing against my ribs. All this time and she never visited. Never wrote me …

Tavell sinks to his haunches before me. "She didn’t know." His voice is as soft as newly unfurled petals. "Once a refugee is accepted into the network, they must cut all ties with family and friends. The risk of someone talking and the authorities finding out is too great. And the network would never pass on such news as a family member being in prison. It would cause nothing but pain when she cannot do anything."

I stare at his grey eyes and see nothing but truth in them.

"Is she … happy? Do you know? Is she well?”

Tavell smiles, and it transforms his face. “Keeva’s mother, Lady Mya is in charge of ensuring those who have been resettled are doing well. We don’t just get them out of Lapana and say, ‘Good luck to you.’ She reports that Cassia is happy. In fact, I believe you are going to be an aunt.”

My fury snuffs out in a wink. I don’t even try to stop the tears that roll down my cheeks. Cassia is safe. Safe and well. Everything that has driven me over the last year, everything that holds me together, leaves me in a whoosh. I am a burst balloon, and bits of me scatter across the rough concrete floor.

“I informed Lady Mya when you joined the Guards,” Tavell continues. “For this news, we made an exception, and she sent a com to Cassia. Cassia was thrilled. Thrilled you had found your place.” Tavell stands and gives a pointed glance at my vest and belt on the ground. “*Have* you found your place?”

43
Rill

TWISTY EMOTION EBBS AND flows as I try to gather myself. I reach for the vinegar that usually fills my core, but it trickles through my fingers and disappears in a mist.

Tavell's question confronts me. My jaw see-saws, but no words come. For several seconds, the only sound is that of cooing pigeons.

Taking advantage of the silence, Keeva throws her shoulders back and aims a raised chin at Tavell. Despite the ridiculous hat she wears and the groom's coat, her stunning beauty shines, and she looks every bit a lady.

"My father, brother, and mother are all part of a secret network to help Hismish find a better life? And you, Constable Nash, assist them in this undertaking?" Her voice is clear and holds a demand for answers.

With a breath, I feel a link to Keeva fall firmly in place. Both of us have family who lied to us. Family who had not seen fit to include us in something undeniably weighty. I understand the emotions that flick across her face. Lord Luca and Lord Finn are not demon summoners, yet they still betrayed Keeva. Her mother, Lady Mya, too, it seems.

Tavell shifts his weight and clears his throat. "This is not how they would have liked you to find out, Lady Keeva." He takes a breath. "Your mother and father have always had a strong dislike for King Ryker and his laws—this you know. His tightening of the Magic Class license system, the segregation it wrought, the suppression of good people—it irked them. But the difference between your family and some others who whisper their disapproval behind closed doors is that your father decided to do something about it. He started his ..." Tavell eyes Keeva, his cheek twitching "... secret network of helping those born on the wrong side of the borders. Hismish, yes, but he also arranges new lives in Lapana for citizens from other regions within the kingdom of Conpieta. The movement is more widespread than you might think."

Tavell's words are for Keeva, but they speak to me, working like an herbal salve. Keeva's father, the Earl of Tarr, *helps* my people and others who are oppressed. It is hard to believe. My entire outlook must shift to fit in this revelation.

"Uncle Sean and Aunt Pippa too?" Keeva asks, sliding the hat from her head and clinging to it in a white-knuckled grip.

"No!" Tavell spits the word in a rare loss of control. But it takes him only a second to collect himself. "No, Lady Keeva, your Uncle Sean knows nothing, and we must keep it that way."

"But Uncle Sean has a kind heart, and Aunt Pippa—"

"Your Uncle Sean is easygoing and well-liked, I know. I think the man could chat with the angriest or saddest of men and have them laughing in no time. But, milady, you must know he likes to drink. You know he likes to spend his evenings in a tavern—any tavern will do. He loves to talk, and once he's had a few drinks .... I'm sorry, but he can't be trusted."

Keeva's proud carriage falters.

"The lives of your father, mother, and brother depend on absolute discretion. And, while your aunt may be the kindest woman I have ever encountered, it would be utterly unfair to involve her and tell her she must keep it from her husband."

I watch Keeva take this in, then give a regal incline of her head.

Tavell smiles briefly. "Your father works to make things better on two fronts. By assisting the oppressed and by the local amendments to the Magic Class bill he is hoping to pass next week during the Ryker Festival."

"Oh," Keeva breathes. "Commander Lewis said King Ryker has taken father's Liberty Law Grant away ... as punishment for not catching the demon summoner quickly."

Thunder crosses Tavell's face, and he rubs a hand over his ginger-shadowed jaw. "That's ... unfortunate and the delay is ... sad, but your father won't let it stop him. He will present the bill next year. The point of all this, Lady Keeva, is that what your father is doing is dangerous. If he were to be found out, he would not only be stripped of his titles but would also be imprisoned. Your brother was only brought into the scheme a year ago. Your father was not only trying to protect you by not involving you, but he also wanted someone who could plead ignorance, even under examination from a diviner. In short, once Finn was aware, he wanted to leave someone who could take his title as Earl. Or Countess, in your case."

Keeva's throat bobs. "My father thought I could become the Countess of Tarr? He ... believed me capable?"

"Yes. He felt you had some growing up to do—don't all fathers think that—but yes, he thought you would fill his shoes perfectly well. If things went awry, he believed you would make a fine Countess."

"Is that why he was at the guard house?" Sabella blurts out, breaking her stunned silence. "To speak to you about ... this scheme?"

"How did you know ... oh, the witness who reported seeing him there?" Tavell asks.

"No," Sabella says. "Not because of the witness. Because of this." Sabella pulls the button from her pocket. "Rill found it in the GH storeroom. It's his, isn't it?"

Tavell examines the button, and his face turns stiff. "Did you show anyone ... tell anyone about this?"

"No. But it's why we are all here. We started to think Lord Luca had something to do with demon summoning. We worried he had taken Finn. Keeva followed them to this place once, so we thought we'd start our search here."

Tavell jolts. "Taken Finn? I figured you were looking for him ... to talk to him .... what do you mean, taken?"

"He's missing, Constable," Keeva says, clasping her hands tight, the hat bunched into a mass of wrinkles. "No one has seen him since the early hours of this morning."

"The Earl was at the GH. To see me. We were planning another transfer of a Hismish man, but we decided to put it off until the summoner was caught. It seems he lost his button while he was there. But, right now, I am more concerned about Lord Finn. Tell me everything."

44

Rill

I FORCE MYSELF UP off the floor, and the three of us tell Tavell everything. When we finish, he wears a grim expression.

"I agree. Someone has taken him. Perhaps because he got too close to the truth. But we can find him." He fills his cheeks with air and expels it in a rush. "The king's guard will be after us, though. We will need to avoid them at all costs as they will not care one fig that we are guards. Or that you are Lady Keeva."

We exchange looks and shuffle feet, the enormity of our situation pressing uncomfortably.

"How will we find him?" Sabella asks. "Time is running out, and with the king's guard after us ..."

Tavell raises a hand to silence her but smiles. "Unless I am mistaken, we have the perfect combination of elemental magic here. But we need to be in this together." He eyeballs me with a questioning stare. "Are we in this together, Rill Narin?"

I rake a hand through my hair, feeling trapped. My emotions swirl like a dust devil sending grit and leaves first in one direction, then another.

"You have a choice," Tavell offers. "If you do not wish to be a citizen guard, we can say you are unstable—that your nerves were frayed from your time in prison."

I know he means it as a ruse, yet indignation fills me. As if I would break that easily.

"It will allow you to return to your old life in Ikra." Tavell rests one hand on his Jack and slips his other thumb into a pocket.

Back to Ikra or to stay with the guards. My cottage calls to me. I can return to my home in Wolf Woods. I can tend my garden, sell my herbs, and be free. I can be safe.

Cassia and I moved to the cottage from the village after citizen guards had come to Ikra to undertake a routine illegal magic check. Poor Ralph, our local potato grower, had been found guilty of using magic simply because his potato plants gave a good yield. Yet, Ralph had no magic. He was just a good farmer. They arrested him and hauled him away. He died in prison a few short weeks later.

It was hearing of his death that pushed me and Cassia to move away from the village. I *did* use earth magic to grow my herbs, and it was only a matter of time before I was caught. Besides, our home in the village that we had shared with our mother and father was filled with the ghosts of our past. Mother had died in that house; father had left us ...

The cottage in the woods was built by our last Head Witch, Genevieve, in the days before King Ryker decided to divide his kingdom into sanctioned and non-sanctioned. When she heard the guards would come for her, she melted away into the woods and was never seen again. Cassia and I turned the abandoned cottage into our home. Safe from prying guard inspections—no guard liked to wander Wolf Woods—we'd fixed and painted and decorated the best we could.

And now I could return.

But I would live there alone. I would live in another home filled with ghosts. I would grow herbs and be alone.

I had rejected my community then—I'd tried to escape—just as my father did. I had clung to my love for my sister and thought nothing else mattered. But my prejudice of the sanctioned had fed my hatred until it had outgrown my love.

The Earl has been helping the Hismish. Everything I believed about the privileged has been turned on its head. Clearly, the sanctioned are not all bad people. I couldn't deny that I had started to like Sabella. I had started to believe this might just work out. But the opportunity to find Cassia had been a big part of that. Now ... well, she didn't need finding. Could I be a guard? Could I embrace that life?

"You are a Class Five witch," I say to Tavell. "You could have been the Head Witch at your village."

He blinks in surprise but nods.

"Why did you become a guard?" I am adrift and seeking something solid I can catch hold of.

Tavell rubs his cheek. "Yes. I am Class Five. And yes, in my community in Fauster, it was widely accepted I would become their next Head Witch. Fauster is not held back by King Ryker's laws—even he knows better than to subjugate a Pegasus breeding community. Which meant I was ignorant to what it was like throughout Conpieta. I liked practising magic, but ever since I was a boy, all I ever wanted was to see the City of Simgra and become a guard. As soon as I was of age, I applied. I nearly got into the Simgra guards too, but ... well, something ... *someone*, happened." A kind of sad anger softens his features, but he shakes it free.

"The details of that are a story for another day. So, instead of getting into the Simgra guards, I was offered a place with the Tarr guards. I moved here with a great sense of excitement. I was going to help people and prevent crime and dark magic. What I didn't understand was how oppressed the unsanctioned communities of Conpieta were. I didn't realise I would be expected to arrest people for using basic spells just because they were born on the wrong side of an arbitrary border." His hands curl into fists.

"I was horrified and nearly left the Guards. But I realised I could still do some good. Being a guard meant holding the power to mitigate some of Ryker's laws. And so, I worked hard to become the best guard I could—to make myself beyond reproach. Still, I wasn't careful enough and word reached Lord Luca of a guard who helped the Hismish. That was when he approached me and asked if I wanted to assist him. That's the simplified version anyway. Ultimately, Rill Narin, I became a guard for the same reasons you told me two days ago. I wanted to bring justice to the people. All the people. Regardless of birth or wealth." He crosses his arms, and for once, his intense gaze holds only patience.

I glance at Keeva. Lady Keeva who does not allow webs to build in her mind. And the webs in my mind have gathered many insects. It is time I dust them away.

I feel the decision fall in place. I need to put my prejudices and hatred aside. For the first time in my life, I experience the power of a goal. A real goal. Not just where I might get my next meal, or a messy desperation to find my sister, but a direction I can take that could even be called destiny. I retrieve my vest and belt from the ground.

"I want to be a guard. If Sabella will still be my prime." Will she forgive me for the horrid things I said?

Sabella gives a smile, small, but it reaches her dark eyes. "I'd be proud to call you my fledge."

Relief fills my chest and something else ... I think it is gratitude.

My attention snaps 'round when Tavell claps his hands with a single echoing smack.

"The day is getting late. We need to find Finn and then the summoner for I am sure one will lead to the other. I have no doubt he will seek to harvest souls again tonight, and despite what Commander Lewis says, I don't think we have discovered who the summoner is yet."

Sabella, Keeva and I straighten. We have a purpose, a function. Despite everything, we are needed.

"Sabella, you are a Red Witch, so we have fire. Lady Keeva, you are blessed with air magic, am I right?"

Keeva nods.

"Rill, you are Earth, yes?"

I dip my chin. He is good if he can read the elements that feed our powers.

"I am Water, and so we have all the elements. Together, we can cast a powerful divination spell to locate Finn."

He goes to one of the desk drawers and withdraws a big chunk of chalk.

Then he finds a relatively bird-shit-free section of floor and draws a symbol. In each of its corners, he chalks a representation of wind, fire, water, and air. At its centre, he simply writes, Finn.

"Stand in a circle."

We do as he says.

"One at a time, draw on your element. I'll go first." Tavell squints, murmuring something under his breath.

I watch in fascination as his eyes turn green and tears glisten. He leans forward and lets them drop onto the symbol.

May water's spirit guide our way,
In fluid motion, on this day.
Embrace its essence, pure and kind,
A source of life, forever entwined.

The scent that is always a part of Tavell, ginger and pepper, grows in intensity, and I breathe it in. This feels right. It is like a drink of water in the desert. Sweet, needed, and life-blooming.

Sabella goes next. With a glance at me, she gives a nod and conjures a tiny ball of flame in her palm, then drops it onto the symbol. She raises her hands, and suddenly, she is passion and power.

May fire's essence guide our path,
From its warmth, and from its wrath,
Its strength and courage never wane
We let your spirit forever flame.

Sabella's magic comes with a rich warm scent of juniper, sage, and smoke.

Then Keeva closes her eyes and holds her hands out, palms facing skyward. Seconds pass, then a breeze tickles my ears, lifting my hair as it goes. It rushes past with a sweet peaches and cinnamon smell. Everyone else's hair rises too, and Keeva pulls the currents in, making a tiny whirlwind over the symbol. Bit by bit, she lowers it to the chalked symbol.

With gratitude, I now command,
The power of air is my demand.
Respect its force, its unseen might,
A sacred dance, eternal flight.

A rush comes over me. I can practice magic without fear. I allow it to rise within and relish the feeling. Calling on nature and the life-giving earth, I draw the dust from the air, pulling it in until a gauzy ball of dirt forms. With reverence and delight, I breathe in my own musk, amber, and sage woodsy aroma and release the ball of earth onto the symbol.

With gratitude, I now decree,
The power of earth, rooted in me.
Respect its might, its nurturing grace,
In harmony, we find our place.

"Repeat after me," Tavell says, and raises his hands.

Visions, arise like ripples on the lake,
Show me the steps that Finn may take.
Through symbols, whispers, and signs profound,
Guide me to the place where he is found.

Sabella, Keeva, and I chant the same words with Tavell, and a mighty thrum vibrates through my bones. Our magical scents collide and melt together in a delicious mixture of power.

We repeat the incantation three times, and a smoking vision rises from the centre of the symbol. It shimmers and flickers and takes form. The form of Lord Finn. It hovers in the air, and beneath it, more smoke swirls and rises, gradually forming the buildings that make up the city of Lapana. Slowly, the bending, warping smoke body of Finn floats over the three-dimensional smoke map. It drifts to the docks on Carlver River, then disappears into one of the buildings.

"There he is," Tavell says. "But it's not good. That particular depot houses shipments for The Carlver Slicers."

He looks at me. "They *are* slavers. If Finn is with them, he's in a lot of trouble. We need to get there now."

With tension pressing, we race from the warehouse.

45
Sabella

WHEN WE EMERGE FROM the crumbling warehouse, my stomach turns over with a violent flip that propels my whirling thoughts into a frenzy. The sun is arcing low in the sky, and we yet must rescue Finn and find and stop the summoner. Concern threads the group, and we half-run, half-walk. We can't afford to draw too much attention, but precious time is slipping away.

The sinking sun has done nothing to cool the city. If anything, it has grown hotter with a baking wind that swirls grit in our faces, and I wonder if a storm is on its way. I can't separate the pressing heat from the pressing tension, so I ignore my sweating face and my dry mouth.

I shoot a fleeting glance at Rill. Her feet turn over faster than everyone else, her legs being shorter. She's declared herself my fledge, and for the first time, it feels official. Any misgivings that she will sabotage her tests are gone. Relief and excited anticipation clash with the apprehension of the current situation. Mixed in with those emotions is the astounding information we'd just learnt. And even though I understood she had been knocked flat by distressing information, even though I knew she had been acting out, what Rill had said about me had dug deep, right down to my bones. Because she was right. I have spent my life trying to be smaller. The guards are my crutch, and I *do* live in constant fear it will all end. But worse, I have smothered the core of my being—my fire magic. As terrified as I am, it is time I let myself blaze.

Courage is not the absence of doubt, but action despite it.

I now wonder if Tavell had always meant I needed to embrace my fire magic. He knows about the child I injured in the orphanage when the unending bullying had finally caused me to snap. Yet, he insisted on training me in fire magic and did so slowly and patiently. But I'm sure he knew I held back.

I swipe sweat from my forehead and push my eddying thoughts aside. Danger awaits us, and we need to rescue Finn. The man I love. I need to concentrate singularly on what we are doing.

In front of me, Tavell slows to a walk as we round a corner, maintaining a constant scan of our surroundings. Ahead of us now are glimpses of Carlver River sparkling in the late afternoon sun. The divination spell revealed Finn being held in a depot on the edge of the West District. Once we reach Carlver River, we will cut east a short way.

"It will be well guarded," Tavell says as we head down the street at a brisk walk. "We'll try to use stealth, but I doubt that will work. The Carlver Slicers didn't earn their reputation by being lax in their security." He rubs his cheek, his chest heaving from the punishing pace. "I just hope the depot is not warded."

"Wards are my thing." Rill offers. "There's a chance I can take them down. Or, at least, create an opening to allow us in."

"Excellent," Tavell replies.

He wears an expression I became familiar with over the three years I was his fledge. He is formulating a plan.

"We all have to be ready to use force," Tavell says. "Maybe even deadly force."

I know the thought doesn't sit easily with him. Hell, it doesn't sit easily with me either.

"If we don't find Finn and they transport him on their next boat out of Lapana, he'll almost certainly never be seen again." There is grim determination in Tavell's tone.

Suddenly I am OK with using whatever force is necessary. My chest tightens. In a short space of time, I've gone from thinking the man I love *is* a slave trader to finding he is being held *by* slave traders.

"Was Rill right? Are you in love with my brother?" Keeva asks, panting. It is like she guesses where my thoughts are.

I dare a glance at Tavell. He will think me ridiculous, but it seems the secret is out, so—

"Lord Finn and Sabella have been seeing each other for ... what, six ... seven months now?" Tavell wears a smirk, but it isn't unkind.

Of course, he knows. The man is a bloodhound.

I suck air into my tight chest. "I am in love with Finn. And I believe he loves me too."

"Is that why you go with me to the prison?" Keeva looks at me with sorrow in her eyes. One hand presses the top of her head to stop her hat from flying off in the rising wind.

"He is not why I go to the prison with you, Keeva. I took my rostered month in accompanying you and, as you know, offered to continue to do so even after my time was served. That was well before I met Finn." I draw a ragged breath of hot air. "I continue to go to the prison with you because ... well, I like you." I don't want to tell her I have only ever had one friend before. I don't want to tell her just how precious our friendship has become to me.

"And your feelings for Finn. Are they the sort that makes you think we could become more than friends? Do you think we might be family one day?"

I blink in surprise. "It's a nice thought, Keeva, but I am not stupid. I know the Earl of Tarr won't be permitted to marry a woman from Keplon with the pedigree of being an orphan."

Keeva looks thoughtful, and my heart aches. We have two years left, and then Finn will become the Earl of Tarr. He will be expected to marry a pretty, privileged woman from Lapana. From the moment it started, our relationship has had a use-by date. Initially, it was simply the thrill of banging the Earl's son. A good-looking man who is great in bed—Agnis save me, he is *amazing* in bed. I just hadn't expected to fall in love.

The streets are filling with other pedestrians now, heads bowed against the roaring wind, and we dodge workers heading home for the evening. The day is nearly at an end, and the gnawing worry I will never see Finn again makes me ill. I can live with not being his wife. I *cannot* live with him being sold to the highest bidder.

Urgency fills me, and I push my aching legs to surge ahead of the others.

The damp, oily smell of the river hits me, and I resist the urge to run. We are close, and I want nothing more than to find Finn. Not only to discover what he knows of the demon summoner but to know he is safe.

When we round the next corner, the river lies directly at the end of the street, and Tavell brings us to a halt, ducking into a side alley. He looks around carefully and tilts his face towards the rooftops.

"The Carlver Slicers will have guards on lookout. Sneaking in won't be easy. We need a plan," he says.

"Diversion?" I whisper, my heart thumping uncomfortably.

Tavell nods. "I think that may be the only way. I'll go straight to the front door. They'll know I don't have a fledge yet—the Slicers make it their business to know everything about the guards—and so turning up by myself won't raise suspicions. If they have Finn in there, and I've no doubt they do for the spell showed us, they'll be edgy. I'll play to that. Say I've had a report that they hold Lord Finn. Suggesting I'm there for any other reason will scream diversion."

I don't like it. Tavell approaching on his own sounds dangerous, but there doesn't seem to be any other options, and we are running out of time. Plus, Tavell is a Level Five witch. No doubt he can defend himself.

"Fledge Narin. Tanglers can usually *feel* the presence of others. Do you think you could sense the position of the guards?"

Rill blinks with surprise. "I ... don't know. I've never ... we're not permitted to do magic in Hismish. I've never had the chance to practice …" She trails off, looking miserable. "No one knew. I kept my black magic secret."

Tavell frowns, a shadow of sadness crossing his features. "Tangling is not black magic. It is rare and feared and illegal for all but a chosen few who are strictly controlled by the king's guard. But unlike, say, necromancy or voodoo, or demon summoning, it is not black magic."

Rill's normally flat expression falters. A war of emotions seems to take hold of her. Disbelief, hope, relief.

"My soul is not black?" she finally whispers, yearning clinging to her every word.

Tavell's face softens. "Absolutely not." He chews on his cheek, seeming to war with himself for a moment. "You know, strictly speaking, you can apply for a Level Five license and do the required training, but it would mean disclosure of your magic. Your life would no longer be your own."

Rill cocks her head. "I don't believe I need a license to discover who I am."

Tavell looks impressed. "I could not agree more. And licensed or not, I am happy to teach you. Just as I do Sabella. But if that is your decision, I suggest keeping your tangling magic a secret. We three know, but I would take pains to ensure no one else finds out."

Rill snorts. To be fair, I am sure she had no intention of telling anyone else. I know I sure didn't.

Rill raises her brows. "I could not agree more." Her lips twitch with her mimic of Tavell's earlier comment. "But it seems a little unfair. You know my magic, yet we don't know your Level Five magic." She looks thoughtful. "If I guess it correctly, will you confirm if I am right?"

Tavell purses his lips. “Alright.” He folds his arms. “But you only have one guess.”

Rill grins. “I only need one. You are a truthsayer, aren’t you?”

46

Sabella

TAVELL'S MOUTH DROPS OPEN, then he flicks a worried glance my way. With a look that feels like an apology, he draws a deep breath.

"Yes," he exhales.

Now my mouth drops open. A truthsayer? But that would mean ... oh gods, Tavell knew every time I lied to him. Which has not been often, but recently, I told a very big lie.

About Rill. And Keeva. And who had witnessed demonic murder.

I glance at Keeva. Her slender hands are clasped, and she is gnawing gently on her bottom lip. I imagine her thoughts are similar to mine.

But Rill smiles. "OK. Now we all hold secrets." She slowly draws her gaze over us. "Bound together."

Suddenly Tavell chuckles. "Indeed." Then he gives himself a shake. "Your lessons start now, Fledge Narin as we are in rather a hurry. Take a deep breath, and close your eyes."

Rill hesitates for only a second, then does as she is asked.

"Reach out," Tavell uses his gentle teaching voice. "Like you would if you were going to tangle with someone. Can you feel us? Not to tangle with, but just feel us?"

A slow smile spreads on Rill's face, softening her angles. "Yes," she breathes.

I swear she grows an inch right before my eyes.

"Just do that again, when you get closer to the depot," Tavell says. "Don't forget to reach up to the rooftops, too. You won't know the people you feel, but you'll sense if someone is there."

Rill opens her eyes, and there is a gleam in them that wasn't there before.

"Go 'round the back," Tavell says. "The guards will be too well trained to leave their posts just because I make a fuss at the front door, but they might be distracted enough that you can freeze them without any trouble."

Tavell gives us all an intense look. "Get in. Get Finn. Get out." He bobs his head in an encouraging nod. "Let's go."

With square-set shoulders, Tavell strides from the alleyway, and I swear the wind parts to allow him through. He sure knows how to look impressive.

Keeva, Rill, and I skip over one alleyway and wait until we hear raised voices. Tavell's voice comes first, loud and authoritative, and we dart, creeping closer to the back of the depot building. Until we hit an invisible, quietly humming wall.

"Wards," I say through gritted teeth. "Rill, see what you can do."

With hands stretched before her, Rill appears to be palpating the wards. Her fingers work in a kneading action, and her lips move in near-silent mumbling. I force my feet not to dance with impatience. After what feels like an age, Rill takes a step ... and is through the wards. On the other side, she extends her hands again.

"Step through when I say," she says, her voice low and urgent.

Keeva and I ready ourselves, looking a bit like runners at the starter line.

Seconds tick by ...

"Now."

We step through. The wards squeeze at me, pressing tight even around my head and face like I am pulling on a tight sweater. Then with a light pop, we are on the other side.

"Hope we're not in a hurry when we come back this way." If we are pursued when we leave with Finn ...

"Not a problem," Rill whispers. "These wards only protect against people coming in, not leaving. We'll be able to pass right through."

"Well, that's something," I say, and we set off once more towards the back of the depot. We stop before we round the rear corner. The wind roars now, sending buildings creaking and loose items crashing. I work hard not to jump with each bang.

Keeva, on the other hand, startles violently with each thud, yet at no point does she cry out. In opposition, Rill, despite her glowing red face, looks completely calm, and in total control. She barely seems to notice the grating out-of-tune chimes the wind sets off around us.

"Rill," I murmur. "Can you feel any guards?"

She stills, closing her eyes, then nods. "Two at the back door and two on the roof. But the ones on the roof are on the river side of the building." She speaks so softly, I have to lean in to hear her.

I peek around the corner quickly. Two men with large swords at their hips guard the door. No doubt Tavell is correct—they will not be distracted easily—but they also look relaxed, leaning back against the wall, deep in conversation. They probably rely on the wards to stop most intruders. From here, I can't hear Tavell at the front of the building anyway. So much for distracting them.

"We don't want them to identify us if we can help it," I say. "Rill, we use our Jacks together. You take the one on the left. I'll take the right. On my mark."

I find a rock on the ground and, staying hidden around the corner, throw it hard and high, aiming for the roof of the opposite building. I cringe, waiting for a second that seems much longer, hoping I have thrown it far enough. Then the rock lands with a thud and a rolling clatter.

I peek around the corner again, and sure enough, both guards are looking skyward towards the roof. "Now," I hiss. I raise my Jack, and Rill smoothly falls in beside me.

Together, we point at the Slicer guards.

"Immotus," we intone together, and the guards are instantly fixed in place, faces tilted upwards.

"Come on," I say, and the three of us scramble for the door.

I push it open, heart leaping in my throat, and peer inside.

Stretching before us are rows and rows of racking that stand nearly as tall as the towering ceiling. Between the rows, seemingly never-ending corridors filled with cold shadows. Crates and sacks and boxes of merchandise line the racks.

We creep inside, and the smell of coffee and tobacco hits first, but the odour is mixed with dampness and dust and ... villainy. It is the only way I can describe it. The place smells villainous.

I look right and left, and not seeing anyone, I take a step. My footstep rings out on the concrete floor, flying and echoing down the stacks like a thunderclap. I grimace and rise to my tiptoes.

Close by, voices sound. Rough, men's voices. And they are coming closer. I cock my head, listening, trying to determine from which direction the men approach. They are only a few rows over. With a jerk of my head to Keeva and Rill, I tiptoe away from the voices, then turn down a row and speed up my dancing, tiptoeing pace.

Here, an overpowering, sickly smell of sugar coats my tongue, and my stomach roils. I gulp as we press on, creeping down the tight aisle, trying to ignore the sensation that we are being watched. Trying to shut out the memories of hiding from the other orphans who loved to torment me in unimaginable ways. And trying to shut out the sensation the racks are swallowing us like morsels of food for a great beast.

I'm not in a gullet. I'm not in a gullet.

The men's voices change. They become clearer and ring out more, and I guess they have emerged from between the racking and are now near the back door. I pause, holding my breath, hoping they'll move away. Instead, they come closer.

Gesturing wildly to Keeva and Rill, I find a gap between the crates and squeeze into it, the rough wood of the crates scraping at my hands. I stand rock still, hoping the shadows will hide me. A vein in my temple pounds uncomfortably.

Keeva and Rill scramble like mice also, stepping lightly and finding their own gaps to hide in.

It is cool in the depot, but sweat beads on my forehead. I don't dare wipe at it for any movement might make a sound that will reveal us. My heart beats in my chest like a drum, and I hold my breath to slow its bass rhythm. I try not to worry about how the hell we are going to find Finn without being discovered by the Slicers.

The men's voices drift towards us, and peeping through the gap between the two stacked crates beside me, I watch. Shapes appear at the end of the corridor and hover. The rise and fall of their voices make it sound like they are chatting. Shooting the breeze rather than looking for intruders. That is good, but the guards at the back door could unfreeze at any moment, and there is no doubt they will raise the alarm. I really want to get further away. But to make progress, we must continue down the corridor that holds us like a trap.

A moment later, the men move away, and I immediately wiggle out and scoot further along the narrow corridor until near darkness envelopes us. Keeva and Rill are right behind me. I stop and listen. I can hear no voices. No footsteps.

"Any idea where we might find Finn?" I whisper.

In the murky light, Keeva and Rill's faces are deeply shadowed. We stand in a tiny circle, heads bent close.

"I imagine there would be rooms on the exterior walls," Keeva says, quiet as a breeze. "We need to get out of the racks, but then we'll be exposed, so ..."

A feeling of hopelessness comes over me. But Finn needs me, and I am a guard after all.

It is time I blazed.

"Come on. We chance it."

I turn and only just smother a scream.

Standing in the corridor is a Slicer. He wears a wicked grin that, in the darkness, looks more teeth than lips.

47
Sabella

SHOCK HOLDS ME. I stare at the slicer, sure my eyes are playing tricks on me in the dark.

"Nolan?"

Nolan Fawn laughs, deep and filled with menace. "Didn't see that coming, did you, Peak?" His normally smooth voice is gone, replaced by guttural words that scrape against my ears. His carefully cultured accent is supplanted by a lower-class dialect.

He still wears his guard uniform but without his vest or belt. He's undone the top buttons of his shirt, rolled up his sleeves, and the departure from his usually precise presentation is marked.

"Don't look so fuckin' stunned. The guards can only take you so far. Sure, they got me away from my pathetic parents and their lowly factory jobs, but I'm not settling for just one step up. I want more. Riches, prestige ... power. Everything the Slicers offer. But, oh, how wonderful that you came here. How wonderful that I found you." He smiles again, his teeth once more glow in the dimly lit depot. "You'll be looking for the baby lord, I'm guessing."

In a snake-like movement, he reaches out and grabs Rill by the wrist. She struggles against his grip until he presses a knife to her throat.

"Settle down, Ikra scum. I'll take you to Lord Finn." He makes a horrid, wet, sucking sound and slurps at his teeth. "I'm sure he'd like the company and Boss Slicer 'ill be happy as a siren at a shipwreck with the money he'll get for you lot. Ladies are in great demand. 'Specially ladies as fine as you." He sinks his nose onto Rill's head and ... smells her.

Repulsion and fear hold me stiff, though my chest heaves. Keeva presses close to me, her body trembling.

"Come along, or I'll slit this one's throat." Nolan grins again, and a line of drool rolls off his bottom lip.

Without his carefully applied guard exterior, Nolan Fawn is gross ... and clearly deranged. Rill saw through his mask. I kick myself yet again that I did not.

Beside me, Keeva's shaking body stills, and I feel her straighten. "Slitting her throat would rather reduce your profit, would it not?" she says.

Nolan blinks at her, only visible because the gleam of his eyes disappears for a second.

"Talk fancy, don't ya?" He peers closer at Keeva, squeezing the knife even tighter against Rill's throat. Rill brings her hands to his wrist, her eyes wide with panic.

Nolan reaches out and whips the hat from Keeva's head. Then he gives a heart-stopping, evil chuckle. "Well, I'll be fucked. If it ain't the baby lady. Oh, but this just got a whole lot better."

The cold freeze of horrifying dread covers me. This is going horribly wrong.

"The guards know we are here, Nolan. If we don't return, they will descend on your … organisation and undertake a thorough investigation. And if Lady Keeva goes missing, you can be sure the Earl won't rest until the culprits are found. You really want that much attention?"

Nolan throws his head back and roared with laughter. "First of all, the Earl don't seem concerned about his baby lord. Doubt he'll care about the little bitch. And secondly, Commander Lewis sent us all out to look for you, Peak. It will be a feather in my guard cap if I take you in."

Ice slides along my bones.

Then Rill catches my eye. "Look after my body," she says, clear as day. A second later, she crumbles to the floor, Nolan pulling the knife clear of her throat as she drops. He stands, stunned like he's just woken up and isn't sure where he is.

I take advantage of his disorientation, grab his arm and, spinning him around, I apply a choke hold.

"Drop the knife," I mutter between clenched teeth. I still don't want to make too much noise and bring others running.

Nolan immediately drops the knife. "Sabella," he squeezes out around the press of my forearm on his throat. "It's me. Rill."

Realisation dawns, and I release Rill-occupied Nolan.

That took me way too long to figure out.

Keeva stares at Rill in Nolan's body. "Wow," she murmurs.

Rill looks down at her body on the floor. "Help me hide … myself." She bends and threads her arms under, well, her arms.

Breaking our shock, Keeva and I help, gently lifting Rill's body and tucking her in beside a crate.

"Don't forget to come back and get me," Rill says in Nolan's horrid, abrasive voice. She picks up the knife again. "Now come on. I've got an idea. Walk in front of me and act like you've been caught."

I catch on quicker this time and, holding Keeva's arm tight, fall into the act of being terrified—which isn't entirely an act. We quickly make our way to the end of the stack corridor.

As we approach the front of the building, we hear raised voices coming from outside. I grin. One of the voices is Tavell, still making a scene. I only hope he is safe. When we reach the end of the corridor, Rill steps forward, taking advantage of the safety of being in Nolan's body, and looks around. After a second, she is back between the racks.

"Left," she whispers. "There are guards. And I'm guessing I know who they're guarding."

I collect Keeva's arm again and allow Rill to grab me by the collar, pressing the knife to my neck.

"Look what I found," Rill says when we get close to the slicer guards. "Baby lady and a guard. Juicy bits of flesh for the sellin'."

The guards fall for it. Why would they not? With hungry smirks, they move aside to reveal a room made of bars.

And on the floor, looking groggy and boneless, is Finn.

48
Sabella

"FINN!" I TRY TO run, but Rill *growls* at me and presses the knife tighter to my neck. "Settle down, bitch."

The two slicer guards, who reek of body odour, guffaw at the comment. One pulls a set of keys from his belt and smoothly unlocks the door. He swings it open and moves aside to allow his comrade to shove us into the cage. The second I feel the knife leave my throat, I swing an elbow at the second man, while Rill—in Nolan's body—shoves the slicer with the keys up against the bars. A beat later, he is frozen in place when I use my Jack on him. Quickly, before he recovers from his surprise, I point Jack at the other guard. "Immotus," I cry and create a statue out of him.

Keeva rushes into the cell and squats beside Finn. "Finn. Finn!" She shakes his shoulders.

I fall in beside her and gently lift Finn's head. "Finn," I breathe, and relief that he is alive washes over me.

His eyes peer at me, confusion furrowing his brow and contorting his mouth. "Sabella?" he murmurs, his voice dry and papery.

"Can you stand? We need to get out of here," I try to keep the panic out of my voice.

Finn's eyes roll about in his head. "Where ...?"

Rill is suddenly in the cage with us. "We don't have time. Hold this." She sheathes Nolan's knife, then slips her arms under Finn and lifts him like a baby. Nolan is clearly quite strong.

Walking quickly, despite the weight she carries, Rill leaves the cage and, avoiding the frozen Slicer statues outside, darts back toward the stack corridor where we left her body.

Keeva and I exchange looks and then dash after her.

We reach the right stack corridor without being spotted, and Rill sets off down it at pace. She is panting now though, and I worry if she'll be able to carry Finn so far. But I worry for nothing because Rill soldiers on relentlessly.

Reaching the place where we'd left her body, however, she lowers Finn and, obviously exhausted, nearly drops him. Thankfully, he seems to have come around more because he manages to catch himself before he hits the deck. He leans against a stack on shaky legs.

"What, in the name of all things holy, is going on?" he asks between clenched teeth.

"You were taken. By the Slicer gang," Keeva replies. "We think they were going to sell you ... into slavery. You don't remember anything?" She goes to Finn and checks him for injuries, palpating his body in the darkness. "Are you hurt?"

"I'm … alright." He shakes his head like he is clearing it of cobwebs. "I … remember leaving the library. I was going to see Uncle Sean." He gasps. "The library records. They showed Alex accessing the Heinous Section. But he didn't, I'm sure of it."

"We know," Keeva says. "I got your message. In the box on the mantle."

Finn stares at her. His eyes roam to me and then to Rill, and they fly wide. "Who is that?"

"It's OK," Keeva says. "He is … a friend of ours. Sort of. I'll explain later."

So much for keeping Rill's secret.

Keeva stands directly in front of Finn and waves a hand in his face, trying to keep his attention. "You don't remember leaving me a message?"

Finn frowns. "I remember thinking someone at the manor was involved. That it was all more dangerous than we first thought. I'm not surprised I tried to warn you … but I don't remember doing it, no."

"Uncle Sean said he never saw you. So, somewhere along the way, someone got to you. Probably meddled with your memories. Maybe the same person who meddled with Hanna's memories."

"We must move," I say. I've listened long enough. "We'll catch up on everything once we get out of here. Rill, are you going to leave Nolan's body now?"

I ignore Finn's confusion at my comment.

Rill shakes her head. "No. It might be useful to be in his body when we try to get out the back door." She grimaces. "Though his mouth tastes absolutely revolting." She shudders. "But those two guards outside, the ones we froze, will be on high alert now. I can't believe they haven't raised the alarm already."

And as if her words were an invitation to fate, shouts and the sound of running feet ring out. We all crouch. Way ahead, towards the back door, a dozen or so men run past. None look in our direction.

"They're going to check the cage where they kept Finn," I say. "We gotta go."

Rill bends to collect her body, but I stop her. "I'll carry you. You're little and light, and it would be better if you were ready to fight."

Rill just nods and helps me slide her inert, soulless body from its hiding place. I heft her into my arms.

"Can you run?" I ask Finn who nods, grim determination on his face.

"I'll *make* my legs work."

And so, we all run.

The frenzied shouts of excited slicers make the rippling echo of our footsteps less noticeable, though we still make a horrific thudding sound as we go. But I am solely focused on getting out. Not sneaking.

When we reach the back door, I am relieved to find no gang members block our way out. But there *will* be at least two Slicers waiting outside.

"Put my body down," Rill says to me, and I lower her gently to the floor. "You've used your Jack three times, so I'm guessing it is out," she says and nods towards her body. "Use my cudgel and freeze one."

I slide Rill's Jack from her inert body.

Rill slides Nolan's wicked-looking knife from the sheaf on his hip. "I'll take care of the other." Her expression is grim ... and just plain bizarre being that it is Nolan's face. "Keeva and Finn. Stand back. This might get messy."

Keeva and Finn tuck in behind me.

"Ready?" Rill asks.

I gulp and nod, trying not to grip the cudgel too tightly.

With a deep breath, Rill belts out the door, shouting, "They're here. Help me get 'em."

The two Slicer guards burst through the door, and I waste no time. I extend Jack, aiming at the closest one.

"Immotus!"

He stops dead in his tracks.

But the other still comes, sword at the ready. A shaft of light catches the blade, and it winks at me. Terror grips me, but I let my training take over. I widen my stance and prepare to block the sword with my cudgel. I am all that stands between the armed Slicer and Keeva and Finn. I will not let them down.

The Slicer's sword arcs through the air ...

Then he suddenly collapses in a crumpled heap. Behind him, Rill stands in Nolan's body, his knife in her outstretched hand drips with blood. As if in shock, she drops the weapon with a clatter, her chest heaving.

Nausea rises in my stomach. Did Rill just kill the man? I look down at his still body, willing him to be alive and hoping him dead at the same time. Filled with dread, I sink to my haunches to check his pulse ...

"Run!" Keeva and Finn yell at the same time.

All at once, the sound of approaching footsteps pierces my shocked mind, and I glance up … to see dozens of Slicers round the farthest stack. They run toward us, and all brandish either swords or wands.

Scrambling, I go to heave Rill back into my arms, but the Rill-controlled body of Nolan stops me.

"No. Get ready to knock this idiot unconscious. He's strong, so don't hesitate."

I ground myself and palm Jack, trying in vain to ignore the horror of the pounding footsteps coming closer.

The second I notice movement in Rill's body on the floor at my feet, I look back at Nolan Fawn who stands with eyes wide with confusion. I don't hesitate. I swing Jack, connecting with his head in a sickening crunch. He goes down like a sack of sugar from one of the shelves.

I urge the others towards the door, panic rising as the Slicers get closer and closer. I can see their faces now, and they are beyond angry. They shout and caged electrical lights above makes their swords glint and their polished wands gleam.

Time to blaze.

A hard lump lodges in my throat, but I swallow it down with such determination, it is like it crumbles to pieces. My hesitation vanishes, and I raise a hand … and send a stream of red, roaring flames at them. As if something unlocks, I feel my self-imposed chains fall away. My fire is part of me. It is who I am. A gift from the goddess, Agnis. It feels right and simple, and I focus it, control it … until the stink of burning flesh fills the air. Retching and with eyes watering, I douse my flames with a snap of my fist.

Suddenly, Finn's arm comes around my waist, and he hauls me out the door.

"Run," he bellows, and we all set off at a frenzied gait, pushing hard against the searing wind.

"This way," he says, and on legs that are still wobbly, he half staggers, half runs towards another depot close by. Within seconds, we are hidden between high walls. Not even rooftop lookouts would spy us. Yet, Finn keeps running.

"There's a place ahead. Someone I know. They will hide us." He pants as he runs and uses the walls on either side of him to right himself each time he weaves on unsteady legs.

"One of your Hismish helpers?" Keeva asks as we jog.

Finn nearly stops in surprise. "You know?" He speeds up again. "Good. I've always wanted to tell you. I'm glad you know."

I notice Keeva's small, puffing smile, and I am glad Keeva and Finn have no secrets anymore.

Finn runs around two more corners and, coming to a halt, taps lightly on a bright orange door. It flies open, and a middle-aged woman in a bright pink apron urges us inside.

"Come in quickly," she says. "Constable Nash is already here."

49
Keeva

I ENDEAVOUR TO STILL my shaking hands as the lady ushers us inside the tiny entrance foyer and pulls the door tight behind us, turning the lock with a snap.

Creeping about the Slicer depot, I felt more scared than I'd ever been in my life. And more alive. I cannot comprehend how something can be so horrible and so amazing in equal measure. Thank Saleal we found Finn and got him out. Come morning, he would have been on a boat bound for a life of slavery had we not rescued him. Overwhelming relief at the close call mixes with a swelling pride that I'd help rescue him. For the first time in my life, I have accomplished something real.

"Tavell!" Sabella cries out when the red-headed constable appears in the hallway that leads off the foyer.

He is a vibrant kind of man. His yellow-green skin and red hair somehow make him luminous. He is a man of contradictions. As intimidating as my father, he also possesses a kindness that is more like Uncle Sean. And the man is sharp. Even now his steely eyes dart, checking to see if anyone is hurt. But he also retains sleek control which is calming. Sabella always speaks of him with respect and gratitude. Not only did he train her well, but he helped her get Diarissa. I can see why Sabella holds him in such high regard.

"Thank Kikara. I was just about to come search for you." Tavell's deep voice matches his broad build. "Lord Finn. You look like you need to sit down."

His comment jolts me from my thoughts. Finn is swaying, like he might collapse at any second. Sabella and I move in concert, catching hold of him at the same time. The lady who had greeted us beckons a plump finger.

"This way. Sit. I'll fetch a bracing cup of tea."

I hook an arm under Finn's elbow, and Sabella does the same on his other side. Following the homeowner, we guide him through the narrow hall and into a tiny lounge to the left.

Rill follows, stepping as lightly as ever. I am glad she is back in her own body. Coming to grips with her being inside that horrendous slicer in a guard uniform—the one they'd called Nolan—was disconcerting, to say the least.

We lower Finn onto a pink velvet armchair where he promptly slumps, his head lolling like an understuffed rag doll. Sabella crouches beside him, and while she doesn't touch him, she gives the impression of clinging to him just the same.

How did I never know?

The lady of the house appears a moment later with a drink. Not tea, though down the hall—presumably from the kitchen—I can hear the kettle coming to the boil.

"Drink this," she says to Finn and all but thrusts the glass under his nose. Fine, curling tendrils of smoke rise from the glass. "Memory magic takes a toll on your body, particularly if it is clumsily performed. Unless I'm much mistaken, your memory was taken by a hack." She tsk-tsks with a motherly shake of her head. "But this tonic will fix you right up."

Finn doesn't hesitate. He accepts the glass and downs it in one giant gulp.

"Right. I'll get that tea now." The woman wipes her hands on her pink apron and bustles off with the movements of a woman used to being busy.

I stand by Finn, watching him, concern pressing uncomfortably on my skin and mind. But with every passing second, he recovers. His vacant look shifts, like he is coming into focus. Then with a deep breath, he sits up in the chair, looking much more like himself. He zeroes in on me.

"Hello, Kee." He gives a crooked, half-dimpled smile. His face is smudged with dirt, but it is nothing a wash will not fix, and he is unharmed.

"Hello, Finn." I channel my father and make my voice clear and even, like I am calm and in control. Nothing is further from the truth, but Finn doesn't need to know that.

He turns to Sabella and reaches out, clasping her hands in his. "Bella."

It is all he says, but I hear the tenderness in his voice. Saleal save us, he is just as smitten with Sabella as she is with him. A smile tugs at my lips, and at the same time, my chest tightens. Sabella is right. The relationship can never go anywhere. Our father will never permit it.

"Lord Finn." Tavell's commanding voice draws my attention back to the pressing issues at hand. "What do you remember?"

Finn swivels his head to Tavell who stands with Rill to one side of the small drawing room. "As I told the girls, I don't remember anything after leaving the library this morning." His breath catches in his chest. "It is still the same day, isn't it?"

Tavell nods, and Finn visibly relaxes.

"The records in the library, completed by Hanna are false. I am sure of it. I believe her memories have been tampered with. If we can look into her mind and see, we'll likely discover who the demon summoner is."

He turns back to Sabella by his side. "Unless you caught him last night?"

Sabella shakes her head, and it is like the air leaves her body when she sags and crumples.

Finn squeezes Sabella's hand. "What happened ....?" Then grim understanding crosses his face. "Who died?"

"We kept the summoner off the streets, right enough. But forced him into the GH. Captain Wallace and his fledge, Eli Palmer, were killed."

"Gods above. Bella, I'm so sorry." Finn darts a look out the window. The light is turning golden as the sun kisses the horizon. "We don't have much time. We need to find out who it is. He will strike again tonight. He'll be particularly determined. If he harvests another two souls tonight, he will be granted whatever favour he desires."

50
Keeva

The lady providing us shelter reappears balancing a tray of steaming tea for everyone, but Finn leaps to his feet.

"We don't have time for tea. We need to go. It's a long walk back to the manor. We need to look into Hanna's mind ..." He snaps his gaze to Tavell again. "Keeva tells me you are a Level Five." Finn's mouth twitches. "Which you might have mentioned, you know." He gives a grim smile. "Can you look into Hanna's mind and ...?"

"Drink, Lord Finn," Tavell says firmly. "The rest of you too. Then we'll leave. It won't take as long as you think, milord. Connie, here, has a dirty apparition booth. It will take us to the foot of Manor Hill."

Connie sets the tray down on a worn coffee table and hands out cups of tea. I am grateful for mine as racing around in the heat and sneaking into the Slicer depot has left my mouth as dry as cotton. I sip on the hot liquid, and I am even more grateful to find it well-sugared.

Sabella too, gulps at her tea with anxious urgency.

"Tavell," she says, licking her lips as if the lubrication is needed. "Constable Nolan Fawn was at the depot. He's working for the Slicers." I can see Sabella has been knocked flat by his betrayal.

Tavell's intimidating side flares, his face twisting with disgust. "Did he see you?"

"He captured us. He held a knife to Rill's throat and was going to sell us. He didn't care that we were guards or that he was taking Lady Keeva." Then Sabella smiles. "But Rill took care of him. She ..." Sabella stops herself because we had agreed to keep Rill's secret.

"Connie. Would you give us a minute?" Tavell softly requests.

Connie immediately leaves the room and pulls the door closed behind her.

Still, Sabella hesitates. Finn doesn't know of Rill's magic.

"Go ahead, Sabella," Rill says. "Lord Finn witnessed it, so I don't think there is much to be gained from secrecy now."

Sabella's smile conveys relief. "Rill tangled with him and used his body to help us rescue Finn."

Finn's face lights with understanding, and he gives an impressed nod to Rill who squirms a little under the scrutiny.

Tavell looks at Rill too, a kind of fierce triumph on his face. "Good job, Fledge Narin." He nods thoughtfully. "When this is over, I'll make sure Fawn is taken care of."

Everyone continues to drink and talk at the same time. I let the conversation of Tavell and Sabella bringing Finn up to date melt into the background. Rill stands to one side of the room, outside the circle of chairs and sofa. Outside the circle is a good description. I take my tea, balanced in its saucer and join her.

"I'm glad your sister is well and safe," I say.

Rill flicks her eyes to me, gives a tiny nod, and buries her nose in her cup.

"Having family keep secrets from you is disquieting," I continue. "I believe it will take some time for the hurt feelings to dissipate."

Rill places her cup in the saucer with a clatter. "My feelings aren't hurt." Her firm, bland expression returns, and I sense the expression is a part of Rill's wall to keep everyone out.

I smile. "I see. But in truth, I was referring to my feelings. Finding out the people I love kept such big secrets—well, while I understand why, that understanding doesn't stop the hurt. And then there is the confusion. I was so sure I knew my family. Now I discover I don't know them as well as I thought. It is ... disconcerting."

Rill downs the rest of her tea in three large swallows and presses the back of her hand to her mouth, like she worries she has dribbled. She puts her cup and saucer on the occasional table next to her, nearly tipping the cup over. She is clearly not accustomed to using a saucer.

"I shall have to settle into a new way of viewing my family," I continue. "Rather like getting to know them all over again. Which is something to look forward to, I suppose. Almost ... exciting. Having something to look forward to—even if the something holds a dose of anxiety—can help one relish life. And I admit, I had been finding life rather ... empty of late. Despite this whole, horrid situation, I am glad to feel I have come alive."

Rill runs a hand through her hair, shooting me sideways glances.

"When this is over," I say, "I would like to visit the Hismish villages. Oh, I shall continue going to the hospital, orphanage, and prison ..." I rush on when Rill winces " .... but I'd like to speak to the Hismish. Not in an act of charity, but to hear their challenges and grievances. Visits outside of the city break none of King Ryker's laws, and while I understand talking won't solve any of the Hismish issues, I cannot help but believe that being heard is a good first step."

Rill turns to face me directly now. I have her full attention.

"I would love you to accompany me, Rill. You have one day a week off, and we only need to take a few hours. I'd appreciate it if you think you can spare the time—"

"Yes," Rill says, cutting me off. "I'll come."

"Excellent." I finish my tea and, after retrieving Rill's cup from the occasional table, place both empty dishes back on the tray they'd been brought in on.

I return to stand with Rill once more, ready to bring my attention back to the room and the animated conversation that is flying between the others.

"Thank you, Lady Keeva." Rill tugs on her guard uniform. "I ... think you're right. Having something to look forward to is good."

I tilt towards Rill, gently bumping her with my shoulder. "Unless we are in public, call me Keeva."

I am rewarded with a fleeting smile.

"But it's not Alex! Tavell, surely you could do something ..." Finn's loud words grab our attention.

Someone obviously just told Finn that Alex has been arrested.

"The king's guard are here," Tavell says. "They have taken over the Tarr Guards. I have no sway anymore. Commander Cadel Lewis is in charge."

Finn sweeps a hand over his hair. "Fuck."

"Finn!" I can't help it. I'd never heard Finn swear before. He ignores me.

"What's more, they are looking for *you*, Finn. They believe guilt drove you to run away. In short, you are a suspect."

"And father," I add.

"What?" Finn is angry, and I understand. Anger still swirls in my belly in a most unladylike way.

Finn throws back the last of his tea and appears completely recovered from the memory-tampering magic. "We've all had our tea, Tavell. Let's move."

Tavell calls for Connie, and she shows us to her dirty apparition booth which has been created in a wardrobe. I give a grim smile. Until two days ago, I had no idea any unauthorised booths remained in Lapana. My father had told me they'd been discovered and decommissioned a long time ago. But then again, Father hasn't exactly been honest with me ... about a lot of things.

51

Rill

I EXIT THE APPARITION booth behind Sabella and follow her out of the hut, grimacing against the wind that has turned into a gale.

We are at the top of Manor Rise, a short distance from the plateau on which the Earl of Tarr's manor is built. It sits in prime position, literally lording over Lapana. The richest families live on Manor Rise in large, fancy homes. I lift my eyes to the earl's mansion above me. From this vantage point, I look almost directly at the rocky foundations that sit beneath the manor's wall. It's an uninspiring view, so I swivel to look instead out over the city.

Daylight is fading fast, and the purple of dusk bruises the sky and darkens the mass of terracotta roofs below. To the east, where the jagged outline of the Haunted Peaks rips across the horizon, black clouds gather—ominous and predatory. A shiver ripples through me, and I focus on the city.

I've never realised just how big it is. Even looking at it from Diarissa's back last night—it had been too dark to see it as a whole. A tiny thrill ripples—I will get to explore Lapana in my role as a citizen guard. As Sabella's fledge. The idea is still so new that I grapple to come to grips with it, but I can't deny a buzz of excitement. Keeva said it was good to have something to look forward to, and she was right. I am filled to the brim with it. I have not had anything to look forward to for years, and the feeling nearly overwhelms me.

My head whirls, and my heart dances with everything I've learned in the past few hours. With the knowledge Cassia is alive. With the decision to become a guard. With the revelation my soul is not tainted with black magic. Trust doesn't come easily to me, but somehow, I believe Tavell, and even that realisation shocks me. And I tangled with that Slicer—openly and in front of others. I am not used to sharing secrets and being a Tangler has always been my deepest, darkest secret.

And then there was Tavell teaching me about my magic—my level five magic. It may have been the quickest, simplest lesson in the world, but it was a sparkling gift, as precious as a diamond. I can't stop practising. In the safe house where we'd had tea, I had reached out, sensing each person in the room. Closing my eyes, I do it again now, and sense Lady Keeva and Lord Finn emerging from the apparition hut behind me. A thrill of power goes through me. Their footsteps are soundless—the wind lashes at the surrounding foliage, creating a raw, vigorous song—yet I know they are there.

Just like the swaying bushes, my thoughts lash—Cassia, Fledge Narin, tangling ... a demon summoner on the loose. I press a palm to my long fringe to stop it from whipping my face and just ... breathe. I need this moment. My armour has failed, completely fallen apart ... and a few seconds to gather myself are precious.

At the edge of the city's buildings, Carlver River marks the city's south border. Beyond the river, upon a narrow band of land known as Lapana Strip, a looming grey stone building—Lapana prison. Its menace is not obvious at this distance, but I can still smell it. I can still feel the steely cold of my cell. I can still hear the march of prison guards and the screaming nightmares of the prisoners. It might not have a physical hold on me anymore, but the mental hold will bruise me for some time.

Beyond the penitentiary, yellow patches of farmland and tiny houses dot the pastures. Wolf Woods and Ikra are out there somewhere, too far and too tiny to see. I take a deep breath, letting the strong wind fill my lungs, and I sit firmly in the moment. Spice, pine, and sweet citrus—the smell of summer flowers—mix with the taste of approaching rain.

But the sun is low, and long fingers of shadow extend over the view like the hand of a giant hag reaching for me. With the fall of night, the summoner will emerge to complete his payment to the demon. I turn back to the hut when I sense Tavell emerging from it.

He waves his hand at Keeva's brother, Finn, in a gesture that suggests he lead the way. Finn immediately sets off at a run, and I will my tired legs into action.

The road from the apparition hut to the gate of the manor is viciously steep, and soon everyone pants. Teeth gritted against burning thighs, I push on. I need to work on my physical fitness if I am to be an effective guard.

It takes nearly ten minutes to reach the manor gates, and my chest is not the only one that heaves.

"Good afternoon, Guard," Finn approaches the sentry on the west gate. Despite being winded, he still speaks with the kind of voice one would imagine from a Lord in Waiting—strong and compelling.

But the response from the guard is not what I expect.

He squints into the late afternoon sun, then his eyes pop wide, and he slowly draws his short sword. Finn goes still, and I wonder if the sword is spelled like a Jack.

"Lord Finn," the guard says, his stance and voice loaded with discomfit. "I am placing you under arrest for demon summoning."

The group tenses.

Tavell steps forward. "I am Senior Constable Nash, and I assure you, Lord Finn is not the summoner. In fact, he has information vital to finding the summoner, so we need to pass."

The guard, however, manoeuvres himself, putting more space between him and Tavell. He grimaces and draws a whistling breath through his teeth. "I have orders from Commander Cadel Lewis, I'm afraid." Then he tilts his head back.

"Lord Finn!" he shouts. "I have Lord—"

His voice suddenly vanishes. He flings his arms out, straight and stiff and drops his sword. His chin thrusts forward, like he is reaching for oxygen—like he just ran up that damn hill. Then he clutches at his throat. It's a sight I am all too familiar with.

Keeva stands with hands extended, and the crackle of magic and the scent of peaches and cinnamon are snatched at by the howling wind. She is using her air magic to take the air from the guard's lungs. Her face is tense, but she hangs on until the guard passes out.

When he crumbles to the ground, Keeva returns our stunned stares.

"We don't have time for any nonsense," she says by way of explanation and gives her shoulders an unapologetic jerk.

There is so much more to Lady Keeva than one would ever imagine. The woman who visits the prison with sweet smiles and benevolence is only a small part of who she is.

"I know another way in," she offers. "Unless they've discovered the entrance, it will be unguarded. Quickly now. The guard won't be unconscious for long."

Indeed, the poor man is already stirring.

Keeva spins, but Tavell raises a hand to stop her.

"We don't want him to raise the alarm." He bends and places two fingers on the guard's forehead. Once more, the buzz of magic surrounds us. Tavell's magic feels different to Keeva's—heavier, older and thicker with its ginger and pepper aroma.

Moments of time, swiftly depart,
Banish the memory with a fresh start,
Return to duty, guard the ground
Our presence forgotten, nowhere to be found

The guard sits up, slack-jawed, his eyes vacant.

Tavell signals to Keeva to move, so she does, leaving the unfortunate guard sitting on the ground looking confused. The man has only had a few minutes of memories removed, but if Finn's post-memory-snatching state is anything to go by, the guard will still be discombobulated.

I tuck in behind Sabella who follows Finn. Tavell brings up the rear, and his thumping footsteps ripple up my spine, and instinct urges me to run faster.

We run around the manor wall, keeping to the swishing bushes. Then Keeva makes directly for a small mound with jasmine flowing over it like a flowery waterfall. She pushes aside the jasmine to reveal an entrance and, without hesitation, enters the narrow tunnel.

"This was an old air shaft to a root cellar," she says, keeping her voice low. "I imagine it would have been too narrow to allow passage when it was first built, but age and weather have crumbled its walls and worn them away, making the shaft wide enough to pass through."

Inside, the wind cuts off, and our feet crunch on dirt and stone. The musty smell of the tight, dark passage reminds me of prison. It lacks the odour of death but still makes my skin crawl, and I concentrate hard on why we are here and try to keep my breathing even. We slow now, as everyone treads carefully in the darkness.

Thankfully, it isn't long before the passage opens up into the root cellar, dimly lit by a light shaft that allows the reddish glow of sunset to fill the room. Keeva crosses the floor with the sort of confidence that tells me she has used this sneaky entrance more than a few times. On the opposite wall of the root cellar, there is a rusty door that Keeva leans into, pushing hard. It swings open with a squealing creak that makes my teeth sing.

"This will take us to the staff level of the manor," Keeva says, leading the way into another narrow passage, except this one is formed with brick and stone.

"Goodness, Kee. You really did figure out a way to get in and out of the manor unseen," Finn says with something that sounds like pride in his voice.

"You'll block it up now won't you," Keeva replies.

Finn doesn't answer immediately, and Keeva keeps talking.

"It would be an intelligent decision. It is too great a security risk, and I'll have no need for it any longer." She reaches a flight of stone stairs and ascends.

"After we get to the servants' level, we'll have to go up one more floor to reach the library staircase. The servant's passageways don't have access to the library with its Heinous Section and horrible artefacts." She shudders. "Hanna's quarters are on the library level, so assuming she is finished for the day, we'll find her there."

I have heard tales of the Heinous Section of the Earl's library. Every child has. They make for terrific and terrifying bedtime stories. In fact, they were some of my favourite, most thrilling stories, yet I am not at all sure I want to visit the library in real life. But then again, the thought of a collection of books—a whole room of them—is enticing.

The stairs finally spit us out into an empty kitchen. Strange that it is empty at this time of the day. Shouldn't there be a collection of Hismish staff cooking up the evening meal? I look around, and my stomach squeezes, for the kitchen window frames near blackness. Night has fallen. We have no time to waste. The window brightens for a split second, followed by a distant rumble. The storm is nearly upon us, and I clench my jaw against the ominous sign.

"This is the winter kitchen," Keeva explains, ignoring the thunder. She walks swiftly across the flagstone floor to yet another door. "The staff will be in the summer kitchen. If we stick to the servants' passages for as long as possible, we shouldn't be bothered by anyone."

"Lead the way," Tavell says.

52
Keeva

THE WINTER KITCHEN JOINS a corridor, and I walk swiftly until I reach the end. With nightfall, the summoner may take another soul at any moment, and I cannot abide the idea of another person dying and their soul becoming trapped in hell for eternity. Failure is an unthinkable horror. And yet, I can't shake the feeling we are out of time. Even after we reach Hanna and Tavell looks into her memories, we may not find what we need. And if we do, it might still be too late. It feels like evil is swelling, riding the approaching storm, and we have no way of fighting it.

The door to our right leads to the laundry, while the door to our left will take us out of the servants' sections and upstairs to the manor proper. I push the door on the left open with desperate force and run up the stairs. A bad feeling has slid under my skin, and it is like I am drenched in viscid anxiety. I do not care that my body aches from a day of walking and running, that my head aches from lack of sleep and fear, or that I am quite certain I smell like a dock worker toiling in the sun. Barely controlled, sickening dread drives me forward.

Reaching the manor proper, our group flies through the wide hallways. The thick carpet—stretching before us like a running track—absorbs our pounding footsteps. I take the next corner … and run straight into the broad chest of my father. I bounce off him, and Finn only just catches me before I land on the floor in a mess of windmilling arms.

"Thank the gods." Father's arms come about Finn and me, and he squeezes us like we are oranges for juicing. He kisses me on the top of my head. "Keeva." Then he kisses Finn. "Finn." He plants yet another kiss on my cheek, his white whiskers tickling my face. "I was sick with worry, I …" He suddenly pulls away, though his hands stay on our shoulders. "Where were you?"

Tavell is beside us. "Lord Luca. It is a long story, and we don't have time. We must get to your librarian as quickly as possible. Every second is vital."

It is brave of Constable Nash to speak to Father this way, but he is right. We've not a moment to lose, and Anja, Goddess of Time, will grant us no favours.

Father takes in our pinched faces, tight lips, and clasped hands. "Right. Let's go then."

Now Father leads our group, but when he doesn't move quickly enough, Finn and I soon overtake him.

We reach the door that leads to the library and start our descent. More and more stairs, down, down into the lowest level. Down into the cool darkness. Down to the library.

Finally, we emerge into the short hallway that leads to Hanna's rooms to the left and ends with the ornate library doors. A muted drumming sound fills the hallway, and I realise the rain has arrived. We are several floors down, but its distant, insistent beat matches our urgency, and we veer left, yet the library doors make me halt. Like lovers torn asunder, they are ajar. The crafted hands that are the door handles reach not for each other, but forlornly into empty air.

The tiny hairs on the nape of my neck stand on end, and I turn to the others. "The doors shouldn't be open. I mean, perhaps Hanna is ..."

Father strides past me to the library doors, and every part of his body is tense. Tavell hurries to join him pulling his cudgel from his belt as he goes. Rill, Sabella, Finn, and I follow closely, unease rising from us in plumes.

At the doors, Father peers into the library, and suddenly, Tavell catches his arm and pulls him back with such force, I am forced to skip out of the way. Crouching, coiled in readiness, Tavell pushes the door open slowly, his cudgel extended before him.

And the smell hits us. A horrible scent of ...

"Brimstone," Rill says, her voice tiny and strained.

My stomach contracts so viciously, I think I am going to vomit. The Summoner and the demon are here? In the Manor? Goose-bumps rise on my skin.

Tavell pushes the doors to the library open, and the odour intensifies. I cover my mouth, my eyes darting around the shadowed library in sheer terror. Only the lights above Hanna's desk to our left are on, leaving the rest of the massive library in blackness. I only just hold back a squeal when Tavell flings out an arm in a gesture that tells us to stay put.

"Wait here," he says, his voice thick with dread. "Milord. Can we get more light?"

Father immediately thrusts his arm inside the door and flicks the wall switch.

Lights burst on and ripple down the stacks, turning the library from terrifying to … slightly less terrifying. Tavell looks about carefully, then enters the library with Father following.

"No, milord, it may not be sa—"

"It is my library, Constable. Do not presume you are in charge."

Tavell looks ready to argue but then gives a sharp nod and moves left. Father veers right.

I watch from the doorway standing beside Sabella. She is trembling … oh, but no, it is me who trembles. I draw a steadying breath and will my body to be brave. Finn stands to one side, shifting from one foot to the other, his head swivelling from Father to Tavell and back again.

Moving past Hanna's desk, Tavell suddenly halts. He lets out a breath and slumps, hands on knees, taking deep breaths through his mouth.

Father and Finn rush across the floor, joining Tavell.

"Gods above." Father's hands flex rapidly.

Pressing knuckles to his mouth, Finn turns away.

I glance at Sabella and Rill, and as if deciding in unison, we walk slowly to join the men.

The sight, hidden just around the librarian desk, is bone chilling. Hanna lies, half on her side, her intestines spilled from her belly like sausages in the butcher's shop. Blood flows from her, spreading in curves and narrow fingers as it follows tiny imperfections on the floor. A shiver ripples through me from toes to head. There is something else wrong with Hanna's body. Her lower half points one way, while the upper half goes the other. The demon has snapped her spine, twisting her so she looks like the gnarled branch of an old tree. Beside her corked body, ringing the blood, the floor is blackened.

Poor, poor Hanna. To have a life of service end this way. My heart aches.

Sabella moves and lays a hand on Rill's shoulder. Under the bright, white electric lights, Rill looks even paler than usual, yet there is a determined rage beneath her shock. She nods at Sabella as if to say she is alright.

"Blood looks fresh," Sabella says, and she does a visual sweep of the library.

"The smell of sulphur is strong, too," Tavell adds. "This was recent. Fledge Narin, is this how it smelt when you saw Thorn killed?"

I jolt. Gods. Tavell knows. He'd figured it out. I dart a look at Rill who doesn't seem at all surprised.

"Yes," she answers.

The reality of what Rill witnessed hits me. And to think she'd seen the bodies at the GH too. I shake off my revulsion and move to her side so Sabella and I flank her. No doubt it is of little use, but it is the best support I can offer her. And that's when I notice the iron gate to the Heinous Section is wide open. I point a shaky finger.

"That ... that wasn't open when we came in? Was it?"

Everyone turns.

"Burning hell," Rill murmurs. Her face is pinched like she is fighting against the evil that seeps from through the open gate. "Why would anyone *ever* come to this library?"

I understand. I felt the same when I sat at the table with Finn last night. "When the gate is shut, the black magic cannot get through," I say.

Then, a loud, echoing bang rings out.

I scream, and everyone else jolts.

For a split second, I think it is thunder, but no, the sound comes from down the stacks towards the back of the library. It is followed by running footsteps, and the hairs on my arms stand up.

"The summoner," Tavell grinds out.

53

Rill

Burning hell!

I can't decide what is worse—the waves of evil that flow from behind the open gate Keeva had pointed out, or that the summoner is here in the library.

Indecision crosses Tavell's face even as his feet move. He takes two steps in the direction of the echoing bang, then stops. "We need to leave. It's not safe ..."

"He only needs one more soul," Finn says. His posture is rigid, his face tight. "Then he can claim his reward. We must stop him, and now may be our only chance."

"We can lock him in ... lock the library," Tavell says. For a change, his expression is a picture of indecision.

The Earl, Lord Luca, points a finger. "Whoever it is managed to get into the Heinous Section—the most secure area in all of Tarr. I doubt a locked door will hold him."

The infamous Heinous Section. That explains the blackness emanating from it, like an invisible finger curling, beckoning and yet repelling at the same time. I swallow thickly. We must end this. God knows we've done a poor job in preventing deaths. We must stop him from harvesting his last soul and getting his reward. The idea is unthinkable.

"Let's get the evil bastard," I say.

Keeva and Sabella nod in keen agreement, their faces set with determination.

Tavell runs a hand back and forth over his neck, glancing at all of us in turn. Another bang ripples through the giant library—it sounds like a book hitting the polished, parquetry floor—and Tavell swings his head. "Right. Pair up and search the library. Finn, you're with Rill. Sabella with Lord Luca, and Lady Keeva is with me." He nods at Sabella and me. "Use your guard whistle if you find him."

Oh shit. I pat my vest pockets, trying to remember where my whistle is.

"Top left," Tavell says as he walks past me. He gestures sharply with his hands like he is directing traffic. "Use any magic you must to keep yourselves safe ... though not fire, Sabella, not in a library. Rill and Finn go left and start with the furthest row by the wall. Sabella and Lord Luca, I want you to weave your way down the stacks by taking all the cross aisles. Lady Keeva and I will go right. Move up and down the stacks methodically and watch he doesn't get past you. We should be able to herd him, get him cornered ..."

He trails off when we all tear off down the towering stacks of books. Enough instructions. It's time for action.

Lord Finn and I fall in beside each other easily and walk smartly down the furthest row to the left, heads swivelling, eyes wide. The guard whistle has a ring on the end, and I slip my finger into it and hold tight. If we find the summoner, I want to be able to call Tavell. As a Class Five witch, Tavell is the only one who can take the summoner down, and I sure don't want Finn or me to become the last soul harvested.

The taste of paper and dust and parchment fills my panting mouth. Any other time I'd be in heaven with all these books—I am gobsmacked by how big the library is, by how many books there are. But right now, the shelves are just giant towers to hide behind. Frustration builds when we get to the first intersecting row. Gods. The damn place runs like a city of crisscrossed roads. The summoner could easily slip past ... but we just catch Sabella and the Earl disappearing around a corner, heading to the next cross aisle.

Footsteps ring out, clopping on the wooden floor and echo so much it is hard to tell if they are our own steps echoing back or if the sound is the steps of the others. Which also means we can't hear the summoner. Above our heads, the muffled drumming of rain urges us forward.

The thunderclap of another book hitting the floor makes me leap from my skin—what the hell is the summoner doing? Flinging books around? Finn and I exchange a look. His chest rises and falls rapidly, a mirror to mine. We walk even faster. At intervals, along the stone wall on our left, little alcoves sit tucked into the wall. Each has a small table and a few chairs. Thankfully, it only takes a glance to ensure the summoner does not crouch in one.

An odour fills the musty library air—a mixture of smoke and stagnant water. Eye-wateringly unpleasant, it scrapes at the back of my throat, and I cough.

Then the lights start going out.

In a random pattern—a light here, another there—bulbs burst in a shower of sparks. The shadows widen and deepen with each extinguished light. The summoner is using magic—magic that smells bad, and I *know* it comes from a black soul—to shatter the lights. As if to prove me right, a few more explode right above us plunging Finn and me into darkness. The stacks loom beside and above us, black, like a cliff face at night. For a second, panic rises, then I remember Jack. I pull the cudgel from my belt.

"Lux," I cry, and it throws a welcome light.

"Thank the gods," Lord Finn says, his cultured accent becoming frayed.

I stare towards the ceiling and the remaining lights that cast out in feeble fingers. Turning back to the library's entrance, I note that the lights there remain. Shit. The summoner is making a path for himself to escape.

"We really should have left someone to guard the door," I murmur.

"Agreed," Finn replies. He has obviously come to the same conclusion as me. "But I won't leave you alone."

"No. We stay together. It's possible the summoner is hoping to separate us."

Trying to calm my racing heart, we continue, but now I have to sweep Jack in front of us and into each damn alcove. The darkness slows us, and misgivings build. The summoner has us, like mice in a maze, just like the cursed Slicer Depot. Easy pickings to take his last soul. I clench my teeth and swallow noisily.

"How big is this library?" I mutter between my tight teeth.

"It lies beneath the whole of the manor. We are ..." Finn hesitates like he's trying to get his bearings. "... nearly at the end of the first row."

Gods ...

"Hello? Is anybody here?"

The male voice comes from the library entrance, and Finn and I spin towards it.

In the cavernous library that acts like an acoustic magnifier, I hear a light switch being flicked, and we are plunged into utter darkness. Then another click and the undamaged lights turn on again.

"What is wrong with the lights? Hello!"

This time the call is louder.

"Sean?" The Earl of Tarr calls from somewhere within the shadowed stacks.

"Luca? Where are you?"

Beside me, Finn goes rigid. "Uncle Sean," he murmurs. "Gods above, he's perfect prey for the summoner." He takes off at a run, rounding the first row and heading back down the second towards the library entrance.

Shit.

I follow, carefully checking the alcove in the back wall, before heading towards the front of the library.

I'Kuna, please prevent the summoner from getting past us. Please keep Keeva's uncle safe.

A loud crash sounds—louder than a book—and then Lord Finn uttering a swear word reaches me. With fear rioting in my veins, I run, my Jack extended before me. Ahead, Finn is in a pile on the floor.

"What the hell happened," I ask when I reach him. "Are you hurt?" I offer him a hand which he shakes off and gets to his feet.

"I tripped ... on ..." he looks to the floor where I have directed Jack's light "... a book. Why is the name of the gods—"

"He ... he is slamming them onto the floor." I interrupt, though I am talking to myself more than Finn.

The tight, uncomfortable feeling we are being herded, drawn and directed by the bang of books intensifies.

Voices drift from the front of the library, and Finn once more takes off at a run.

I follow more slowly at a jerky walk. I'm on edge, and every tiny sound has me whipping about to look. Eventually I draw closer to the front of the library and sense ... a faint but familiar presence. I whirl around, extending Jack in a trembling hand. But there is no one. I stand frozen for a moment, trying to recognise what I feel. But it is gone again. I could use my newfound sensing power. I only need to close my eyes and feel. But closing my eyes when there is a demon summoner on the loose seems like a mistake. Instead, I keep going, checking over my shoulder every few seconds at the shadows that chase me.

After what feels like an age, I reach the front of the library, relieved that the lights still on in the main area illuminate my way. I extinguish my Jack, suddenly feeling a bit silly, convinced my imagination has gotten the better of me.

Even before I can see them, I hear Lord Luca and Keeva talking to this Uncle Sean—the one Tavell said must not know about helping the Hismish. The one who is a much-loved drunk. It is a mess of voices, all speaking at the same time. I peer around the end of the aisle and get my first look at Uncle Sean.

He is dressed like I assume a Baron would be, except he has no jacket over his dark waistcoat, and his tie is undone, dangling down his starched white shirt that shines under the electric lights. "I was so worried about you Keeva," he says. "You too Finn. And that awful Commander Lewis kept saying you might be involved." He tsk, tsks and weaves lightly on his feet. Probably drunk. But his words are kind, and he looks at them with an expression of tenderness.

The weird feeling rushes over me again. It is stronger this time. A warning, like an electrical buzz in a thunderstorm. I crouch, muscles coiled, and check behind me again, yet there is still nothing. But every tiny hair on my body is standing on end. I am convinced the summoner is nearby.

I peer back into the main area. Everyone else is there, standing in a circle talking, and I have the disturbing notion they are caught in an invisible Sorrow Spider web—a larder for a giant spider to feast upon.

"The summoner is here?" Uncle Sean continues, fluttering a hand against his chest. "That is ... highly disturbing." He spins on Keeva. "Keeva, my dear, you shouldn't be here. Luca, I'm surprised you would allow her to remain in such a dangerous situation."

The Earl draws himself up. "My daughter rescued Finn, placing herself in great danger to do so. I think she has earned the right to see this through." His tone is a mix of pride and ... condescension.

He is all Earl talking to a subject, even though the subject is his own brother.

Keeva's face shifts with surprise and then pure happiness, and I get the sense she does not often win words of praise from her father.

I go to leave the stacks and join the group when Sean lifts his monocle and looks over to the open gate to the Heinous Section.

I turn cold, from my toes to my head, and my heart slams against my ribs.

From a distance, the movement looks like a salute. A salute like the summoner gave me in Carlver Alley.

It can't be. It is not possible. But even as I think that a certainty settles over me. His voice ... it is the same one that chanted in Carlver Alley. His build is the same. His expensive clothes are the same. And it explains the creepy feeling that pebbled my skin when I drew close.

Keeva's uncle is the summoner.

In that second, I catch Tavell's eye, and he gives me the slightest shake of his head. He knows something is wrong—and he wants me to stay hidden. Perhaps his truthsayer magic has alerted him. Sean will not know Sabella has taken a fledge, and Tavell doesn't want him to know there is one more in the library. But what does Tavell expect me to do? Why would he want me to stay?

"Where is—" Sabella's sentence cuts off when she gasps.

Constable Tavell has lifted his hands to the skies, and he ... shines. He sparkles like a dewy spider web on a frosty morning. His normally kind face has turned hideous. His nostrils flare, and his eyes take on evil darkness that even from my vantage point is horrifying.

I clap a hand over my mouth in gut-churning confusion and distress.

"I am the summoner!" he bellows. "All of you, into the Heinous Section." His voice has changed too. It booms with sheer power and malicious intent, and for the first time, I understand what it is to *quake in my boots.*

"Tavell? What—?" Sabella's question is once more cut off by the biting look Tavell directs at her. Her face is all confusion. And fear. And sorrow.

Tavell's magic fills the library. Its power, raw and terrible. Pepper and ginger soak the air, and I press my hand harder over my mouth and nose when I sneeze. My eyes water, yet the smell is not foul. Not filled with decay like the smoke and stagnant water stench from earlier.

"Into the Heinous Section. Now!" Tavell roars at everyone, and they all jump in unified terror. Keeva clings to Finn, and Lord Luca stands with his fists curled, his expression that of abject disbelief. Sabella looks like she is about to cry. But Sean ... he looks ... amused?

Tavell thrusts his hands forward, and magic ripples outward. Suddenly, everyone turns into rag dolls, relaxed and compliant. Ensorceled, they turn as one and make for the open gate to the Heinous Section.

Finn enters first, followed by Keeva and Sabella.

Fear grips me. Everything about this is wrong. Tavell is not the summoner. He can't be. He was with us when the demon took that poor librarian lady.

Tavell's outstretched hands push and pull like he has puppets on wires. Lord Luca goes to step over the threshold with Sean close behind … then … chaos.

Sean, in a mirror of Tavell, extends his hands, one towards Lord Luca and one towards Tavell. In an instant, Tavell is lifted from the ground and swept into the Heinous Section like a leaf riding the wind. In the same moment, the Earl of Tarr flies in the opposite direction across the library, his arms flung wide in shock. He crashes into a table with force and tumbles to the floor, moaning.

I jam a fist into my mouth to prevent crying out in shock.

Sean pushes the gate to the Heinous Section shut and locks it in one smooth movement … physically with a key and magically with the flick of a hand. The swaying has disappeared. The friendly expression on his face has vanished.

"Nice try, Constable Tavell, saying you are the summoner. But even your magic cannot win against the power of darkness."

Tavell wraps his fingers around the curling iron of the gate, the frightening persona he'd donned a moment ago is gone. "No, Sean. Don't do this."

But Sean just laughs and turns back to Lord Luca who is a crumbled heap on the floor.

"Now dear brother, we need to have a chat."

Fuck, fuck, fuck.

54
Rill

FINN AND KEEVA BANG on the curling ironwork of the Heinous Section wall.

"Father!" Keeva cries.

Sabella and Tavell both lean a shoulder into the locked gate, but the ancient ironwork is strong and won't budge.

"Uncle Sean? What are you doing?" Finn doesn't shout, but the agony in his voice fills the library.

Gods. Think, Rill. Think.

I grip my cudgel. It is out of freezing magic, but perhaps I can run out and smack Baron Sean over the head. I try to catch Tavell's eye from where I cling, half behind a book stack, but his eyes are fixed in anger on the Baron.

Why? Why did Tavell lead them into the Heinous Section? I replay the scene. Tavell spelling them and then ... Keeva's words replay. *When the gate is shut, the magic cannot get through*. Oh! Tavell wanted to get everyone to safety behind the wall worked in hieroglyphs. They'd be safe from the demon. Something had tipped him off about Baron Sean, and I can only assume he was going to face him down once everyone else was safe. But the Baron outsmarted him. And out magicked him.

Which leaves me. *Fuck. Fuck. Fuck.*

Lord Luca struggles to his feet from the splintered table. One of his arms holds the other tight to his body. He takes a step with a nasty limp that makes me grimace.

"Sean ... I ..." Lord Luca's voice is strained.

"Oh no, no. I will do the talking for a change, and you will listen." Sean turns to the group locked in the Heinous Section. "Finn. Keeva. I never meant to do this in front of you. I tried so hard to keep you out of it. But it would seem the Slicers are imbeciles and Keeva, dear, your stubbornness made you ignore the death threat, so here we are."

"Uncle Sean?" The look on Keeva's face is heartbreaking. It is like watching her mind gradually come to believe this unbelievable situation. "You, you ... it cannot be true." Tears roll down her pale face.

"Why can't it be true? Because I am your *sweet Uncle Sean*." The Baron adds a friendly, slightly drunken lilt to the last few words and plenty of sarcasm. "You underestimate me, just as everyone does. You overlook me like I am nothing more than a piece of convenient, comfortable furniture." He spins back to Lord Luca whose breath comes in ragged pants of pain.

"I am the summoner. I am the one who has been harvesting souls. And my dear brother, you were always going to be the last soul I took." He swings back to the others. "I just did not expect to have an audience." A whiff of hesitation enters his voice, and I hold my breath hoping he might yet have a change of heart. Then he chuckles, and it is a truly horrifying laugh that chills me to the bone. "Never mind. You are secure for now. I am sure my employer will advise me as to what to do with you."

Employer? Shit. They, whoever they are, won't have second thoughts. They will order all witnesses killed. I must stop this. Closing my eyes I draw a steadying breath. I need to think clearly. When I open my eyes again, I study the library like it is a puzzle and not a nightmare.

"Why?" Lord Luca asks and winces when he tries to take another step.

"Why? Why? But of course, you would have no idea. My brother, the ignorant, arrogant, self-important fool. Well, I'll tell you. Because you have the very two things in life that I want. The Earldom and Mya."

Mya? Lady Mya? Keeva's mother?

"Mya was supposed to be mine! You know this. You know she was invited to dinner by our father as a match for me. Yet, she took one look at you, the older brother headed for Earldom, and looked right through me. Oh, you cared not. Didn't care that I loved her. That I still love her!" Sean paces back and forth.

Lord Luca takes another limping step and moans, his face crumpling in pain. "But you married Pippa. You love Pippa. You ... you never showed any interest in Mya after that first dinner."

"Pippa? My consolation prize?" Sean throws his head back and laughs. "She came from a regional family. Oh, Father tried to wrap her up in a pretty bow, but she was from inferior stock, and that was even more apparent when she turned out to be barren. A dry, pathetic husk."

"But Aunt Pippa is ... wonderful," Keeva says from behind the iron wall. "You always seemed so happy with her." She and Finn press their faces to the metal of their cage.

"Ha! I fooled you, didn't I? Pretending to be the affable Uncle and the loving husband." He tugs at his tie, undoing the knot, and pulls it from round his neck. "Thank goodness the whores of Lapana gave me some comfort." He laughs again. "And not a few children, I might add." He flings the tie away and moves towards the librarian's desk. "Bastards of course. But nice to know I am virile."

I tuck in a little tighter behind my bookshelf when Sean moves, worried he'll see me. I am nearly useless as I still don't know what to do, but if he sees and captures me, there is no hope.

He ducks behind the desk and picks up something from a shelf. Slowly, like a horror story in one of my beloved books, he straightens ... and his face and bald head have disappeared. In its place, the summoner's mask.

My stomach clenches at the memory of the last time I saw it. Then, with a sweep, he pulls a black jacket from behind the desk and, throwing it around his shoulders, is now all in black.

"You don't look well, brother. Shall I be kind and end your suffering?" His voice takes on a hollow sound behind the mask, and a shiver runs down my spine.

He is right though. Lord Luca is swaying on his feet and looks ready to faint. He still clings to his arm and favours one leg. Yet, he hobbles in a pivot to face Sean.

"How? You ... you are a Level Two."

Sean waves a hand. "A simple matter to fix when you have access to the Heinous Section. Black magic cares little for the power of the witch. It has its own power."

Oh gods. If he's been dabbling in dark sorcery, it is no wonder his soul has turned black. No wonder his magic smells rotten.

He prowls towards Lord Luca while slowly doing up the buttons of his jacket. "The Slicers helped me, too. Procuring dark artefacts for me." He stops and cocks his head. "I did not tell you that, did I? I have become good friends with the Slicer Boss. Or perhaps friend is the wrong word—we are ... useful to each other. I provide him with secrets and names of valued citizens who would bring good money as slaves, while he brings me artefacts and other support." He reaches the buttons near his neck, pulling the jacket tight under his jowls. "Like distracting the guards with murder while they were looking for me last night. Like taking Finn." He turns to Finn locked in the Heinous Section. "You are Mya's son. I would not hurt you. You were only going to be held while I finished my harvest, then released."

Finn opens his mouth, anger contorting his face, but no words come.

Sabella was right. The murder in the alley last night, staged to look like a demon attack, was a gang hit. At Sean's request.

"You were going to make the demon take me," Keeva cries out, a mix of anger and agony lacing her words. "You ... pursued me ..." Her voice cracks, and she sobs silently, breathlessly.

"Oh yes, Keeva, darling." Sean's tongue curls around the word *darling*, coating it with syrupy condescension. "You gave me *quite* the fright when I saw you in Carlver Alley." He smirks. "But for Mya's sake, I called the demon back and did not pursue you. I chose a dirty booth and a poor Hismish village to finish my work. No one would know me there."

Keeva's sobs catch, and I think my heart stops dead at the same time. He didn't follow me in Keeva's body. Just as Sabella suggested, it was pure coincidence. *Burning hell.* If I hadn't taken Keeva to Ikra ... I stop my thoughts cold before they can beat me bloody. Everything that happened was meant to lead me here.

Sean does up the last of his coat buttons. “You know, I was going to poison you, brother. The Slicers were going to get me an untraceable poison. One that made you suffer, too. One where you would die in agony.” He rubs his hands together in delight. “But then I was given another opportunity. You haven’t asked who my employer is. Would you like to know?”

Lord Luca stares at Sean with shuttered eyes.

“I will tell you because it is too delicious not to share.” He claps his hands together in one giant smack. “It is ... King Ryker!”

A wave of shocked anger floods over me. King Ryker ordered Baron Sean to summon a demon to take souls? But why ... then it comes to me in a snap. It is King Ryker who wants the favour. Yet, Sean must be getting something out of this besides killing his brother.

“In return for summoning the demon and taking souls, the king is going to give me a title. I will be the Duke of Tarr. Yes, dear brother. I will become higher than you. Not that you will care, because you will be dead. Then I will marry Mya. Oh, don’t worry your great pig head—I will take care of Keeva and Finn." He swings his head to the locked Heinous Section. "I will have to kill the constables, however. I can't have them on my heels."

I notice Keeva is trying spells on the lock, even as tears flow down her face.

"But enough. It is time." Sean extends his hands and begins muttering a few words. Then, his voice rises, and magic flows into the library, swirling and pressing. The taste sits on my tongue, a metallic burn that makes me want to gag. I blink, and in the split second my eyes are closed, the demon appears.

Heat hits like a wall of bricks, blasting at me even sheltered behind the stack. The reek of brimstone fills the air. Between Sean and Luca, the red-eyed, dog-headed demon squats, its snake tail hissing and flicking. The demon licks at the air, boring its glowing eyes into Lord Luca ... and it smiles.

"A soul for the taking," the demon says in a bone-scraping voice that goes straight through me, infecting me with sticky evil.

I have run out of time. I must do something. But I have no ideas except ... I can put myself between the Earl and the demon. It will mean roaming the nine levels of hell for all eternity. But not doing so will cost Lord Luca his life.

Shit.

Two days ago, the decision would have been easy. I would have let Earl Luca Dalton die. I thought him the enemy. I thought him evil. But the last two days have challenged my beliefs. Changed them. A searing sorrow hits me ... what I had become was hardly any better than Nolan Fawn. His bitterness had turned him into an ass. And bit by bit, my bitterness would have done the same. Goodness knows it had already lost me my sister.

The demon creeps towards Lord Luca, a malevolent grin contorting its ghastly maw.

I draw in a deep breath … and leave the safety of the stack.

I run, desperate to reach Lord Luca before Sean can use his rotting, black magic against me.

Catching my movement from the corner of his eye, he spins around and flings his hands towards me. Skidding on the polished floor, I slide under a table, narrowly missing the stinking black magic that flies overhead. Even as I get to my feet, a shudder ripples through my body. The darkness in his magic is grotesque. And he draws his hands back like two snakes about to strike, ready to direct more at me.

I draw on my own power and the magic in the air, and murmuring a quick spell, I create a ward that splits me and Lord Luca from Sean and the stalking demon. Not a second too soon either as the demon hits the ward, sending it wobbling. The monstrosity tips its head back and howls.

I continue to pour all I have into the ward as I shuffle and finally reach Lord Luca's side. Now I wrap the ward around us like a bubble. Standing beside him, I can clearly see how much pain he is in. His face is pinched and pale and sweaty. His eyes are filled with terror, and I am sure his fear is the only thing keeping him conscious.

The demon swipes a claw at my ward, and it wobbles once more but holds. The demon hisses with a high-pitched sound that vibrates the floor beneath our feet. It claws at us again, and my ward shakes violently.

"Who the hell are you?" Sean demands, his face glowing red with rage.

"I am Rill Narin of Ikra, Fledge Constable for Sabella Rivers," I declare. Energy pours from me like water flowing down a drain. Magic demands much, and after the last few days, I have very little left.

"A fledge? From Ikra? So, you are ... nothing. Nothing at all." Sean throws dark power at my wards, and I feel the magic hit like a hammer, sending shocks up my arms. I gasp but hang on.

"The demon may take my soul," I cry out. "But you will be caught and put in prison. You will not get what you want. I am the opposite of nothing. I am ... everything!" And for the first time in my life, I believe it.

The demon throws itself up against the shield, shrieking like the creature from hell that it is. It goes into a frenzy, slashing repeatedly at the wall of magic, and I know it is going to fail. I cannot hold for long against an agent of the underworld.

"Open the gate! Open it!" It is Sabella screaming. She rattles the iron walls that hold her, her features twisting in agony.

Keeva is still wiggling her fingers over the lock, her lips moving with the spells she chants. But they can't help me. I only have one hope. And that is to shrink my wards so they cover Lord Luca only. Then offer myself to the demon.

I dared to hope I might have a life of purpose ahead of me. That I might find my place within the citizen guards. But part of that purpose is to be ready to put myself in danger to save others. Maybe it is my fate. To save the Earl of Tarr.

"Keep saving Hismish," I whisper to him.

And I step out from behind the wards, bringing them in tight behind me, wrapping them around the Earl to protect him.

Now I stand before the demon. Its serpent tail whips back and forth.

"Nearly had you once before." It flicks its forked tongue out. "Taste is the same, but body is different." Its eyes narrow. "Trickery? You dare try to trick a demon? I shall take you anyway."

"No!" Sean roars. "No. I summoned you to take him!" Sean points a fierce finger at his brother.

"You cannot control me. I take whatever soul I desire." The creature steps closer. Its red eyes burn. Smoke rises from its body. The snake tail flicks a forked tongue.

My heartbeat slows, a dense clump, clump, like life itself is already leaving me. Then, in a mini explosion, my chest bursts with wild racing beats that slam against my ribs. A shudder takes over my body, making even my lips wobble.

There is no dignity in death. I would have preferred to stand tall and calm, but death was not made to be faced calmly. The world shrinks about me, and I withdraw, hoping I might not feel it when the demon opens me up. When my guts spill onto the pretty parquetry floor. One or two more steps, and the creature will be on me.

I withdraw so far, that I barely notice the soft coolness that slides into each of my hands. It is only when the coolness squeezes that I look. To the gate of the Heinous Section that stands open. To the two girls who stand beside me.

"Together," Sabella says.

"Together," Keeva says.

55

Rill

A RUSH OF MAGIC pours into me. Purifying heat in one hand and the fresh coolness of air in the other. The gift of energy fills me and soothes my trembling body. The calmness I desire comes to me. This thing, this fragile new friendship between Sabella, Keeva, and I is like a magic of its own—a ternion of power. I draw on it. I draw on their strength. Their power melds with mine, and with a deep breath, I slice the space between the demon and us with a shielding ward.

The near-invisible wall shimmers with Sabella's fire magic like a haze on the horizon. It whirls in eddies like tiny dust whirligigs with Keeva's air magic.

Tavell rushes to Sean who stands several steps behind the demon, shock written all over his face. He raises a hand towards

Tavell who, ready this time, bats the magic away like it's nothing more than an annoying buzzing fly. But Finn is not so lucky. Clipped by his uncle's magic, he is tossed through the air like a discarded apple core, but Tavell reaches one hand out and *pulls*. Finn hits the bars of the Heinous Section, but softly with a tiny plink. With another wave of his hand, Tavell raises a ward of his own, cutting Sean and the demon off from him and Finn.

Sean tilts his head back and screams. "Fuck you all!" he says. "I should have killed you, Finn. I should have known you would have too much of your father in you. You too Keeva. Your stubbornness is pure Luca."

Keeva's hand squeezes mine tighter, and tears fill her eyes. "You .... you killed ... Thorn. And the others ..."

"You wouldn't understand," Sean spits the words across the room. "You who have everything." He curls his fists. "You wouldn't understand!"

The demon throws itself against my shield, yet it barely wobbles. The creature goes into a frenzy, slashing repeatedly at the warded barrier of earth, air, and fire.

Like a lull in a storm, the demon suddenly stops attacking the shield. It turns slowly and stands, snarling and slathering. In that moment, Sean realises. He is the only soul the demon can reach.

"No! No, you bastard. I summoned you. You can't take me."

He chants, the same rhythmic chanting I heard in Carlver Alley. He is trying to send the demon back to hell.

But in a movement so fast it is barely visible, the demon launches at Sean, talons outstretched ... and rips him to shreds. The monster lowers his head to the Baron's tattered body and sucks upon him, drawing the soul from Uncle Sean's dying body.

Then, in the blink of an eye, the demon vanishes, leaving behind smoke and stink and flesh and blood.

I continue to pour magic into the wards. The one before us and the one that wraps Lord Luca. The demon is gone, but I can't let go. It's like when your fingers have gripped something for so long, they become stiff. The shimmering of white flame in the wards stops. The swirling eddies of air stop. The weight of shielding Lord Luca falls solely on me, and my knees buckle. I moan and keep drawing magic from within even though I am empty.

"Rill. The danger is gone. You can lower the ward," Keeva says, sobs snagging at her words. I am vaguely aware she no longer holds my hand, but instead, her fingers wrap around my arm.

"Rill. Rill! It's OK, Rill." Sabella gives me a little shake.

But my eyes stay on Sean's broken body, and I can't stop. I can't stop strengthening the ward.

"Fledge Narin." Tavell's deep voice vibrates through the air and into my skull. "We need to attend to Lord Luca. You must drop the wards so we can help him." He doesn't shout, or rage, but the power behind his voice is extraordinary.

I haul my gaze from Sean's bloody body and bring it to Tavell. His grey eyes are soft and consuming. He nods lightly at me and tips his head towards Lord Luca who stands behind me.

"We've got this now, Fledge. Stand down."

Stand down.

For the first time since my mother's death, I have someone to share the weight. After she died, I picked up the burdens of life for my father and for Cassia and refused to set them down. I carried them even after my father left, even after Cassia left. I carried them into prison, piling them on top of my own burdens. Now I have people who will take over. Who will allow me to rest. With a whooshing exhale, I let my ward fall.

Finn, Keeva, and Tavell surround Lord Luca, but Sabella stays by me. Her strong arm slips around my shoulders. Habit makes me want to shrug it off, but her warmth feels nice and I … leave it be. I even soak it in a little.

"Sit," she says and gently directs me to a chair.

I sit and watch as Tavell, Finn, and Keeva lower Lord Luca gently onto the floor. Fair enough as I think he has, at long last, passed out.

Tavell orders Finn to fetch a healer, and he rushes from the library, giving his uncle's body a wide berth.

"You saved his life," Sabella says. Then she gives a shaky smile. "Not bad for a new fledge on her third day."

Suddenly, I giggle. Not because it is funny because none of this is, but perhaps because stress leaks from my body, and sagging relief rushes in to take its place. It feels so ridiculous. I fought a demon. In the Earl's library in his manor on the hill. I risked my life to protect his. Three days ago, I'd been a Hismish prisoner. The lowest of the low. Giggles bubble up in my chest and force their way out. Sabella must think me mad.

But she smiles and even gives a chuckle of her own. "Crazy few days, hey."

I nod and try to get a grip of my silly, giggling body.

When, a short time later, the doors to the library are flung open, I assume Finn is back. Instead, Commander Lewis of the king's guard strides in the door. Following him are the same guards that searched the guard house stable a few hours—a lifetime—ago.

Lewis pauses at Sean's body and glances over at the broken librarian. Then his black eyes find us, his sharply trimmed beard slicing at the air with the movement. His intense gaze drifts over me sitting in a chair with Sabella standing beside me, then to Keeva and Tavell, both on their knees beside Lord Luca. He snaps his fingers, and three more people rush into the room.

All three are women and wear the black uniforms and white aprons of healers. Two carry a stretcher between them. Gods. They'll have to carry Lord Luca up all those flights of stairs. Exhaustion lies heavy on me, and I can barely concentrate on the conversation between Commander Lewis and Tavell who has left Lord Luca to the healers.

I hear enough to know their voices are ... heated is not the right word ... fierce is more like it. Both have an aura of power to them, and both use it, their magic and self-assurance clashing and banging and weaving together. However, in no time at all, the healers have Lord Luca on the stretcher, and Commander Lewis, to his credit, orders his men to carry the stretcher up the stairs, relieving the healers of their burden.

Cool arms are suddenly flung around me. "You saved my father." Keeva squeezes me. "Thank you. I will never forget what you did. Never."

A surge of rightness comes over me. I did the right thing in saving the Earl. I did the right thing in deciding to be Sabella's fledge. And my reward is two people I am pretty sure I can count as friends. I look up into Keeva's red-rimmed eyes.

"I am very glad I did, Lady Keeva."

Weeping anew, she gives me another tight hug.

And I hug her back.

56

Sabella

We sit in the fancy upstairs room under a blanket of thick, disbelieving silence. Keeva's Aunt has stopped crying and stopped asking why. No one could answer her anyway. So now she simply sits, staring at nothing, her tear-stained, red-rimmed eyes are empty. Keeva is beside her, perched on the arm of the chair, a hand resting on her aunt's shoulder, although the woman seems unaware of her.

I sit on a sofa opposite them with Finn at my side pressing close, his face blank with shock. My fingers brush against his, and he immediately clutches my hand without hesitation. Clearly, any secrecy around our relationship has evaporated in the flaming horror that was the last few days. Even still, I know with time, propriety will see furtiveness reestablished, so I savour the warmth and strength of his hand on mine.

Rill stands by a window with one buttock resting on the deep sill by an open window, bathing in the cool night air that follows the storm, now abated. She stares too, but out towards the city like she might find meaning from it. I doubt she will because there is no meaning to be had. The summoner was Keeva's uncle, Lord Luca's brother. It is beyond comprehension.

Tavell sits on the edge of a straight-backed, wooden chair, his fisted hands resting on his knees. He too, stares at nothing in particular, but emotion ripples across his face. Shock, grief, and anger follow one another in a never-ending, circling parade.

Commander Lewis ordered a thorough search of the library once Tavell filled him in on what happened. He also ordered a search of the Baron's rooms for clues that might explain why he did what he did. No one bothered to argue with Commander Lewis. Everyone was content to let him take over the investigation, our dislike for the man no longer seeming relevant. To his credit, the tough kings-guard leader showed some empathy. Or, at least, he was slightly less arrogant. His tone less condescending. And it hurts me to admit, but the man is extremely efficient.

As if my thoughts summon him, the Commander enters the room, a few slips of paper in his hand.

"We found these in the Baron's room. They are obvious forgeries."

The announcement brings Tavell to his feet, and he takes the offered documents from Commander Lewis. He reads, then snaps his head up, a look of shock on his face.

"These are from King Ryker," he says, his voice incredulous. "He ... he asked Sean to obtain the Map of Allurement, whatever that is." Tavell shakes his head and reads on. "He did indeed promise to make Sean Duke of Tarr as a reward. That ... that is impossible."

I glance at Pippa. This is her husband they are talking about. Her swollen, tear-stained eyes stare at Commander Lewis.

"As I said, the document is a forgery," Cadel says. "It is not from the King." He moves beside Tavell and points. "See here. The seal is wrong. This line should be wider ... and this line here ... it doesn't exist on the King's seal. The paper too, it's not the official paper used in King Ryker's communications."

Tavell fingers the document.

Cadel presents another piece of paper. This one is a narrow, com-box printout. "We also found a com-box hidden in his room. We printed all the messages, but there were only three. The first Baron Sean sent. 'To obtain the Map of Allurement, the demon Garmr must be summoned to harvest six souls in three nights.'"

Lewis glances at Pippa with discomfort before looking back at the strips of paper in his hand. "Then whoever was posing as the king sent this back. 'Proceed with soul gathering.'" Cadel's lips twitch. "The last com from Sir Sean simply states, 'I will happily do as you ask, your Majesty.'"

Keeva's aunt leaps from the chair, her knees knocking the coffee table and rattling the cups on the tray. She presses her palms flat to her stomach like she can hold her distress at bay. "I was well aware of who my husband was. I was aware of his drinking, his dalliances. I accepted him for who he was the moment I fell in love with him. But ... this, this is not him." She collapses back onto the chair, sobbing softly. Finn gives my hand a pat, then rises, moving to be the one to comfort his aunt this time.

"It was the black magic, Aunt Pippa," he says. "It taints, and he was corrupted by it."

I have a strong feeling Sean was corrupt long before he dabbled with black magic, and I am sure Finn knows this. But he is comforting his aunt in any way he can.

Keeva brushes at her clothes. "At least whoever impersonated the king, did not get the Map of Allurement. Uncle ..." Her voice breaks, and she takes a deep breath to steady herself. "... Sean didn't obtain it." Keeva's lips wobble. "What is this Map of Allurement? Does anyone know?"

Blank faces answer her.

"The Baron mentioned the Slicers were obtaining artefacts for him," Tavell says, handing the papers back to Commander Lewis. "Perhaps this map was one of the things they procured for him."

I watch the Commander. His face twists like he is having an internal struggle, and his dark eyes stare at nothing, then he comes to attention with a snap of his heels. "I shall leave some of my men here to assist the citizen guards in dealing with the Slicer gang. The Slicer boss and this Constable Fawn you told me of will be brought to the capital for questioning. I, however, shall return to Simgra to investigate. It is a serious crime to impersonate the King, not to mention to demand killing by demon in his name. Additionally, the king's scholars may have knowledge of this Map of Allurement. I shall keep you informed of the outcome of my investigations." He hesitates. "I will recommend to the King that Tarr's Liberty Law of the Festival is reinstated. Please pass that on to Lord Luca." He turns to go but pauses. "Your guard, Alex Albo, has been released." He gives his jacket a sharp tug, then marches from the room.

Thank the gods he found the com-box. Thank the gods he believes us. Thank the gods he is gone. I hope I never cross paths with the vile man again.

Keeva sets about righting the teacups her aunt upset and exchanges a look with Finn. "Perhaps we should enquire if a healer can be spared to help Aunt Pippa," she murmurs. When Finn dips his head in agreeance, she makes for the door. It opens before she touches the handle, revealing her personal guard, Alex Albo.

"Alex. I am pleased you have been released. Welcome home," Keeva says.

"Thank you, Lady Keeva. I just wish it were under happier circumstances."

Keeva lets her head drop for a second, then squares her shoulders again.

"But I have a surprise for you," Alex says.

And with that, a stunning, well-groomed woman sweeps into the room, and Keeva immediately flings her arms around her. The two embrace fiercely, joined a second later by Finn.

I go to Rill by the window where she is looking at the new arrival with nervous curiosity.

"It's Keeva's mother," I say. "Lady Mya."

57

Rill

Keeva's mother, Lady Mya, is a powerhouse. She greets her family, then in a matter of minutes, she rallies the servants and arranges for Keeva's aunt to be taken to her room and seen by a healer. The man with the long, rather unfortunate, face—I think it is Keeva's guard who was arrested—is sent to bathe and rest. Lady Mya then orders fresh tea and food to be delivered. Staff move promptly and with eagerness, and I sense Keeva's mother is well respected.

"I expect every drop of tea drank and some food eaten, too," she tells the room. But her words hold love, and her face shines with determined tenderness. It is a strange and powerful combination that reminds me of Ikra's village elder, Esme.

"I have just come from your father. He has suffered a broken arm and leg, but he will make a full recovery. The healers have given him a draught, and he will sleep now." Her expression shows raw emotion beneath her efficiency.

"Finn." Lady Mya looks at her son. "There are funeral arrangements to be made. For all the victims. Please put a proposal together on how we can assist. I think we should organise a memorial gathering for all the victims of the demon. To be held the night before the Ryker Festival. Once I am satisfied you have eaten, can you begin planning? We don't have much time, so we must be prompt."

Finn nods. "Yes, Mother."

She approaches me. "You are Fledge Narin, I assume?"

I slip from the windowsill and give a little bob. "Yes, milady."

"I believe I owe you thanks. You saved my husband's life and soul."

I don't know what to say. Lady Mya is a handsome woman, dressed in the finest gown, and I am more than a little intimidated. It is obvious from where Keeva gets her proud elegance.

"She most certainly did, Lady Mya," Sabella answers, and I give myself a mental kick. I am a grown woman, and Sabella should not have to answer for me.

"It was my pleasure, mil—"

An ear-splitting scream cuts me off.

The scream fills the room and bounces off the walls. I slap my hands over my ears. The sound seems to go straight through the skin, flesh, and bones of my hands, drilling into my eardrums like a sharp spike.

Finn and Keeva pale.

They both mouth two words at the same time—words drowned out by the scream—and tear from the room.

With my heart thumping, I, and everyone else, follow. The scream is no quieter in the corridor. In fact, it is the same everywhere. No matter how many stairs we take, no matter how many doors we go through, the scream is everywhere. It fills every nook, every cranny. Staff and guards appear at corners and in doorways, their eyes frantically asking the same question.

What is it?

But Finn and Keeva seem to know, rigid dread painting their faces.

They descend several flights of stairs at pace, and I realise we are heading back to the library. Now dread fills me too.

Reaching our destination, Finn throws open the double doors and runs in with the rest of us close behind.

Thank heavens, the bodies of the librarian and Sean have been removed, though blood stains and black scorch marks remain. The scream, if it is possible, is even louder in here, and the sound holds me in a vice grip.

Finn scrambles behind the front desk by the door and places his hand on a metal cabinet. It springs open, and reaching in, he pulls a lever. The scream, mercifully, ceases.

But he and Keeva are still stressed. Still panicked. They make straight to the Heinous Section where the door swings wide open.

Burning hell. Lord Finn had locked it carefully before we left the library.

"Mother, stay here," Finn says.

Lady Mya bobs her head.

"I will stay with her." Sabella takes up the post at the matriarch's side.

Tavell gives a grim nod, and Finn and Keeva step into the area beyond the wall from which such evil emanates.

With a gulp, I follow, drawn and repelled from the place in equal measure.

My stomach shrinks to the size of a pebble. I push against the blackness that hits me and stay close to Keeva.

Finn seems to know what he is looking for—what he fears—because he goes directly to the furthestmost row on the right. He creeps down the corridor, keeping away from the glass cases that line the wall.

I understand why he shrinks from the cases as horror sits in my bones, and suddenly, the smell of my prison cell seems sweet compared to this.

Finn doesn't muck around though. He passes each case with the quickest of glances. Until he doesn't. He reaches a case that freezes him in place. It is shattered, shards of glass scattered all over the floor.

Tavell and Keeva fall in beside him.

"Oh no," Keeva says. "Is that ...?

Finn nods, one hand rubbing his chin vigorously. "The Claw of Whiron." He points to the claw that extends towards the ceiling. Its taloned fingers splay open, its palm facing the ceiling. "And the document is missing. A document I now assume to be the Map of Allurement."

Well, shit.

58
Keeva

A WEEK LATER, SABELLA and Rill visit me at the manor in what has become my study. The room had been my piano room, and it still is, for the grand piano stands in its usual corner. However, it now has company with the desk I requested positioned in the opposite corner.

"Good morning," I greet them when they are shown in by Alex. I rise from behind the desk and offer both girls a hug. The friendship we've formed is firm and seems only to be growing.

"Are you ready for the memorial?" I ask.

Sabella nods. "Though Rill seems to think the guard dress uniform is a bit over the top."

Rill flings herself into a wing-back chair, swinging her legs over one of the arms and resting back on the other. "I can hardly breathe in the thing." She makes a motion with her fingers to her neck like she is tugging on a tight collar. Then she gives one of her rare smiles. Smiles that are slowly becoming less rare. "But I will admit it does look smart. The victims deserve smart. So, I will endure it."

Sabella gestures towards my desk and the piles of books and scrolls upon it. "Have you found anything?"

I wander to the desk that resembles Finn's scholarly mess more and more each day. It is no wonder since he has been my teacher, showing me the finer points of quality research. "Nothing in the history books. But I did come across something in the Book of Myths. The Map of Allurement is purported to show the bearer how to get to the Shrine of Simgra in the Black Roil Islands." I give a wry smile for I am struggling with the ludicrousness of it all.

"What do you mean? An actual simgra?" Rill props on her elbows, straightening a little. Her expression is incredulous and fascinated.

"Yes. A unicorn. It is written that once every thousand years, a simgra is born, and they can be summoned to the Shrine of Simgra ... if several other conditions are met ... though I've yet to discover what those conditions are."

Sabella gives the most un-lady-like snort. "Someone wants to go after a mythical unicorn? They must be nuts."

I sigh. "I agree. I will undertake more research. Perhaps we are missing something." I run a finger over a bulky leather-bound book, praying for it to share its secrets with me.

"Have you heard anything further from the Commander?" Sabella asks gently.

I can't help but wince. "Yes and no. He returned to Lapana briefly and, as you know, has arrested the slicer boss and Constable

Nolan Fawn. Fawn not only worked for the slicers ... but also admitted to arranging for a rival gang member killed and arranging it to look like a demon-killing. Albeit on order from ... Sean but still ..." My throat tightens. I can no longer call him *Uncle* Sean.

Sabella exchanges a look with Rill who just raises her eyebrows in response.

I shudder at the memories of the creepy Slicer Depot. "But the Commander seems to think he may know something about the demon's granted favour. About the Map of Allurement. They are interrogating him further."

"How is your aunt?" Rill asks.

Bless her for asking.

"She's gone to stay with our cousins for a while. She found being here, in the manor she shared with Unc— ... Sean, too hard to bear." I shake my head. "I had no idea. No idea that Sean slept around, that he fathered numerous illegitimate children. She knew though. Yet ... she still loved him." I take a breath. "I thought I knew him. I didn't."

I roll my shoulders. "But enough of that. Rill, I have a present for you."

Rill swings her legs off the arm of the chair. "What? Why?" She frowns.

The poor girl will take a long time to learn that good things can happen. That they can happen to *her*.

I smile. She saved my father's life, and I want to give her something. I only hope I've made a good choice.

"Here," I hold out the wrapped present to Rill.

Hesitantly, she accepts it. She weighs it in her hands and flashes me a look like she has already guessed what it is. Then she gently unwraps the paper, careful not to rip it, and stares down at the gleaming new book in her hands. The gold lettering of its title, *Legends Unleashed - A Collection of Extraordinary Adventures* reflects the overhead lights.

"Sabella told me you have a bookshelf in your room at GH to house the textbooks you must study. I thought it would be nice to have something other than textbooks on the shelves." I hold my breath.

Rill looks up from the book, her carefully constructed bland expression is gone. In its place, welling eyes and a wobbling lip. "How did you ...? My mother gave me this book as a present when I was little. It's ... my favourite."

My breath catches in my throat, and I go to Rill in a rush. "Oh, Rill. I didn't know ... about your mother. I saw the book on your table in your hut, and it looked so well loved, I just thought ... I'm sorry if I upset you."

A tear rolls down Rill's cheek. "Upset me? This is the nicest gift anyone has ever given me." She gives a wry smile. "Even better than fruit. Thank you, Keeva."

Then, with an awkward lunge, Rill wraps her arms around me. I hug her back and, over her shoulder, see Sabella dabbing at her eyes. I give Rill a squeeze and gently untangle her.

"Before I forget, my father wants to see you both." I smile, because I know what he wants.

"I need more help assisting the citizens of Hismish."

Father sits in a wheelchair in his study with its substantial desk and serious furniture in dark colours. The portraits of previous Earls, all painted in muted colours, line the walls.

Finn, my mother, and I perch on straight-back chairs, allowing Sabella and Rill to sit on the sofa. Not that it is much softer. My father doesn't encourage lounging in his place of work. Typical that he'd choose this room for such a serious conversation.

"Constable Rivers and Fledge Narin, would you be willing to join Tavell, me, my wife, and Finn in our efforts? Keeva has already said yes. Consider your answer carefully. What we do is against Conpieta law, and you will be in serious trouble if we are caught." He looks pointedly at Rill. "Prison is likely."

"I'll do it," Sabella and Rill answer at the same time without a moment's hesitation.

Father chuckles. "Well, alright then. We will meet again after the Ryker Festival." He taps a finger on the plaster cast encasing one leg. "One last thing. What I'm about to tell you must not leave this room. No one else, not even Tavell must know. I confess I was reluctant to inform you, but Keeva tells me we must not have secrets."

My heart pounds with the enormity—and the uncertainty—of what I know my father is going to say. It pounds with the gift he is about to give.

Father looks at Sabella with a genuine smile. "Finn has informed us you are very much in love. So, I wish to share our plans to allow you to marry, should you choose."

59
Rill

"FIND US A TABLE, and I'll get the drinks," Sabella says, before moving smoothly—powerfully—towards the drinks bar that sits to one side of the guard mess hall.

Looking around, I automatically search for a vacant corner table, then catch myself. This is not the common room of Lapana Prison. I don't need to fear attack. Cook Calista dashes about dishing up hors d'oeuvres, winding her way through the sharply dressed citizen guards. There are no raised voices, no pending riots. The room is filled with delicious smells from the plentiful food, and not one dish comes with dead floating maggots. I purposefully choose a table right in the middle of the crowd and sink onto the chair, returning greetings and smiles from some of the guards, including the new captain who transferred from the township of Basima to take up the position.

We've just returned from the memorial for the demon's victims which was even better than I thought it might be.

Many people from Ikra came to Lapana as special guests of the Earl. They came with hair damped and carefully combed, their clothes clean and neatly repaired. They fidgeted with downcast eyes and tense postures, but Keeva and her mother went out of their way to make them comfortable. Keeva's charm, in particular, worked wonders, and soon enough they'd visibly relaxed.

The service hadn't mentioned Keeva's Uncle Sean during the roll call of the dead. He may have been one of the demon's victims, but he was also the summoner and mentioning him would not honour the others.

All the guards turned out, of course, to pay their respects to their Captain and his fledge, Eli. And while I had complained about the dress uniform, I admit all the guards looked sharp as tacks. I wore my newly trimmed hair slicked back and stood with considerable pride. Spine straight, shoulders back.

The victims had all been cremated and had private services, but when asked, the families had willingly turned over the ashes to Sabella. After the memorial service, Diarissa made a magnificent appearance, led in by Tavell. She stood before the crowds, flaring her wings and lowering her head in a bow. Murmurs from the crowd said she looked like an angel. Then Sabella mounted her and took to the skies, scattering the ashes to the winds.

When the ceremony was over, I spoke with the people of Ikra. I introduced Keeva and told them we'd be coming to visit every couple of months. Though there was a good deal of mistrust, the

Ikraites also seemed cautiously interested in visits from the Earl's daughter. I can't help but hope it is the first tiny step of a new kind of society.

Sabella places a drink before me, pulling me from my reverie. I take a sip, pleased to find Sabella fetched me a fruit punch as I am not a drinker.

"What are you drinking?" I ask.

"Fruit punch, too," Sabella says as she sits. "Wine would be an ill-advised choice." She grins. Her dark eyes shine with soft amusement.

Tomorrow is the first day of the Ryker Festival and will be a busy time for the guards. I find I am looking forward to my duties. Normal guard duties without a demon summoner on the loose.

Tavell emerges from the milling guards with a large mug of beer in hand and joins us at our table.

Sabella and I exchange a barely repressed smirk of amusement when he pulls a long draught. He clearly cares little for a busy tomorrow.

"Lord Luca asked us something this morning," Sabella tells Tavell. Aware we are surrounded by potentially listening ears, she chooses her words carefully. "Rill and I have agreed to assist." Of course, she holds back the other secret Lord Luca shared. A secret that fills Sabella with heady hope.

Tavell smiles. "Good. I'm glad he will receive your assistance." He gives Sabella and me a slow look.

"I need to go away for a bit. My hometown is in trouble, and their head witch has asked for my help. Hopefully, I won't be gone long, but I'll feel better knowing you will be assisting the Earl in my absence."

"I hope everything goes well and you can help your friend," Sabella says.

"Oh, he's not my friend. We despise each other. Back home, we are known as the Foes of Fauster."

Foes of Fauster is coming in 2025

Acknowledgements

I am filled with gratitude as I sit here, penning the acknowledgments for another completed book. The support I've received along this journey has been nothing short of incredible, reminding me that it truly does take a village to bring a story to life.

First and foremost, my heartfelt thanks go to my editors. Rachel Hunt, my developmental editor, took on a rough draft and with her insightful comments and suggestions, challenged me to delve deeper into plot development, character arcs, and thematic elements. Her guidance was like a compass guiding me through uncharted plot challenges. I'm equally grateful to Mandi Oyster for her eagle eye, meticulous attention to detail during the second edit, helping me polish the story to its finest shine.

To my dear critique partner and fellow author, Jenny Sandiford, your unwavering support, endless ideas, and constructive feedback is like fuel for my creative engine. I often find myself saying the same thing in every acknowledgment, but it's because your contributions truly are gold to me. I couldn't imagine this writing journey without you.

A special thanks goes out to Jenny Sandiford, Liz Highland, and Katherine Fairbrother for beta reading and providing such insightful feedback. Your input has been incredibly helpful in shaping the final version of the book.

To my ARC team, I extend a massive thank you. Your rockstar enthusiasm, support, and the wonderful reviews you've written have helped me share *Ternion of Tarr* with the world. You are all the BEST!

My gratitude also extends to my husband, Dave. Your endless patience, whether it's listening to me talk through plot concerns or helping me with various technical type questions, is unmatched. You are my real-life superhero.

To my awesome family and friends, your constant encouragement and excitement for my work lifts me up in ways I can't fully express. I am deeply appreciative of your support.

Last but definitely not least, to all you wonderful readers who've taken a leap into the fantastical world of Conpieta, your excitement and kind words make this crazy writing journey worth every twist and turn. Thank you for joining me on this adventure—I promise there are more magical surprises ahead!

About the Author

Bethany Arliss is an enthusiastic nerd with an unwavering passion for all things fantasy and sci-fi.

Nestled amidst the breathtaking landscapes of the Otway Ranges in Australia she rules over her kingdom alongside her trusty side-kicks: a dashing husband, a dynamic duo of furry canines, and a feathery flock of chickens who are surprisingly well-versed in interdimensional politics.

Never miss a beat of Bethany's fantastical adventures! Become an honorary member of her nerdy brigade by subscribing to her newsletter at https://bethanyarliss.com/

Don't worry, she promises not to teleport you into another dimension without your consent (unless you're into that kind of thing). Get ready for exclusive sneak peeks, and more nerdy goodness than you can shake a wand at!

Also by

Shadow Fractures Trilogy

Aracron

Sanda

Essence

COMING SOON

Simgra Series

Foes of Fauster

Kin of Keplon

Elders of Erian

Beaux of Basima

Clash of Conpieta

www.ingramcontent.com/pod-product-compliance
Lightning Source LLC
Chambersburg PA
CBHW030603310726
48979CB00003B/558
* 9 7 8 1 7 6 3 5 4 2 1 0 5 *